HOW
Angels
Die

HOW
Angels
Die

A NOVEL BY

DAVID-MICHAEL
HARDING

How Angels Die

By David-Michael Harding

This book is a work of fiction. All of the characters are fictitious, and any resemblance to actual locales or persons, living or dead, are coincidental.

A
Q&CY
BOOK

Available at qcybooks.com
and amazon.com

Printed in the United States of America

December 2011
Second Edition

1 3 5 7 9 10 8 6 4 2

Library of Congress Cataloging 2011934837
ISBN-13 9780615503325
ISBN-10 0615503322
WGA 141084-00

For
Courtney & Amanda

PROLOGUE

The room was absolutely still. Occasionally an unconscious sniffle would erupt and seem like an explosion of sound. Renault was sitting in a worn, overstuffed, red leather armchair. His legs were crossed at the knees, still muddy and damp. He sat back deep in the chair's comfort but found none. One arm rested limp across his lap while the elbow of the other pressed into the chair's arm, holding his hand up to his face. A single finger pressed against his lips, and the thumb gracefully held the old man's chin. His eyes were cast down and saw nothing in the room and everything beyond. Memories flashed. Most were good, others less so, but each was as vibrant as if it were happening again right now, right in front of those distant eyes.

Sophie was curled up on a small bed a few feet away. Her knees were pulled up to her stomach, and both hands clutched a dainty handkerchief with a frilly lace border to her mouth. Her once exquisite makeup was all over her face, and her eyes were red and swollen. The fingers fidgeted with the handkerchief as if feeling their way for something.

Renault had been to the woods already. He had knelt beside Paul's torn body and wept as his hands clutched the bloody black sweater of the young man he had at first mentored then come to love as a son. He was unable to provide the normal direction to the grave diggers. It didn't seem to matter any longer.

"Renault?" Sophie called from the bed for the second time.

"Yes, dear? I'm sorry. What did you say?"

"Did he suffer?"

"No. Not for moment."

"That's good," she commented slowly as though trying to find solace in the cold facts. "He suffered enough."

Renault barely nodded.

Several more moments passed in silence before a hesitant knock came at the door. Before either could answer, it opened slightly, and Claudine stuck her head in. Her hands gripped the edge of the door tightly as if she could buttress the wood and shield herself from what waited on the other side. She wanted to ask if what she'd heard was true, but one look at the tear stains on Sophie's face and the question was no longer necessary. Without a word she burst in and fell across the bed into Sophie's arms. They didn't speak, but held each other as both began crying for the other's loss.

Renault stood and walked by. As he did, Claudine reached for him and gripped his arm. Neither spoke. Renault only nodded again, patted her hand, and slipped away deeper into his grief as he closed the door and wandered around the room.

"How? Why?" Claudine questioned from behind a veil of trembling tears.

"I don't know, honey. I don't know," Sophie answered as she hugged the girl now left fatherless for a second time.

***

1

The old green bicycle assumed an exaggerated sway as Claire
stood on its pedals trying to conquer the hill. The sun rose
steadily as it crept down her body. It began by grabbing
at Claire's tweed cap, snatching and releasing, snatching and
releasing, as she pumped up and down on the bike. At the crest
of the hill, the last hill, and gratefully so for her eighteen-year-old
legs, the sun's brilliant light broke over her face. She squinted and
looked down, employing the brim of her cap to do its job. It did,
and Claire concentrated on her black boots pumping at the pedals
as the grey stony pavement slipped by in a slowing blur beneath
them.

Her speed continued to wane, but the hill eventually succumbed.
With the summit, the sunlight also triumphed and enveloped her.
The warmth of the early June sun combined with the slow straining
ride to heat Claire's body and flush her cheeks. She paused on the
crest to catch her breath and survey the French countryside of her
birth.

The city was laid out before her like a giant board game, the
streets and roads crisscrossing the land like trails for game pieces.
On the far side, the game board ended where it butted the English

Channel. From her spot at the crest Claire watched the white lines of waves breaking appear and vanish near the beaches. They were so far away that there were times when the ocean seemed not to move at all, an illusion played out by light and distance.

Those beaches had been wondrous playgrounds when Claire was younger. They had been the world's biggest sandbox for her, her sister Monique, and their many friends. Claire had chased and been chased by her only sibling up and down and around and around that sand for what must have seemed endless hours for their mother and father. But those wondrous days were long removed from Claire's city now. Even on warm, bright days such as this, the beaches were empty except for the concrete pill boxes of the German machine gun nests and miles of barbed wire that stretched along the shore. The beach-goers had long since been driven away, underground or into reluctant servitude.

Back on the game board the houses and factories stood testament to the people, unseen from this distance, who still resided and worked there. These were her people, her kind. French, through and through. But among them was a virus, a cancer, and even from the faraway hilltop Claire could see and feel its presence.

She squinted against her friend, the warming sun, and shaded her eyes in support of the hardworking cap. Some way off she could make out vehicles moving, apparently slowly, again tricked by the distance. While their speed was hard to determine and their destination unknown, their color reached out to Claire across the valley and up the hill to slap her in the face. The cars, trucks, and half-tracks meandering through her city like warring ants invading a foreign colony were grey — German grey. And invaders were exactly what they were.

Claire could scarcely remember a time without war — or talk of war, threat of war, fear of war. And its latest face, occupation, was as hideous as war itself. There were nearly as many deaths now as when the German armies first approached the borders and the Luftwaffe dropped their incendiary bombs from the sky. Now, however, the deaths were less pronounced, less dramatic, and the foreign press didn't notice them. Gone were the days of overt battle and fierce fire fights for desolate stretches of land that heretofore no one cared about. They had been replaced by quiet days of blank uncertainty as Germany's grip tightened around the throat of France. Yet in the subtle strangulation of a nation, many died invisible deaths.

The regular German Army had been replaced as well, at least in part, as large numbers of its members had been drawn to the east to battle the Russians. In its stead rose black-suited soldiers whose battle plan differed strongly from open confrontation, bombing, and bullets. Unlike those in grey headed to the front, the black uniforms seldom fraternized with locals beyond rape and torture. These were the German SS and the Gestapo, secret police who turned citizen against citizen and often family against family in a perverted attempt to turn France against itself. It was a form of death from within, or so they must have thought. The Gestapo were the eyes and ears of Berlin and the black uniformed SS were their executioners. A shiny black staff car, like a specialized black killer ant among the hundreds of vile greys, glittered in the distance, revealing the Gestapo's presence.

Questioning and arrest in the street had supplanted gunfire and artillery on the battlefield, although it occurred to Claire that the end result was often the same. At least on a battlefield one could claim the dead or the part that remained. Those arrested during this dragging foot of war that lingered over France just disappeared. They vanished into railroad cars like a magician's pretty assistant into a magic box. Her father, Sean McCleash, spoke of internment camps to the east where all those arrested were being held. To her face, Claire heard her father say that when the war ended, those folks would be released and allowed to return to their homes — the assistant always reappeared at the end of the trick. It seemed logical, as they had done nothing wrong, certainly nothing illegal, but when Sean McCleash spoke of these camps he did so in hushed tones, after which he made the Sign of the Cross over his thin chest and checked the lock on the door. The lock checked, he would glance around the curtain through the front window into the dark street. He knew more than he said, Claire reasoned, and she doubted that she would ever again see the entire families she had witnessed being rooted from their homes by the Nazi invaders.

Her own family had been untouched when judged by the perverted standards of war and the occupation. There were no sons or brothers to be killed or taken prisoner, and her father, as Irish and as un-French as one could be and still live within the country's borders, was "beyond the age of able-bodied men," or so a recruiter had once said. Claire smiled to herself at the remembrance of that declaration and the vicious diatribe that followed, delivered at the hands of her father, on the poor civil servant who thought he had done the senior McCleash a tremendous turn in sparing him from war.

Absent a veteran for a father and minus brothers who might have carried the McCleash name into battle, Claire believed it fell to her to represent the family's interest in the war. However, it needn't have been this way. Many young girls lived where Claire lived and lived as she lived, with parents and families not unlike her own and maintained a life apart from the Germans. This was actually supported by the occupiers, who needed the citizens to see to it that the country was fed at the very least. Though the prime commodities, and often more than that, went to Berlin, many French conducted their lives and their businesses in a manner not much removed from the time before the Germans flew their flag over Paris. Claire's own mother still darned socks and mended shirts as she always had done, though now the French work shirts had become uniforms, and the simple colors of her neighbors had been replaced by the grey of German soldiers. It seemed the invasion hadn't put an end to the need for a talented seamstress.

Yet Claire's private world had taken a turn, and the better or worse determination of it was far from resolved. One might have considered, and reasonably so, that growing up in an air of conflict had made Claire what she had become. At six she had played on the kitchen floor with her older sister. As they squirmed and wrestled and sang around the chrome legs of a new Formica-topped kitchen table and the feet of their parents and neighbors, china cups and saucers clattered and talk of impending war with Germany dribbled off the table's edge. The words fell among the sisters and festered there over time. The sores would not break the surface and bleed for several years until 1940 when a cursed tyrant sent his legions against France in earnest. Then, amidst sporadic gunfire, sirens, and dashing feet, Claire cried like thousands of others through day and night as grey trucks carrying grey soldiers stole her country, and sometimes her friends.

During the first days of the invasion Claire hid, somewhat voluntarily, from the activity in the street. She listened to the whispers of her parents and the blaring sirens wailing across the city. Both made her tremble. One day she chanced a look through the front window curtain, drawn tight since the invasion, and watched in confusion as a neighboring family with a girl just her age was loaded, rather harshly, into a large grey truck. As the truck sped away and the family left the neighborhood, unknowingly for the last time, Claire's father discovered her at the window. She had braced herself for a lashing, but none came. Instead, he cradled her in his arms and sank into the dark green Victorian-style chair that was his throne and cried. He had never hugged her so tightly for so long and never had his tears lost themselves in his daughter's hair. These things a child remembers until she grows old enough to understand. Even then, the memories remain, but Claire had felt them shift from foggy confusion to fuel for an inner fire.

The early days of the occupation slipped into weeks and months, and the McCleash family turned the pages of their calendar with a solemn reverence for lost time. With another month gone, curiosity, boredom, and the temptation offered by fear bid Claire to peek out more and more from behind the drapes of the family's windows. On the heels of these timid glances up the street came the inevitable ventures into what was becoming a new country. The Nazi presence was everywhere. Their bland trucks skirted up and down Claire's familiar roads leaving dust storms and litter reeling after them. It was these trucks that became the center of attention for Claire and several other budding teenagers. Protected by their knowledge of the city, the children of France began tormenting the trucks in the manner they may have pestered a tied hound in earlier days.

For Claire it began when a slight stick she was carrying seemed almost involuntarily to leap out and scratch the grey skin of a parked half-track personnel carrier. She instantly dropped the stick and sprinted away until she reached the safety of her house. Even then she ran until she was in her room, crouching on the floor in the corner. The shadow of safety cast by her bed held her at length while she listened for screeching tires and rattling gunfire erupting from the street in front of her house. None came. When she dared stand to check the window and the street below and found no signs of gathering grey or black uniforms, a warm rush coursed through her lithe frame and she sank to the floor once again, smiling.

It wasn't long before trying to hit the black crosses that graced the grey doors with rocks tossed from hidden places and rooftops became the local sport of choice. With the clang of a hit, a chorus of young voices would resound the feelings of all France. On the day when an errant throw missed its mark and instead shattered a windshield, forcing the truck under assault to veer into the gutter, the same rush of emotion that had captured Claire on her bedroom floor surged through the entire group.

The troublesome youngsters became teenagers and aged quickly, spurred by war, and their games grew with them. It was discovered that trucks with broken headlights could not move in the dark, whereas to Claire and her friends the night was an ally. So windshields and headlights suffered mightily until one afternoon an accidental escalation rocketed the bothersome antics of the group, from buzzing gnats to be halfheartedly shooed away, to the hunted — prime targets for the secret police.

Unthinking soldiers were stopped in a narrow alley when a garbage can dropped from a rooftop careened off the hood of their truck. The foolhardy driver stepped from behind the wheel into a barrage of bottles, stones, and bricks being hurled from above. One projectile or another, and from whose hand no one was certain, struck the German in the head. He instantly dropped to the ground, and a pool of blood spilled out from his broken skull. The brave and the reckless peered over the precipice of the building. Claire was among them, secure in both categories. She witnessed the single dying soldier, but for her he became all of Germany. There was a way to stop the Nazis, and she had found it at age fifteen.

When the driver's companion opened fire at the rooftop, Claire's compatriots darted away, but she remained, staring into the gunfire, never flinching. That calculated act remained with her through the years, a constant companion as she rained her own diminutive terror down on the occupying military. Now, from the hill, it was invoked yet again as she looked down on her infected city.

**

2

Three young Resistance fighters, one in old brown leather shoes with laces broken and retied, raced up the stairs two at a time. German soldiers in shiny black high-top boots with rifle muzzles jumping ahead of them followed within seconds. Shots rang through the house, and a Resistance fighter, the owner of the broken laces, fell. The Germans were on him before his heart could stop, and another bullet entered his eye as he looked up at his executioner.

"Go! Go! Go!" Sergeant Sneitz yelled. "They went up!"

The sergeant, a despicable man who drank often and bathed little, whipped his two companions into a lather as he stood over the one-eyed dead man. "Hurry, you assholes! And don't hit her! I want her, and I aim to have her!"

Two privates, Herbeart and Timic, ran up to the third floor ahead of him and encountered no opposition on the way. In seconds they had cornered the two fleeing fighters, one a young man and the other the object of the chase for Sergeant Sneitz. Herbeart, heretofore lost in the passion of the chase, suddenly realized the couple posed little threat. They may have been members of the Resistance, a great many young people were in one sense or another, but these

were unarmed and merely walking up the boulevard when Sneitz
had spotted the woman. Now they were running for their lives, and
the route they'd chosen was the wrong one.

The last room had no weapons, not even a stick or a chair to
fend off the pursuers. And still the young man, like a frightened
animal driven to a corner, turned and jumped at the soldiers. Private
Herbeart, the youngest of the Nazi trio, fired out of instinct. His
partner pulled his trigger as well, and the young Frenchman withered
against the wall and waited to die. In moments his wait was over.

Sneitz sped into the room just behind the shots. "If you shot
that whore..." Then he saw the girl was unscathed. "Good job!" he
said as he lowered his weapon and patted Herbeart's back. "Now we
can have us a party."

For the girl, resisting the soldiers proved more painful than the
attack. She tried, initially, but the sergeant invoked her cooperation
with several well-placed punches to the face. The rape began while
Herbeart and Timic searched the two dead men. Herbeart found a
few francs on the dead man leaning against the wall and stuffed it
in his pocket, carefully hiding the fact from his partners.

The sergeant was finished in minutes. Then the rape was passed to
Timic while the girl stumbled through various stages of consciousness.
When Timic had finished with her, Herbeart had seen enough.

"Next!" Timic yelled triumphantly.

When Herbeart didn't follow suit the others began to ride him.

"What's the matter, soldier?"

"Nothing."

"You aren't a queer, are you?"

"No, but...damn, she's almost dead."

"So?"

"I'm not touching no dead girl."

Sneitz kicked the woman in the side, and she uttered a tired
moan. "See? She isn't dead."

"I'll pass."

"You fairy, Herbeart!"

"Damn!" the young soldier said as he stormed out, chased by
more taunts. No sooner had his boots hit the stairs than one last

gunshot was triggered in the house. The report spun Herbeart on his heels, and he raced back to the room. He came into the doorway at the same time Timic tried to leave. They bounced against each other and faked to one side then the other, each anxious to go by in the opposite direction. Exasperated, Herbeart pushed Timic back into the room. Only then did he see the widening pool of blood streaming from the girl's head.

"Damn, Sneitz! What the hell's the matter with you?"

"She is...was, a part of that Resistance thing. Now she isn't. Let's go."

Herbeart stood stock still, staring at the blood as it moved across the floor, coming for him.

"I said, let's go!" Sneitz ordered.

"She was just a kid."

Sneitz looked back at the girl. Her pants were down, one leg torn free from them, and her shirt was pushed up. "She was old enough. Probably same age as you, Herbeart."

That realization struck him hard, and the puzzled look on his face deepened. Timic saw it and grabbed his arm. "Hey. C'mon. We got work to do."

Timic succeeded in pulling Herbeart toward the door, but as soon as the retreat began, the sergeant stopped it. He lowered his rifle barrel across the doorway in front of the two soldiers. "Herbeart, you forget anything you're thinking. You go soft on me and you're apt to get hurt in a firefight some night. A bullet's a bullet. Doesn't matter where it comes from. Follow?"

"Don't worry about him, Sarge," Timic said with a laugh. "He just needs a little R and R. I'll take him to the Lights Club tonight and get him drunk as hell. Tomorrow he'll be right as rain."

Sneitz didn't say anything else, nor did the others. The soldiers fell in behind their sergeant and left the house to their conquests. The blood pool gave up trying to reach the men and slowed. Minutes later it stopped entirely and soon turned almost black as it dried on the floor and the hair of the pretty young girl.

***

3

Claire's breath was her own again, but before she left her vantage point on the hill she doffed her cap and discreetly peered inside. Tucked beneath the inner headband was a letter she had secreted away many miles and many hills before. She adjusted it slightly, more of an assurance to herself than security for the note, then pulled the cap back down tight over her tied-up hair and pushed on.

This side of the hill proved a comfortable friend and pulled her effortlessly down toward home. As the bicycle picked up speed it was swallowed by the increased traffic nearer the city. Freed from pedaling, Claire was able to concentrate solely on navigation, which was warranted as the grey cars and trucks seemed to care little about the lone bicyclist.

The air of the Germans was, however, not one of complete indifference. Even in her corduroy pants, boots, and baggy jacket, the curves of Claire's young figure were strong. Though she always preferred her pants to her sister's flowing dresses, today, on this two-wheeled sortie, her clothes had a purpose. She had hoped her unadorned appearance would help keep her from drawing the attention of passing Germans. As a result of the exploits of Claire and her young countrymen, the Nazis had become more cognizant of the Resistance and therefore more willing than ever before to stop and question the citizenry, especially pretty ones.

As she raced on, aware of increasing stares both piercing and passing, Claire hunched even further over her handlebars to conceal the curves of her breasts. She ducked her head to hide her face and glanced up only enough to save herself from crashing as the traffic swirled around her.

A convertible German field car — long, grey, low to the ground, its top down in the sun and bursting with a load of young zealous soldiers, slowed as it approached Claire head on. She heard the motor relax and looked up into the lewd stares of half a dozen soldiers. The car slowed nearly to a stop when it came abreast of the bicycle. Two soldiers leaned heavily out of the car and crudely swiped at Claire's bottom.

"You like to ride, baby?" they shouted in broken French. "I got something for you to ride on!"

The nearness of the pass forced Claire onto the grassy roadside and nearly into the ditch. The bicycle teetered on the uneven ground, but Claire forced it ahead. In the car, the driver was being goaded to stop. He resisted his comrades' playful punches until his hat was pushed down over his eyes. As he slammed on the brakes and halted the creeping car, several of the soldiers clamored out the back onto the wide trunk and shouted at Claire who once again stood on the pedals and encouraged the bike ahead.

"Come back, sweetheart! I need riding, too!"

"No, no! Me, you sweet thing! How about dinner?"

Claire glanced over her shoulder as a third soldier snatched a candy bar from his pocket and jumped off the trunk. He jogged toward Claire dangling his prize. "Forget them, darling. I've got chocolate!"

Claire heard him and looked again, but more to judge the distance than the bait. The soldier took the glance as a positive sign and continued toward her as his partners laughed behind him. Claire's legs responded to the closing threat and pumped all the harder, easily outdistancing the candy suitor.

"But I've got chocolate!" he yelled woefully as he lumbered to a stop and the pursuit ended.

Claire cycled further on until she was easily out of reach. The soldier began returning to the car, which pulled away slightly as he approached. The candy-bearing soldier was soon forced to jog after it then run outright, shouting obscenities at the driver as his ride picked up speed. Claire stopped when she heard the commotion and straddled the bicycle as she looked back at the childish spectacle. She shook her head as her vanquished intended was forced to relinquish his precious chocolate in exchange for re-admittance to the car. The entire carload caught sight of Claire watching from her safe distance and threw her kisses. Then they laughed heartily at their sport and drove away while Claire watched, fuming. She squinted to better see the faces in the car, but they had become a blurring mass of grey.

"Perhaps we will get together some night," she said softly as she tugged at her cap and felt the letter hidden in its lining. "Perhaps we will."

The bicycle and Claire departed company with the car and was soon absorbed by the ebb and flow of traffic as the city wrapped its arms around her. Rows of tightly spaced similar-looking houses lined the narrow streets on either side as Claire pedaled the bicycle toward home. She continued her leaning and weaving navigation until she turned up a cramped side street and coasted from the thoroughfare onto the sidewalk.

Before she stopped completely, Claire stepped through the bike's frame and hit the ground in stride. She moved hurriedly up the stoop of her parents' house wheeling the bicycle alongside. The pause at the door was only enough to work the lock; then she stepped inside, pulling the bicycle in with her.

The house was dim despite it being only late afternoon, but Claire's eyes would soon adjust to the subtle light of the foyer. This open hallway and the attached living room still rested behind pulled drapes four years after the invasion and those first ugly days. Had the curtains opened, the sun would have shone on a room neat and clean but lacking in décor, almost Spartan in its simple functionality. Impending war and war itself had prohibited Sean from furnishing it to the level he wished for his wife and children. He had the money, tucked away for rainy days, and worked part-time when he wanted at the local postal delivery office where in his prime, in better days, he had labored as a carrier and retired as a manager. The McCleash money was currently hidden in the house, out of sight from the invaders who had early on pilfered the banks. The house itself — though plain, simple, and anonymous on the street — was paid for. It was his. But Sean and his family understood it would remain so only until such time as the Third Reich decided otherwise or the British and Americans bombed it in an effort to dismantle the German war machine.

The bicycle leaned against the wall, enjoying a well-deserved rest as Claire sent a standard glance in the direction of her father's chair. She didn't expect to find him there, and she was right, but the look was really an assessment of his pipe rack, which consumed the better part of a smallish end table that sat alongside the worn and comfortable chair.

The neat row of pipes, eight in all, served many functions beyond their designed intention. To Sean the various pipes were carriers of different tastes and different sensations to the mouth, nose, and hand. They had been years in assembling and had become comfortable friends to him and guardians of simple pleasures. But to the women of the house the pipes provided a wealth of information. They were both a barometer of the patriarch's temperament and a geographic locator of sorts.

When the radio sent music through the house, Sean held a rather dainty pipe with a hand-carved bowl and delicate stem that he seldom drew against. Rather, he seemed to wave it about like a maestro's baton, keeping rough time to the tunes. Yet when the limited news dispatches concerning the war interrupted the songs, the dainty pipe found its way back to its cradle and was replaced in Sean's hand by a dog-eared pipe with a robust stem suitable for grinding teeth. He would listen to the German propaganda and puff hard and fast, transforming the pipe into a locomotive's smokestack. At the end of the rack rested a glorious handcrafted carved white clay pipe from Sean's Ireland. This wonderfully fragile piece was reserved for holiday smokes and very special occasions only. Even after countless years on the pipe rack's throne, the white clay was scarcely discolored by tobacco. Holidays were few given the occupation, and to Sean there was nothing to celebrate.

Claire took a step toward the pipe rack and the information it offered, but was interrupted by the sound of her sister's voice calling out strongly from upstairs.

"Claire? That you?"

Monique's voice brought Claire up short, as if the youngest McCleash were bracing for a battle.

"Who'd you expect?" Claire tossed up the stairs in the first line of defense.

"Hurry along," Monique came back. "We'll be late."

"Late for what? And where's Father?"

As if on cue, Monique appeared from upstairs on a narrow landing halfway up the steps. She wore a shimmering maroon dress, which was as yet unbuttoned from her collar to her waist. A gleaming white camisole bursting through the front of the dress sat low and tight on Monique's ample breasts. She cast a potentially fierce glance at her sister then tossed her chestnut hair to the side and concentrated on a troublesome earring. As she primped herself in a full-length mirror that resided on the landing, she chided her sibling.

"I don't know the answer to the latter, and you know full well the answer to the former," Monique said to the mirror. "You're to go with me to the club. Now, get out of those boys' clothes and into the dress I've laid out for you."

Monique settled with the irksome earring and buttoned her dress to the top as she continued, "Being a few minutes late is fashionable, but too late..." She unbuttoned several of the topmost buttons, cupped her breasts and pushed them up. "Yes, too late, and well, let's just say the pickings may be slimmer."

Claire realized the words she was about to say were certain to ignite another argument and buffeted for the storm she knew was about to descend from the landing. However, the words were suddenly, albeit temporarily, squelched in her mouth by the admiration she felt for her sister as she looked to the landing. Claire recognized Monique's beauty and stunning figure, but also her command. As she watched her sister in those brief seconds, Claire found herself following the outline of the clinging maroon dress.

Monique's hips were full and the dress tight. Claire considered that it wasn't the type of snugness that came from too many parfaits, but rather it was the style of firmness that caused a yearning in men and invited them to ask for a dance and hope for breakfast. Monique knew what to do when they asked, for dances and more, and it was this ability to both excite and disarm that captivated Claire, although as sisters are prone to do, she was loath to let on the depth of that admiration.

What she did allow to show through was her contempt for Monique's practice of dating Germans. For her own brand of enemy contact, Claire relied on guns, not dancing. It worked, of course, was more final, and, to Claire, more fitting. She thought her sister's way took less of *something*, but she wasn't always certain what that something was. Guts. Courage. Nerves of steel? To lie in wait and pull the trigger. Versus Monique's seductive moves, delicate mannerisms, careful words. Was that a skill?

For all her intended resolve against the trip to the club, Claire could now only manage a weak attempt at misdirection. "These aren't boys' pants, are they?" she said as she brushed at the corduroy.

Monique pivoted toward the living room and thrust her hands onto her hips. "Move!"

"I'm not going," Claire said.

Almost ignoring her sister, Monique turned her attention back to the mirror and resumed primping. "It's been all argued out. You told mother you'd go. And Claire, please, there isn't time. We have to stop by the nunnery."

Claire had been ready to give in as she had the evening before when the plan was battled into existence by Monique and their mother. Now, however, she had unexpected ammunition. "Hold it. I might have said I'd go to the club. Repeat, MIGHT. But I never said anything about the nunnery. The deal's off."

Monique spun from the mirror again. Her face reddened slightly beneath her exquisite makeup, and she stepped menacingly down two steps toward her sister. "Listen to me. I haven't the inclination nor the time for one of your famous political tantrums. We are going to the club, and we are stopping at the nunnery. Now get dressed!"

Claire recognized the tone in her sister's voice and the set of her jaw. Pursuing the argument would be fruitless. She was overmatched and outgunned, and she knew it. "Alright. Alright. Don't get in a tizzy over it. Gee whiz, you'd think I cussed out the Pope or something."

With steps as plodding as a dying elephant's, coupled with an overemphasized sway to match, Claire reluctantly began climbing the stairs. "I'll go, but I'm not going in the nunnery. I hate that place, all full of those little German bastards."

Monique reached out and gently touched her sister's arm as she passed. The voice that had been so stern moments before evaporated, and the glare she had shot down the stairs vanished in an instant, replaced by a hurt in her deep brown eyes. "Please don't say such things, Claire. They're just children."

The change of attitude was marked and didn't go unnoticed by Claire. She had lost the previous battle, but the anguish in Monique's eyes betrayed a weakness which Claire targeted.

"Children, yes. German children. Father says they're from Nazis raping schoolgirls. He says they should send them back to Germany where they belong."

It was Claire's turn to grab her sister's arm. The effort was strictly for dramatic effect. There was no compassion. "Once I heard Father and some of his friends say the children should be...eliminated!"

"Don't say that."

"It's true! Father said that in the Great War there was a bunch of German bastards born, too. And now they've grown up. They went back to Germany because that was the only country that would take them. They trained them all as Gestapo, you know. Father says that now they've returned to France to kill and rape again. He says..."

"I know what Father says, but we're talking about children. It's not their doing they're here. Do you think they chose to be born into a war? Or chose to be born at all?"

"And do you think all those girls chose to be raped?"

"You don't know that all those children are the result of rape."

"They must be. No decent girl would be seen with a Nazi after what they've done to our country." Claire's eyes slid disapprovingly, but nervously, over her sister.

Monique recognized the intent of the speech and the glance. "They're just children," she said as she turned away. "The nuns have an awfully difficult job raising them with people like father around."

"And me!" Encouraged by her slight victory Claire left the elephant behind and bounded up the steps, continuing her bantering as she entered her bedroom at the top of the stairs. "I agree with father. Send the little bastards back to Germany. I hate them all. Them and all Germans. But you don't, do you? You don't seem to mind Nazis at all. In fact, I think you like the sons of bitches, especially the officers."

Claire set her cap and its secret letter carefully on her bed next to a neatly laid out glistening blue dress, which she callously pushed aside so she could sit. As she abused the dress, her sister appeared in the doorway.

"What's that supposed to mean?"

An intense stare had taken the place of Monique's mournful eyes. Claire saw it and immediately retreated. She shrugged meekly as if unsure how to end a conversation she herself had begun. Looking for an ending, perhaps on the floor, Claire ducked her head and began untying her boots. Beyond her, Monique stepped away from the door and went down the hallway to her own bedroom.

The boots were only a short-lived reprieve for Claire. Monique soon reappeared in the doorway, running a pair of silk stockings through her fingers. "Here," she said as she tossed the stockings on the bed. "Put these on."

Claire carefully picked up the stockings and examined the delicate weave. She put a hand inside and brushed the fine hose against her cheek. "Silk stockings...I wonder what you had to do to get these."

Monique crossed her arms, closed her eyes dramatically, and leaned against the doorframe. "Not much," she said. "And I got a lot more than just stockings."

"I'll bet you did, but at what price?"

"No price."

"No? I didn't realize they were giving away dignity these days. I must be mistaken. I thought self-respect was still valuable."

"It is. And I still have mine. I have everything I've always had."

"Except your virginity."

Monique stepped to Claire's dresser and began straightening her sister's ragtag cosmetic collection. "Oh, grow up, Claire." She picked up a few disjointed blushes and liners as she addressed Claire's reflection in the mirror. "If you go on a date..."

"Fat chance."

"I said if."

"I heard you, but you don't have to make it sound so...so if-y."

"Regardless. Let's say you go out on a date. The gentleman takes you to dinner then to a film. Naturally it's his treat."

"Naturally."

"After the film you stop at the club for a few drinks and some dancing. You spend more of his money."

"Your point being?"

"By the time the night's over you've spent his entire week's wages, right?"

"Hopefully," Claire laughed as she bounced to the edge of the bed as if hearing a good story.

"And what does the now broke date want in return?" Monique teased.

"I know this one! I know this one!"

Monique raised her eyebrows suspiciously. "I'm sure you do."

"Well, I mean, I don't know personally, but I know what they're after."

"And do they get it?"

"No! Of course not!"

"How about a kiss goodnight?"

"Sure."

"How about some real passionate kissing in a dark corner on the way home?"

"Sounds kinda nice," Claire said dreamily.

"And then he runs his hands over you. Very gently..."

Claire closed her eyes and smiled to herself. "Yeah..."

"And then..." Monique said softly as she crept to the bed. "You rip your clothes off!" she screamed as she flung herself on Claire and pinned her to the bed, fighting to kiss her sister's neck. "And you roll around on the wet grass and hump each other like dogs in heat!"

Claire screamed as well but quickly recovered and flung Monique off her onto the bed. While her sister rolled in laughter, Claire scrambled to her feet and tossed the stockings in Monique's hysterical face.

"That's not funny!" Claire said as her own face reddened, initially from embarrassment, but also from a timid anger.

Monique regained her composure and propped herself up on an elbow, gently fondling the silk stockings. "But consider it, Claire. The poor slug's spent every cent on your date and in exchange you're going to give up at least a kiss and maybe a lot more."

"A little more."

"Okay, for you, a little more, or so you claim."

"Monique!"

"Alright. A little more. You're still talking about what you can get and giving them at least some of what they want. Am I right?"

"You make it sound awfully sterile. Like a date is some kind of legal business."

"Isn't it? You give, you get. It's business."

Claire walked to the dresser and began thoughtfully examining the cosmetics Monique had so neatly arranged.

For her part, Monique stayed on the bed. She gently stroked the stockings as she again watched Claire in the mirror, but now their positions were reversed.

"What about...love?" Claire asked. "You know, what about feelings and things?"

"All that comes later, if at all."

"And then what of 'business?'"

"Out the window!" Monique said as she set aside the hosiery, got up, and went to her sister. "When love enters the equation, forget everything I said."

Claire was noticeably relieved to hear the latest advice. "Well, at least that's good to know. I was beginning to wonder if I was going to have to keep a tally book by the bed after I was married."

"No, no book." Monique laughed, hesitated, then pointed to her head. "Keep your husband's records up here."

Claire pushed her away. "Now you're getting silly."

Monique went back to the bed, sat, and leaned back on her hands. "Husbands aside, most dates are just exchanges. Business. Agreed?"

Claire turned from the mirror and leaned heavily against the dresser. "To save an argument, agreed."

"You take what you can and give up as little as possible in return," Monique repeated.

"Okay, and so?"

"So," Monique continued, "I'm just saying what's the difference if you get the gifts, or the date, or whatever, up front and give them some of what they want later or you have sex with them first then get what you can? You're still peddling your ass, now aren't you?"

Claire's arms flopped down to her side, and her jaw dropped. "God, Monique, is that what you do?"

Monique got up uneasily and stepped back to the doorway. She shuffled her feet in an unaccustomed fashion and stared at the polished hardwood floor as she answered. "No...Not exactly."

"Then what, exactly, do you do?"

The pause that proceeded Monique's reply was weighted and didn't suit the sisters or the room. This room had eavesdropped on them many, many times since they began sharing it years before when Claire first left her crib. And even after, when Monique, accused by Claire of abandonment at the time, moved out and down the hall to her own room, this small bedroom would collect the two when a situation or a circumstance suggested a sisterly talk was in order. In those talks, ears fine-tuned for hearing familial voices, listened intently as the sisters provided the right words or at times, just a shoulder. But the war had escorted those days into the past.

Monique remained in the doorway. She eventually lifted her head and spoke in a soft, but clear voice. "I do what I can for the Resistance."

Claire felt the heft of her sister's answer and followed with her own respectful pause. She took Monique's place on the edge of the bed, but found she couldn't contain herself as her thoughts formed words in her mouth.

"C'mon. Now who needs to grow up? You sleeping with Nazis. What does that do for France?"

Instantly on the defensive, a firmness crept back in Monique's voice. "You'd be surprised what attentive ears can learn on a pillow."

Claire snatched up the stockings and jumped up to her knees on the bed. She held the hosiery out to Monique and shook them at her. Though she wasn't angry, her voice was quick and impassioned. "Don't do this anymore! Come with us! Work with the active Resistance. It'd be great! You and me!"

Monique sighed deeply, but found a smile for her intense little sister. "Darling," she said wryly as she spread her fingers before her. "Look at these hands. I can't play with guns. I'm afraid I'd break a nail."

"Stop it, Monique. This is serious."

"I am serious! Do you know how much a good manicure costs these days? Why, you have no idea."

Claire lowered her head in defeat. Her hands dropped into her lap, and she absently tugged at the stockings. "Aww, c'mon, Mo..."

The shallow smile abandoned Monique's lips, replaced by a tender look of care and compassion. "You haven't called me that in a long time."

"No?"

"Maybe years. I kind of miss it."

"Yeah?"

"Yeah."

"Sorry."

Monique stepped into the room again and slowly approached her sister, whose body betrayed the exasperation she felt. "How come you never call me Mo anymore?"

"I dunno," Claire muttered as she continued her handling of the stockings. "Just grew out of it, I guess."

"When you were a baby, you couldn't say Monique. You could only get out the Mo part. I always liked it though. It was something just between you and me. Whenever I heard someone yell Mo, I knew it was you."

Claire chuckled a little and looked up. "Yeah, I knew you liked it. I remember how if I really wanted you to do something, I'd call you Mo."

"And I'd do it."

"Yeah, you would," Claire continued softly as her attention once more drifted to the stockings in her lap. "But I guess it doesn't work anymore."

Monique moved close to her sister and tenderly covered Claire's hands with her own, unconsciously gripping the silk stockings between them. "Honey, I'm no soldier. I can't carry a gun. And I can't do the things you and the others do. So I do what I can. Okay?"

Claire rose slowly, not pulling away from her sister's clasp. Monique's hands fell away regardless and the stockings with them. The fine hosiery slithered through Claire's fingers and dangled from Monique's manicured nails. She stared at the silk a moment then gently laid them on the bed next to Claire's cap as a pile of hastily discarded clothes began to grow beside her sister.

"It's not okay," Claire said as she stripped. "Not with me. I want you to know that. But if you won't listen to Father, you're not going to listen to me."

The reference to her father peaked in Monique a rush of emotions that ran a wide gamut. Fond memories of love and devotion were bordered by anguish and heartbreak. Even the most precious memories had been tampered with. Seeing them now in her mind's eye, the events were seasoned with ugliness, as if one could believe such a thing possible. Long ago, fear had unseated trust between father and daughter and had served to bury every hint of the old relationship. Long periods of silence had replaced the laughter that had once flowed so easily between them. Now, mournful periods of silence were unending and only interrupted by Sean McCleash's lectures regarding his eldest and her rendezvous with German officers.

Monique returned to the door as Claire stepped into the dress and awkwardly pulled it up. "You know, Monique, you can be awfully strange."

The words brought Monique to a slow stop in the doorway. She momentarily let the resurgent thoughts of her father pass and concentrated again on her sister. Though she didn't speak, she did raise an eyebrow at Claire's suggestion.

"Think about it. What do you do during the day?" Claire asked rhetorically. "I happen to know you go to that nunnery and help out with those orphans. You play nursemaid to them, I suppose. Then at night you dance with the same Nazis who rape our country and infest us with those identical little bastards. How in the world do you keep your sanity?"

The rush from Claire set Monique back as her footing was still awkwardly slipping across her father's opinion of her. She uncharacteristically hesitated with her reply and tried to skirt away from the real issue of fraternizing with the enemy by forcing a weak smile. "I don't know. It's not as bad as all that."

"Yes it is. You live a life with bastards — bastard children in the daylight and bastard members of the Third Reich in the dark."

Monique's smile faded. "I wish you wouldn't put it that way. The children..."

Only half dressed, Claire went to her sister and grabbed her arms. The passion returned to her voice, but now it carried with it a desperation that suggested she would not ask again. And in that not asking there was a fear.

"One last time. Join us. The satisfaction of killing a Nazi has got to be better than babysitting their brats or sleeping with them."

"I can't, Claire. I'm no killer."

"Neither am I! I'm a soldier."

"I can't do that. I'm sorry."

"Are you? I wonder. I really and truly wonder."

Monique stood a minute longer in Claire's grasp, but her conviction was undaunted, and the resolve in her voice melted away her sister's hopes along with her arms.

The youngest McCleash went to the bed and began lazily pulling on the silk stockings as Monique turned away. "Hurry along. We'll be late."

As her sister disappeared down the stairs to the family's living room, Claire recklessly applied the minimum amount of makeup. She hastily brushed her soft brown hair, which, in spite of the rough treatment, came to life around her face and shoulders. As she stepped to the bed and retrieved the clandestine letter from the cap, Claire squirmed into her seldom worn dress shoes.

In the room below, Monique had slipped into her father's chair. Her head rested against the well-worn back cushion, and she closed her eyes. The breath she drew carried with it the musky smells that were her father. It was clean working man sweat, coupled with a very plain cologne supplied in days past by his children on Christmas and his wife on the occasion of their anniversary. Around the particular scent was the ever present aroma of tobacco and the pipes whose smell whispered for her attention.

She opened her eyes and looked at the old but neatly arranged rack of pipes. After a thoughtful examination, Monique very carefully slipped the white clay from its place and held it closely, exploring every minute carving and age-worn scratch, each one an indicator of a time apart from the present.

Claire didn't pause to check her look in the bureau mirror nor did the full-length mirror on the landing stop her on the way to the living room. Only when she bounced into the room did Monique force Claire's attention back on herself.

"Why, Claire," Monique said over a broad smile as she lowered the clay pipe to her lap. "It's a transformation. You look absolutely stunning."

Forced to pause mid-entrance, Claire glanced quickly at herself and brushed away a wrinkle in her dress. "You don't have to act so shocked. I am a girl you know."

"And you look every inch of it."

"Yeah, yeah. Thanks," Claire said, waylaying the praise, but secretly relishing each and every nuance of the compliment.

The dress had indeed done its job nicely. The shimmering blue material cascaded over Claire's curves and flowed around her waist and hips, propelled by the slightest of moves. All this while the letter flipped back and forth in her hands.

Claire sought to compound her new status as dress wearer by adding the importance of the letter and her role in the chain from author to the head of the Resistance. She tapped it demonstratively against her palm. "I've got to drop this off at the safe house. Supposed to go directly to Charlemagne herself."

Until now the dress had overshadowed the communiqué, but when Monique did notice it, it repelled her, representing as it did the Resistance, her seamy work, and the resulting conflict with her father. Much to Claire's dismay Monique was riveted again by the white clay pipe.

"You remember," Monique said, as if addressing the pipe and not her sister, "when we were little we weren't allowed to touch this pipe? All the rest were okay, you know? If you wanted to play Father or do something silly, it was all right to have one of the others, but not this one. Remember that?"

The dreaminess in Monique's voice asked Claire to set aside the importance of the letter and momentarily stay Claire's own fleeting dash to center stage. Claire moved, albeit cautiously, toward her father's chair, Monique, and the pipe. The letter, temporarily demoted, was still in front of her as if it and a suitable distance would shield her from blame should Monique's hand slip and the McCleash touchstone – the clay pipe – tumble to the floor.

"I wouldn't touch it now," Claire said through a laugh that did little to hide her seriousness. "If that breaks you're still going to get a whipping."

"He probably would whip me, wouldn't he? Like he needs another excuse."

The words were punctuated by the pipe being carefully slipped back into its place alongside the others. Monique withdrew her hands slowly and examined them as she sighed. "Father hates me, Claire," she said as she dropped her hands with resignation onto her lap. Her eyes were fixated on her hands, fingers, and nails in an abstract way.

The words did much to bring Claire close. She crouched down in front of Monique and rested her own hands on her sister's silky knees. Claire attempted to rouse her sister from the sadness that enveloped her as surely as if it had been smoke from the white clay pipe.

"Father doesn't hate you. He just hates the things you do."

"I only do what I can."

"I don't know about that, but I do know Father loves you."

"Not like he used to."

"Things are different now. The war has brought changes in all of us. But soon the Americans will come and we'll get back to the way it used to be. You'll see."

Monique sat quietly and seemed not to hear. Memories drifted in and out of her head, clouding Claire's well intentioned words until a thought took root and flooded her with remembrance. "Claire, you remember when we were little and we used to dance for Father all the time? We'd sing and dance and Father would clap the rhythm?"

"You danced. I clapped with Father. You were the showgirl. I couldn't dance. Still can't."

"Yes. I suppose," Monique answered absently. "I'd dance around his flower bed out back. Remember how he'd never let us pick any? Why was that?"

"I guess he wanted them to stay put. When you pick them, they die. When they stay in the bed, you can enjoy them a lot longer. The speech went something like that I think."

Monique continued without acknowledging Claire's recollection. "And then Mother would bring out some of her little finger cakes and we'd have a party."

"I remember. God, those things were good! I could eat a hundred of them. When they're tiny like that they don't make you fat. You can eat as many as you want."

Claire's playful comments brought a smile to her sister and edged her a short distance from her melancholy. With the comfort of the distance, Monique gave Claire a disbelieving look.

"It's true!" Claire laughed.

"Regardless. Do you remember those times? Back when things were simpler?"

Claire patted Monique's knee and stood abruptly. "C'mon you. You're talking like it was fifty years ago. You're barely twenty-one and reminiscing like we're in the parlor of the government old-age home! Let's go if we're going. I've got to get this to the safe house, and I suppose you still want to stop at the nunnery."

Monique shook her head, trying to cast off the cobwebs of the recent past. The dream slowly cleared. "You're right. It just seems so long ago."

As she spoke, Claire stepped into the foyer and retrieved two light summer coats. "It's the war. And those damn Germans." She draped one coat over her arm and held the other out to her sister, inviting Monique to join her.

"Don't curse. It isn't ladylike," Monique said as she moved to take the coat.

"When I talk about Germans I don't feel ladylike."

"Let's get out of here," Monique answered as she pointed back to the pipe rack. "Father's walking pipe is missing. He could be home any minute. If he catches us dressed like this, we'll both be in for a whipping."

Claire answered by moving toward the door. She cautiously opened it, stuck her face out, and looked up and down the street. Monique poked her head out over her sister's shoulder and joined in on the surveillance. Not seeing their father, the pair slipped out the door and hurried away from the shadow of their house. The same streets that had first cradled and nurtured the girls in the early years and then come to haunt them with the advent of the Nazi presence quickly swallowed them as they made good their escape. Though assured of forgoing an immediate altercation with their father, Monique tossed a quick glance over her shoulder as she rounded the corner that would leave their neighborhood behind. Had Sean McCleash slipped onto the street unnoticed behind them, she would have had the luxury of preparing Claire for the inevitable scolding that would have been certain to come. As it was she sighed unnoticeably in relief and hustled up the boulevard at her sister's side.

***

4

Foot traffic increased as the sisters walked on, and they soon found comfort in the anonymity of the crowd. The people around them were all French or apparently so. Certain among them were German, or perhaps worse, German sympathizers, though the distinction wasn't an obvious one. All this was by design. In the years following the initial invasion, and indeed prior, the Gestapo had attempted to place spies over the breadth of France. Few were actual members of the Third Reich. Most were born French and considered by the invaders as converts to the cause of German supremacy. Understandably, the bulk of the country, the "true French" as Sean was apt to call them, considered these converts traitors.

While the lives of everyone, German and French alike, had changed beyond measure as the war became a part of their daily lives, few could boast a change as dramatic as those born to France who now gathered intelligence for the enemy. The modification for these people was more an emotional one, at least at the onset. They rode a line between their own selfish desires and the needs of their country. As often happens to those who find themselves astride a fence, they would eventually take a hard hit to the groin.

Few French, if any, were sympathetic when this eventuality struck. Cowing to the wants of a superior invader to advance one's private interest, even if that interest was food for the family's table, would elicit the harshest of responses from the natives. The care of the Germans toward these people, whom they considered necessary evils, wasn't much better. Distrust and pressure to produce almost always culminated with betrayal, real or imagined, followed closely by exile or death. It was one of the few certainties of the war, that once committed to espionage, the fate of the traitors was sealed, regardless of their initial intentions.

It was these people that the sisters looked for as they discreetly slowed their walk. They took turns scanning the crowd for any hint or clue that someone was watching them. Practice had taught them ways of looking into faces without their glances being returned, as direct eye contact might be a warning to someone inclined to look for such things as the sisters themselves were inclined. When they accidentally caught an eye, their painted lips jumped into smiles, easily disarming and dissuading and driving out thoughts of anything other than that pretty face. But today, all was quiet.

The pair stopped near the entrance to a narrow alley. Conversation had slowed with their steps, but once they stopped, Monique launched into a dialogue that would have been senseless save for the situation.

"So I told them I thought the apartment was fine. A touch small perhaps. I'll just have to adjust."

As she spoke, Claire surreptitiously glanced into the alley. Monique continued her dribble until the look in Claire's eyes confirmed that all was well. The sisters then drifted to the corner, and the conversation renewed itself as Claire checked down the street. Her eyes rested on the front of a nondescript row house. It was still, and the street in front was nearly empty.

Claire flashed a nearly invisible nod at her sister, which prompted the two of them to retrace their steps to the alley. Without looking back, and at a determined but casual pace, they stepped into the seldom used back street. Once they were out of range of the prying eyes on the main street, they hastened their steps until they reached the back door of the house Claire had observed from the corner moments before.

This was the Resistance safe house for this section of the city. Countless others dotted the country, but their locations were far from permanent as the Resistance was forced to move them often. The houses were actually far from safe, but the name stuck. Too often the Germans learned of a house's location and raided it, usually leaving the building burning in their wake. Given the confines of homes in neighborhoods like this one and others in the city, adjacent houses often caught fire as well. This was of little consequence to the Nazis who relished a good burning as a way of purging France of what the Germans took for blight and the French took for patriots. Because of the potential for fires and also the fear that the Gestapo would retaliate in other ways against the nearby homes, suspecting them, usually wrongfully so, of being affiliates, the formation of a safe house was not totally embraced by the neighborhoods into which they fell. Due in part to this reaction, the path of a home's induction as a safe house into the Resistance was very gradual. This seemed to ease the transition of the house and, to a smaller degree, the neighborhood from civilian to paramilitary duty.

The owners of the various houses were seldom compensated and, as often as possible, the actual owner had no direct affiliation with the Movement. It was vital that as much figurative distance as possible be set between the house and the Resistance, leaving location as a secondary consideration in the selection process. Owners, however, to the man and to the woman, gave up their homes readily, many times moving completely out for safety's sake. For some it was the only way they could contribute to the effort. For these citizens, losing their homes, first to the Resistance then to the Germans and perhaps fire, was accepted with a glad heart.

This particular safe house was typical. It was as nondescript as any other on the row. The front stoop blended in with countless others but was special for a secret it concealed. Lost along the risers of its steps was a miniscule vent. It was all but invisible from the steps themselves and entirely so from the street. Like the house

itself this was all part of the design, and also like the house, the vent
served a purpose well above its original intent.

Below the house in its basement was the current war room of the
French Resistance for this region. The hidden vent was its lifeline to
the streets. A tube ran from the vent through the subterranean walls
of the house and opened into the room in which decisions about the
future of France were being made with increasing regularity.

The intelligence information those decisions were based on was
often passed from person to person across the country. However, as
the proximity of the safe house drew closer, hand-to-hand passes of
notes were often deemed too risky. Then an intelligence officer in
the Movement or perhaps a child bearing German troop placements,
arms shipments, or intercepted communiqués would sit briefly on
the steps of the safe house and deliver a message under the noses of
the Germans, but out of sight of their eyes.

For the moment, staying out of sight was also the concern of
the sisters. They had moved hurriedly through the alley and now
Claire was reaching for the simple latch on the back door of the safe
house. The plain door gave way easily, but also triggered a silent
alarm in the house.

Once inside the alley entranceway the sisters found themselves
facing a second, more secure door. The alarm had summoned
security guards that checked on the visitors through a peephole.
The girls were instantly recognized, and the main door to the
safe house unlocked, but not opened. The sisters heard the latch
slip, but they waited another minute, allowing the guards to
retreat to their posts hidden from view in upstairs windows with
machine guns leaning against the sills. Protocol called for the
girls to wait — the less faces that recognized other faces, the
better off for all.

Beyond the doorway was a short darkened hall that opened into
a large living room. Claire led the way and entered a quiet beehive
of activity. Young men and women, most dressed in dark clothes,
moved around and through the room quickly and noiselessly. Some
carried papers and maps, some weapons, and others just coffee cups.
In the center of the bustle was a large table that held a collection

of the carried items. Empty cups rested near maps that were held down at the corners by gun stocks and rifle clips.

The appearance of the sisters triggered a soft hum of recognition. As various members of the movement passed within arm's reach they stopped to hug Claire or grip her arm in silent acknowledgement. Of the many who passed few said a word outside of a soft hello and fewer still acknowledged Monique beyond a negligible nod.

Sophie, whose figure rivaled Monique's, stood against the far wall chatting quietly but in a lively manner with a younger girl. In sharp contrast to the dark clothes of those around her, Sophie wore a bright pink dress that flowed as she moved. Though her flouncing manner and appearance might have indicated otherwise, Sophie was a ranking member of the Resistance. Her specialty was intelligence gathering, which benefited the Movement and left her with silk stockings gently tucked away in dresser drawers. Monique was her protégé.

When Sophie saw Monique she excused herself from her companion and skirted across the floor. Unlike the others, Sophie passed Claire and embraced Monique fully and warmly as they exchanged cheek kisses.

"Darling," Sophie said through a caring smile. "You look absolutely a picture!" She held Monique's hands and took a slight step back glancing up and down her student's body. "That dress would entice Goering to give up the fuehrer's home phone number. You'd better keep your wits about you."

"I will," Monique answered without a hint of shyness at the flattering comments.

"Being careful?" Sophie asked as though quizzing a past lesson.

"Very careful. And you? You're dressed to conquer the world. Will I see you stepping from the door of a colonel's villa tonight?"

"You'd have to be there to see that, wouldn't you?" Sophie replied playfully.

"One can never tell where the night will lead."

Though Monique was clearly being comical Claire rolled her eyes and turned slightly but markedly away from the pair of professionals.

Sophie saw the move and added more incentive purely for her own pleasure. "The door to his villa? I don't think so. His bedroom maybe!"

Satisfied with her shock treatment Sophie turned her attention to Claire, but deferred and motioned back to Monique. "You look out for your sister here. She's a true saint."

"I'll try," Claire offered cordially. "But I'm kind of out of my element tonight."

"You'll do fine," Sophie said offhandedly. "It sure beats careening down some dark road in the middle of the night with bullets whistling by your head."

As she finished speaking, a handsome young man dressed in black from head to toe slipped through the room seemingly unnoticed by all but Claire. As he completed his stealthy exit he made brief eye contact with Claire who absently responded to Sophie's suggestion.

"Oh, I don't know...We all do what we can."

Sophie didn't see the cause or take notice of Claire's distraction. Rather, she continued her interest in the sisters' presence.

"What brings you two here anyway?"

Claire responded by turning slightly away from the room and slipping her dress up to retrieve the letter from the top of her stocking. Sophie glanced around the room and down at Claire's exposed thigh.

"Nice stockings, Claire. New?"

Claire dropped the hem of her dress and held up the letter. "New to me. They're Monique's."

Sophie smiled knowingly at Monique and playfully patted her arm. "Good work, girl."

"I learned from a master."

"Thanks," Sophie said as she cocked her head to the side. "I think."

Claire purposely ignored the veiled references to the ladies' enterprises. Instead, she tried to command attention with the letter, tapping it vigorously against her hand.

"Is Charlemagne in?"

The name wrenched Sophie from her playful mood. "I'm afraid not, but I'll see she gets it," she said as she reached for the letter.

Claire held it back noticeably, acting as though she hadn't heard or hadn't believed. "I was hoping to give it to her personally. I pedaled my butt off to get this here and, well, I've never met her."

"Yes, dear, I know," Sophie answered compassionately. "I'm afraid that's how it'll remain." She saw the disappointment register across Claire's face and quickly added. "At least for now. I'm sure you'll meet her one day soon."

But Claire was not yet ready to relinquish control of her only tie to the head of the Resistance. "Are you positive I couldn't just drop this off to her? I'm...I'm sort of a...a fan. Ever since the Nazis came I've been hearing about Charlemagne and the Resistance."

"I know, dear. But those who head the Movement must be very careful." Sophie clutched Claire's arm. "Not about you, but rather for you." She eased her grip on Claire and looked to Monique for help then back to the younger McCleash. "See, sometimes the less we know the better off we are. Understand?"

Claire didn't respond, but handed the letter to Sophie and walked away. Monique and Sophie looked after her steps and watched her exit the room through the same doorway the young man had used moments before.

"Monique, talk to her," Sophie begged.

Claire made her way down the hallway, stopping periodically to peek into the rooms that sprouted from it. She listened intently at a closed door then slowly cracked it open. It was dark inside. Her hand skimmed up and down the inside wall groping for the light switch until she found it. When she turned on the light she saw the young man in black, Michel, immediately before her. He smiled easily and reached for the light switch, covering Claire's hand with his. Using her hand as his own he flicked the light back off then eased Claire into the darkness and into his arms.

Michel closed the door with Claire's body as he pressed firmly into her. Their lips sought out one another in the dark and they kissed. Their hands cradled each other's faces until they fell to other things. Claire roughly squeezed his upper arms. Her hands danced back over his shoulders to his face then raced across his chest and again to his arms as passion filled them and the room.

Michel's hands dropped away from Claire's face and brushed along the length of his young lover's arms until they slipped onto her hips and down to her thighs. There they began to creep beneath the hem of the tight blue dress.

Claire's response was immediate, but not total. Her hands jumped down to Michel's wrists and gripped them tightly, stopping their advance.

"You look so good," Michel said as he nuzzled Claire's neck.

She let her head fall backward offering up her throat to her lover. "How can you tell in the dark?"

"Then you feel good," he said as he pressed his hips hard into hers. With the pressure Claire relaxed her grip, and Michel's hands slipped beneath the blue dress and squeezed her thighs through the silk stockings.

"So do you," Claire breathed as she arched into him.

They kissed and touched in the dark for several minutes. Flames began to lick at the dress until Claire slowly but firmly pushed Michel back until she could rest her arms on his chest.

"Down boy."

Michel smiled in the dark, but grabbed Claire roughly and pulled her close. "I never saw you in a dress before. Is all this for me?"

"I wish it was," Claire said softly.

Michel eased slightly out of the embrace. Even in the dark she could see the question on his face.

"I'm going to the Club of Lights with Monique."

Michel's hands froze on his lover. They stopped their pursuit and, unnoticed in the dark, one went to the light switch. He flicked the light on and stepped incredulously away from Claire. She shielded her eyes from the sudden brightness with one hand while the other pulled the hem of the dress back into place. All the heat that had been passion just moments before turned to ice with the switch of the light and the expression on Michel's face.

"You're kidding."

Now it was Claire's turn. "Why are you looking at me like that?"

The mutual responses of shock were pushed aside and in their wake lines had clearly been drawn.

"I'm looking because I'm trying to find Claire, the fighter. I want to ask her if she's forgotten about the Resistance."

"I haven't forgotten. That's what this is about."

Michel started to step backward then nearly rushed in on Claire. "The hell it is! And forget the Movement a second, what about us?"

"Stop being so dramatic. You act like I'm going on a date."

"Aren't you? I know what Monique does. Is that what you want to do?"

Claire clenched her fists, turned her back on Michel, and stomped further into the room. "I can't believe you'd ever think that!"

Michel followed her. "Why not? You get all dolled up to dance with German officers — dance and who knows what else. And you do it in the company of the biggest prostitute in all of France!"

"She's not a prostitute!"

"Then what is she?"

Claire cooled for only an instant. "I don't know. She does what she can."

"She's a whore!"

Claire wheeled on him. "She's my sister!"

Claire's words echoed between the walls and fueled the anger on her face as the young lovers locked eyes in the small getting smaller room. Michel was more than upset, though he did trust her. It was the possibility that frightened him. Monique's influence on her sister was great and Michel knew it. But he also knew that Claire would not waver once committed. He had seen it many times as they matured in their work. So after a cold minute Michel allowed her to win the short-lived staring contest and looked away. The simple victory stymied Claire's anger and allowed her to quietly approach her lover. She stepped gracefully around him until she was able to rest her hands flat on his chest.

"Don't do this, Claire," Michel pleaded the lost cause.

"I told Monique I'd go."

"Please?" he asked in a whisper as he gently held her.

Claire smiled at the child-like request and answered in her own soft voice, the anger now completely absent. "I'll be home early. Everything will be fine."

"Do I have to beg? Don't go with that..."

Claire put a finger over his lips and silenced him. "Don't do this to me, Michel. Don't make me choose."

Michel lovingly gripped Claire's hand, kissed it, and pulled it away from his lips. "Would it be so bad? Is it such a tough choice?"

Claire answered by kissing his cheek and stepping toward the door. "Nothing will happen. Relax. Okay?"

She opened the door and was already in the hall when she stepped partially back inside. Michel met her near the door, and she rewarded him with a kiss.

"I'll see you tomorrow," Claire said softly. Then she looked up and down at Michel's black clothes and knew the look of a guerilla's uniform. "Be careful tonight." Another quick kiss and she pulled the door closed behind her.

"You too," Michel said faintly to no one.

***

5

Back in the living room, Claire stopped to talk with a small group of guerrilla fighters rather than go to Monique and Sophie. Just beyond the group was Paul, a rugged fighter in his mid-thirties, old for the work he did. His face was chiseled, handsome by all accounts, and his powerful arms filled his sleeves, but his eyes were nearly dead, as cold as a snake's, and he walked with a noticeable limp. He seemed to never look directly at anyone, or away from anyone, but somehow saw everything. His experience as a fighter had kept him alive, and his hatred of Germans kept him dressing in black whenever the needs of the Resistance beckoned.

Back in the early days of the war Paul had fallen in love with another fledgling guerrilla, Valerie, Sophie's younger sister. With matching soft brown hair and glorious high cheeks beneath deep brown eyes, many mistook the sisters for twins, though Sophie was several years older. Their diverse roles in the Resistance foreshadowed Claire and Monique's, and Valerie would have become a fine teacher for Claire had the Germans not intervened. On a cold and drizzly afternoon in the fall of 1940, the Gestapo routed the Resistance from a safe house. Too long in one place and a loose tongue had led the Nazis to the door. In the melee that followed, Paul and Valerie found themselves in the streets with German soldiers nipping at their heels.

Five minutes before, the couple had been lying on an old bed upstairs in the safe house. Words were soft and slow between them, like the lovers they were, talking and dreaming as if saying things would make them real. Then there came the abrupt sounds of crashing and splintering doors as the Gestapo rushed the house. Gunfire erupted from the floors below and instantly each knew what was happening. Having been lured by passion into the seclusion of the upstairs bedroom, neither had their weapons. Even if they had, Paul would not have hesitated in opening the window and coaxing his lover out onto the roof. To stay and fight the encroaching enemy would be fatal, either immediately or shortly thereafter, following the torturing interrogation that would be certain to precede it.

The pair slipped along a shallow rooftop two stories high while shouts and bullets ricocheted inside the safe house behind and beneath them. When they reached the end of the building Valerie looked back at her lover.

"We're out of roof."

Paul looked up the main street and saw German trucks approaching. In the alley behind the house he saw a Frenchman in a dark blue beret. He recognized him immediately as Renault, his mentor and a senior member of the Resistance. Renault had been headed to the safe house when the gunshots had stopped him. Now he was in the alley, trying to find a way to help. Paul waved him back, and Renault stepped out of sight into a shallow doorway.

There was no more time to look for another way off the roof and nothing to look for had time permitted. The window was the only safe way, and it would be full of German guns any second. Paul quickly slid down the incline of the roof to the edge. He peered over and down at the ground, nearly twenty feet away. A short distance to one side, at the base of the building, was a row of garbage cans.

"Come down here!"

Valerie followed, thinking another lower rooftop must be waiting. When she slid up next to Paul she looked over the edge and back at him.

"I can't do that. It's too far."

In reply, Paul kicked at the rain gutter that circled the rooftop to test its strength.

"I'm going to hold onto the gutter. You climb down me to my ankles then drop on those garbage cans. It won't be far to the cans. Then stack up a couple for me and I'll drop."

"We'll kill ourselves!"

Paul looked over his shoulder at the escape window. "You want to wait for them? They'll kill us both right here."

"Paul..."

Without giving her a chance to finish, Paul clamored over the side of the roof and hung by the gutter. "Hurry! I can't hold on long!"

As gently as possible Valerie began the descent over her lover. She too gripped the rain gutter, carrying as much of her weight as possible until the last moment. Her legs circled his waist until one hand let loose of the gutter and clutched at his clothes.

"Are you ready for me?"

"Yes," was all he said.

"I love you," Valerie whispered as she kissed his cheek from behind.

"Tell me later, can't you?" Paul laughed ever so slightly.

Valerie dropped her remaining hand to his clothes and felt them sag on his body with her weight. Paul's fingers cut into the edge of the gutter but held on as Valerie lowered herself down. She crouched on his feet and wrapped her arms around his legs. First one foot slipped off his, then the next. She slid down his legs until her hands were gripping his boots. Up above, blood was beginning to trickle out from beneath Paul's fingers.

"Go!" he encouraged as firmly but as quietly as he could.

Valerie looked down for a second and judged the fall to the garbage cans. It was still a long way, but a sudden burst of gunfire from the house pushed her and she dropped.

The cans scattered beneath her like bowling pins, but did their job. She spun away onto the ground, rolling out of the fall like a paratrooper. In a flash she was on her feet stacking the cans as high as she could like a banged up metal safety net. The timing was close. No sooner had she pushed the top can in place than Paul released his fragile grip on the steady gutter. The drop was longer and harder than Valerie's. He hit the top can, and though it slowed him it knocked him away from the others. His arms flailed at the cans to catch his fall while his right leg abandoned its partner and shot out to the side for balance. His left foot stretched down for the ground as if to shorten the distance. At least he wouldn't land on his head.

When his foot smacked the ground the speed and shock turned his ankle and knee. If not for the racket of the tumbling cans he and Valerie would have heard the tearing of tissue and cracking bone in his left leg. With the collapse of the leg the rest of Paul's body crumpled down in a heap.

Valerie was on him before the cans ceased their squealing. As she pulled him to his feet the damaged leg folded up like an accordion and he went down. While they each took a turn holding the knee, feeling for protruding bones and the like, the crashing of the cans, twice now, had summoned German soldiers from the safe house.

"Let's move, Paul. Up you go."

In the attempt Paul felt the knee give way again. "You go. I'll catch up," he winced as crippling pain shot up his leg and into his back.

"Not a chance," Valerie lectured in a flurry. "You get up or I swear to God I'll sit down right now and wait for the Gestapo. Either you get up and move or I'm theirs. You decide, but you better do it goddamn fast!"

Paul could only look at Valerie as the sweat, born from pain, ran down his face.

"What's it going to be, mister?"

At that, Paul began to struggle to his feet. She aided him greatly, and with his torn knee against her, the pair started to hobble quickly up the alley behind the house.

Renault had seen the couple's leap and entered the alley to help, but the escape was far from complete when the first soldiers found their way out the rear of the safe house, drawn by the beckoning garbage cans. They spied the limping couple fifty yards away, but did not notice Renault straight beyond. The soldiers shouted for them to halt before immediately opening fire.

Renault flung himself into a narrow space between two houses, but there was no such protection for the couple. There was also little run left in Paul and no abandonment in Valerie. The length of the alley would be their undoing. Without hesitating, Paul crashed through the nearest door with Valerie tucked under his arm. Splinters of broken casing were like confetti on the pair as they slid across a polished kitchen floor.

Bullets whistled through the alley in front of Renault as Paul and Valerie scrambled off the stranger's floor. Neither stopped as they limped together through the kitchen and into the front of the house, intent on leaving through the main door. Paul's dim hope was to delay the Germans long enough to find a sanctuary somewhere beyond their sight. But as the couple passed through the living room they came face to face with a frightened mother crouched in a corner holding two children. The boy, about eight, hid his face, but the little girl, perhaps two or three years older, looked up at the interlopers.

"Don't be afraid, Mommy," she said firmly. "They're French. Not German."

"But they're coming," Paul ordered. "Hide the children...and yourself. Hurry!"

Without waiting for a reply, Paul and Valerie ran out the front door while the woman pulled her children across the floor to a plain closet. The front door, the closet door, and what remained of the back door, all moved at once. Paul and Valerie vanished into the street, the children were secreted, and the Germans burst into the kitchen. The last man in was Private Herbeart. He lingered with the others, accessing the room for the wanted and to protect themselves from attack. Across the alley, Renault waited to hear gunshots. When none came he slipped deeper between the houses.

The slight delay of the anxious soldiers gave the fleeing fighters time to cross the street and enter yet another house, this one apparently abandoned. The plan was to again race through the house and out the other side to divert any pursuing Nazis, but Paul's leg was failing him miserably and Valerie could no longer support his bulk.

"We can't run," she told him as the escape stalled in the battered house.

"You can."

"But I won't."

"So we hide here?" Paul asked as he looked around the disheveled home.

"We do. And hopefully they'll miss us or move on. Maybe they've had enough blood for today."

"Nazis never get enough blood," Paul answered as he struggled for the staircase. "Let's get to high ground."

Across the street the frightened mother was facing Nazi guns.

"Where are they?" a black-suited soldier screamed as he grabbed the poor woman's hair.

Her answer was her own scream as the soldier jerked her across the room away from the closet door and onto the floor. Though flailing, her eyes gave away her children's hiding spot. As the first soldier held her, another silently gripped the handle of the closet door. Private Herbeart and another soldier aimed their weapons at the closet, certain they would find the Resistance fighters inside. Herbeart, the most junior member of the group, licked his dry nervous lips, his eyes wide above them. When the door was flung open instant reaction almost brought death to the children, but the soft colors and tiny sizes of the intended victims held up the bullets. With three machine guns trained on them the children cowered in the corner of the closet, out of sight of their mother.

As disappointment registered on the faces of the hunters, their superior, Lieutenant Rheinholt, burst in the back door with a host of black uniforms. The Nazi lieutenant, who served as the local head of the dreaded black-clad SS soldiers and Gestapo, was a short man, thin, with a sunken face and tiny cruel eyes. His uniform was the standard black fare, impeccably neat and pressed, with a bright red swastika band gracing his left upper arm.

"Where are the two from the alley?" Rheinholt ordered as he came into the front of the house. "I was told a man and a woman?" The hurried officer was looking from face to face over the woman on the floor for an answer.

The SS soldier at the closet door looked at the children. "In here," he said jokingly. "But they seem to have shrunk."

Herbeart laughed, pleased at the opportunity to relax. But the smile faded fast when Rheinholt looked quickly in the closet then sharply slapped the face of the soldier at the door.

"You think this is funny?" The question, and the man who sent it, did not want an answer. "Search the house."

Trying to redeem himself, the joking soldier, his face still smarting, addressed his lieutenant. "Sir, the man appeared badly injured. I don't believe they could have gotten far."

Rheinholt looked harshly at the transgressor then issued more orders sending a number of soldiers into the street. "Secure the rest of the houses in this sector for one square block. Begin searching the perimeter."

Only now did Rheinholt look at the mother. "Where are they?"

"I don't know..."

To encourage the woman the soldier who held her tightened his grip.

"I don't know!"

Rheinholt held up his hand, and the soldier's grip eased slightly. Then he motioned to the closet for the children. As they were pulled from their hiding spot the lieutenant continued the interrogation. "Where is your husband?"

"You killed him."

"Did I?" Rheinholt answered as the boy and girl were shoved to his side. They reached for their mother and her for them, but all were restrained by stronger arms.

"You mean, he was killed fighting against the country of Germany, not that I killed him myself."

"You are all killers and butchers."

"I see," Rheinholt said as he knelt beside the children. "What's your name, little girl?"

"Claudine."

"And how old are you?" the lieutenant asked pleasantly.

"Ten."

"Did you see a man and a woman come through here?"

The little girl nodded.

"And where did you hide them?"

"Leave her be! You filthy dog!"

Rheinholt looked away from Claudine to her mother. "You have a poor opinion of us."

"You are pigs. I spit on you." And the woman did, the spittle catching Rheinholt in the face and unknowingly sealing her fate.

As the soldiers rushed for her, the lieutenant again held up his hand to stop them. While the room watched, he pulled a hanky from his pocket and slowly wiped his face.

"Without a man to tend to you...to meet your needs," Rheinholt said as he neatly folded the hanky and returned it to his pocket. "You have grown aggressive...Perhaps you would like some of my soldiers to take you upstairs and temper your spirit."

"Do with me what you want. Beat me, rape me, kill me like you killed my husband, and my children and all the children of France will rise up one day to avenge our deaths!"

"Perhaps you are right," Rheinholt said as he ripped the pistol from his gun belt. Without another word the lieutenant placed the gun barrel against the back of the boy's head and pulled the trigger. Blood and bone exploded from the child's face and showered his mother. He fell to the floor without a sound as the ringing in the soldiers' ears was replaced by the screams of both mother and sister.

"He will avenge no one," Rheinholt said without pity. "I ask you again. Where are they?"

The woman fell to her son's body. Her hands faintly touched the gaping wound in his head in disbelief, as if trying to put back the shattered pieces. When the woman's only answers to Rheinholt's questions were cries, he grabbed the girl by the back of her neck and forced her down on top of her brother's body. He rammed her face into the bloody mess that had been her brother's head as he screamed. "Do you want me to feed this one to my dogs? Where are they?"

The woman was in shock. She tried to hold the girl and began tugging at Rheinholt's fingers to loosen his grip on the child's neck. The girl was crying, the mother was pleading, and the lieutenant threatening.

"Where are they?"

The lost mother broke herself from grief long enough to reply. Blood was on her hands and face as she looked at Rheinholt before lowering her head, ashamed to be revealing anything to the Nazis and terrified if she did not.

"They went out the front door...as soon as they came in. I don't know where they are, sir. I didn't see..."

"You lie!"

"No! I was tending to my children."

"Liar!"

"They ran out and closed the door behind them! I...couldn't... see..."

The woman collapsed over both her children, weeping and pleading with her tears. Rheinholt released the girl and stepped away. He slammed the closet door in disgust. "They're not here," he muttered as he stepped toward the front door. "But they're not far. Bring the woman."

Paul and Valerie had heard the single shot from Rheinholt's pistol as they settled in an empty room on the upper floor of the abandoned house a few doors down and across the street. Valerie went to the window and carefully peeked out at the house they had broken through. As she watched, black-suited soldiers emerged, weapons at the ready, scrutinizing the nearby houses, including hers. She continued to monitor the Germans as she spoke to Paul.

"That was from the house with the kids."

"Jesus..."

Valerie looked at him, saying without words that the fault was theirs.

"We didn't know, Val."

She nodded and looked again out the window. "They'll be coming for us."

"I know," Paul said as he tried to examine his leg.

She saw him and came to his side to help. "Let's have a look."

But the examination was a short one. Paul's knee had swollen so that his pant leg was tight around it.

"Something's broke in there. I can't even bend it."

"We'll just wait until dark. I'll slip out and bring back some help to get you out of here."

"Maybe if I rest a while. Jesus, it's killing me!"

She hugged him and kissed his face. "I know it is. Hold on 'til dark."

"And if they don't wait until dark?" he said as he motioned toward the window and the street beyond.

"We'll worry about that later."

The gap in the conversation was filled with their eyes searching each other's faces. In their looks was the knowledge of what would happen to them when the Nazis came. There would be torture for both, worse for her, then a bullet if they were lucky, death in a concentration camp if they weren't.

Paul began to drag himself across the floor. "Help me downstairs."

"Why?"

"I'll distract them out front. You go out the back and run like hell."

"Forget it."

But he continued to drag himself. "Help me!"

"No!"

"Goddamn it, Valerie!" he said as loud as he dared. "Get me to the door!"

She reached for him, and he relaxed, but her grasp was only to jerk him back into the room. His leg twisted, and he almost passed out from the pain. When he regained himself he was nestled in her lap.

"No heroes, Paul. If we make it, we make it together. If we don't...we don't. Together."

"That's foolish. Goddamn foolish," he said gently.

"Isn't it, though?"

"I'd leave you."

"No you wouldn't."

Paul could not argue, but a realization was settling over them both. "You know what'll happen when they come," he said softly.

"I know," she said as she held him tightly.

"I can't let that happen to you."

"If they come, we'll make such a fuss they'll shoot us both right here, together."

"Me, yes. You, no. They won't shoot you...not at first."

Valerie squeezed him very tight and her armor began to slip. "I know that."

Outside, the Germans were loading captured fighters, most wounded in one fashion or another, into a truck as they cleaned out what had been the safe house. Two additional trucks waited nearby, one for captured weapons and intelligence and the other for bodies. The truck for the dead would carry more Resistance members than the first.

The prisoners loaded quietly, having been calmed by fists, boots, and the butts of German guns. As two of the trucks pulled out of the way with their cargo, the already dead and others destined to be so, the third truck pulled up on the sidewalk and began accepting weapons and ammo from the belly of the house. Soldiers not assigned to the weapons recovery split into units of fours and fives and began searching the houses on the street for the escaped couple.

A few houses away Lieutenant Rheinholt led the procession from the home with the shattered rear door. The woman, lost in a dreadful numb stupor, came out behind him, a soldier on either side. Claudine was clinging to her mother's bloodied dress. The woman's hands, also bloody, massaged her daughter's shoulders and held her close, whispering words of encouragement that she herself did not believe.

"Listen to me!" Rheinholt bellowed into the instantly quiet street. "We are looking for a man and a woman. They are escaped prisoners. If you know where they are hiding, come forth now. Do not attempt to hide them. They will be found and you will be made to suffer for any assistnace you render them."

Though many heard, no one moved on the street. Most residents just tightened their drapes and checked the bolts on their doors. Paul and Valerie heard Rheinholt as well. They didn't speak and waited for the German's next command.

"Very well," the lieutenant said stoically. "Bring the woman into the street."

The soldiers forced the woman to her knees along the sidewalk. She woke from her nightmare enough to struggle. Her daughter was caught in the conflict. As her mother battled with the soldiers, Claudine began to scream and cry frantically as she too fought the enemy.

"Take that child back in the house," Rheinholt ordered Herbeart. "Shut her up. I don't care how."

The young soldier tore the girl from her mother's dress and stuffed her under his arm. He bounded up the stairs into the house, grateful for not having to witness what was about to happen.

Once back inside the house he closed the door with his body and leaned against it. Unknowingly he was holding the girl out toward her brother's mutilated body. Claudine screamed all the louder at the sight. Herbeart put his hand over her mouth, and she bit him. As he winced and grabbed his hand she broke free and ran to the window. She saw Rheinholt standing behind her mother, his pistol in his hand. A soldier was on either side of the woman. Each man was holding a twisted arm, pinning Claudine's mother to her knees as she screamed and pleaded.

"This woman has been found guilty of aiding in the escape of convicted criminals. The punishment for such crimes against the Third Reich...is death. If you know where the criminals are hiding, tell us now and spare yourself a similar fate."

Herbeart snatched Claudine up from the window, but she clutched at the curtain long enough to see the smoke spew from the lieutenant's pistol. The report of the gun was muted slightly by the house, but Claudine witnessed the red puff of blood erupt from her mother's head before she went limp. The child screamed uncontrollably as her mother's body continued to be held up by the soldiers who gripped her wrists.

"Goddamn it!" Rheinholt screamed as he turned toward the house. "Go in there and shut that little bitch up!"

Another soldier, bloodlust in his eyes, ran up the stairs to the house, pulling his pistol as he did. He dove into the front room and found Herbeart holding the girl in front of him, his hand firmly over her mouth. Tears from Claudine's eyes were running down her cheeks and over the soldier's hand.

"Give her to me!" the soldier with the pistol said.

"For what?"

"The lieutenant said to give her back to her mother," the soldier smiled.

"She's dead."

"Right. And this little noisy kid is about to join her."

Herbeart held the child away as the pistol reached for her. "Jesus, I thought we were soldiers! We don't kill children!"

"Don't we? Where do you think all those kids we've been stuffing in those trains go? Summer camp? Give her to me!"

The junior soldier continued to hold her, Claudine's hot breath blasting from her nose, fanning against his hand. He could hear it as his hand felt it. In his arms he could feel her tremble even as her tiny fingernails dug into the skin on the back of his hand.

"Give her to me!" the other threatened, thirsting so for blood that he appeared ready to shoot a German soldier just for the pleasure of killing a French child.

"I'll do it!" Herbeart shouted back. "The lieutenant gave her to me!"

He did not wait for a reply. Instead, he jumped with the girl in his arms over the body of her brother and darted through the kitchen. He crushed pieces of the door beneath his boots as he left the house that would never again be the same.

When Herbeart entered the alley his footfalls immediately drew the attention of Renault, who was creeping along between houses, still trying to assess what could be done. Renault froze until the sound of the running boots passed him, then he chanced a look out from his hiding spot.

The little girl's legs dangled limply around the running man, and her arms flopped around his shoulders making no attempt to hold on. Renault took her to be dead. When the soldier vanished around a corner down a converging alley, Renault pulled his knife and took flight after him.

As Herbeart sprinted down the alley he looked back over his shoulder searching more for his own kind than an intended enemy. Not seeing anyone, he focused on the back doors of the houses nearest him. With no criteria in mind, he stopped short at a simple back stoop and rapped quickly at the door.

A few seconds too many passed, and Herbeart knocked again louder and faster. An elderly couple opened the door together. The old man stepped in front of his fragile wife at the sight of the uniform. "Go away from here," he said. "We've done nothing."

The request was ignored as Herbeart plunged the little girl into their arms. "Take the child. Hide her well! You'll learn soon enough!"

"No!" the old man answered as he held the girl back out to the soldier like a bag of potatoes. "We see nothing! We know nothing! We stay alive!"

Herbeart shoved Claudine back inside and the man with her then grabbed the door and pulled it closed as he jumped away from the stoop. His feet carried him running up the alley back toward the safe house before he could again be refused, but he heard the door open behind him and glanced over his shoulder as he ran. What he saw was the old man setting the girl on the back steps like the night's trash.

The sight brought Herbeart's feet to a stop, but as soon as the door to the old couple's house closed, it opened again and the aged woman stepped out. Slowly and apparently painfully, she picked up the little girl, limp from shock, and took her inside. As the door closed behind them once again, Herbeart took off toward the corner of the alley. He had no way of knowing that Renault was approaching the same corner from the opposite direction.

The reluctant soldier spoke to himself as he ran on. "Rheinholt would kill me," but as he rounded the corner Renault was waiting, knife in hand. The momentum of Herbeart's run coupled with Renault's strong arm to drive the knife into the young man's chest and pierce his heart. Surprise and shock left him motionless until the damage inflicted by the knife could take full effect. Renault expertly twisted the knife in the dying man's chest, and its blade ripped the flagging heart.

As Herbeart collapsed he clutched the hilt of the knife over his killer's bloody hand.

"Die, baby killer!" Renault tormented. "Where'd you dump her, you miserable bastard?"

Herbeart did not have time to explain, not that it may have mattered, clothed in grey as he was, nor did he have time to cry out, but he looked over his shoulder and pointed toward the old couple's house with a bloody finger. In another moment the hesitant soldier died, and Renault withdrew his knife which he unceremoniously wiped on Herbeart's grey jacket.

Renault stood and looked down at his handiwork for a moment, then his eyes shifted around him. "If your friends find you, they'll burn the entire block, or maybe only a few houses since you were just a private. What do you think, huh?" Renault asked the corpse as he nudged it with his boot. "No opinion, ah? Well, I think we should hide you."

At that, Renault sheathed his blade and took hold of Herbeart's body. He dragged it down the alley toward the door of the old couple. When he began to pass it the old man stepped out. He and Renault locked eyes over the dead man. The Resistance fighter dropped the arms of the young soldier and waited.

"I have stayed away," the old man mumbled. "Now my wife, she says we have stayed away too long."

With those words, the wife appeared beside him in the doorway. Claudine, eyes still wide above tear stained cheeks, pushed in between the two. Renault's jaw went limp, and his shoulders dropped as he looked from the child he thought was dead to the dead soldier at his feet.

"We are in it now," the old man continued as his wife nodded and held the little girl in front of her. Renault could not reply, but the old man began his entry to the Resistance with vigor. "And it feels good," he said clearly as he came down the steps. At their base he turned back to his wife. "Take her inside. She has seen enough death for a lifetime."

The old woman complied and took Claudine into the front room where she held her on her lap in a straight-backed chair. While she talked softly, introducing herself, her husband, and their home, she heard the coal door open at the rear of the house. When she heard muffled voices and the sound of rough shoving, the woman began to hum a lullaby, held Claudine's head against her breast, and placed a free hand over the child's other ear.

Paul and Valerie were holding each other as well. They remained settled in the same room where they had heard the reports from Rheinholt's pistol. Paul's powerful arms circled Valerie's waist as he sat on the dusty floor between her legs, his head laying gently against her breasts, which heaved with nervous breaths. She cuddled close to him, stroking his hair. They could not see each other's face; neither saw the other's tears.

"Val?"

"Yes?"

"I never thought it would be like this."

"Thought what would be like this?"

"Getting caught like a rat. Trapped in a filthy box."

"Who says we're caught?"

"I do...and you know it too."

"Yes, I know it."

"I don't want you to hurt."

"I know you don't."

"Won't you please run?"

Valerie did not answer.

"Are you thinking about it?" Paul asked.

"No. And don't ask again. It may be foolish, but that is how I want it. I love you. If they take you from me, I would die of a broken heart."

He hesitated. "Would you like to make love?"

She hesitated. "Perhaps."

"If you were pregnant you would have to leave, to save our baby."

"But I'm not."

Paul adjusted himself in her lap and saw the water in her eyes. "We could change that. Right now."

Valerie shook her head. "No, Paul. That's a nice trick, but it won't work. Besides, who says I would even escape? They could catch me and still do what they want. No. No more talk."

Paul's head fell back to her breast. "I don't want them to hurt you."

"We'll fight when they come, like I said. We'll both be in heaven within a minute of each other. Whoever gets there first has to wait for the other."

"I wish I had my gun," Paul said with a quiet resolve.

"Tough guy Paul wants to take a few with him, does he?" Valerie said as she smiled and squeezed him.

"No," he answered slowly. "It would be for us."

There was scarcely breath between them. Thoughts whirled in their heads as the sounds of Nazi boots and voices came close to the house.

Valerie eased her lover up in her arms. She kissed him and held his face. "Paul, if they come — when they come — rock me to sleep. Hold me, won't you? Squeeze tight," she said as her hands went to his and brought them to her throat. "I don't want them to hurt me," she cried. "And I won't leave you. I love you." The tears came in earnest. "Squeeze me tight and rock me to sleep." Valerie's voice became a choked whisper. "Rock me to sleep..."

Paul nodded yes. With each drop of his chin, new tears escaped.

"Will it be quick?" Valerie asked with a cracking voice.

"Yes."

"Will it hurt?"

"No. You will be asleep in a few seconds."

"And will you come to me as fast as you can?"

"I'll be right behind you."

They kissed there on the bare floor. It was as long and loving an embrace as the world had seen. But it could have climbed yet higher mountains had the door to the house not been flung open below them.

The couple jumped in each other's arms. Instinctively they shuffled quietly across the floor to a far corner of the room previously occupied only by a ragged and dirty blanket. When they reached the wall their positions had been reversed. Valerie was now sitting between Paul's legs. His arms were around her, his right up high above her breasts. Both of her hands grasped his arm and alternated between pats of assurance to a tight restraining grip.

There were sounds in the house now, clamoring steps and voices. The steps were quick and ran from room to room below them. Paul's arm slipped further up until it brushed Valerie's throat.

"Not yet!" she cried softly, then heard the anxiousness in her own voice. She stroked the muscles in Paul's forearm. "It's okay, my love. I'm fine. I'm ready."

"I love you," Paul said into her ear as he adjusted his arm until the crux of his elbow rested firmly against his lover's throat.

"Don't make me wait," she whispered.

"I won't."

Paul tightened his grip as the footsteps found the stairs.

"I love you, Paul. I love you so."

The steps hit the second floor and Paul's strong muscles contracted hard. Paul pulled Valerie's head against his chest and tucked his fist hard under his own chin. She tried to gasp, but could not. Her hands clutched at his arm, but they were no match for his strength. The door to the room burst open, and a black-suited soldier leveled his machine gun at the couple as he shouted for his partners. The message was relayed out of the house and across the street. In seconds, Lieutenant Rheinholt and others were running toward the front door.

Valerie was stiff, as every muscle fought against what she had voluntarily asked for. Her mouth was open, but she could neither breathe nor speak. The blood to her brain was being cut off, and she was fainting quickly. She felt Paul's kiss against her face and the tears on his cheek. Then the soldier with the machine gun began to fade. As he screamed at the couple he disappeared entirely, as did the rest of the world.

***

6

Paul held his lover's throat as tight as he could despite what the soldier and the machine gun were screaming. The shouts brought the rest of the soldiers on the search detail and Lieutenant Rheinholt from the street. The racing soldiers also captured the attention of several neighbors who peeked from behind pulled curtains in anticipation of another execution.

"Release her!" the soldier screamed again and again as he shook his weapon at the couple, locked in a fatal embrace on the floor.

"Screw you," Paul answered coldly.

"Do it now!"

Paul's answer was to squeeze tighter.

"Now!" the German screeched as Rheinholt and others crowded in the doorway around the soldier. "Release her or die where you sit!"

"I'm coming," Paul whispered, and he kissed Valerie's cheek.

The soldier aimed his weapon at Paul's head.

"Are you waiting?" Paul said softly into his lover's ear. "I'm here."

"Wait!" Rheinholt howled. "Wait!"

The soldier lowered his gun, and Paul raised his head. His mouth hung open and his arm relaxed ever so slightly around Valerie's neck.

"Get him away from the woman," Rheinholt ordered. "Hurry!"

A stream of uniforms flowed into the room. Paul clenched his arm again, but the time for reaction from Valerie had long passed. The first soldiers grabbed her legs and his, pulling the couple apart. Paul kicked as hard as he could, but the broken knee would not help ward off the attack.

With both arms wrapped around his Valerie, to protect her from the soldiers in a way only Rheinholt had recognized and with only one good leg, even Paul's strength was no match for the horde. The soldiers used their guns like clubs against his back, head, and legs as they tried to wrench Valerie from him. He had completed his task, but Paul held her for himself and against what he saw in Rheinholt's eyes.

"Get him off of her, you idiots!" the lieutenant shrieked. "He's killing her!"

With several soldiers now on Paul, ignoring Valerie's listless body, the battle was nearly over. One arm was ripped free leaving Valerie dangling in the other and tossed about as the soldiers fought against Paul's strength. A well-placed rifle butt to an obviously wounded knee sent Paul to the brink of passing out and allowed Valerie to be pulled away. His groan signaled the end as the Germans pinned him face down to the floor. He no longer struggled, but smiled through his fainting stupor as he looked across the floor directly into Valerie's vacant face.

"I'm coming, Val," he whispered.

Rheinholt walked into the room for the first time. He looked down at Valerie's body and put the toe of his shiny boot under her belly. With an easy flip he rolled her onto her back. Her eyes were white, rolled back in her head. She was not breathing. He knelt down and placed his fingers against her throat. Not feeling a pulse, his hand slipped off her neck and very gently brushed the hair from her blanched face.

"Pity. Such a beautiful woman."

"Leave her alone," Paul growled from the floor through gritted teeth as he tensed.

Rheinholt smiled and continued stroking Valerie's hair. "Or? What will you do? Save her? You've already done that, haven't you? That was your intention, was it not?"

Paul didn't speak, and his struggling lessened as Rheinholt stood up from Valerie's body and walked over to him. The lieutenant knelt again, this time in front of Paul.

"You are a hard man, but I suspect you loved this woman. You must have, to do what you did. To kill her."

He stood and walked around the room thinking out loud as Paul and the others watched him. The soldiers' eyes jumped from the body to Paul to the lieutenant in rapid succession, not certain of what to make of the things they had witnessed.

"You are prepared to die," Rheinholt said. "No, let me rephrase that. You expect to die, wish to die. Did you plan this...this...little murder-suicide of yours? My suspicion is that you expect to follow this woman to the grave. And you would like for us to accommodate you."

The scheme was laid bare bones on the floor of the dirty room. In the lieutenant's words Paul discovered that the ending of his life would not come as he and his lover had expected. The fervor of the euthanasia and the wrestling match with the Germans had subsided. All that remained was Val's body on the floor with the smell of urine and feces emanating from it. And surrounding it, smelling nearly as sickening in Paul's nostrils, was the knowledge that Rheinholt had found him out.

"Place the prisoner under arrest for murder. Remand him to the custody of the local authorities. He is to be tried for the murder of this woman. We are all witnesses."

"No," Paul muttered, but the words did nothing but bring Rheinholt crashing down next to him. The lieutenant grabbed Paul's hair and wrenched his head backward.

"Oh, yes! I know you! I know the kind of animal you are!" He pointed Paul's face sharply at Val's body. "Look! Any man who can do that would never break, even under my...special treatment.

And after days and days I would have nothing, and you, you would die miserably. But that is just what you want!" Rheinholt crimped Paul's neck even more. "Isn't it?" Then he threw Paul's head forward and stepped away. "No, you will live, not for an hour or a few days, but for a long time. You will die in prison. In two prisons. One of stone and one of your own making."

Rheinholt walked by Valerie's body and waved at his nose. He knelt and picked up the ratty blanket with the tips of two fingers and tossed it over her. "Bring up the truck of corpses from those bastards' wretched house. Get this stinking bitch out of here. She shit herself. And cuff this animal. Place him under a suicide watch, around the clock. You will be tried, and you will be convicted, but mostly you will live. You will live to suffer."

The lieutenant left the room to his soldiers. Paul's struggle began again, but several blows to his knee and as many to his head reduced him to a form as limp as his lover's. The Gestapo cuffed the unconscious man behind his back and the soldiers carried him down the stairs. The sounds of their cursing Paul's weight and the shuffling of boots on the stairs masked the slight cough that came from beneath the dirty blanket.

***

7

Natei, a boyish fighter in the circle at the current safe
house, tugged playfully at Claire's dress.

"Nice outfit," he teased.

Claire brushed his hand away then in a flash gripped the back
of his neck with one hand and stabbed the extended fingers of the
other up under Natei's jaw, causing him to wince in pain. The others
smiled as Claire pressed her knife-like hand against his jawbone.
"Glad you like it, Natei. But remember, the prettiest snakes have
the deadliest bite."

She withdrew her hand and smiled at herself as Natei touched
the sore spot beneath his jaw and suffered a weak smile himself. "I
can see that."

Paul passed within reach to the side of the group. "You're still
one of us," he said as he patted Claire's shoulder, ignoring the dress.
His words brought stares to the group and bestowed confidence and
justification to Claire.

When Paul limped out of earshot, Natei spoke again, but this
time he used a hushed voice. "He speaks. I've been here almost a
year and never heard him say a word."

Renault's short and stocky frame, capped by his constant blue beret, was suddenly behind the young fighter. "He speaks little and kills often. Do well to learn from him."

"Learn?" Jon, Natei's older brother, asked. "How can you learn anything from him when he doesn't talk?"

"By watching," Renault continued. "By watching."

"Yes, but if he would talk to us perhaps we could learn quicker," Claire chimed.

"Watch instead."

"Team me with him, Renault," Claire suggested. "There's a lot I could learn from..."

"No!" Renault said sharply. "You stay away from him!"

The harshness startled the entire group. After the words escaped, Renault felt their intensity and countered, "Paul has a death wish. He is very, very good at killing Germans, but he will not live to see the end of the war." The senior fighter took Claire's arms and held her, almost as in a distant caress. "You are the future of the Movement, with or without that dress. We need you and others like you. Paul will continue as he must, but on his terms. Understand?"

"Yes, sir."

"Good, now—" Renault cut his words short when two men in German uniforms appeared from the hallway and strolled into the main room. They garnered little attention and paid the group of fighters no mind.

"I wish they'd wear a goddamn bell or something!" Renault said sternly. "After all these years I cannot get used to seeing our boys in those uniforms. They walk in, and I reach for my knife. Every damn time."

He walked off, following the uniforms and complaining all the way. "Hey, boys? Why the hell don't you whistle or something?"

The group laughed at him as Michel joined them from the hall. "What's the joke?"

"Renault," Jon laughed. "Every time he sees a uniform in a safe house he gets crazy."

They all looked and chuckled at the Resistance leader, watching him as he chastised the phony German soldiers.

"What did he mean?" Natei said quietly. "You know, that Paul had a death wish?"

No one answered.

"What? Is it a secret or something? I think maybe he's shell-shocked. Acts kind of nutty most of the time if you ask me."

"No one's asking you, Natei," Michel said firmly. "Just leave Paul alone."

"I don't understand. He's our best fighter, according to Renault. And what's this death wish? He walks around like a zombie most of the time, like he just lost his best friend."

"He did."

"He did?"

"When?" Jon picked up for his brother.

"About four years ago. In the early days. Paul and his fiancé were trapped. He did what he thought he had to do and..." Then Michel checked himself. "She got killed. Paul was captured. His knee was already broken so they beat on it until he passed out. That's why the limp."

"Are you kidding? How'd he escape?"

"He didn't. They let him go, made him go really."

"What?"

"He was to be tried for murder, but the police couldn't assemble a jury. I guess the Gestapo got tired of torturing him. They'd seen what he...that he blamed himself for her death. Some ruthless bastard decided the worst punishment for Paul would be to make him go on living. And they were right. Finally the local police released him to Renault. If it wasn't for him, Paul would have killed himself four years ago."

"Christ," Natei said slowly as he stared across the room at the killing idol.

"Just leave him alone. That goes for everybody," Michel said as he registered with every face in the crowd. "Leave him alone."

They would all follow his advice. When Paul was in the room the youngest fighters still collected near him, as near as they dared, in hopes of learning something from him that for a few would propel them to greatness, but for the others, would just keep them alive.

While the small band of fighters continued to discuss what they had just heard and repeatedly laugh and mimic Claire's knife attack on Natei, much to his chagrin, Claire saw Paul slip through a door that led to the basement, the war room and, presumably, Charlemagne. Claire moved away from the group, intent on passing through the door as easily as he had. But as she reached for the doorknob a hand materialized from nowhere and caught her fingers before they could turn the latch.

"You can't go down there right now." Claire followed the hand and saw that it and the voice belonged to Sophie.

Claire immediately pulled her hand back. "Why?"

"There's a meeting."

"I need to see Paul."

"He's busy."

Claire's temperament was rising. "Look, Sophie, I'm not after him if that's what you're worried about."

"I'm not worried," she answered, increasingly tired of Claire's brackish attitude. "Paul does what he wants with whoever he wants. It makes no difference to me."

"I bet you wish he felt the same," Claire answered with a bite.

"No I don't, but it's none of your business how I feel."

"And it's none of your business where I go," Claire answered as she reached again for the knob.

Sophie grabbed her wrist. "If you open that door, I'll have the sergeant-at-arms bar you from the house."

"You can't do that."

Renault spoke up from behind Claire. "Yes, she can."

The women looked from each other to the senior official. Renault took both the wrists and pulled them apart. He released Sophie immediately and motioned her away with a look.

Renault turned Claire toward him and hugged her. He kissed her forehead then shook her the slightest bit. No one could see it, but Claire felt the force.

"Claire, you are one of the finest soldiers we have. I want you to do...your...job."

"Yes, sir," she answered somewhat sheepishly.

He removed his hands and walked away leaving Claire alone by the door, implying a trust that was not all that strong. She looked at the door and thought of the impressive, but invisible Charlemagne just beyond, then felt Sophie's eyes on her. Claire met her glance and shot darts at her with her own eyes then abandoned the door and huffed away to her own kind.

Monique shook her head at the goings-on and then exchanged kisses with Sophie amid last minute warnings and advice. She stepped up to her sister and without words said they should be going. The fighters gave tough-guy hugs to Claire, many verbalizing their condolences for the duty she had drawn at the insistence of her sister. The women in the group eyed Monique harshly while the young men, pretending to do likewise, secretly lusted after the curves accented by the shimmering maroon dress.

Reunited, the sisters exited the safe house through the same back door they had entered. They cautiously navigated the alley for the second time that day and re-entered the main street, quickly blending in with the flowing foot traffic.

Several minutes passed without a word between the pair. It could have just been in the interest of security that the sisters continued to eye their surroundings for any indication that they had drawn attention to themselves or the safe house. But a greater share of the silence grew from the widening gap between the two over their eventual destination and the work they would do once they'd arrived. Monique recognized this as the root of the extended quiet and hoped to bridge the gap with a radical change of conversation from that which each had held in the safe house.

"Who's the guy back there?" she asked as they continued up the boulevard.

"What guy?"

Monique raised her eyebrows at her sister.

"Oh, him. Michel. Just a friend."

The look from Monique was comical, displaying obvious disbelief.

"He is!" Claire said loudly, as though trying to convince herself. "Or at least he was."

"Why do you say that?"

"He didn't want me to go to the club."

"You've been to the club before."

"Not like this."

Claire immediately thought that she'd like to have her last words back, but of course it was too late.

Monique's eyes fixed straight ahead and lost the gleam of girlish teasing she had begun to muster. "You mean, not with me."

There was another pause, equally as poignant, before Claire answered. "Something like that."

There were a few more steps that served to move the sisters away from the awkward hurt.

"How'd you leave it with him?" Monique finally asked.

"Not too good."

Monique leaned forward as she walked and looked into her sister's face to judge the degree of hurt. It was there, but not too deep in Claire's generally bright eyes. Monique straightened away from Claire's own stare.

"What?" Claire said forcibly.

"Just friends, huh?"

"Yes! I hardly know him!"

Monique didn't say a word for several steps then she spoke quietly. "Claire?"

"Yes?"

"Your lipstick's smudged."

Claire stopped in mid-stride, her feet stuck on the sidewalk. She dabbed a finger at the corner of her mouth, looking straight ahead as if her reflection waited there. Her sister watched with a growing smile. When Claire realized she'd betrayed herself her hand dropped in unison with her head. And like her sister, a soft smile started. Then, relaxed and comfortable with Monique's easy jab, the smile blossomed into a brilliant, slightly embarrassed grin. Laughter erupted from them both as Monique tossed her arm around her little sister and the pair again stepped off on their travels.

The laughter had just begun to stop bubbling when Claire tossed a different coin into the fountain. "Sophie's a bitch."

"No she is not," Monique defended. "Why would you say such a thing?"

"She thinks I'm after Paul."

Monique smiled. "I doubt that."

"Yes she does. Hey! You don't think Paul would be interested in me?"

"I know Paul. He's only interested in killing Germans."

"But he and Sophie are together a lot."

"There's a reason for that. They are very close friends. That's all. He doesn't even date."

"Why?"

"Broken heart I suppose."

"He'd probably go out with Sophie if she didn't date so many Germans herself."

"No. She reminds him too much of Valerie. Self-imposed torture. It's both heaven and hell for him to be with her. Or as close to either as he can get — though he continues to tempt whichever would have him." Monique's thoughts came up short, as though she'd pulled a curtain back too far. She recovered by seamlessly shifting gears. "And Sophie works, she does not date."

"I doubt if Paul, or if not him any other man, sees it that way."

"And there's the rub, isn't it?"

"So why doesn't she stop?"

"Stop what?"

"You know...with the German officers."

"Ask Paul when he will stop killing Germans. When he stops, she stops."

Claire walked on a few more steps, closer to the destination and the carefully crafted words in her mind. "It's not the same."

Monique needed no yards for her words to form and no time buffer to protect herself. "It is the same. It is very much the same."

The words invited no response or reaction. They were a statement, plain and true, at least to Monique and the other women like her. Whether they sought truth or justification, it carried them and allowed them to continue as clearly as Paul and Claire were permitted by their credo to kill again and again.

Turned back at this front, Claire chose another. "But she could have let me see Charlemagne. She actually grabbed me by the basement door! Wouldn't even let me go downstairs!"

"So, it has nothing to do with Paul."

"He went down alright."

"I mean your dislike of Sophie. You're mad because she wouldn't let you down to the war room."

"Well, no, but for Christ sake! I'm not going to tell anyone! You know that."

"Of course, but how easy it is to keep a secret if there is no secret to tell."

"Keep a secret if there's no secret? What does that mean?"

"Think about it."

If Claire thought about it at all, it was fleeting. "I'd never tell anything. No matter what. They'd have to kill me before I'd tell."

"I don't think even the Gestapo has figured out how to do that yet."

"Do what?"

"Kill you then make you tell."

"You know what I mean."

"I do. Sophie has a job to do just like us. You do yours, I'll do mine, and we'll let Sophie do hers."

"You sound like Renault."

"Then listen to us!"

"But I wouldn't say anything," Claire pouted.

"Yes, yes," Monique said as she stuck her lip out in an exaggerated version of her sister. "I know. It's a terrible thing that darn old Sophie did. Just awful. She's so mean to you."

"Knock it off."

"Knock it off," Monique echoed.

"I mean it!"

"I mean it."

Now Claire couldn't help but laugh at the common sisterly taunt they had tortured each other with for years. "You're such a—"

Monique grabbed her sister. "Sweety!"

"Hardly! You drive me nuts!"

"In your case, that's a very short trip."

"Funny."

***

8

With several blocks of easy laughter and sisterly ribbing behind them, Claire and Monique found themselves hand-in-hand in the shadow of the spire of St. Catherine's Cathedral. As the shadow engulfed them Claire's hand came away from her sister's.

The tower of the ancient church was perched a hundred feet over the mammoth stone structure. Years had done little to deface the stonework aside from stains and color, which only added to its character. The war too, had graciously left the church unscathed, on the outside anyway. Inside, it had undergone several changes. The cathedral had become, as many churches had in this time, a Mecca for those whom the war had impacted the deepest. It had witnessed the funerals of hundreds of young men who had grown up fidgeting in its pews beneath the firm stares of their parents. The church had also listened as atrocities committed in the name of war had painfully trickled, and sometimes gushed, from the mouths of parishioners wracked by pain and doubt.

The walls of the city's Holy Mother heard the petitions of her children every day at masses that were seemingly unending. On many days the benediction of one all but became the opening processional of the next, such was the depth of need. Though the masses were constant, attendance was not always so. The Gestapo, always fearful that the church and its leaders were instrumental in the Resistance, occasionally lodged a small garrison near the church to observe, check papers, and overtly harass the worshipers. Generally the true Resistance knew when such an ineffectual plan was in the offing and advised the denizens of the city accordingly. Subsequently, the Germans were left to haggle with toothless old women wrapped in black shawls who gave as good as they got and frightened the imposing Gestapo soldiers nearly as much as any battle.

But when unimpeded by the Germans, the pews filled with souls and the rafters filled with prayers sent heavenward by pleading and desperate hearts. Petitions for the dead of war commingled with pleas for the release of their country from the grip of the Third Reich. And dancing in and about these offerings were hesitant prayers from Resistance fighters looking for absolution from things they were trying to justify under the name of war. The stones of St. Catherine's had always said, "Thou shalt not kill." Now, hidden soldiers, many in their teens, others in black shawls, and still others in pretty dresses, came to ask God if He made exceptions for soldiers.

Next door to the sanctuary proper was a much lower building of matching stone. In better days it had served as the church's community center and also as home to its priests and nuns. Now it was employed as a catch basin for the lost children of the war — young boys and girls orphaned by German bullets and babies left with French girls who believed that the tryst with a handsome German soldier would last a lifetime.

The nuns had surrendered their quiet life to crying children when the war descended on the city. Their service to God and Mother Church now came in the form of caretakers. The women in draping black habits saw to education and training, blind to lineage. The children themselves, protected in the cloistered walls, were blind as well. Growing in a tiny world free from prejudices, they had not learned to hate for hate's sake. They had learned only the language of worship and play, oblivious to the disparity in features that signaled "different" to most and "enemy" to some.

While the nuns had at least temporarily stymied bigotry they often found themselves confronting sometimes larger and certainly more immediate problems. Most were as basic as food. The original war effort had placed a burden, though one taken without complaint, on the resources of St. Catherine's. Following the occupation, any stores that had been laid in were soon bled off by the invaders to support Germany's home interests. As a result, the nuns came to the city and often the Resistance for help. All were eager to assist — assist the French orphans of war, that is. The illegitimate German children were another matter.

The Sisters of St. Catherine's painted with broad brushes though, and managed to keep food in tiny stomachs and clothes on little backs independent of political sentiments. Meager donations and volunteers struggled to help the nuns keep up with the growing numbers within the old nunnery. All the while, the Germans, through killing and lust, provided an endless supply of hungry mouths and French tears, from eyes young and old often to be dried with the frayed edges of black habits.

Monique hadn't noticed Claire's release of her hand, but she quickly recognized the reason behind it when she reached the top of the stairs to the nunnery alone. She turned back to her sister who was still waiting at the base of the steps eyeing the church tower.

"Hurry up," Monique ordered.

Claire hugged her own arms and rubbed them as if they were cold. "This place gives me the creeps."

"You're such a baby."

Claire's eyes skated over the nunnery. "I hate this place."

Monique's eyes followed Claire's, but more to see if anyone or even the stones themselves had heard her sister's blaspheming. "Don't say that!" Monique said in a near whisper. "It's a church!"

"Oooh, a church," Claire said as she pretended to quiver nervously under the eyes of the old cathedral.

"Stop it, Claire."

In reply, Claire began to swing her arms back and forth, occasionally clapping, as she pivoted away from the nunnery and meandered slowly around on the sidewalk. "I'll just wait out here."

This was not acceptable. Monique retreated in a jog down the steps and grabbed her sister's reluctant hand. "Oh no you don't. I want you to meet someone." Claire feigned weakness as Monique pulled her up the stairs and through the weathered oak door.

The pair stepped into an expansive room with a high ceiling above a shiny marble floor. The center of the large room was empty, but the sides were alive with young children too numerous to count. They sat at short-legged tables facing the wall on crude benches built low to the floor. On the tables, beneath stubby little hands holding tiny pieces of broken chalk, were dusty and cracked slate tablets. The sheer number of children seemed to command noise, but the room, even with its ancient marble floor, could barely muster a whisper.

Every small eye glanced at the sisters, openly or covertly, until the guiding hands of the nuns, islands of black amid the sea of little ones, pointed back to the slates. The nuns themselves stole looks at the pair, whose stylish dress set them far apart from the surroundings. Claire had never visited the nunnery, but Monique was a regular volunteer and yet the glowing dress and bright lipstick made her painfully out of place.

Across the wide room, Sister Arlene, the Mother Superior, recognized Monique immediately through the makeup and after dutifully assigning her young students to the care of another came to greet her. She walked with her arms folded in front of her until she was close enough to reach out and cover Monique's manicured hands.

"So grand to see you, dear!" the old nun said with soft enthusiasm. She paused a moment and tilted her head to the side as to reveal a well known secret. "Someone's been asking after you."

"I figured as much. Unfortunately, things have kept me away."

"I know they have. And she understands as well. The main thing is that you are here today. But you are not alone, I see," the nun said as she took notice of the younger McCleash.

"Mother, this is my sister. Claire."

"Oh, my stars! You can't be little Claire! Just look how you've grown. I haven't seen you in such a long while. You must not frequent mass as I'm certain to recall such a lovely young lady."

"Thank you," Claire said shyly.

"Do stop in for prayer and communion. During these difficult times our relationship with the Heavenly Father is more valuable to us than ever before. Wouldn't you agree, dear?"

Claire's mind had already drifted away from the conversation.

"Dear?" the nun repeated.

Monique stepped in for her sister. "Yes, you'll get no argument from us on that point. Right, Claire?"

"Oh, right. Certainly."

Sister Arlene tried to do her part to dispel the awkwardness, but Claire made little attempt to hide her disdain of the children around her, the orphanage, the church, and, at present, even the elderly nun.

Once again, Monique stepped in to move the conversation in a new direction. "Is she about?"

The sister tore her gaze from Claire's distant face and focused again on Monique. "I'll see to her."

Before Sister Arlene could step away Monique pushed a small roll of German currency into her hand. The nun looked down discreetly and saw the tightly rolled money. "Bless you, dear. Someday we will use their money to start the fires in our trash barrel. But for now the children have great need of it. God bless you. I'll be right along."

Sister Arlene appeared to glide across the polished floor. Her feet were invisible beneath the long black robe, and it took only the smallest amount of imagination to make one believe she was hovering inches above the floor as she moved out of the room through an open archway.

"Nuns are spooky," Claire said as she hugged herself and rubbed her arms again. "How do you stand it here?"

"Now who's strange? You sneak around in the middle of the night with guns and bombs, but a sweet little old lady scares you. How can that be?"

"I repeat, nuns are spooky. C'mon, you paid your penance. Let's go." Claire punctuated her words with a step toward the door, but Monique caught her arm.

"Wait. Here she comes."

Monique was looking back across the room to the archway where Sister Arlene had reappeared. The nun was resting her arm around the thin shoulders of a little girl whose blonde curls contrasted greatly with the black sleeve of her guardian. The child's face was blank as she surveyed the room until she spied Monique. Instantly the little face erupted into a brilliant all encompassing smile, and she bolted from the nun.

"Walk!" Sister Arlene called out sternly, which immediately corralled the little feet and reduced them to a brisk walk.

Monique had already squatted down in anticipation of greeting the little girl. Claire towered above and scowled at the stiffly approaching child. "Blonde," she said bitterly. "Blonde Nazi father."

"Hush!"

The words barely had time to escape Monique's mouth when the little girl launched herself into the arms of her benefactor.

"Where have you been?" the girl asked through teeth clenched in her tightest hug. "You didn't come see me for a long, long time!"

"It's only been a few days! Let me have a look at you." Monique held the girl out in front of her and brushed at her dress, smoothing away new wrinkles compliments of the dash, jump, and hug. After she had been made presentable, Monique turned the child toward Claire. "Here, do you know who this is?"

"That's Claire."

Monique stood and urged her on. "Very good. Introduce yourself."

The little girl curtsied and smiled. "Hello. My name is Essey."

Claire looked away and shifted purposely in her stance. "That's nice. C'mon, Monique. We've got to go."

Essey turned from Claire's rebuff to Monique, her little face already drained of the delight from moments before. "You have to leave already?"

Monique tried to soften the harsh blow Claire had delivered. "I'm sorry, sweetie. I do, but I'll be back tomorrow. I promise."

"Promise?" Essey asked slowly over a pouting lip.

"Promise," Monique repeated. "You go and play. I'll see you in the morning. First thing!"

"Promise promise?"

"Promise promise."

Essey sighed and took what comfort she could from the sincerity of Monique's words. "Oh, okay," she drew out slowly.

"You run along and play now. I'll see you in the morning." Monique crouched down again and exchanged hug for hug and kiss for kiss with the little girl. Essey turned to hug Claire but ran into her outstretched hand instead.

"Sorry, kid. I don't hug. C'mon, Monique." With that, Claire headed toward the door leaving Essey standing where the affront had stopped her.

Only a heartbeat passed before Monique snatched Essey away from the rebuke. She tried to make up for the rejection with another round of hugs and kisses. "Don't let that bother you, honey. You know that's just Claire being Claire. She doesn't mean anything by it."

"She acted like she mean-did it."

"Yes, I know. She can be quite convincing. But we've talked about Claire before. You'll have to trust me. She's a softy."

"You sure 'bout that?"

They hugged yet again, and through it Monique tried to relay a positive answer, but she never lent the feeling words because they would have been weak and she wouldn't have believed them herself. She had never seen her sister so cold. The war had brought changes to everyone, she knew that, but it was only in tiny events like this that Monique caught glimpses of this new hardened Claire. What she saw frightened her, but it also made her mad.

"Okay, you. Off you go," Monique said as she turned Essey toward the tables and patted her off with a playful swat on the butt. The little girl's feet shuffled reluctantly, but slowly carried her into the quiet turmoil of the lost, the unwanted, and the nuns.

Once the room had swallowed the child Monique turned her attention toward the door where Claire paced like a tiger in a cage. Monique approached quickly, passed her belligerent sister, and hit the door hard. As she burst through she chided her sibling roughly. "That was rude."

Claire followed her sister through the slamming door. "Rude? I told you I didn't want to meet any of these little German bastards. I don't need any reminders that the Nazis are raping our country."

"Cut it out, Claire."

"I would like to meet the brat's father, though."

Monique stopped at the base of the stairs and turned back to her sister. "Now, why would you want to do that?" she asked with a burst of sincerity.

"To kill him, of course."

"Stop it, Claire! Just stop it!"

The sudden vehemence in Monique's voice caught Claire off guard. It was a moment before both recovered and Monique could continue in a voice more accustomed to her. "I don't ever want to hear you talk like that again. I've told you, I don't care for it."

The words brought Claire up short on the steps, but like her sister, she recovered and blared down the stairs. "You don't care for it? You don't care for it? You think I care for this?" she said as she motioned to her stockings and dress. "You think I care to get dolled up like a goddamn whore so some German son of a bitch can paw me over?"

The muscles in Monique's face tightened as she stared down her sister, but the nunnery and the cathedral behind Claire caught her attention and steered the conversation away from the fight that was certain to come, if not today then soon. Monique relaxed and her shoulders fell as she sighed. "You promised mother you'd go."

Claire stomped down the stone steps. "Oh yeah, I promised. Promise promise," she mimicked cruelly.

The words tore through Monique's dress and dove into her heart while the callousness behind them continued to shock and surprise. "What's happened to you?" Monique asked.

The question caused Claire to spin on her heels. She accented her words with a pointed finger. "Me? What's happened to you? You're the—"

Her words were broken off by the opening of the nunnery door and the appearance of Sister Arlene and a second nun. The pair walked reverently down the steps and through the scene of the impending row.

"Good day again, ladies," the sister said firmly. The other nun did not speak but nodded as they unintentionally stepped between the feuding pair and on up the sidewalk.

Monique didn't let Claire resume her attack. "Let's get this over with," she said as she stepped away.

The pair walked on in silence, a marked contrast to the frolicking mood they had been in as they walked these same blocks minutes before. Though the evening June air was warm and pleasant, both women buried their hands deep in their light coats and their shoulders hunched against an unseen cold wind. There had never been this distance between the two. And each considered that it might be too easy to blame the war and the Germans for their trouble.

The quiet held between them as the streets gave way beneath their feet. After a long quiet time they were within sight of the Café of Lights. Monique nudged her sister. "Try to smile."

Claire flashed a quick phony smile then let it fade just as fast. Monique just shook her head.

Up the street at the club the doorman was busy. Parties of soldiers were filtering in and out. Couples came and went. Every man was in uniform. There were no exceptions. As the sisters approached, Monique managed a smile for the doorman who returned it as he held the active door. "Good evening, ladies. Welcome to the Café of Lights."

Monique's transformation continued as she stepped through the door. When she emerged on the other side the hurt was buried, and she had successfully painted on a pleasant face. Claire came into the club as angry as she had been in the street, and the scene before her did nothing to change her mood.

The floor of the club seemed to be alive and moved like choppy waves as dancers bobbed to the music while others moved in and around the vast rooms. Waiters and waitresses in black pants and skirts, white tops and black ties, darted and weaved their way through the mass, deftly balancing trays of drinks and appetizers. The dance floor was lower than the rest of the club and was the focus of attention for most. At one end of the floor a band, each member looking sharp in a crisp tuxedo, churned out renditions of popular tunes from a small platform.

The musicians' black and white attire was the perfect backdrop for the dancers. The women, all French, wore bright summer dresses with short sleeves or thin straps above flowing skirts. Every color of the rainbow was represented in fine order. Blues danced beside pastel pink and sun-bright yellow with red as though it didn't matter. The dresses flashed and winked their splashes around glimpses of silk thighs and the alluring tease of bouncing breasts. Women's hair, after hours of struggle to obtain the right style and look, now shook to the music and was matted at the temples by beads of sweat brought on by the vigor of the dance, alcohol, and impending passion.

Every man on the floor was in a grey German uniform. In such contrast were the male members of the troupe of dancers to the women that despite their blandness, or perhaps due to it, the ensemble complimented one another nicely. The men danced slower than their partners except for the odd unruly enlisted man whose legs and hips had been oiled by liquor and beer into such a state that gravity and physics, not to mention good taste and ethics, seemed suspended.

Rank however, remained constant. Although alcohol loosened hips, only on rare occasions did it do the same for tongues. Foot soldiers sat with foot soldiers, non-commissioned officers with non-coms, and the officers with themselves. Unintentional jostling on the dance floor and accidental bumps in the crowded club were acceptable but seldom occurred without being followed by a harsh glance from the higher rank. This play took stage throughout any evening and the soldiers were kept wary by the quickness with which the participants could change. A sergeant would be bumped by a private and revel in his superiority only to turn away and run into a lieutenant and be subjugated to his own treatment. The more levels that existed between the ranks, the greater the fear or disdain. Minus the uniforms and rank, the club could have been anywhere in the world and held a large degree of the same posturing, for effect and for women, as might have been done in the smoke of a fire outside a cave a hundred thousand years prior. But in the modern smoke of the club the collar ornaments and shoulder patches were so distinct as to permit the hierarchy of the battlefield to easily carry over onto the dance floor. Occasionally reason gave way to drunkenness, and the gap of rank seemed inconsequential. The fights were always over a girl, whether officially or the result of distant jealousy. Still, this was generally the exception in The Café of Lights. It seems there was enough fighting to be done outside.

And so it was that the war was moderately suspended in the club. It was relegated to a far second among chief topics. The winner's circle was now occupied by affairs of the heart, or with the veil of propers removed, affairs period. The soldiers plied their trade with a dimming flash of uniform and rank while the girls flirted and toyed. As the women teased, the men were left to stumble for words in conversations only meant as fillers before they chanced a reach beneath the Café's starched tablecloths and caressed a soft thigh.

The recipients of those secretive touches had their own reasons for being at the club, and they were as varied as the colors on the dance floor. Most looked for a little laughter and fun to counterbalance the despair outside. Though their country's economy was battered beyond recognition many of the women had jobs, but they were often jobs that had once belonged to absent or dead fathers, husbands, brothers, or other missing Frenchmen. Their work was often difficult and underpaid if paid at all. The club and a strong drink, even if offered by a hand protruding from a grey sleeve, was a welcomed respite.

The vacuum in the workplace was replicated in the social circle. Several young ladies danced their way into the hearts and beds of the wanting soldiers for simple pleasures. Many were seeking only an hour's worth of human touch, but some sought true love and in their minds transformed the German grey into shining silver and military cars into white horses. These women were often the ones eventually left most shattered while their French sisters, those who smiled, danced, and loved away the weary nights, continued on as long as their looks and legs allowed.

Of these, nearly all were amateurs — looking merely for laughter and lovemaking. The strict professionals, the whores, were not allowed, openly anyway, to solicit in the Café. Lastly, there were those like Sophie and Monique who were skilled professionals as well, though their clients, who grinned like sly foxes as they dressed in the foggy French mornings, never realized how exorbitantly high a price they had paid for a woman's momentary favors.

While the ebbs and flows of the early mating rituals continued around them, Monique and Claire began edging through the club toward the tables. Claire took her sister's elbow, a bit too tightly, and leaned toward her ear as she spoke, her free hand motioning toward the dance floor.

"See that? That's what Germany brings to France," she said with contempt dripping like venom off her tongue. "All the bright colors are French. The grey is Germany — dull, stupid, grey. They bring nothing but misery. Do you see it?"

"I see people having a good time."

"Then you're blind."

"I can see fine, thank you."

"You only see what you want."

"And you don't?"

"I see the truth."

"Stop being so dramatic. Enjoy the music."

Claire continued to glare at the German dancers as the sisters moved for an open table. She stepped alongside Monique at a break in the crowd and spoke again, a little too loudly. "Do you know what color besides grey looks good on a Nazi?"

Rather than provide encouragement by admonishing her, Monique played along quietly. "Is this a joke?"

"Not really."

Monique hesitated with a sideways glance before continuing. "I'll bite. What other color looks good on Nazis?"

"Red. Blood red. Their own, of course."

"Of course," Monique answered as she shook her head. "God, you sound more like Father every day."

"Is that so bad?"

"Tonight, yes. It isn't wise to say things like that in here."

"Then maybe I should leave," Claire said as she half-heartedly turned in the direction of the door.

"Fat chance," Monique said as she pulled Claire toward an empty chair. "Have a seat, little sister, and learn from a master."

Monique slipped gracefully into her seat while across the small round table Claire flopped down roughly. "Oh, this ought to be good."

A frail-looking waiter, who moved with quick darting motions and a para-military bearing, suddenly appeared beside the table. He snapped a towel beneath his arm and brushed vigorously at the tablecloth, smoothing the tiniest of wrinkles.

"Good evening, ladies. Miss Monique. As always, it will be a distinct pleasure for me to serve you. And for you and your companion, complimentary shrimp cocktails," he said as he plucked two prepared glasses and an equal number of tiny forks off a passing waiter's tray. "Courtesy of a misplaced shipment bound for Berlin and table number twelve!" The waiter and the sisters shared a laugh as Claire all too openly looked around the room for an annoyed German waiting for a shrimp cocktail.

"Anything special to begin your evening?" he continued. "Or shall I wait a few moments for one of these swine to bolster the courage to approach your grace?"

"Jean, you're teasing again. I'll have white wine. You select for me, please."

"And your lovely associate?"

"Excuse me, Jean. This is my sister, Claire. Claire, this is Jean. The finest waiter in all of France."

Jean snapped to attention sharply and politely bowed his head. "I am known as Jean Luc, loyal only to a free France and my customers. It is a pleasure to meet the sister of Miss Monique." Jean Luc took Claire's hand and bent to kiss it. As he came close to her he whispered. "It is also a pleasure to meet someone whose convictions mirror my own. The hope of our country lies in your hands and others like you. But be careful, as your reputation grows, so does your vulnerability." He kissed her hand, rested it gently on the table, and stood back with a sharp click of his heels. "I will be your waiter and attentive servant, Miss Claire. What may I bring you?"

It was a moment before Claire focused on his question. She was stunned, but pleasantly so by his remarks. "Oh, uh...just a beer."

"Excuse me?" Jean asked as if he really hadn't heard.

"She'll have white wine as well," Monique interjected.

"Very good, ladies." At that, Jean Luc vanished into the atmosphere of the club snapping his fingers and issuing orders to busboys as he went.

Claire leaned toward her sister excitedly. "Did you hear what he said?"

"Not all. Thank God," Monique answered as she looked around.

"How'd he know?"

"Jean hears and sees much with his towel."

"He works with the Re—?"

Monique cut her off. "How can you be so stupid and still be alive?" she whispered fervently. "Don't ever even say that word! Not here, not anywhere! To no one! You hear me? No one!"

Claire cowered for the first time that night. "You're right."

"Then you wonder why Sophie protects you the way she does."

The sisters quieted and let Claire's mistake slip away into the music. Monique relaxed shortly and rested one elbow on the table. "You have to adjust your thinking. And given your tendencies, it will be no small feat. Lesson number one," she continued as she pointed after the darting Jean Luc. "That is the last drink you buy. And the only one you drink. From now on you have the drinks bought for you, but you don't drink them. Perhaps a sip or two from each at most. Then after half an hour you ask for a fresh one."

"Oh, that's rich! Father will be so happy I'm only a prostitute not an alcoholic."

"Hush up and listen." Monique scanned the club as if searching for a target. "Lesson number two. Nothing below a lieutenant. Absolutely no enlisted men. None. No matter how handsome he might be."

"I don't get it. Not that I want to."

"Enlisted men don't know anything. Just lieutenants and up. Captains are excellent. Majors even better. And colonels, well, if you can get a colonel you're really on to something."

"Oh, God, a shopping list of whoremongers."

"Pay attention! Officers know things. And they love to talk to soft attentive ears. You make them think they're the smartest officer in the service. Whatever rank he is tell him he should be the next one higher. Get them talking and they won't stop. Oh, how they love to impress us! Act enamored by their conversation and they'll tell you the combination to Hitler's safe if they have it. God, men are dumb."

"No. This is dumb."

"No it isn't. It's important. All you have to do is talk to them. They'll do all the work. You'll see it's actually quite easy."

"Don't you mean sleazy?"

Monique tightened her brow at her sister. "Just talk. That's all. You'll soon find that you won't be able to shut a lieutenant up even though they may not have a lot of what we want. Now colonels on the other hand know plenty, but they're a tight-lipped bunch. I suppose that's how they get to be colonels. But pressure, applied correctly, can loosen their tongues."

"After you loosen their pants, right?"

"Don't make this harder than it is. Let's just leave it as talking for now. Dance and have a good time. Agree with what they say and take mental notes. For bigger fish and bigger rewards you have to use more bait. That's the only difference."

"Not to me it isn't."

"With intimacy comes a trust. You can use that to your advantage. Pillow talk has made and broken more men than battle."

"It's repulsive."

"It's important."

"I can't do this," Claire said as she started to get up.

Monique grabbed her arm and held her. "Sit still. There's a couple of lieutenants trying hard to look like they're not, but they're coming our way. Practice."

Sure enough, two young officers were working through the mix of crowd and tables, taking a roundabout way to the sisters. They leaned heavily on their drinks, sipping them often and smiling over the rims at no one. Throughout their charade they looked often in the direction of the McCleash table. Though she had watched their approach as deliberately as if they had been planes on a radar screen, Monique feigned a pleasant surprise when the junior officers finally found their way and the nerve to approach the table.

The closer they came the quieter Claire grew. When the officers finally stepped up and said hello Claire had scrunched herself deep into her chair and was considering the notion of invisibility. Monique, on the other hand, was in full swing. As she talked and teased, Claire couldn't help but be amazed at what she heard come out of her sister's mouth. When Monique produced a cigarette from her purse, though Claire knew she didn't smoke, Claire's mouth fell open. Though still repulsed by the scheme she had become a part of, watching her sister skate so skillfully through the Germans was only two steps short of fun.

"So, where are you stationed?" Monique asked as she held her cigarette and leaned forward in anticipation of a hurriedly produced light. In her leaning, Monique revealed considerably more cleavage, which sped up the lieutenants' heartbeats but hampered the production of the match now caught in a shaky, fumbling hand. The temptress seductively touched the officer's hand, settling its quiver as she stole the light for her smoke.

"Oh, we're not stationed in country. We're news correspondence officers."

Monique wanted to laugh out loud at the notion of their work — typing press releases, being told what to say so the German people could be told what to read. Instead she leaned back and drew ever so slightly on the cigarette as she sized up the men before her. Regular correspondence officers might dispatch important documents, but even they'd never be able to access them. Certainly all the information would be coded. Intelligence could decode many messages she knew, but nothing could come from news dispatches. For her labors with these two she would gain nothing except a sweaty over-exuberant youngster who would probably shoot his cum long before he shot off his mouth and neither projectile would be worth a damn. Monique laughed at her analogy and allowed a smile to bubble to the surface. These were nobodies, glorified typists, but then again maybe good for something.

Her laughter was out of place, but she excused it quickly. "Excuse me," she said as she touched her lips with her fingers. "Too many drinks on the way over here tonight. Wine makes me silly."

The explanation and smile eased the tension of the officers just as Jean Luc returned with the previously ordered drinks.

"You look very happy tonight," Monique's lieutenant said with a smile as he took her drink from Jean's tray and placed it in front of her. "Here. Drink up. Be silly. I love your smile."

"Oh, I always smile in the presence of a gentleman," Monique said as she began rifling through her purse, taking great pains not to find her money. Claire recognized this part of the ploy and actually smiled herself for the first time since entering the world of The Café of Lights.

As Jean skillfully flipped paper coasters on the table and gently placed the sisters' drinks on them, relocating Monique's, the lieutenant dove for his money clip. "Here, allow me." The confidence in his voice would be short-lived.

"Thank you so much," Monique said slyly. "What a gentleman."

Jean grabbed the lieutenant's money, dropped his arm, rolled his eyes, shook his head, and turned away laughing.

The officers looked after him and tried to erase the obvious thoughts they were having. Monique brought them back with well-placed compliments, blatant flirting, and the occasional forward lean. The work was well rehearsed, though not recognized as such, and very skillful. Through all the subtle wordplay Monique intentionally never asked the two men to sit. As she continued to hold the attention of her lieutenant, the second shifted his focus to Claire, who had yet to speak.

"You're kind of quiet. I like that," he said with a smirk across his lips.

The remark touched a nerve. Claire instantly felt violated, even by the soldier's attention. Her face held the fiercest gaze she could manage and burned into his eyes as she struggled with what to say or do next. Beside her she could scarcely hear and even less understand the droning of her sister. The sounds of the rest of the club had disappeared entirely.

She was unarmed for the first time in weeks on a night spent working for the Movement — if this was indeed considered work. But the lieutenant had a sidearm. Claire's eyes shifted to the officer's weapon and studied it as her thoughts raced on to the beat of the unsuspecting German's babble, meant to coax her into his arms. She could try to snatch the gun then and there and kill him now, but the risk would be tremendous. Monique could get hurt in the shooting, and she'd be caught for certain. The Resistance could be exposed as well. All for a single dead typist.

No, she thought. *I'll play this game. I'll invite him to take me for a nice ride in the country. Then when he takes off his gun belt in anticipation of taking off his pants, I'll tease him. "Is this your gun?" I'll say as I stroke his pistol. "Or is this your gun?" I'll say as I ease down his zipper. And when he laughs and reaches for me, all confident and hot, I'll shove the gun against his temple and send his own bullets through his horny little brain.*

"Hello in there?" the lieutenant said as he tapped Claire's temple with his finger. "I said, would you like to dance?"

She jumped and brushed his hand away from her head. There was a rush through her, not unlike the feeling that came when she raided with the Resistance. Ignoring the repeated question, she pointed at the officer's pistol.

"That's a Luger, isn't it? The P-08?"

Her suitor was taken aback, but recovered enough to look down at his side. "Uh, yes. Yes it is."

Claire moved slowly and ran her fingers across the butt of the weapon until only her middle finger hung near the action. "Makes a nice neat hole. Not a lot of knockdown power though. Not like the Americans' 45, but then again you have the advantage of a larger capacity clip." The same finger now moved to her mouth and hung on a protruding lip. "Or not? I can't remember. Isn't that silly! Yours, I should think, was manufactured in Berlin or maybe Karlsruhe. Do you know?"

"Uh, no I don't." The lieutenant played his role to perfection and stood up straight, away from Claire. For her part she increased the tempo.

"You ever see what a 45 caliber bullet does when it slams into someone's temple at close range?" Her index finger was firmly pressed against the side of her own head as her eyes widened. The lieutenant's eyes widened with hers as Claire pulled the trigger on her play pistol and let her head fall limp, her tongue roll out, and her eyes cross.

"Denise! Please!" Monique said with a noticeable nervousness in her voice. "You'll have to excuse my friend. The combination of too many drinks and too many stories from the front." She leaned back in her chair behind her sister and slowly twirled her finger around the side of her head. "The war affects us all differently," she said as she made an odd face and pointed discreetly to Claire.

The lieutenants could only manage shallow, painful smiles. The first politely excused himself, promising to return to Monique for a later dance. The second only stared at Claire's drooping head and still crossed eyes as his partner pulled him away by the arm to begin the search for easier, saner prey elsewhere in the club.

"Claire!" Monique whispered harshly. "What are you doing?"

"I hate Germans. I can't pretend to be nice to them."

"Well, you'd better do better than that! One more chat about guns and the Gestapo will be hauling you off for questioning. Now wouldn't that be just marvelous? You and your guns."

Sergeant Sneitz, completely drunk, suddenly sprawled across their table. "Hi ya, sweetheart," he slurred to Monique. "Wanna dance?"

Claire pushed back from the table, repulsed by both the look and smell of the man. Monique held her ground and was unflappable. "No thank you, sergeant."

"Awww, c'mon, Frenchy. Whaddaya say? How's about you and me goin' for a midnight ride in the country?"

"I said no thank you."

"Why not? I'll show you a good time, baby."

"I'm sorry. I'm waiting for someone."

Behind Sneitz, Private Timic and another equally drunk friend began to laugh. "What's the matter, Sarge? I thought you were gonna charm her."

"Yeah, you said you'd charm the pants off of her."

"Or the dress!" The pair laughed all the louder at their own joke and fell into each other hysterically. The sergeant followed by leaning closer to Monique, who remained strong and proper.

"That's right, Frenchy. Let's take that ride. Then we can get you outa that fancy dress and have us a real party." He roughly grabbed her arm and began jerking her out of the chair. "Let's go!"

Monique twisted her arm away and Sneitz stopped momentarily as if shocked that he'd been met with such resistance. While he collected himself Claire nudged up to the table and discreetly slipped a shrimp fork into her hand. She fingered it nervously beneath the table, testing it for the best possible grip. She wouldn't shoot a lieutenant tonight for fear of retaliation, but she could test this sergeant's hide to see if he was well done.

Sneitz recovered from Monique's rebuff and lunged for her. She responded quick as a cat and tossed her drink squarely in his face.

The sergeant's companions roared behind him as he licked the drink around his mouth and wiped his dripping chin on his grey sleeve. Claire's muscles tightened, and she gripped the edge of the table with one hand, preparing to propel the other toward the German's throat if he moved again. He moved, but it was a feint as if to step away, then he returned fast and pulled back his hand to slap his hesitant date. But at the height of the sergeant's swing someone grabbed his wrist.

The sergeant stood dumbfounded. For her part, Monique recoiled into her chair, but Claire leaped across in front of her sister with the tiny fork jutting out of her hand. In the move, she bumped the table roughly and spilled her drink.

His snatched wrist kept the restrained sergeant from moving forward with his intended slap and into the tiny tines of Claire's fork. The rush of movement from all sides froze as if it were a still picture.

Monique's savior was a major. His features were chiseled and his grip on the sergeant's wrist was tight, but his voice was calm and almost matter-of-fact as he stared down at the smaller man.

"There a problem here, ladies?"

Monique looked squarely at the stymied and drunken sergeant with the wet face. "I don't know. Is there a problem?"

"Naw," Sneitz answered as he eyed the major's collar ornaments. "No problem here, Major. These whores was gettin' lippy is all."

Claire bristled as she stood her ground, fork in hand, while Monique feigned shock. "I beg your pardon!"

"Perhaps you and your men ought to move along," the major suggested.

Sneitz crudely jerked his arm from the major's grasp, and the drunken party moved a comforting distance away. "Sure thing, Major. Sure thing. Damn, French whores."

"Sergeant. I suggest you leave. Immediately."

With each retreating step the sergeant's words grew bolder. "Officers' whores is what they are! Won't even dance with an enlisted man." Sneitz pointed beneath the table. "That's how you got them fancy silk stockings, isn't it, Frenchy? Fucking officers!"

"Get out! Now!" the major bellowed as Claire dropped back into her chair with her fork and pulled her legs up under the table.

"Yeah, we're going. We're going. Damn French whores. That's all they are."

The trio of banished men slowly exited the club, all the while staring back at the sisters' table. The major returned their glares until they disappeared then turned gallantly to the table.

"Are you ladies alright?"

"Quite. Most rude however," Monique said as she faked a nervousness that caused her to pat her hair and adjust jewelry that didn't need it.

"If it's possible I would like to apologize for the actions of my countrymen. Please know that not all Germans share their opinion of the French."

"Thank you, Major. You are most kind. Won't you please sit down?"

"Thank you. I believe I will."

Claire rolled her eyes as her enemy pulled up a chair next to her sister. "Oh, Christ," she muttered under her breath as she fingered her tiny fork.

As the major settled in he looked beyond Monique to Claire. "I think it's the sergeant who should be thanking me, not you. If I hadn't stopped him I'm afraid there'd be a soldier somewhere struggling to pull a fork out of his throat."

The major chuckled with Monique and didn't hear Claire's quiet threat. "There's still time," she whispered.

Suddenly the major became very formal. "Please excuse me, my name is Pieter Von Strausser. At your continued service."

"My...," Monique said as though terribly impressed. Then she held her hand to her chest. "I'm Monique, and this is my friend, Claire."

The major extended his hand and took Monique's tenderly. He did not kiss it, but bowed his head slightly toward her as she spoke. "Absolutely charmed." Then he released the soft hand with great hesitation and eased slightly up out of his chair to reach across the table toward Claire.

"Claire," he said politely. "My pleasure."

The major's reluctance to release Monique's hand was mirrored by Claire's hesitation to take his. The fighter looked at the hand with loathing, but slowly took it and to the major's surprise squeezed tightly.

"Me too," Claire answered coldly.

The major felt the awkwardness of the grip, but lost concentration on it nearly as soon as it released him as Monique deftly leaned in between the two soldiers. In seconds she had totally captivated the unwary major.

Over the next several minutes Monique plied her wares with practiced precision and in the process spun a web for the blinded officer. As the couple exchanged basics and moved on to open flirting, Claire tried to make herself small. When she couldn't stand it any longer she stood up. Monique broke away from the major and grabbed Claire's arm, but the fledgling intelligence officer in silk stockings tore it away. "I'll be back," she said disgustedly.

Monique's smile and cleavage dismissed any questions about Claire from the major's mind. While the couple returned to their flirting, Claire worked her way to the bar. It was awash in grey, but parted politely for the pretty French girl who walked a bit stiffly in her high heels.

As soon as she hit the rail Claire motioned for the bartender. "Whiskey," she ordered as he stood in front of her.

"Whiskey?"

"Did I stutter?" she asked harshly.

"Whiskey it is."

Claire stared down at the bar, ignoring the countless eyes peering at her from their grey fortresses. When the shot glass touched down in front of her she pushed her money forward, picked up the drink, and downed it in one gulp. She gave a short dry whiskey breath and pushed the glass toward the bar keep.

"Another."

The bartender retrieved the whiskey bottle from its place on the back bar and filled the glass. This time he held the bottle at the ready in case Claire was going to repeat. The nearby soldiers waited, too, but rather than wait to fill her glass they had thoughts of a soon-to-be drunken pretty girl and her misplaced inhibitions. Both the bartender and the soldiers would be disappointed.

Claire went through her money again and tossed just enough beside the waiting glass of whiskey. She cradled the drink in both hands then turned her back to the rail.

From her station at the bar, Claire watched her sister step away from their table and into the major's arms. As Monique began to sway on the dance floor, a corporal who had watched Claire's drinking habits with delight moved closer to her. He smiled when he brought Claire's eyes away from Monique and the major.

"Hi," he said pleasantly.

"No thank you." And the corporal's dream ended before it began.

Before he or anyone nearby could recover, Claire left the bar and returned to her empty table. She set the drink down too hard, and some of the elixir jumped over the rim of the shot glass. As she took her place she licked her fingers and looked for Monique on the dance floor. She discovered her there, lightly stepping and swaying with the major.

As Claire looked on, Monique's easy gait and ability to fraternize with such apparent ease totally transfixed her. Claire was appalled to even sit in the same room with Nazis. Her eyes shifted from her sister, now wrapped in grey and surrounded by the chords of a slow romantic waltz, to the far reaches of the club.

Gathered in all the corners, in every nook, were soldiers. Not unlike men in dance halls around the world and across time, they lined the walls and ogled the girls. Each held a cold drink which they would have traded in a second for a warm hand. Each also held onto something else — the hope that one of the flowery dresses would somehow become so enamored by their look, stance, or hidden charm that they would ask them to dance, to drink, and make love. They knew the hope was slim at best, but for the possibility, however remote, they held out, waiting and leaning, watching and dreaming, sipping their slowly warming drinks, and laughing too loud.

The laughter found Claire and brought her to concentrate on its source. She would stare intently into a grey mass and wish for her eyes to be rifle sights and her stares bullets, but then more boisterous laughter from another part of the club would snatch her away from her victims. With each shifted gaze the fire burned a little hotter, partially fueled by the warming whiskey in her stomach.

To Claire the men became nests of roaches, grey instead of black. They moved slightly against the walls, not anxious to give up prime spots from which to see or be seen. They were huddling together for security against the rejection of the flowery ones, real or imagined, but Claire saw them as conspiring against her, the Resistance, and France.

"What a delightful bombing could take place here!" she mused. "If there was a way to keep Monique and the others away just one night." But there was no way, no way of certainty. If not Monique then it would be one of the other girls who presently whirled across the floor in colorful blurs. And then there'd be the matter of the waiters. And the busboys. All French, each and every one. But each one catering to the Nazis.

Claire shook her head no in wonder and spoke quietly to herself: "How do they do that?"

She washed down the words with the whiskey then without speaking continued the thought. "They must know what these bastards are doing in the hours when they're not here. How do they smile so easily at the faces that killed their friends yesterday and will kill their families tomorrow?"

A young lieutenant, willing to brave the harsh and vacant stare that had deterred a dozen others in the moments before, stepped up to Claire's table and dared ask for a dance. The spell was broken, and Claire focused, albeit slowly, on the lieutenant. Thinking he had not been heard, he asked again.

"I was wondering if you'd like to dance?"

Claire came out of her trance slowly. Her eyes focused on the face before her and deemed it pleasant enough. In another place at another time she would have been flattered, but here in the club, the grey of the German's uniform soon obliterated all else.

Despite the clouding of her vision, brought on in part by the strong drinks, Claire scanned the uniform before her for the insignia of an officer. On his collar were lieutenant's bars. She extended her hand with a delicacy that did not match her words. "Why the hell not," she said as the whiskey took full effect. "It'd make my sister happy, right?"

"I can't say, but it would make me happy."

"Don't be so sure," Claire said as the lieutenant took her hand and escorted her from the table. "You could wake up dead."

The comment was not totally absorbed by the junior officer. His comprehension was hampered by desire and the rush of success at having come off the club wall and bagged one of the bright dresses. Claire could have said, "Yes, I'll dance, but afterward I'll eat you like a mating spider." And even if it could have been true, he still would have escorted her to the dance floor.

The newest couple in the club made their way through the crowd like so many others before and spilled into the dancing scrum. The music was soft and slow as the lieutenant slipped his arm around her waist. He pulled her toward him, but the distance wasn't an unacceptable one for dancing. Still Claire was repulsed and looked for an excuse to make a scene. She was prepared to push away and slap the young officer's face when she caught Monique watching her beyond her suitor.

Monique was swaying slowly in her major's arms, but had effortlessly positioned her partner so she could observe her sister. Now she was looking around the major's shoulder, intently watching Claire dance. When she caught Claire's eye she flashed a slight smile and gave an approving nod. Claire returned the acknowledgment by crossing her eyes and letting her tongue loll from her mouth as she dropped her head on the lieutenant's shoulder. Her student's apparently painful entrance into the world of covert intelligence brought an impromptu laugh from Monique. She covered her mouth as the major gently held her out in front of him.

"My dancing is so funny?" he smiled.

"Oh, no. You dance wonderfully," Monique smiled in return as she pulled herself back into her newest partner.

The feel of her body next to his erased any subsequent questions about the source of the laugh, just as Monique had known it would. A touch, a caress, a kiss, or the slight exposure of a thigh or breast had many times proved useful in squelching questions. She had used her hands and her lips as erasers on blackboard minds so many times it came without thinking and with such a gentleness and sincerity, not once could she remember having to answer difficult or revealing questions. No, in this world she was the one to ask the questions. Her dates, her quarry, need only dribble their answers down the front of their unbuttoned shirts and trousers.

But for now there was only the waning music and the obligatory applause of the dancers. As Monique and her major moved from the dance floor she looked through the disbanding dancers for her sister. She found her, but was flooded with short-lived disappointment as she saw Claire across the club handing her ticket to the coat check girl.

While she was waiting for her coat, Claire turned back to the club and caught her sister's questioning face. Monique mouthed the word, "Why?" though the answer was never in doubt even when the argument turned into agreement at last night's shouting match in the family living room.

Claire smiled sickly, shook her head in an easy no, and shrugged her shoulders. The clerk touched her with her coat, and she turned to take it. As she slipped it over her shoulders she blew Monique a kiss that said despite the evening they were still sisters and best friends. As Claire turned to the door Sophie entered on the arm of a captain.

"Calling it a night already?" Sophie whispered as the captain checked her coat.

"Just too far out of my element, I guess."

"Don't worry. It'll come," Sophie said as she patted Claire's arm.

Claire wanted to say something clever and to the point, like "I hope not" or something worse, but Sophie's arm was being taken from behind by the captain. So instead she smiled and pointed across the floor. "Monique's got a table over there somewhere."

"Oh, I don't think I'll intrude just yet," Sophie said as she waved across the floor to her student who was working back to her own table.

"Shall we?" the captain asked, motioning further into the club.

"Indeed. Claire? Are you leaving alone? Perhaps the captain could ask one of his lieutenants to escort—"

"Thank you, but I'm meeting someone."

"Oh, very good. Have fun!"

Claire's goodbye was a flashing faint smile as Sophie and her captain were absorbed by the throng. The newest, but soon to be retired intelligence officer, stayed in the club just a brief moment longer looking after Sophie as she, like Monique, eased through the crowd and the Germans. The entire scheme remained disgusting, but they had such grace and carried themselves with an air of remarkable confidence. Claire again felt the sense of awe that came over her as she watched her sister primp in the mirror hours before. Then she turned on her heels, tightened her coat around her, and stepped out the door into the cooling night air.

Inside, Pieter was still escorting Monique back to their table as Sophie and her captain searched for one of their own. The major held Monique's chair appropriately as she slipped into it. As he sat, never removing his eyes from her, she turned slightly, looking for Sophie. Now Pieter followed her eyes and watched with her as Sophie and her escort disappeared across the club.

"Friend of yours?"

"Yes. I was going to ask her to join us if she couldn't find a table, but I guess she's all set."

"Nothing against your friend, but I'm glad she found her own table."

"I'll accept that as a compliment."

Pieter smiled and nodded an acknowledgement as Jean Luc materialized beside the table. "Anything from the bar, Major?"

"Yes. Bourbon."

"And the lady?" he said, disguising the fact that he knew Monique as a regular.

"Monique?"

"White wine, please."

"Very good, madam."

Jean disappeared under a flutter of his snapping towel and fingers. Before the couple could launch very far into advancing their conversation, Jean reappeared with the drinks. The major's was a double - purposely placed oil for Monique to work with, compliments of the ever diligent Jean Luc.

Unaware of the stacking odds, Pieter stirred his drink as he searched for words in a game he was not conscious of. While he planned his course of action, preparing to thrust and parry, flank, assault, and regroup, Monique, far better prepared, went to work on hers.

"Tell me, Major, what do you do when you're not rescuing damsels in distress?"

"Oh, military things," he said as he raised his glass to his lips.

"That doesn't tell me much."

"Perhaps that was my purpose," he said as he drank triumphantly.

"And perhaps I was just being polite," Monique said as she coyly dropped her eyes and face as though he'd hurt her feelings.

His reaction was immediate. He reached across the table and gently clasped Monique's hand. "I'm sorry. I didn't mean it like that. The war has made me cynical."

"And rude."

"No. I could never be rude to a woman as lovely as you."

Monique did not respond — rather, she waited, giving the poison time to work. In seconds, her venom had reached his mind and though he slowly pulled his hand back from Monique's, he started to talk.

"I'm an administration officer. A lot of paperwork, scheduling shipments, and transports. Nothing too glamorous I'm afraid."

"That would depend on your definition of glamorous."

"Most people, certainly civilians, think all the excitement is in the Luftwaffe and the Panzers or on the front lines."

"My idea of excitement doesn't mean being in a position to kill someone or get killed."

"You might not believe this, but I tend to agree." The major's words slowed and he diverted his eyes for one of the first times all evening. Monique took note of it. "To tell the truth, what I do, even though it's well removed, generally, from the action as one might say, can still trouble me."

"How so?" Monique said as she took her turn in reaching across the table and covering a hand. The major stroked the back of her manicured fingers as they rested on his.

"Sometimes I think about the men and weapons I arrange transport for. I know what they'll do. And I know that many of the men I send won't come back."

There was no true caring behind her words, though the keenest ear could not have heard otherwise as Monique clenched the major's hand tighter. "If it bothers you so, then why do it?"

"Tradition, if nothing else."

"Tradition?"

"My family, the Von Straussers, have been fighting for our homeland for generations."

"Von Strausser. Sounds as if it should have 'Baron' before it, certainly 'Colonel.'"

"Thank you," the major answered shyly. "Perhaps one day. But I wouldn't be the first 'Baron Von Strausser.'"

"Perhaps then you could be the first 'Baron Von Strausser' who does not fight."

There was no reply. The major digested the words as he looked out over the crowd. Monique was left to search her own mind for the origins of the statement. It had surprised her. She had never cared whether a German fought or didn't. She cared only for France. Pieter shifted his eyes back to Monique without moving his face, which was stern but rapidly melting. Suddenly he leaned hard toward her and took Monique's hand once again. "You're very easy to talk to."

"Anytime."

"Tomorrow?"

"Perhaps."

Then he reconsidered. "Oh, actually tomorrow might not be possible, but beyond it are a great number of certainties."

"There are very few things certain with this war around us," Monique said in her softest voice. "Still and all, a quiet dinner would be a pleasant diversion, wouldn't it?"

"It would at that, but..."

"You've already made plans with someone else?"

"Yes. If you consider the German Army 'someone else.'"

"Ah, the famous Von Strausser devotion to duty."

"I'm afraid so."

Monique spoke beneath a well placed set of batting eyes. "Perhaps if you are close enough, when you are finished..."

There was a pause as Pieter ran through the events to come the following night. He spoke almost absentmindedly, unaware that Monique was logging each word. "Are you familiar with the Clovington Turnpike?"

For her part, Monique registered a blank look and lied. "No. Why?"

"I have a troop convoy headed out that way for the coast tomorrow night. I generally accompany my transports if possible. I wonder how far it is from here?"

"One is never far from the coast in this part of France."

"That's true, isn't it? Could I give you a call when I'm finished?"

The answer took the form of Monique rummaging through her purse for a pen and a scrap of paper. She wrote gracefully, fully aware that Pieter was watching, hypnotized by the simplest gesture. The paper came up between her fingers and was flamboyantly extended toward the major then snatched back. Monique rubbed the paper seductively against her neck, raising her chin and closing her eyes as she did so. Not content, she retrieved a tiny bottle of perfume from her purse and dabbed the fragrance near her telephone number. Again she held the paper out to Pieter who took it and held it under his nose before he even read it.

"My, how delightful."

"Just a name and a number may not be enough to get you to keep your promise."

"You needn't be concerned about that, I assure you," he said as he began reading the note aloud. "Monique McCleash, ICB-829." He smiled and slipped the paper into his breast pocket. "McCleash doesn't sound very French."

"My father's people are from Ireland."

"A thousand shades of green. Isn't that what they say?"

"My father says ten thousand, but that's my father."

"I understand it's a lovely country. Have you been?"

"Just once, when I was young, but my father returns often, at least he did, but for the time being the occupation prevents him."

"My apologies to your father."

"He loves his 'Emerald Isle,'" Monique said through a gentle smile, imitating her father's accent and instantly lost in memories of days when the relationship was not strained.

Pieter laughed a little at the attempt. "It's good to be proud of one's country. Don't you agree?"

"Oh, he is definitely proud. But still, he was kept from it by 'me darlin' French lass.' That's what he calls my mother."

Pieter took Monique's hand and gently held it to his lips. The kiss was slow and soft. "I can see how such a thing could happen to someone. Love of country or not." And he kissed her hand once more.

***

9

Several blocks away Claire was trotting up the front steps of her house. She entered the dim foyer and slipped off her coat in one fluid motion. The coat landed on the nearby tree as she headed past her bicycle for the stairs and her bed beyond. A faint light coming from the kitchen diverted her. On the way to the open doorway she glanced at her father's pipe rack. Even in the pale light she could see it was full. The McCleash patriarch was in.

Gauging her father's presence and mood by the pipes always made Claire smile. Tonight was no exception. A tender look broke over her as she thought of her father and his rough and rustic charm. His tongue was quick like hers, and he was a bit of a rabble-rouser, again like her. God how she adored that wiry man with his stout arms, sharp wit, and callused but tender hands. It was him that had taught her, directly and through example, to be what she now was. The journey did not seem a long one, and he had generally made it fun.

She pulled her shoulders back with pride as the kitchen light fell on her shoes. Her father would be proud of her for leaving the club as she did. He would laugh with her and pat her shoulder when she relayed the story of the sergeant and her fork. The story began even before she entered the room.

"Hey, you should have seen..."

But when Claire stepped into the kitchen, there, seated at the simple table with the chrome legs, was her mother.

Claire's smile vanished along with her cocky storytelling attitude. The surprise at finding her mother was only half the cause. All the affection she had for her father was mirrored by an equally intense dislike for her mother. It hadn't always been so. The divide that now pulled the air from the kitchen had begun as a crack when Claire tossed the first rocks at the German trucks. While Sean McCleash had cheered, Claire's mother cringed. The disapproval in Estelle's voice blossomed into shouting matches with both Claire and her husband. Monique had aligned with her mother, and the division in the family was cemented.

Estelle looked up at her youngest daughter from the dim light of a single lamp set on the table. Around the light were short piles of grey German uniforms, some neatly folded and others haphazardly strewn about which had either enjoyed the attention of Estelle's sewing needle or waited their turn.

Though she looked up to greet Claire's face, her fingers continued to dance with the needle and its long tail of thread. Estelle's hair was greying at the temples and was pulled back in a tight bun away from a face that had traded beauty for thin lines of character. Still she was attractive, though tonight, and every night since the occupation, the face was tired. She wasn't heavy, but thought she carried more pounds than she should. Sean said, "More to love," and he meant it, so there was no real concern in her thoughts. Her dress was neat and clean and still well pressed after a long day that had now extended late into the night.

Tension sprang up in the room as soon as the women saw each other. Though the pair had clashed often with increasing harshness, Estelle still loved her daughter with the dangerous life. The affection was not returned, however, and was deteriorating into disregard. This fissure was growing increasingly obvious in the McCleash home and was ready to ignite yet again in the simple kitchen.

"Oh, I thought you were Father," Claire said in a voice dripping with disappointment. Her last word was still escaping her mouth as Claire turned back to the living room.

"You can talk to me, can't you?"

Estelle's words brought Claire up short in the doorway just as they had throughout her childhood, but now the years, her brashness, and the war had made Claire bold.

"Not really."

"You used to be able to talk to me."

"You used to listen."

"I still can."

"I'm tired. Goodnight."

Again Claire tried to step away, but as before, her mother's words stopped her as surely as if a door had closed in front of her.

"You look lovely, dear. Have you been to the Café?"

Claire remained frozen in the doorway, her back still to her mother. "Yes," came out through lips that tightened behind the word. What followed was an uncomfortable and prolonged silence.

"And?" Estelle questioned as she continued working.

"And what?" Claire exploded as she spun and faced her mother with both teeth and fists clenched.

"How did it go?" Estelle asked in a gentle voice, trying to diffuse her daughter's growing anger.

"If you mean did I screw any Nazis, the answer is no!"

Estelle dropped her mending into her lap and looked at her daughter with sorrowful eyes. "Claire. Why do you say such things?"

"Me? Why do you want me to give myself to the same sons of bitches who are destroying France?"

"I never said that."

"Well that's what Monique does, and you treat her like she's an angel!"

"Your sister does what she can for the Resistance."

"The Resistance? What do you know of the Resistance? A silly housewife who mends the enemy's clothes for pennies." Claire swiped at a neat pile of German uniforms and sent them sprawling across the table and onto the floor. "I'm no seamstress to the bastards! And I'm not their whore! I'm a soldier!"

Claire wheeled back to the living room, but Estelle was hot on her heels. "Yes. Yes you are, Claire, but dresses are better than guns. Safer."

"No! I'll never cater to the Germans!" Claire shouted as she vaulted up the stairs.

"Wait!"

"Or bow down and mend the same uniforms that kill French! Not now, not ever!" She slammed the bedroom door to emphasize her point.

Estelle stood with one hand on the banister looking up the stairs, but she knew Claire would not come out again tonight. Another moment passed before Estelle let her hand and hopes slip away from the railing. She walked slowly back to her work in the kitchen while the furrows in her brow deepened.

The sole light greeted her and reminded her of Claire's outburst as it shone on the clothes scattered across the table and the floor. She bent down on aging knees and picked up the grey pieces, folded them neatly, and stacked them on the table. Then, as before, she took up her place at the table and drove her needle deep into the grey flesh of the German uniforms.

Upstairs Sean had stumbled from his bed, disturbed by Claire's shouts. His hair was wild and his eyes sleepy around a face that still bore pink wrinkles left by a pillow crunched up around his head. The flannel pajamas he wore were well faded, threadbare in spots, and slightly askew on his thin frame. He paused at Claire's bedroom door and cocked an old ear against it as he tapped softly.

"Go away!" Claire answered sharply to the knocking.

"It's Papa."

The door opened immediately. "I'm sorry, Papa," Claire said. "I guess I got a little loud."

"Aye, ya did. Ya did," he said, the accent as thick as molasses.

"But Papa, she doesn't understand. She doesn't know the Resistance. What it means to me to fight!"

Claire gave way to her room now, and her father followed.

"Oh, I don't know," Sean said in a voice that still carried a sleepy gravel.

"She doesn't! She sits around here and actually stitches the holes in their uniforms so they can put them on again to kill us. Why?"

"Your mother's a fine woman, honey."

"She fixes their uniforms, Papa!"

"Aye, but there are reasons."

"No, Papa! Nothing is worth that. Do we need the money so badly that we have to sell our dignity? Sell it for pennies?"

"Of course no, but still in all, everybody must do that which they can. Do you understand, me little girl?" Sean ran his gnarled fingers through Claire's hair and pushed it back from her face.

She sensed that her father was attempting to lessen the gap in the house, and she wasn't prepared, fresh from the fight with her mother, to allow it. There was a way to turn her father and she knew it. And she wasn't above salting his wound a little in order to stem the tide she felt was turning against her.

"She wants me to...to do things...with Germans. Like Monique does."

The change was immediate and profound. Sean looked above his daughter's head as if reading a message on the ceiling. He sighed deeply and licked his teeth behind his lips then flexed his jaw as if testing it, readying it for a blow. He began to nod his head, slowly at first, but faster as his face reddened.

"I know," he whispered as he turned away and moved toward the door. He stopped at the hallway and ran a hand over the dark wood of the door casing. "Claire, ya mind your father here now. Ya stick...to...your...guns...Stick to your guns. Take that in all the ways ya want. Ya hear me, girl?"

"Yes, sir."

"Don't be givin' in t'them for no reason ner nobody."

"I understand," Claire said, glowing inside from the victory.

"I'll tend to your mother," Sean said as he turned and reentered the room. "And ya might as well be forgettin' 'bout your sister.

She's got 'er mind set in a bad way. God will deal with 'er in His own good time fer the things she's done."

"Yes, Papa."

Sean kissed her forehead tenderly and patted both her shoulders at once. "Now ya better get to sleep. Tomorrow there's more rocks to be pitchin', aren't there now?"

Claire smiled at the memory and nodded like a child. Her father smiled with her and left the room without another word.

Alone again, but feeling like a real soldier once more, Claire closed the door behind her father and slipped out of the dress. She reached for a hanger from the closet but caught herself. Instead she tossed the dress on the bed, sat down beside it, and roughly began taking off the silk stockings Monique had given her. Purposely or otherwise, the stockings had several runs by the time Claire pulled them off. She wadded the stockings and the dress together in a ball and threw the mess into the corner of her room on the wings of a vow not to wear a dress again until all the Germans had been driven from France or preferably killed.

For now, one of those Claire wished to eradicate was dancing slowly with her sister under subdued lights. The brass in the band had muted their horns and the drummer used his softest brushes. Pieter held Monique as tight as he dared, and she responded by nestling her carefully painted face into his shoulder. When the song ended the couple applauded politely with the rest of the dancers.

Again they weaved through the crowd retracing their steps to the table. He stayed in character and eased Monique's chair out. She caressed the back of the chair slightly then picked her purse up from the table as she spoke.

"Would you excuse me a moment?"

"Of course." Pieter paused then touched Monique's arm. "Is everything alright?"

She smiled disarmingly and leaned toward him as she whispered. "I have to powder my nose."

Pieter smiled, a bit embarrassed, and Monique slipped off through the crowd. He settled in his chair and tapped and tightened a pack of cigarettes against the back of his hand.

The ladies' room was three-quarters full of primping, gossiping women. Giggles mixed with hard glances at the hair and dresses of the competition. Monique passed by it all and was pleased to find an empty stall. She entered it quickly, not unlike the others, but once inside she fumbled through her purse for her pen. She held the pen in her mouth and continued to rummage for a scrap of paper. In her hurry, a lipstick case fell to the floor drawing the attention of several women outside. She hesitated and grimaced at her clumsiness then bent quietly and picked up the offending piece. Outside, the gathered women paused only briefly, exchanged nondescript looks, and returned to their bantering amid rushed adjustments to their makeup.

She placed the paper on the stall door and held it firmly while she printed hurriedly but as neatly as possible: *Troop Transport - Clovington Turnpike - Tomorrow Night - Heading to Coast*. She returned the pen to her teeth as she quickly folded the note. Then she stopped, unfolded the paper, and put it up against the stall door again. Her pen hesitated over the note then wrote another word: *Invasion?*. Monique watched the word for a moment as if it might reveal something, having been set out in the open, but it did not. So the pen went back to the purse and the note was folded over the word and tucked in her bra.

Then she froze, except her hands. She stared at the unusual quiver in the delicate fingers with the painted nails. She had done this a hundred times, a thousand. There hadn't been this nervousness for years. Women took forever in the bathroom. Everyone knew that. There was no need to rush. And yet here she was blasting through her purse for a paper, dropping things, and scribbling as though time were about to expire on an examination. She took a deep breath, still staring at her hands.

"Calm down, you idiot!" she whispered to her palms as she turned her hands over and back, but they didn't answer. She filled her lungs again and let the breath escape slowly.

"Okay. Okay. Slowly. Move slowly. Move slowly and think quickly. That is the key. Move slowly. Think quickly."

Monique tugged and brushed at her dress to straighten it, flushed the unused toilet, then opened the stall door. The bathroom was as full as before, but the faces had changed. Few took notice of the lovely lady in the maroon dress as she dabbed at the lipstick in the corner of her mouth with her little finger. She cocked her head from one side to the other checking her look, ran her fingers through her hair as if they were a comb and as if it changed anything, then headed away from the brightly lit vanities into the darkened club.

Once outside the confines of the ladies' room Monique positioned herself to see Pieter from a vantage point where he could not do likewise. From across the club, she watched for a moment as he sipped his drink and flicked the ashes from his cigarette. Finding him occupied, Monique shifted her attention to locating Sophie. The crowd was lighter in the rear of the club, and she moved easily but a bus boy was busily clearing Sophie's table as Monique walked up.

"Excuse me," she asked. "Where's the lady who was sitting here?"

"Gone," the boy said as he continued clearing glasses and wiping the table. "Walked out with a captain about five minutes ago. Didn't stay long enough to finish their drinks."

Lost in a thought that centered on the notion that she would have given her message to Sophie, Monique cupped the unbuttoned neckline of her dress and touched the note. The information could not wait. Preparations needed to be made and quickly. She would have to use another avenue to the Resistance tonight. There was another moment's hesitation at the empty table which allowed a second thought to arise in her mind, then she returned to her major.

As she moved back to the table her fluid movement through the crowd caught Pieter's eye. He wasn't alone. Other men watched in envy, not unlike like Pieter himself, each dreaming, with the help of their liquor, of falling in bed, in love, with such a woman.

"Miss me?" she said as Pieter helped her with her chair once more.

"I'd be a fool not to."

"You are the charmer, aren't you?"

"You make it easy."

"What I have to say next may change all that."

"Oh?"

"Not to worry," she said playfully. "I've had a wonderful time."

"That's good to hear."

"It's just that I have to be going."

Pieter checked his watch. "It's still relatively early. Are you sure everything's alright? If I've done something…"

"Oh, heavens no. It's been a lovely evening, but I do have to work tomorrow. And as I remember, so do you."

"I'm hoping to remedy that."

"I'm hoping so as well, but for now I'm afraid I'll have to say goodnight."

Monique stood abruptly which snapped Pieter to his feet just as quickly. From a distance one might have thought an argument had ensued save for the pleasant smile on Monique's face as she extended her hand. "Perhaps tomorrow then?"

He took the offered hand graciously. "Allow me to see you home."

"That won't be necessary."

"But I insist. It wouldn't be proper to abandon such a beautiful lady to the streets after she's graced me for so long."

"I only live a few blocks. I'll be fine, but thank you."

"I'm afraid you'll have to let me," Pieter continued, oblivious to Monique's growing anxiousness. "If not I'm certain to follow you."

This conversation was no longer cute. Being followed was very serious to someone who worked as Monique did. Even Pieter's words, meant to be playful and charming, struck a harsh chord that made Monique's stomach tighten.

"You'd follow me?" Monique asked in disbelief.

"I'm afraid so."

Monique could only stare at the moonstruck major who smiled like a mischievous little boy.

"Well, you needn't," she said. "But it doesn't appear as if I can stop you."

"If it would make you more comfortable I'll walk a half block behind."

A nervous laugh escaped Monique's throat, but Pieter, so overcome with her, failed to sense it.

They went for their coats with his hand barely touching the small of her back as part guidance and part attachment, demonstrating to the rest of the men in the club that she was with him. Though none could know with certainty if he would make love to her that night, in the walk across the club Pieter projected the air that she was his girl and that sex was a given. None need know that the couple had just met.

For her part, Monique felt the touch on her back and the stare at the curve of her hips. She didn't exaggerate the sway though, as easy as it would have been to torment both Pieter and the others. What sway existed was natural, subtle, and extremely erotic all on its own and Monique knew it.

As expected, Pieter retrieved her coat and assisted her with it, continuing the assumed role of gallant gentleman. She tightened the belt on the light coat and walked ahead of her escort through the door of the club and into the streets.

"Which way is home?" he asked.

She pointed. "Rue la Blanc."

"Shall we?" Pieter said as he took up his position on the street side of Monique and offered his arm. She slipped her hand comfortably through his arm, and the couple stepped away from the busy foot traffic of the café. In moments the bright lights began to fade, taking with them the noise and bustle that defined the club.

The cool early summer air was refreshing, as it always was when she exited the club after a night of dance. On so many evenings the air plucked at her cheeks and drove away any romantic notions that had begun to take root on the dance floor or over the rim of a wineglass. The freshness of the night air had often served to remind her of the assignment that had brought her to this hunting ground in the first place. Tonight the breeze was just as fresh, but Monique resisted the call to wake up from the dream that was taking hold of her, compliments of Pieter.

He was a delight, not pretentious or arrogant. Neither stupidly suave or cold. He was charming, witty, handsome, and fun. And, she thought, vulnerable in a way that asked her not to play her hand to the strong suit. In his words and mannerisms, the inflection of his voice, Monique gained a sense that this was a man out of step with his work but pleasantly in time with the beat of her lonely heart. She knew all too well she had to maintain an inner distance from Pieter, but he was making it difficult.

They walked along enjoying the refreshing silence of the quiet street. Words came easily to both and soon brushed away the uneasiness that had overcome Monique in the club. Talk of childhood, of family and friendships, of travel and places seen and places yet to be seen, snippets of the good and the bad, spilled from each with an ease neither had known before. Pieter spoke in a voice as soft as the summer evening breeze. The bearing and confidence that had served him thus far in his life had little use for volume or verbosity. He felt no need to impress this woman with tales of triumph in an attempt to bed her. Instead, he related stories from his days growing up on assorted military bases throughout Germany, while she countered with tales from her past and dreams for her future. Commingled throughout the seamless conversation were reassuring squeezes on a carried arm or a leaning shoulder. Recounted stories that still carried unsettling memories were complemented by comforting assurance. Other remembrances, happy ones, ended with shared laughter. Each story and each smile ended as another brick in a rapidly growing foundation of an intimate friendship.

Streets and blocks passed effortlessly beneath the couple's feet. Their talk continued, having long ago moved away from the sparring flirting that had begun at the café table. But as quickly as the anxiousness had taken her back at the club, it returned. Monique took her arm from Pieter's and thrust her hands deep in her pockets.

"Cold?" Pieter asked tenderly.

"A bit." The answer was a lie. In truth, Monique realized that she had just listened to herself reveal far more about her life in the last half hour than she ever should have. She had walked these streets countless times before on the arms of ranking Germans and had never said more than a few words that were true. Normally she listened, which was the plan — her job as it were. When she was forced into an answer they were routinely vague and shallow. She was, for the purposes of the mission, bright and articulate only enough to be alluring. Certainly most occasions required little of either as she let her hips and curves work their magic well in advance of the need for conversation, but the chance encounter with Pieter had been different from the onset. Business had been somehow relegated to the background and rather quickly so. Traversing this new ground felt foreign. It had been years since a walk in the dark and pleasant conversation had fanned flames in her heart. And still she caught her tongue, hoping it wasn't too late but also cradling a second hope that somehow the exchange with Pieter would continue as it had.

Pieter slipped his arm around her shoulders and squeezed tightly to ward off the fictitious chill. "Does that help?"

She couldn't help but smile. "Some."

A more comfortable quiet enveloped them until they reached the street corner that held the safe house. With no visible hesitation Monique turned up the sidewalk. Pieter fell away from her shoulder and looked up at the street sign.

"I think we go straight, Monique. Rue la Blanc. Correct?"

She didn't stop moving, only turned and began playfully walking backward. "Pieter, can't you tell when a girl wants the night to last a little longer?"

He immediately stepped in her direction, pleasantly surprised. "But the girl I left the club with had to get home."

"Don't tell me you've never heard of a woman's prerogative?"

Monique was still backing up the street as Pieter threw up his hands, smiled at the game, and followed. When he overtook her, she turned into him and slipped her arm back through his.

The safe house was fast approaching on her left. There was the slightest of plans afoot in her mind, but it was clouded by Pieter. As before, an abnormal feeling near anxiousness but rooted far from fear, coursed through her. She had entertained so many Germans in so many circumstances and had gathered and passed information so smoothly that few opportunities slipped away. Even now she knew there was a way to notify the Movement with relative ease, but she advised herself that doing so with Pieter in tow might not be wise. And still there was a gentle tug deep within her that whispered that all would be well. Perhaps it said other things before and after, but Monique didn't hear them. She wanted, needed, to do her job, but she also didn't want the night with this powerful yet endearing soft-spoken warrior who seemed to possess a poet's touch to end. There was no time for more deliberation as the safe house was alongside. If Pieter had felt her pounding heart he might have deemed himself the cause, and of course he was, but not in the way he would have considered.

Monique stopped immediately in front of the safe house stoop and tugged through her dress at the top of her hosiery. "All that dancing has given this stocking a mind of its own," she said over a smile as she put her foot on the first step of the safe house stairs. Hidden on the riser beneath her high-heeled shoe was the small vent.

She pulled the hem of her dress above her knee to access the supposedly troublesome stocking that in truth was fine.

Pieter stared at her exposed thigh and felt a surge common to men in such situations race through him.

Having set the hook with her leg, Monique stared back at the gaping major.

"Pieter?"

"Hmm?" he said as though startled from daydream.

"Would you mind?" Monique asked as she twirled her finger, requesting he turn around.

"Oh! Of course, of course."

Pieter followed directions and gave Monique his back so she could attend to the stocking with some degree of privacy. Much to his delight he immediately discovered that he could see Monique's broken reflection fairly well if he pieced them together from window panes across the street. There was a moment's hesitation as valor wrestled with voyeurism, but the battle was soon lost to more self-indulgent interests. Pieter settled in comfortably to watch the show.

Monique was tensely watching his back, attempting to insure that he remained facing away. Her interest in his back was such that she failed to notice that she was being watched even more intently. With her eyes glued to Pieter, and his clandestinely to her, Monique stepped down from the safe house and reached into her bra for the note she had written in the club's bathroom. In one fluid movement, she squatted, slipped the note into the vent on the step's riser, and stood again, replacing her foot on the same step. As before, she hiked up the hem of her dress, but its allure had been vanquished. Pieter's interest had shifted miles beyond the measure of her silky thigh.

Below the steps of the safe house, safely tucked away in the corner of the basement, Renault, Michel, Paul, Jon, and Natei were leaning over a battered table. As they scoured maps and a few aerial reconnaissance photographs, Monique's note tumbled from a delivery tube onto their pile of ragged papers. As one, all the men slowly turned their faces toward the ceiling.

"Alright, Pieter," Monique said almost proudly, having seemingly carried off her delivery. Pieter, however, did not move. He remained transfixed by the reflection in the window and the flashing memory of what he had seen there.

"Pieter? You may turn around now," Monique offered again, this time nearing a question.

Pieter dropped his eyes from the girl in the glass and turned ever so slowly hoping somehow that when he had done so, a trick played by the reflecting image and the dim light would be revealed. But that would not happen. The stunned major brought his eyes up to Monique's face, easily ignoring the teasing thigh. When Monique had recaptured his attention she dropped her hem and brushed it flat as she stepped down from the riser.

"Shall we go?"

Pieter neither answered nor moved. He stood in continued shocked silence waiting for the dream, now perhaps a nightmare, to be over and show itself as something other than what he feared it was. He searched her face for a sign, an answer, or an explanation, but was only rewarded with her usual smile. Even so, it was enough to sway him, and in his consciousness he felt the sight of Monique bending low to the vent, pushing in the note, being itself pushed back in his mind. She disarmed him so. In her smile there was no hint of larceny or treason. And Pieter believed the smile. Slowly he extended his arm for her.

With her arm slipped delicately through his they stepped away from the safe house as if they had indeed only stopped to adjust a stocking. But the ease that had permeated the conversation of the major a block ago only a minute before had vanished. In its stead was a silence born out of rapid but deep thought, confusion, and a seasoning of distrust and anger.

Back in the lower reaches of the safe house the note that had caused Pieter's dismay was being examined while a short wave radio in the corner of the room hummed. Renault, the most senior man present, held the note in both hands. He was a short thick man now in his fifties with an increase in wrinkles around his eyes brought on by the last four years of occupation coupled with years assembling the Resistance while the German war machine assembled nearby. He was made an inch or so taller by the dark blue beret, a trademark which rode high on his head. Irrespective of his height, there was real power in him. Renault said what he meant and meant what he said and was mean enough to say it when need be. His thick arms in his oft-worn blue and white striped shirt cradled Monique's paper as he read it to himself.

Below Renault's hands lay several maps of the surrounding area, some of which were hand drawn and others of French or German design. Most were in various stages of decay. All the German maps, stolen or recovered as booty from raided convoys, were covered in handwritten French notes, corrections to improper locations and highways. These roads, so familiar to Renault, Michel, and the others, had once carried them to school and to the arms of their lovers. The war had evoked so many changes that the lessons at the end of the roads were much different now, much harsher, and the consequences far more reaching. And the lovers that traveled these roads now often followed hearses, laying precious hearts and bodies to rest under ground that seemed unable to find that same peace and stillness.

When Renault finished reading he set the paper aside and began rustling through the maps. "Where's the Clovington Turnpike?"

Without speaking Paul pointed out a spot on a map with a well-scarred muscled hand. Natei, proudly standing near the vicious fighter, spoke for him though it was not necessary. "It runs to the coast."

Renault's voice was distant. He did not appear to be referring to either Paul or Natei. "I think you may be right," he said softly. "I think you may be right..."

Michel exchanged looks with the other men as though Renault was questioning the obviousness of Natei's comment. "Who's right?" he asked.

"Our messenger," Renault answered without looking up from his search.

Michel scanned the pile of papers on the table and picked up the note. He read it quickly then handed it to Paul, who scarcely glanced at it before dropping it on the maps. Jon snapped it up and read each word with Natei looking over his shoulder, studying as though he was privy to something unusual, as indeed he was. While Jon and Natei read, Michel questioned Renault.

"An invasion?" Michel said almost with a chuckle. "Do you think it's time?"

"Apparently the Germans think so and that's what matters."

Suddenly more serious, Michel snatched the note from Jon and held it out to Renault. "How do we know this information is good?"

"It's good," Renault replied, still not looking up from his study of the maps.

Unable to garner Renault's attention, Michel looked again at the note. "Looks like a woman's handwriting to me. I don't think we should rely too heavily on it." Michel looked to the others for support. Jon shrugged his shoulders to Michel's unasked question and was mirrored by Natei, who then simply stared at the paper. Paul ignored Michel completely and continued studying the maps with his mentor.

Renault let Michel's words hang for a moment then disappear entirely from the air before he spoke. "The information is solid," Renault said with no urgency.

"Yes, but," Michel said as he began to pace around the table, waving the note as if trying to rally the others in the room, "this may be the whimsy of a woman. It may—"

"Leave it alone, Michel." Renault cut him off with a tone that was just beginning to show a hint of impatience. "We've got a great deal of work to do." He pointed out a route to Paul that intersected the Clovington Turnpike. "Here, Paul. I know this spot. We lay charges in the road, here and here, just where they slow for the turn. The terrain is steep on both sides of the road. Have your snipers and machine-gunners on these banks. On either side of the road. Jon, you and Natei mine the road before the curve. Lay the trip wires along the ditches. When the charges are touched off we—"

"Do you know who sent this?" Michel interrupted as he halted his pacing with a snap of the note out toward Renault.

For the first time since the inquiry began, Renault raised his eyes from his work. There was a long pause as he stared intently at Michel, carefully gauging both the young fighter and his own answer. "I may," he said slowly.

"Who is it?"

The question was so sharp it caused Paul to uncharacteristically tighten his eyebrows in concern.

For his short time at his country's work, Natei did not know enough to be surprised. Jon, however, felt his mouth suddenly hang open in shock.

"Why?" Renault said in his same guarded voice as he moved away from the maps and around the table to Michel.

"I'm curious about the person you are so quick to trust."

"You ask too many questions, Michel."

The two men were now face to face. Michel was looking down at Renault, and his voice was full of resolve. "We have limited resources. You know that, Renault. I think we should be very careful how they're deployed. We cannot afford to—"

"Is that it? Is that what you're concerned with? Resources? Numbers? Counting bullets?"

"I think-"

"Or is it possible, let's say, that you are more interested in names than in numbers? Perhaps for the Gestapo even, eh, Michel?"

"That's ridiculous!"

"Is it?"

"It certainly is."

"Says you."

"Don't turn this on me, Renault. All I'm saying is that we can ill afford to invest our time, energy, and resources in the pursuit of Germans who may or may not even be moving as this mysterious writer suggests. We can't jump every time some woman takes it into her head that she's somehow suddenly become privy to information about the Third Reich that our regular intelligence has been unable to gather."

Renault snatched the note from Michel's hand and glanced at it. "What makes you think this is not from our regular intelligence?"

"Because it's a woman's handwriting."

"So?"

"I know the intelligence members in this city, and they are men."

"How do you know them?"

"Renault," Michel said, "I've been with the Movement from the beginning."

"As have I."

"Then you must know—"

"I know nothing! And I know nothing because I choose to know nothing! And what I have known, I have also forgotten!"

"I am not blind, Renault! And neither are you! We can only do so much. We're running low on virtually every munitions we once had in abundance. I want to know our sources — judge their reliability — so we can determine where best to invest what little we have."

"Those are not your decisions. You do as you are told. Same as me. What is important and what we can afford to do will be determined by Charlemagne and the directors."

"Yes. Yes. But if we can filter out the whims of—"

Renault waved the note. "This is not a whim."

"Perhaps."

"Trust me, Michel."

"Trust you? Then you trust me. Who dropped the note?"

Renault looked at the message again, fondling it with both hands. His eyes drifted up slowly and searched out Paul, Jon, and Natei, pausing on each before he suddenly broke his gaze away and returned to the maps. He placed the note on the edge of the table and began tracing the route of the German convoy. He did not look up as he spoke. "Paul? You and Jon. If Michel asks any more questions...kill him."

"Yes, sir," Paul answered immediately as he looked with frozen eyes at Michel.

"Jon? Did you hear me?"

Jon looked from Renault to Michel and back again.

Renault's voice rose. His face was reddening as he looked up from the table. "Jon! If he asks any more questions, kill him! Do you understand?"

Again, Jon did not answer directly. His feet began to shuffle beneath him, and he looked at the floor. Natei stood helplessly frozen.

"You can't be serious," Michel said, thereby saving Jon from Renault's glare.

Renault slammed both fists down hard. The table and Natei jumped. "Goddamn it!" Renault screamed as the veins in his neck bulged to near bursting. "I am deadly serious! And for me, too! If I ever ask too many questions, kill me! Do you hear, Paul? Michel? Kill me!"

Renault took a deep breath and closed his eyes for a few seconds. When he opened them again, he scanned the faces of the men under his command.

"Boys. The Nazis are masters at covert infiltration — spies. We can not, I repeat, can not, be too careful. If one should turn it will mean the gallows for all. And our families besides." He paused again and once more took a breath meant to relax both him and those nearby. "For now," he continued, "we are forced to trust one another." He picked up Monique's message one more time. "I'll send off a memo to Charlemagne on this. Jon, prepare an inventory of what explosives you have remaining. Natei, see what we have for vehicles to get our people out to Clovington. Paul, check the small arms. Then all of you get some sleep. Tomorrow may be a long day."

Natei looked at his watch then to Renault. "It is already tomorrow."

***

10

Time slipped away from Monique and Pieter as well. Silence had prevailed for several blocks and now they were turning up Rue La Blanc.

"A penny," Monique said with a gentle squeeze of Pieter's arm.

"Pardon me?"

"For your thoughts. Isn't that how it's said? Or should it be a groshen?"

"Oh, I suppose."

"But the meaning and intention are the same."

"Yes. I guess they are," Pieter answered absently before another pause in the conversation.

"And so?" Monique queried again.

"So?" replied Pieter, still lost in thoughts far from Monique's word game.

Monique stopped walking halting the major as well. "My penny? Your thoughts?"

"Oh," Pieter said as he started moving again with Monique in tow. "Just thinking about work."

"That family tradition again?"

"I suppose so."

"Well, I'm home so you're spared my lecture again," she said as she looked up at her parents' house.

His eyes followed hers, but he did not comment on the house as he might have had Monique's reflection in the window not jumped back into his mind and force other thoughts aside. He felt Monique saddle up close to him and listened as she spoke.

"I've had a wonderful night. But I do wish I could have made you forget about your work for a time."

Pieter paused and let his eyes skate over her face. "You did, Monique. I did forget. For a time."

Now it was her turn to examine his features. "Is everything alright?"

Pieter shook himself unnoticeably. "Yes, it's ah...I...I have some tough decisions to make tomorrow."

"Does one of them have to do with me?" Monique asked innocently as she gently kissed his cheek. "And our dinner?"

Pieter softened and allowed himself to smile. "I should think it does."

"Maybe this will help you make the right decision."

With that, Monique kissed him warmly. As they parted she stared lovingly into his eyes.

"That was quite a kiss," he whispered.

Monique smiled, turned from his embrace, and sauntered up the stairs to her door. "There's more where that came from," she said in a voice that was overly seductive. "Call me, won't you?"

Pieter stood in quiet awe as Monique unlocked her door, all the while casting a sultry look down the steps. She slipped inside the house as Pieter turned to go. He had taken but a few strides when the sound of Monique's steps, nearly running down the stairs, caused him to turn back toward the house just in time to catch her in his arms.

She was almost giddy. "I'm sorry. I didn't mean that. I did. I mean, part of it I did." She dropped her eyes and studied the ground as if the words she were searching for might be found there. "It's...I mean, I really did have a nice time tonight. And I...I usually don't."

Pieter touched her chin and ever so gently lifted her lips to his. The kiss was a brush of rose petals, the softest either had ever known. As they parted, Monique's eyes remained closed until Pieter whispered. "I know. I felt it too. It's been a delight."

He gradually stepped back, trailing his hand in hers until it fell away. "I'll call tomorrow. If...umm..."

Monique took an almost involuntary step toward him. "If?"

He paused in his retreat then smiled sweetly. "If you promise no more theatrics."

A girlish pout came on her face and she traced a cross over her heart. "Promise promise."

"Goodnight, Miss McCleash, Pride of Ireland. I'll talk to you tomorrow."

"Goodnight, Baron Von Strausser," she said as she walked again up the stairs, this time in a more natural gait but with plenty of prance in her step.

Pieter turned away, buried his hands deep in his pockets, and walked into the darkness.

With the door closed safely behind her, Monique found herself leaning heavily against it. A deep sigh escaped her and she bit her lip before a wide and contented smile broke across her face. She remained that way through another breath then slid away from the door, slipping off her coat as she did. She was distracted by the thoughts of her evening, and walked by the coat tree opting instead to playfully toss her coat across the handlebars of Claire's bicycle.

She leaned against the banister at the base of the stairs and slipped off her shoes before heading up to bed. A dim nightlight greeted her in the hallway at the top of the stairs guiding her as she walked as quietly as possible on stocking feet.

When she reached Claire's doorway she paused and leaned inside. Her little sister was asleep. She tip-toed into the room and pulled a blanket up further around the sleeping girl's shoulders. Claire did not move.

As Monique turned to leave she saw the dress Claire had worn that evening in a rumpled pile on the floor. The stockings were peeking out from beneath. Monique couldn't resist a smile at the last act of defiance and bent to pick up the mess as she shook her head at the ways of her unruly sister. Monique hung the dress on the corner of Claire's bureau mirror. She draped the stockings over her own shoes and took them with her.

The light dimmed more so at the other end of the narrow hallway. Still, Monique stopped at her parents' bedroom and stuck her head around the edge of their slightly opened door. She could not see her parents as she had Claire, but listened in the dark for the distinct breathing of both. Content with the sounds of quiet sleep, Monique withdrew and retired to her own room across the hall closing the door behind her.

A few blocks away the streets gave the appearance of being deserted, but Pieter understood that they probably were not. There was a sense in him that indicated the wary eyes of both the French and German intelligence contingencies were on duty. So he walked along with a brisk purpose of step and direction, not looking left or right, not inviting suspicion, all the while retracing the steps he and Monique had taken earlier. In a few minutes he was on the street where the supposedly troublesome stocking had given Monique cause to stop.

Now he did look about him, but so cautiously that no one, even had they been watching, would have realized so. When he came upon the steps to the safe house he stopped and put his own foot in the exact spot where Monique's had been on his first visit. This time it was his turn to work a charade.

Pieter bent and tugged at the lace on his shoe. He casually adjusted the laces and began systematically straightening and tying, re-cinching the shiny black oxfords. As one hand reworked the lace, the other dropped away from the shoe and felt along the riser of the step. He found the vent easily, but learned little beyond its existence. Frustrated, he moved his foot from the step and crouched so low that the disguise of the shoelace would expire.

All but ignoring the shoe, Pieter looked directly into the vent. There was nothing to see, so he cocked his head, looking again at the shoe, but listening intently. The street was deathly quiet. Perhaps there was the slightest of humming noises coming from the vent, but that was all.

Pieter stood and brushed at the knee of his pants. He moved off, not looking back, though his mind remained at the vent and what had happened there with Monique and her paper. When he rounded the corner away from the house he paused under a meager lamp. He slipped a pen from his inner coat pocket and patted himself down, looking for a slip of paper. He discovered one in that same jacket pocket. It was the note Monique had given him in the club and carried her name and phone number as well as the scent of her perfume. Pieter jotted down the street name and number of the house with the vent and also Monique's house number on Rue la Blanc. He stuffed the note back in his jacket pocket, certain he would return with his army. But then the perfume drifted up to him. Perhaps he would not.

***

11

Four years earlier, two unlucky young grey soldiers were trudging up the stairs of the abandoned house that had given up Paul and still held Valerie's body. Outside, the truck that had collected the dead Resistance fighters from the broken safe house was grinding its gears.

"How is it that we always get the shit details?" the first asked his companion though the answer was hardly in doubt.

"'Cause we have the least amount of seniority."

"That's not much of a reason if you ask me," he said as he plodded on. "I could be the best soldier in the Army, but if I am also the newest I get the shit jobs."

"Now you're catching on."

"It's not right."

The second soldier leaned against the railing on the stairs. "I'll wait here while you go explain your theory to Rheinholt. He's sure to understand."

"My ass! Did you see him slap that private? I thought he was going to shoot him. And that stupid Herbeart was laughing. Surprised the lieutenant didn't knock him right on his ass."

"Rheinholt doesn't pay attention to soldiers who aren't in black. We're nothing."

"Speaking of nothing, where is that Herbeart? He should be doing this, not me. I've got more time in than he does."

"Haven't seen him since he took that kid in the house. But here's another piece of news for you."

"What's that?"

"I'm senior to you."

"So? It didn't save you from having to haul this dead bitch down the stairs, did it?"

"No, but it does mean something else."

"What?"

"I get the feet."

The men walked on up the stairs and into the room. They saw the old blanket over the body. At the midsection it was damp with urine. The smell of feces filled the room.

"Damn it! When I said it was a shit job, I was only kidding!"

"Just grab the arms and get going."

The soldier did just that and felt the heat in Valerie's hands. "She's still warm," he said surprised. Had he stopped to examine her intently he would have discovered a very faint pulse in the wrists beneath his grip.

"She hasn't been dead for more than ten minutes," he said as he took a hold of her ankles. "One, two, three." They lifted her off the floor, blanket and all. As they hobbled toward the door the foot carrier stopped. "You want me to leave you two lovebirds alone for a while so you can say goodbye?"

"You're sick."

"Yeah, right," he said as they moved out the door. "Like you never screwed a dead girl. Probably the only ass you can get."

"Go ask your sister."

"Screw you."

The men were a quarter of the way down the stairs when a realization struck them both.

"Why are we carrying this girl?"

"You're absolutely right."

As one they sat down their load. The soldier furthest down the stairs moved to the side and both grabbed their corpse and bent it at the waist. Then they gave it a shove and Valerie somersaulted down what steps remained. The blanket tangled around her and rode the steps with her. The soldiers, pleased with themselves and smiling, walked lightly down the rest of the staircase.

They resumed carrying at wrists and ankles and took Valerie out of the house to where the large covered truck waited. The tailgate of the truck was already down, exposing a dozen or so of the bloody dead. The soldiers began to swing their body and counted again. "One. Two. Three!" And they threw Valerie up onto the heap.

"Any more?" the driver asked from his window.

"Not yet, but Rheinholt's around somewhere. I wouldn't leave just yet."

"I'll tell the lieutenant you said that," the driver laughed. "Hey, close the tailgate."

The truck roared to life as the tailgate slammed. Then the makeshift hearse bounced away, jostling the bodies in the back and causing them to settle.

Valerie rolled in her blanket down the dead and came to rest against the side panel of the truck. The rumbling of the truck did no more to wake her than the rough trip down the stairs. She was breathing, however faintly, and her heart was forcing life's fluid through her, but the oxygenated blood was reaching her brain too late. Paul's arm had stopped its flow long enough to render her unconscious, long enough to give her the appearance of death, and long enough to starve her brain of life, but not long enough to kill her.

Some form of awakening was beginning to take place in her as the truck rolled on. It was foggier than deep sleep rousing in the middle of the night, when colors are absent and language lost in the giving or receiving. And less comprehensible than being stirred back to consciousness by salts and but a step above the painless, fearless portal before death when all the senses have retired. She drifted in and out of this dreamy state, not in pain, but not cognizant of where she was or who she was.

Eventually the door to the real world would remain open, but Valerie would never walk through it completely. Deprived of memory, void of thought and emotion, she would exist exactly as she was now beneath the dirty blanket tangled with the dead. The ruin suffered by her brain would never repair, and though her heart beat on, her mind and inner heart stayed upstairs in the abandoned house, torn from her with her consent by events closing in, and by Paul.

In due time the truck stopped, ground its gears, and backed up to a makeshift morgue adjacent to St. Louis Hospital, which presently served both the Third Reich and the native French. Like their trip up into the truck, the bodies and Valerie were unceremoniously heaved from the truck bed and dragged across the floor where they were arranged in disjointed rows. Rather than deposit the dead directly into a mass grave or incinerator, bodies of Resistance fighters were held for examination. They were summarily searched for identification and photographed in an attempt to attach a name to a cold face and that name to others involved in what the Nazis termed as illegal activities. Valerie took her place in a line with her urine soaked blanket still tangled around her, though now it was stained with the blood of her friends. The room went dark, the door closed and the truck - dripping blood - pulled away. Silence reigned for several hours.

Valerie opened her dead eyes. The trauma of the day and the time spent on the hard floor had stiffened her, but she slowly sat up, the blanket draped around her shoulders. She did not know why she sat up or how and she did not care. Her eyes adjusted to the poor light filtering in from outside and from a corridor set aglow by a bare bulb emanating from a side room. Driven by nothing more than what a moth feels when it rushes to a flame, Valerie stood up aching. Her mind, lost even to itself, could not recognize the stiffness and pain in her limbs for what it was. She moved slowly as if unsure how to walk and ventured to the light.

The hallway welcomed her and the stiffness in her legs began to ease slightly. Not knowing where to go or why, Valerie drifted into the first open room in the hall, brought on by the bare bulb and its light. The space was a break room for workers who handled the unending stream of dead supplied by the war machine. Uncertain what to do now that she was in the light, Valerie stood beneath the bulb for nearly an hour. Then as her legs began to give out she sank to the floor, stretched out with her filthy blanket, and fell to sleep.

Morning would bring a new cast of characters into what remained of her life. Some would be tender, others not so, but none would know her and none would be able to save her.

***

12

Mission came to the morgue early despite being sick with a cold. This was grimy work, but it was what he had. Years before the French military had rejected him for what a paper had said was "diminished capacity." So Mission became a very average man with a protruding belly, but he came in early this day, summoned by the sirens and stories from the day before. Mission relied on the Nazis for fresh corpses. Whatever he could find on the bodies, he stole. Wedding bands and watches, clothes if they suited him or could be sold — provided they weren't stained too badly with blood, and even gold teeth. On a regular day, Mission could be counted on to be late and generally recovering from a drinking binge courtesy of some poor soul's dental work.

But on this day he had arrived sober, still unshaven and unshowered as always, but in advance of his boss, Nurse Raquelle Pravain, so he could labor in peace. Pravain was a robust, no-nonsense woman who ran a humorless ward. She knew about the stealing, at least some of it, but she permitted it after taking a large cut from Mission for the hospital. Her justification came easily as supplies were always short and always expensive on the black market. Even if Mission drank a share it was better than having the loot go into a Nazi pocket.

If Pravain were here Mission would have to divide the booty, so he came on his own time this morning to pilfer from the dead. He struggled against the rigor mortis still present in the bodies and his constantly runny nose that he wiped on his sleeve, taking what he could. He was singing to himself between coughs and stuffing a couple of watches and rings, a few Francs, and a pair of eyeglasses in his pockets when he stumbled into the break room and discovered Valerie. She was sitting in the middle of the floor beneath the bulb, still wrapped in her disgusting blanket.

Mission was startled when he saw her, but recovered quickly, born out of the necessity of having been caught doing any number of illegal things many, many times in his life. He had a story for her as to what he was doing well before he realized he needed none.

"I was cleaning up in the other room," he said as he pointed over his shoulder, one of the watches dangling from his hand.

Valerie looked at the sound, but nothing more. The lack of expression on her face unsettled Mission, but he came closer, tucking the watch in his pocket as he did.

"You okay, miss?" he asked.

The same blank face answered.

Mission stepped fully into the room and came closer. The smell of blood, urine, and feces was strong.

"That you what stinks? My nose's plugged up and I can still smell it."

The answer came back the same.

Mission reached for her and took hold of the dirty blanket. "This has got to go, Miss. Jesus, look at it. Stinks like shit, if you don't mind me saying."

Valerie moved nothing but her eyes as Mission slipped the rag off her shoulders. "Hold on, now. I'll fetch another."

When Mission returned a moment later with a fresh blanket he held it out full for inspection. "Look at this one. Isn't that nicer? All clean and such."

"Will it hurt?" Valerie said plainly.

Mission was confused. "Hurt? No." He stopped to wipe his nose on his damp sleeve. "Don't believe so. Just a blanket. Better'n that ratty thing you was using."

He slipped the blanket around her and smelled the stench. "Whew! You're kinda poorly, ain't you? You sick?"

Valerie didn't answer.

"Well, you sure as hell smell sick. Kinda sick myself this mornin'. How'd you get in here anyways?"

There would be no answers, not now, not ever.

"Can't you talk too good?" As part of his investigation into her voice, Mission looked at her throat. It was badly bruised, bright red turning all colors of black, purple, and blue.

"You got worked over pretty good, huh?"

Mission bent close through the smell and touched Valerie's throat.

"Rock me to sleep," she blurted out, which made Mission jump.

"Rock you to sleep? What the hell you talking about?"

Valerie just stared at him, and Mission stared back. Then even in his ignorance he saw that something was missing in her eyes.

"You ain't right, are you? Somebody really worked you over good. Goddamn soldiers, I'll bet. Jesus, they probably left you for dead with them others out there."

He settled on the floor on his knees. His eyes looked around him as his thoughts took on action. He sniffed hard.

"You got any money? Maybe I could help you get back home, you know? But it'd cost a bit of money."

Valerie stared, scarcely blinking.

Mission reached for her pockets. "You don't mind if I take a look, do you?" When she didn't object, or even move, he continued. "I didn't think so."

Finding nothing in her pockets he slumped his shoulders, disappointed. "Nothing. Not a single penny. Ain't you something. Know what they'll do with you? They'll toss you in the loony bin, that's what. Here you are without chick ner child. If somebody don't claim you, why you'll be living out your days in the nut house. And you pretty and all."

Mission's mind drifted from money. "Maybe, if no one shows for you, you could stay on here with me. Be my helper. Would you like that? There's always something to eat around here. And I could put you up a bed in a storeroom. How'd that be?"

Mission touched her face and let his hand slip down her bruised throat to her breast. "I'd take care of you, see? And you could do something for me?" He unbuttoned her blouse, slid his hand inside and began fondling her breast. "You don't much give a shit what I do, do you?"

"Mr. Mission!" Nurse Pravain yelled from the doorway behind the kneeling molester.

He jerked his hand back and stumbled trying to get up. He fell sideways and ended up sitting on the floor at Valerie's feet. "I was putting a blanket around her! See there? That's one of our hospital blankets she's got on!"

The nurse saw the blanket but didn't overlook the open blouse and partially exposed breast.

"Hardly!" Pravain said as she stepped forward and reached down to help Valerie to her feet. "Are you alright, missy? He's a pig, just a pig! Dr. Meceraux will see to you, Mr. Mission! He'll see to you, alright!"

"Wait a minute! No need to trouble him with this."

"Are you alright, young lady?"

"She won't answer you," Mission said from the floor as he himself started to follow Valerie to standing. "I think she's messed up in the head."

"Small wonder after what you've done to her."

"No, she was messed up before I done anything. I mean, I didn't do nothing to her, but she was messed up before I did."

Nurse Pravain had Valerie standing now. "Let's button you up," she said as she did just that. "We'll have Dr. Meceraux give you the once over. He'll have you on a steady course quick enough."

The gentle attendant to the sick and the dead took Valerie's hand to escort her out of the room.

"Hold on," Mission said as though a bit perturbed. "I found her. I'll say what happens to her."

"You found her? What does that mean? And wipe your nose."

"Means I found her," Mission said as he wiped his nose again on his driest sleeve. "She ain't got no papers. And she's gone off her head, so if no one claims her I think it ought to be me what takes care of her."

"I've seen what your idea of taking care of her is."

"I'm not joking, Pravain. I found her. She's mine."

Raquelle let loose of Valerie's hand, took a fast step, put both her hands against Mission's chest and crudely rode him to the wall. "What do you think she is, a pet? You can't keep a person just because you found them! And don't you mess with her again or I'll tell the doctor what I caught you doing. It's not like it was the first time either."

"I wasn't doing nothing!"

"Will you leave her be?"

Mission pushed the hands off his chest. "Do what you want with her. I don't want no shit smelling bitch who can't talk anyway!"

Valerie had not moved through the exchange. Raquelle stepped back close to her and took her hand. "Come along with me. Let's see what we can find of the doctor."

"Will it hurt?" Valerie asked.

"No. No. Dr. Meceraux is a fine doctor. Won't hurt a bit."

"She don't mean that," Mission complained around a cough. "Says it all the while."

"Rock me to sleep."

"And that too. Crazy as hell."

"Rock me to sleep."

"See? I told you."

"Never you mind," Raquelle said sharply to Mission.

"Rock me to sleep."

"I told you," Mission repeated softer.

"Well," Raquelle said as she looked oddly at Valerie and her strange words. "Let's see what the doctor has to say first."

The two women maneuvered up the corridors of the hospital hand-in-hand with Mission following behind to see what would happen. Mission coughed while Raquelle talked the entire way, but despite her assurances Valerie asked over and over, "Will it hurt?"

The doctor was found in a ward, surrounded by a sea of beds holding patients with various illnesses and injuries. There was no room for separate sections so the man who had recently had his legs removed — first by a land mine and what remained by Dr. Meceraux — lay next to a child with pneumonia. Coughing was prevalent as was groaning and crying. Medicine and fresh dressings, less so.

Dr. David Meceraux was working through the beds followed by a single nurse. He was in his forties with deep-set crow's feet at his eyes that gave him a handsome character and reading glasses which did not, parked permanently on his nose. The trailing nurse wrote quickly and filtered the doctor's directions to what few additional nurses skittered around the room. With little medicine available to work with and an abundance of injured, diseased, and dying, Meceraux would have remained well thought of had he collapsed or disappeared to a quiet life he could have easily afforded. But he had taken a vow to preserve life, and now he struggled to keep it.

Raquelle, Valerie, and Mission weaved their way through the maze of beds. Mission's eyes jumped from person to person, both curious and offended by what he saw. Valerie looked around her as well, oblivious, showing no signs that she understood or cared. When Raquelle reached the doctor, the smell from Valerie did as well.

"Where is that smell coming from?" Meceraux asked as he looked at the patients nearest him.

"That'd be her," Mission said flatly followed by a sniffle.

"Who?" Meceraux asked as he turned to face Raquelle and her foundling.

Dr. Meceraux had seen all the faces of war and death, but the first sight of Valerie was immediately different. She was dirty as before, had dried blood on her face and hands, and her clothes reeked. But through the stench, the caregiver noticed her empty eyes. It was these blank pools in her face that made her so much in need.

"Raquelle, who is this?" he asked.

"I can't truly say. She was in the break room this morning, just like you see her."

"What's your name, dear?"

"She ain't much of a talker," Mission volunteered.

Meceraux looked briefly at her battered throat. "I can see why. Looks as though someone's tried to rip her head off. Can you talk?"

"Will it hurt?"

"She says that good, don't she, doc?" Mission said with a laugh.

Meceraux ignored him. "Raquelle, let's get her cleaned up and into some fresh clothes. Mr. Mission, scare up some breakfast for her. From the look of her I don't imagine she's had anything to eat."

"Yes, sir."

Dr. Meceraux waited for Mission to move. When he did not, the doctor gave him a nudge. "Well, Mr. Mission?"

"Huh?"

"The breakfast?"

Mission jumped away immediately. He left the ward, but waited outside, peeking in the window rather obviously, waiting to see what would become of the girl he had found.

David saw him waiting, but only cared that he was out of ear shot. "Raquelle, I've heard we received a delivery from the Gestapo last night."

"I counted eleven."

"My suspicion is that we received twelve."

"Oh, my God," Raquelle whispered as she looked at Valerie with new sympathy.

"I'm afraid we must keep this lady's presence close to the vest."

Raquelle digested the directive then made her own proposal. "Doctor?"

"Yes?"

"This will be hard for all."

"I know," David said as he began walking Raquelle and Valerie to the door.

"If we ask the...the people who may know," Raquelle said hesitantly, "we may be brought into question. And they will feel compelled to lie, to protect themselves and others."

"Exactly right. Perhaps worse if we can't help her regain herself. The Germans aren't stupid. They'll be back to photograph the bodies. Do we have a twelfth — it'd have to be a young woman — to lay out for them?"

"No. Not just now," Raquelle said as she looked around the ward with a sadness on her face.

"They'll be missing her. They'll think someone took her body to avoid identification or to give her a decent burial. Whatever the case, there'll be an inquiry. And if someone should come for her like she is, word will spread through her neighborhood of the walking dead girl. Then the Nazis will take her and whoever cares for her."

"So then?"

"Then we do what we can for her and hope she comes around. Comes around enough to help herself and whoever her family is. Damn, this is going to be difficult."

By the time Mission realized the doctor was coming into the hall it was too late to hide. He began to slink away, but the doctor's words stopped him.

"Mr. Mission! Come here at once!"

Mission returned with his tail tucked between his legs. "Yes, sir. I was looking for breakfast."

Meceraux whispered, "Not a word about this young lady to anyone. Understand?"

"Yes, sir," Mission answered, somewhat puzzled.

"I mean it," the doctor emphasized as he shook his finger at Mission. The attendant to the dead nodded dutifully, sniffed at his cold, and continued to shake his head yes even as Dr. Meceraux returned to the ward.

Raquelle stood Valerie near the door and took Mission's arm, walking him down the hall until they had cleared the ears of the ward.

"Mr. Mission. Do you fully understand what Dr. Meceraux said to you?"

"I think so."

"Those were members of the Resistance that came in last night."

"I guess so. The Nazis enjoy killing them the most, and they always bring them here to check them over."

"And then they watch who picks up the bodies, don't they?"

"So?"

"Mr. Mission, that girl is a member of the Resistance. She was left for dead. If the Germans discover that she's alive they'll come back and take her. Probably torture her and kill her proper."

"She can't tell them nothing. She's messed up in the head."

"Do you think they'll care?"

"No, ma'am. They don't care for nothing."

"Do you like our new friend?"

"She's pretty, but she stinks."

"Do you want the Nazis to hurt her?"

"No."

"Then not a word of this to anyone. Not word one. You hear me?"

"Yes, ma'am. Not a word."

Raquelle took another tact for insurance. "Should you forget, there is something I want you to know. If you tell anyone, anyone, about this girl, I will report you to the Gestapo for stealing from the corpses. They will kill you in one second."

"You do it, too!" Mission said excitedly.

"Only for the hospital. And who do you think they will believe? Dr. Meceraux or you?"

Mission was thinking as best he could. Though threatened, he hatched a sudden plan, ingenious to him. "I want to keep what I get."

"How's that?"

"What I find, I keep. And then I keep my mouth shut."

Raquelle looked up the hall at Valerie then back at Mission. She understood that no matter what was said or done today, Mission would eventually talk. He'd get drunk and he would talk. So she bought herself time.

"Done," she said as she walked back to the girl with no name. "Thank you, Mr. Mission. And I thank you for our young friend, as well. Oh, and after we've gotten her cleaned up and fed, stop by the office and I'll give you something for that cold."

Valerie was cared for that day, and on the countless others that followed, by Raquelle and David. Mission was dead within a week — before he could tell those sharing a bottle about the pretty girl he had found. His death was brought on by a supposed simple cold medication Nurse Pravain had given him. When Raquelle heard the news she did not break stride in her routine and that night closed her eyes as easily as ever.

For Valerie, nearly four years would pass in a life and a mind left totally stagnant and empty before a form of redemption would find her at St. Louis Hospital.

***

13

The morning following Claire and Monique's joint venture at the Café of Lights had broken overcast, and the threat of rain greeted the sisters as they came out of their house. Each hit the sidewalk with a different purpose in mind for the day ahead and the days that would follow, but they would walk along together for a time. There was little talk concerning the night before and even less about their plans for the day that had just dawned.

"What time did you get in?" Claire asked with a bit of a bite.

"Late."

"How late is late?"

"Late. Late."

"Did Father catch you?"

"Everyone was asleep, but I don't think he cares that much anyway."

"Get caught coming in at two a.m. and you'll find out how much he cares."

"I don't equate a screaming lecture with caring."

"Then you've forgotten the Irish way."

Monique laughed a little. Claire continued, making up a story, imitating her father's heavy accent, entertaining herself as much as her sister. "Don't ya know that the word 'lecture' comes from the root word 'lec'? Now 'lec' as the whole of the world knows, is the old Irish for 'love'. Now then, lass, have I explained things clear enough, or do I need to be layin' me shillelagh aside your head to be of assistance to i'tall sinkin' in?"

"Fortunately, that won't be necessary."

"See that i'tis and, mind ya, girl," Claire continued, now mimicking her father by shaking an imaginary pipe, "you and that rabble lot you run with keep clear of me flower bed!"

Monique smiled and shook her head as she clapped slowly and quietly. "Very nice. Very nice. You'll have to do that for Father some night."

"Don't count on it."

"Chicken."

"No. Smart. I don't want to get killed."

The words stuck between the two, and they each felt their own smiles fade as they witnessed the same on the other's face. With the smiles lost, their eyes fell to the sidewalk beneath their steps. At the end of the block Monique pulled up short and Claire with her.

Monique reached for her sister's hand as she spoke. "Are you going out tonight?"

"I was about to ask you the same thing."

"You probably wouldn't consider not going," Monique asked in a voice that wavered between pleading and asking.

"Would you?"

"Quite a pair, aren't we?"

"I guess."

"Claire, please think about what I said last night. Think about—"

"No. No, Monique. Don't start again. You go your way and I'll go mine." Then Claire reverted back to her father's accent. "And that's the whole of it," she said with a crooked smile.

"I won't give up."

"Neither will I."

"But at least promise me you'll be careful. No chances. None of that hero stuff."

"Yeah, yeah. I gotta run."

"I mean it, Claire. Keep your head down..."

"...and your powder dry," Claire answered, again like her father.

Monique nodded. "And your powder dry."

"See you later," Claire said as she turned to go. But Monique stopped her mid-turn, grabbing her coat sleeve and giving her a hug.

"Be careful," Monique whispered in Claire's ear before kissing her cheek good-bye.

Claire smiled and pushed herself away. "Worry wart."

Monique watched the younger more volatile McCleash move a measurable distance up the block before spinning away herself. The foot traffic was light, and before long she was bounding up the steps to the nunnery.

Several blocks away, Claire was ascending stairs herself as she walked up the front stoop of the safe house.

If there was one shared element in the sisters' mornings it was that each passed in a blur. Claire found Michel as soon as she entered the safe house. The young lovers talked softly about the night before. All was forgiven when Claire relayed the story of her fork and leaving soon thereafter. Reunited, they tried in vain to find a still room. The entire house was alive with activity. Eventually the couple settled somewhat dejectedly at the long table in the house's onetime dining room and hunched over cups of coffee.

"What's going on?" Claire whispered.

"Planning for a raid."

"When?"

"Tonight."

"Where?"

Michel stopped just short of the answer. "Why?"

"Why? Why what?"

"Why do you want to know?"

"What?"

"Why do you want to know?"

"Because I'm hoping I'm in on it. What kind of question is that anyway?"

"Just wondering why you ask so many questions."

"So many questions? I asked you when and where, for crying out loud."

Michel was quiet for a moment and looked into his coffee.

"What's the matter with you?" Claire asked, her impatience showing clearly.

Michel looked up and grabbed her hand as tightly, but as discreetly as possible. "Nothing, Claire. Nothing. We just had a long night getting this thing together. Renault will fill you in on everything this morning at the briefing."

"But, do you know if I'm in?"

Michel cautiously glanced around the room. "You're in."

As if on cue, Renault entered the dining room. He motioned to several men and women who were standing against the walls in various parts of the accessible downstairs rooms. Heads poked around corners and sought out eye contact with Renault, hoping for a nod or a wave, any sign that they would be included in the evening adventure. Some were rewarded, others waved off. Claire was on the edge of her seat and her nerves as she waited her turn in Renault's eyes.

Any conversations that had been underway were temporarily stymied. Fighters stood as statues, waiting for the nod or a touch on the arm. Michel was relaxed, having known from the arrival of the note that he would play a part. Claire, though reassured by her lover, waited anxiously with the others for Renault's confirmation. It came as Renault passed behind her and gently patted her shoulder as he whispered. "The war room. Fifteen minutes."

Claire stood up immediately. Michel followed and the two moved toward the basement steps with Claire leading the way. When Claire reached for the doorknob, Michel caught her hand. "Just a minute."

Claire looked at him, puzzled.

"Come with me," he said as he left the main room with its table and walked up the narrow hallway. En route to nowhere particular, Michel peeked in an open doorway and discovered an empty room.

"Claire," he half whispered. "Empty."

"Stop that!" she whispered harshly as the house continued under Renault's selection process.

"We've got fifteen minutes," he said as he reached for her.

"No. We've got to get downstairs."

Michel answered by playfully pulling her into the empty room. Her resistance was meager at best and quickly turned into passion as the door closed behind her.

The scene at the nunnery was calmer. Monique and Essey had secreted themselves side by side on short boxes in a tiny storeroom and were in the process of applying makeup. Monique had propped up a small vanity mirror into which Essey was exaggerating her open eyes as she put on black eyeliner. Monique steadied her little hand.

As the rouge came out of the box, Monique heard footsteps in the hall and a strong voice call to her. It was Sister Arlene. Monique's own eyes widened as she put a finger to her lips and turned off the light. In the dark she felt Essey scramble onto her lap.

The pair sat huddled in the dark with Monique stroking Essey's little girl hair to soothe her. The nun's heels clicked toward them, and Essey buried her face tighter into Monique's neck, but the sound grew then slipped away as quickly. The child relaxed in Monique's arms. Another moment and Monique turned on the light.

Essey was smiling widely. "That was a close one!"

"I'll say it was."

"Sister wouldn't like my makeup, would she?"

"Probably not too much."

"So we hide to keep her happy, right?"

"That's about right."

"Hiding things is okay. Do you think so?"

"Sometimes it is, and sometimes it's very necessary."

"I know," Essey said before closing an imaginary zipper across her lips, turning an invisible key, then opening her mouth to toss in the key. She swallowed the key long and hard then opened her mouth wide for inspection.

"Nope," Monique said smiling. "No key."

"It's in my tummy."

"Good job. C'mon. We'd better get back out with the others before Sister Arlene comes searching for us again. But first we'd better clean you up."

Monique pulled a damp towel, brought especially for the purpose, out of the box and began dabbing gently at Essey's face. The makeup came off cleanly leaving the little girl's face glistening and damp.

Claire's face was glistening as well as she eased away from Michel with a soft kiss. "We'd better get downstairs," she said as they each began pulling and tucking and coaxing their clothes back into position, just the opposite of what had occurred minutes before. There was no mirror in the room so they stared at each other, primping and smoothing collars and roughed up hair.

"Presentable?" she asked.

"Delightfully so."

Claire dropped her arms to her side. "I mean to someone decent."

"You're perfect. Trust me."

"Trust you? You who just ravaged me while I fought with the whole of me?"

Michel grabbed her and pulled her close to him. "I like the way you fight."

"If you liked that fight wait until you see what I do tonight."

"To the Germans or to me?"

"Both! Let's get downstairs."

Another kiss and the lovers, still carrying the disheveled look and dreamy eyes of lovemaking, slipped back into the hall.

As soon as they entered the war room in the safe house basement they realized that their time in the empty room upstairs had exceeded fifteen minutes. Renault had already launched into his discourse on the raid but stopped with the interruption. He looked with annoyance at his watch then at Michel and Claire. "I trust you two will be in position on time tonight."

"Yes," Michel answered, followed closely by Claire's echo.

"Yes." And they both lowered their heads.

Renault was ready to launch back into his briefing but hesitated long enough to walk over to the sheepish couple. When he approached, Michel raised his head in anticipation of a confrontation. Claire eyed the floor, both embarrassed and upset with herself for being tardy. Renault ignored Michel and stopped in front of Claire. He cupped her cheeks with both hands and lifted her face.

"How's that father of yours?" he asked softly.

"Very good, thank you."

"Is he still ready to turn the Green Isle red with German blood if need be?"

"Always," Claire smiled.

Renault laughed. "He's a fine man. And you are his daughter, through and through."

Renault released Claire's face and stepped back toward his position, patting Michel's arm as he did. "You've got a tiger there, Michel. If I was thirty years younger I'd take her away from you."

Surrounded by soft chuckles from all but Paul, Renault moved further to the front of the assembly. He paused for a moment then began. "We all have talents. And when we put those talents together no one can defeat us. No one."

The speech was abruptly interrupted by a knock at the war room door. Paul answered it and found Sophie. She touched his arm but looked beyond him to Renault as she spoke.

"There are two soldiers out front."

The room had been quiet before, listening intently to Renault, but now it became a grave.

"What are they doing?" Renault asked.

"Smoking. Talking."

"Where exactly?"

Sophie pointed to the delivery tube.

"Right there?" Renault whispered.

Sophie nodded.

"Watch them. They may be out walking. If they show any interest in the house, let me know at once."

"Don't forget, Claudine is due any minute," Sophie added.

Renault grimaced as Paul looked up at the tube then to his mentor. "They're too close," he said in a voice coated with ice.

"It may be nothing," Renault replied with little enthusiasm.

"It may be everything," Paul said.

Renault saw the fire already beginning to rise in Paul's eyes. He walked toward him and took the soldier's thick arms. "Should we ask them to leave?"

"Yes, sir."

Renault stood on his tiptoes and kissed Paul's forehead. "Be quick and be careful."

Paul did not wait. He slipped out the door without looking around the room or back at Renault. Sophie looked everywhere then raced off behind him. Two other fighters went to the door to follow, but Renault stopped them by silently closing the door.

"No. That won't be necessary."

Having squelched Paul's backup, Renault walked over near the vent to listen. When he could not hear anything he cupped one hand against his mouth and whispered just loud enough at the vent so the audience of fighters in front of him could hear.

"Psssst! Hey, Nazis. The Angel of Death is coming for you." Then he looked back at the room and an ocean of smiles. "It seems fair to warn them. They are only two!"

Upstairs, Paul was at the back door of the safe house. Sophie came through the door from the basement just in time to catch him.

"Paul?"

He stopped and patiently waited for her to cross the room.

"What will you do?" she asked, though she already knew.

"Invite them to tea."

"Let's wait a few minutes first. They may move on. They may be harmless."

"They're Nazis. They're not harmless."

"True, but today for a few minutes, they might be." Sophie took his hand and pulled slightly toward the front of the house. "Come wait with me. If they move away, we'll wait and get them later. Eh?"

Paul was reluctant, but let himself be pulled away from the door and his rendezvous with the soldiers waiting out front.

Sophie perched them both near the front windows. Paul sat on a low couch while Sophie rested against the arm, peering through a crack in the curtains. She could see both soldiers at the front of the house. As she watched, one sat on the steps just above the vent and pulled out a cigarette.

"What are they doing?" Paul asked.

Reluctantly, Sophie told him, knowing her answer would push Paul out the rear of the house. "One just sat on the stoop."

The fighter stood. "Better move."

"Another minute! Another minute. They might be resting," she said as she grabbed his arm.

Paul took a hold of her gently and shook his head. "Claudine is on her way."

"She should be here any minute," Sophie answered dejectedly.

"If she should, then she will and I don't want her to have to deal with those two."

Sophie delayed a breath before she spoke again. "You've been a wonderful father to her."

"I'm not her father."

"You know what I mean."

"I owe her that much."

"She loves you like a father."

"She's a fine young lady."

"She is very rough. Too much like a boy."

"It's her way, but she's a good girl."

"You have the voice of a father."

"Perhaps I can hold his place in some respects, but I had nothing to do with his death. Her mother? Her brother? Those I must pay for. If not for that debt I would have been with Valerie four years ago. That goddamn Renault made me see that debt, so I'm here, but I can't bring anybody back."

"Of course not. And no one's asked you to."

Paul had no comment and let the words drift by. "I'll be back," he said as he tried to pull away.

"Perhaps just another moment or two?" she asked, clutching his shirt.

"No more waiting, Sophie. She's coming."

She had tried, but lost him. Her hand dropped off his sleeve as she acknowledged the inevitable. "Be careful."

He retraced his steps to the door, but her voice stopped him again.

"Paul?"

"Yes?"

"Claudine needs you."

"You will take care of her," he said without looking back.

Sophie slowly shook her head yes, as the truth was the truth. But she had another card, a stronger one, to play before Paul left the house and danced in dangerous arms.

"Val will wait, you know?"

The name caused him to linger. His face came up and turned. They looked across the room and the ghost of their shared love. "I know."

"She'll wait a lifetime. Your lifetime."

He held the doorknob a moment longer then slipped out of the house while Sophie stared at the closed door.

In the basement, Renault continued his pep talk but did so quietly, occasionally eyeing the vent. "They can defeat a single soldier. A lone fighter, out on his own, is quickly tracked down and hung."

Claire interrupted then immediately wished she had not. "Paul is alone."

"He is the exception," Renault said without missing a beat. "Paul is a sniper with a knife, an assassin, driven by demons. For the rest of us, we must understand that many fighters lead in many directions and in no direction at the same time. Many together are strong. We will win tonight. We will win tomorrow. And next week. And next month. And next year, if necessary. And we will keep on winning our battles until we have also won the war. We will not lose."

Oblivious to their planned defeat, the two German soldiers were lollygagging on the stoop, their rifles leaning harmlessly against the railing. One's boot crushed a cigarette butt a few inches from the vent as Paul rounded the far end of the block. No sooner had he done so then Claudine entered the street from the opposite end. She caught the soldiers' eyes first.

Claudine was tall, nearly sixteen now, but from the distance of the block hardly looked like a target for a date. Her clothes, purposely beaten and a little dirty, would dissuade any suitor even had he chanced a closer inspection. Claudine's clothes were much like the ones Claire chose to diminish her sex when it was necessary, but for Claudine the purpose ran deeper. She despised dresses and the girls who wore them. The dresses, like their pretty faces, made them targets. Attractive eyes invited attention and pursuit, pursuit that led through houses and left young boys with splattered brains and mothers dead in the street. For her part, Claudine wore baggy boys' clothes every moment and pushed herself to be homely. She had never worn makeup and her hair was a chopped-top short boy's cut.

So while the hair and shirt might have warded off the soldiers on the steps, what continued to hold their attention was the large picnic basket she was carrying in front of her with both hands.

"Hey, here comes lunch," one said as he slapped his partner's shoulder.

"Perfect timing."

Paul saw the fascination of the soldiers. He speeded his approach and lowered his head as if he had not seen the men at all. He continued to limp toward them conspicuously, intentionally looking and walking very determined. The shuffling gait eventually brought one of the soldier's attention to him and away from Claudine's basket. That soldier touched his partner and discreetly pointed at the limping Frenchman with the hurried step.

"Where do you suppose he's headed in such a hurry?"

"Who cares? Lunch is coming."

The first man continued watching Paul as he came closer. "When he comes by, we're going to ask him."

"As long as it doesn't interfere with my lunch. What do you think she's got in the basket? I'll bet there's a pie. What'll you bet me?"

Paul was certain they had seen him, certain they were watching the muscular man with the bad leg, so he looked up and stopped abruptly.

"Shut up, will you?" the soldier said as he watched Paul holding fast up the street. "This guy's up to something."

Now the second soldier tore himself away from thoughts of lunch. He looked at Paul just in time to see him take a few more tentative steps toward them then blatantly turn around and begin quickly walking back the way he had come.

The move and mannerisms set the hook in the soldiers. One poked the other and motioned toward the retreating man as Sophie continued watching from the window. As one, the pair picked up their rifles and moved up the street, away from the safe house just as Claudine and her basket arrived, unmolested. Sophie jumped across the couch and eased the curtain back further, watching the soldiers until they disappeared from view. Then she went to the door and let in the girl she also felt indebted to.

Renault was speaking to the group in the war room quietly, part for effect, and part for the soldiers outside. "We cannot lose. To lose means we die. And not just us - our families, our children." He looked across the room directly at Claire. "Our parents."

Sophie knocked lightly and let herself in. Renault and the others waited for the report. "Claudine is here safely."

"Have her wait a moment. And the soldiers?" Renault inquired.

"Gone for tea."

Every voice wanted to ask after Paul, but no one did. Renault only nodded to her then went on.

"If we lose, lose one battle, we risk everything that is France. Our religion, our art, our heritage, and our land. The Nazis will take all that we love and twist it until it is ugly and perverted. Goering will topple the Eiffel Tower and make his Luftwaffe from the scrap metal. Hitler will take Rodin to Berlin to adorn his toilet. Himmler will take your daughters and sisters and feed them to his SS."

He paused and looked around the room. "But it won't happen." He smiled, and many faces broke into smiles with him. Relieved of the German sentries outside, their voices, both men and women, rose up from around the room.

"That's right!"

"No more!"

"Never!"

Renault continued. "Those who came before us lit a fuse. We are the explosion!"

Cheers rose up from the small group, picking up on Renault's lead. Fists were raised and shouts filled the tiny room until Renault called for silence.

"That's my soldiers! That's my soldiers! Now, to work!"

As Renault laid plans out on maps deep below the street, Paul led the two hapless soldiers away from the safe house. He was expert at presenting the illusion of not knowing he was being tailed. But in only a few minutes he had led the men to a cramped and vacant alley. When he ducked inside, he knew the soldiers would take the bait and follow in short order. With his knife in hand he waited around the corner. The first to appear would be the first to die.

Paul heard the fall of their boots and judged the distance and the timing. His arm was coiled like a snake prepared to strike and strike it did as soon as the first hint of grey came into view. The wide blade dove six inches into the soldier's chest and back out before the soldier had time to react.

The second soldier turned, but only in time to catch a crushing punch square on his jaw. He dropped like a stone, knocked unconscious. The soldier with the torn heart tried to level his rifle, but Paul let his bloody knife drop to the ground and gripped the barrel with both hands, easily wrenching it away from the stricken man. Not knowing he was already dead, the soldier fought on. He was effortlessly overcome, and Paul ended his life before he could bleed to death by slipping a powerful arm around the dying man's throat.

It had become his way. While the soldier gurgled, fighting little, Paul squeezed on his neck until he felt bones snapping under his arm. The soldier's face reddened and he went limp, but the squeezing continued until Paul's face turned crimson as well from the effort.

On the ground nearby, the second man stirred. Paul released the body in his arm, letting it fall harshly without ceremony, and walked deliberately to the waking soldier. Before the man could regain complete consciousness Paul kicked away his weapon. Then he picked up his bloody knife, squatted down beside the German, and waited for him to recover.

The soldier's eyes opened, and he cleared his throat. It took another moment for him to focus, and what he saw shocked him. The hulking Paul, flipping his knife, was inches from his face.

"Good morning, sleeping beauty," Paul said with a smile. "Nice nap?"

The soldier did not answer, fearing, rightfully so, that any reply would be the wrong one.

"What are you doing on my street?"

The German looked around, not fully understanding. "Walking."

"Walking," Paul repeated. "Why here?"

"I don't know. We were..."

"I know. Just walking."

"Yes."

"Do you want to go for a walk now?"

"Where?"

"Anywhere. Back to your barracks?"

The man saw the form lying in a circle of blood behind his captor. "Yes. I would like to go."

Paul stood up and stepped to the side. His hands, one still caressing the knife, motioned toward the mouth of the alley.

The queasy German stood and looked from Paul to the street then to his dead companion. He took a timid step and Paul spoke up. "Hold it. In order to leave you have to settle with me first."

The soldier watched as Paul moved to the alley entrance. "C'mon. Through me is freedom. C'mon," Paul teased as he tossed the knife from hand to hand, but the soldier would have none of it.

"Oh, unfair advantage you say?" Paul joked as he looked at his knife. "Fine. No weapon." He was only a stride away from the dead man and stepped over to him. "Here. Hold this for me," he said to the corpse. With a savage thrust Paul stuck the knife in the dead man's chest. The sound of ripping flesh and scraping bone turned the stomach of the remaining Nazi. Still, even minus the knife, the soldier did not come.

Paul was impatient. He backed away from the body and the knife, kicking the soldiers' guns further away as he did. When the distance was judged enough, the German rushed to his partner's body and ripped Paul's knife from the nearly bloodless wound. It was his turn to smile as he waved the knife at Paul and began his approach.

"Oh, that's not fair," Paul said with a grin.

The soldier rushed at him, flailing the knife from side to side. Paul made no attempt to avoid his own blade and even offered an arm for the taking. But when the knife slashed at the dangling arm, Paul's other arm jetted forward led by a fist as hard as a rock. The blade cut him slightly, but the minor victory cost the soldier a mammoth punch in the face and in the end, his life.

With a practiced step, Paul caught the staggered German and snapped his knife-wielding wrist like a twig. The blade dropped harmlessly. Like water, Paul slipped behind the soldier and forced him to his knees. His arm circled the German's throat like a boa constrictor and began tightening its coil. The soldier clawed at

Paul's arm, slipping on the blood running from the gash he had just caused.

The Angel of Death leaned close to the man's ear and whispered, "Is there not one of you who can help me?"

The soldier struggled and convulsed against the death grip around his neck, but Paul only tightened his arm and continued, "Send someone to free me."

The German's body began to relax. The hold on his throat tightened even more as Paul pressed his face against the dying man's ear. "Free me...," he cried softly as tears mixed with sweat and ran down the paired faces.

In the war room, Renault and the others were crowded around a map laid out on the table. "Michel, how about the charges?"

"Already laid. Jon is out there now. He'll touch off the first ones and take out the lead truck. When the others stop, Natei has six more charges laid out in the road. There are directional mines along the side of the road. When they abandon their trucks they'll trip the wires."

"Excellent."

Michel pointed to the attack spot on the Clovington Turnpike. "And whatever is still standing will be cut down by riflemen and machine-gunners here and here. On both sides of the road."

"It's been well scouted?"

"It's perfect for us. The Germans are idiots."

"Don't be so sure. They did not cross the Rhine by shear blunder."

"They do not know our land."

Claire spoke up. "Or our people."

"Yes," Renault smiled at her. "Or our people."

Over the course of the next hour, Renault and the others went over the plan that would hopefully end in the destruction of the German convoy. With the charges already in place, the biggest hurdles that remained were transporting everyone undetected to the hillsides and obtaining and dispensing enough ammunition for the job. The movement of people into place would begin immediately. The fighters would trickle onto the hills above the Clovington Turnpike and wait. For the early arrivals, the wait would be a long one.

As the hour drew to a close there was another knock at the door. Michel stepped away from the planning long enough to open it and found Claudine, holding her heavy picnic basket with both hands. The girl and her basket, replete with red-and-white-checkered tablecloth covering, stepped around Michel without a word and moved to the table where she plopped the basket down with a thud. Several of the fighters, licking their lips, began to crowd around her and her basket. Claudine, however, stretched both hands out over the red and white cloth and looked for Renault in the crowd, effectively halting the hungry advance of the fighters. When they found each other, Renault nodded. At that, Claudine began to pull away the tablecloth while the fighters leaned forward in anticipation. But as the cloth slipped away, instead of revealing biscuits and tea, the basket was loaded with boxes and boxes of bullets. There was temporary disappointment on a few hungry faces, but it was quickly set aside as the boxes were passed from hand to hand around the room as the fighters laughed and chided away the disappointed.

Renault worked through the moving boxes and placed his hands on Claudine's shoulders. "Ladies and gentlemen. Listen up." The excitement eased and the room quieted. Renault patted the teenage shoulders beneath his hands. "This is a brave young soldier. She is as true to the Movement as anyone in this room. She had a mission, and she accomplished it without regard for herself, though she has already given up more to the defeat of the Germans than most. Tonight, when you bask in the glory of our victory, remember her and others like her who do what they can so we can do what we must."

The fighters all but pushed Renault aside as they crushed in on Claudine, tousling her hair and patting her back as they congratulated her over and over. Claire squeezed the girl's arm and smiled then reached into the basket for another box of ammunition. Then she retired to a far corner of the room and began feeding finger-sized rounds into an empty machine gun clip.

As Claire reached for another bullet, Monique reached for a large red crayon. She and Essey, long since back in the large dayroom with the others and back also under the eye of Sister Arlene, were putting the finishing touches on their coloring project. The red was to be for the lips of their character, but as Monique put color to paper, a nun, always hovering throughout the room, drifted too near. Essey covered Monique's hand with both of hers and looked with wide eyes from her makeshift teacher to the nun.

"I think it's alright," Monique offered soothingly.

"But it's awfully bright."

"Yes, but it's so pretty," Monique said as she eased Essey's hands away from the coloring.

"They won't be mad?"

"I don't think so."

The circling nun did indeed stop at their table and look at the drawing. "Very nice, dear." Then she tapped the bright red lips of the roughly drawn figure several times. "A touch bright here perhaps."

"Thank you," Essey and Monique said in unison as the nun stepped off to direct the talent at other tables.

When she had moved a comfortable distance away Essey whispered harshly, "Told you!"

"Yes, you did, didn't you?"

"No one believes you when you're little."

"Oh, I don't know about that."

"No, it's true!"

"I believe you."

"No one else would."

"People will believe what they want, Essey, good or bad. But usually, in the end, the truth has a way of reaching everyone."

The little girl sat quietly and doodled with her crayon. Monique watched her coloring and the changing expression on her cherub face. Something was bubbling to the surface.

"Monique? The Germans are bad, aren't they?

"Well, I wouldn't say all Germans are bad, no."

"They hurt a lot of people. The sisters talk about it."

"German soldiers do bad things, yes, but that doesn't make all Germans bad people."

"Are you sure?"

"Yes I am. Why?"

Essey lowered her face. "I'm German."

Monique grabbed her gently and lifted her chin. She looked in tiny eyes that had tears in their corners. "Who told you that?"

"I heard the nuns talking. They said things will still be bad when the soldiers go home because no one will want us. Because we're German."

Monique scooped Essey out of her chair and onto her lap. "Don't you listen to such foolish talk. You're a wonderful girl." Monique held her out at arm's length. "I want you, don't I?"

Essey's chin dropped again. "Not really."

"Of course I do! Why would you say such a thing?"

"I can't come stay at your house."

Monique hugged the little girl. "Oh, Essey. We've been over that a thousand times. It has nothing to do with you. Nothing at all. You know that. Besides, you wouldn't want to leave all your friends behind here, would you? I can't take you all, you know?"

"I know."

Monique sat her back in her chair then fumbled with a crayon. "Here. Let's get things straightened up. It's about time for a nap, don't you think?"

"No."

"I figured as much. How about I read you a story back in your bed?"

"I guess so."

Monique rummaged through some worn books on the table. "How about this one?" she said as she selected one from the pile.

"The Three Little Pigs. We haven't read that one in a while, have we?"

"I know it already."

"I'm sure you do, but maybe I can add a few twists to the story to make it interesting." Monique held the book and took Essey's hand as she got up from the table. "Here we go," she said, as she led a slow moving Essey out of her chair and away from the table.

Essey shuffled along next to Monique as they made their way out of the dayroom and down a hall to a large open room which held a seemingly impossible number of tiny beds. Essey went straight for hers and popped up on its edge. Monique sat the book on the bed and helped Essey remove her shoes. "In you go now."

Essey crawled under the worn blanket and Monique tucked her in before picking up the book. She opened it and began as though reading. "Once upon a time there were four little donkeys. The first little donkey-"

"They're pigs, not donkeys! And there's three not four!"

"I guess you don't know this story as well as you thought. It says here they're donkeys." Monique turned the book toward Essey and back again in a flash. "See?"

"You're being silly."

"No, I swear! It's true. Says right here, four donkeys. And the first one, he lived in a railroad car down by the river. Well, one day this duck walked up and pecked at the door of the railroad car. The donkey says..."

"Monique?"

"Yes?"

"I am German, though."

Monique laid the book in her lap. "Listen, honey. You are half German, that's true."

"My father was German?"

"Yes he was."

"And he died in the war."

"Yes."

"But I'm half French?"

"Yes, I've told you that many times."

Essey threw back her covers and looked herself up and down. "Which half is French?"

Monique smiled. "That's hard to tell. Everything is kind of mixed up, I guess."

"Oh," Essey said, obviously disappointed.

"But in here," Monique said as she pointed to Essey's heart, "and in here," she said while pointing to the little girl's head, "you are French. All the way through. As French as me or anyone. And don't let anybody tell you different. Understand?"

A broad smile broke over Essey's face. She pulled open her blouse between buttons and stroked the skin over her heart. "French," Monique repeated as she touched the skin as well.

"I like this part best," Essey smiled.

"I thought you might," Monique said as she covered Essey again. "Now, back to our donkeys. So, the first one, he says…"

"Monique?"

"Yes?" Monique answered, with a hint of pleasant desperation in her voice.

"Maybe we can finish the donkey story tomorrow."

"You don't like it?"

"It's supposed to be pigs."

Monique laughed. "Okay. Tomorrow then. Ready for a little sleep?"

"I'll try."

Monique stood up then bent down and kissed Essey's forehead. "Night night, Sweetie."

"Monique?"

"Yes?"

"Will you be here when I wake up?"

"I don't think so, honey."

"When will you come back and see me?"

"How's tomorrow?"

"Great!"

"Then tomorrow it is. Do we have a date?"

"A date!"

Monique bent and kissed her again. "See you tomorrow, Essey. Now, take a little nap."

Essey pulled the blanket up tight around her neck and turned into the pillow. Monique stroked her fine hair gently for a few moments then stepped away from the bed and out of the room. She passed through the day room, grabbed her coat, offered a friendly wave goodbye to Sister Arlene, and stepped out into the street.

The weather was deteriorating. Monique pulled her coat tighter against a misty rain dropping from a greying sky. Though the day was overcast, the city ignored it and was in full swing, typical of midday. Even in the bustle, the walk home was accomplished with head down, against the rain, and in contemplation of words echoing in her head. Pieter's were ringing the loudest, even throughout her morning at the nunnery. Monique had been a young girl when last she felt her heart leap at the touch of a man. The war, as was always the case, had changed everything, perhaps even her soul. Once, on grey days like today, time had offered hand-holding walks through the city to the occasional jeers and teasing of friends. Now the nighttime brought her to sleep with men she cared nothing for. She could never have imagined her life the way it had turned since France fell beneath the armored tracks of German Panzers. And now, as if her life needed more complications, there was this new feeling, a fresh love, already taken root and struggling against the odds stacked around it. She was so thoroughly entrenched in her thoughts, she never looked up until her feet, seemingly all on their own, brought her to her front door.

The house was quiet. The empty coat tree stood with its short arms outstretched and accepted her slicker. No sooner had Monique headed across the room to the stairs when a knock came at the door. The visitor had arrived so quickly, on another less thought filled day, she might have immediately considered that she'd been followed. But on this day of daydreams she simply retraced her steps and answered the door.

As Monique opened the door her eyes were full of grey. She saw the German uniform in front of her before she could see the person in it. She felt her eyes widen and her breath escape as if the outside had suctioned against her with the opening of the door. The uniform smiled. Only then did she see the face clearly beneath the shadowed visor of a crisp hat with its polished black bill.

"Good afternoon," the uniform said pleasantly as Pieter snatched the sharply blocked hat from his head.

Monique's shock was lessened only a small degree at recognizing her new desire. She caught her breath, instantly grabbed his arm, and pulled him inside the house. With him tucked inside, Monique poked her head back out the door and glanced swiftly up and down the street. Neighbors had stopped minutes before in their tracks. Some stopped in anticipation of the worst, an arrest perhaps. Others managed faces of disgust, knowing or thinking that the McCleash girl was seeing another German officer. But Monique didn't take notice of any reaction on the street. Her eyes searched only for her father and not finding him, she dropped back inside the house to Pieter. All this without a word, but that was about to change.

"What are you doing here?" she admonished, unable to hide the anxiety rising up in her throat.

"Glad to see you, too," Pieter replied, still smiling, still unaware.

"I'm sorry. I am glad to see you. You can't know how much." She paused only long enough to touch his arm and kiss his cheek like a comfortable lover would greet her mate. "But you shouldn't come here."

"Why?"

Sean McCleash had slipped unnoticed into the room from the kitchen and the backyard beyond. "Because of me, no doubt."

Sean stood beneath the archway leading to the kitchen. He did little to fill the doorway, but his wiry build and complexion, ruddy as it was, united with his demeanor to show that this small man carried grit in his belly. His clothes were slightly damp, as was his neatly combed white hair, from the gathering mist outside. As he stood staring intently beyond his daughter to the grey uniform in his parlor, he placed his pruning shears under his arm and tugged at his tattered gardening gloves.

Monique turned toward her father and directly positioned herself between him and Pieter. Sean walked smoothly into his living room, moving so to see around his daughter and be seen. He finished removing his gloves and held them in one hand, retrieving the shears from under his arm with the other.

"Ya see," he said, "I don't care for me daughter's vile habit of sleepin' with Nazis. I think the lot of ya are blood-suckin' scum."

Pieter replied only by looking at Monique who was painfully caught in the middle. "Father, please-"

"So now I can't speak in me own house?" Sean's voice was rising on every word, and his face reddened as he crossed his floor.

Monique snatched her coat and literally pushed Pieter toward the door. "Let's go."

"That's right," Sean said venomously. "You've come to take me daughter, take her! You'll be takin' her as easy as ya took France!" Now Sean descended on the couple, menacing his shears at them both. "But if ya Nazi bastards ever have balls enough to get your feet wet, you'll find you'll not be takin' me island so easy!"

Pieter opened the door and Monique nudged him out.

"Go on! The whole of ya! If you ever come back, the first shot fired between Blessed Mother Ireland and Germany will be heard in this very house!" Sean had come close with his shears and gave the door a swift kick just as Monique and Pieter pulled it closed from the street side.

The couple beat a hasty retreat up the sidewalk with Pieter looking over his shoulder to see if the shears might still be hunting. Before he could comment, Monique stopped and he with her.

"Would you wait for me?" she said apologetically.

"Certainly."

She squeezed his arm for strength then turned and headed back toward the house.

"Hey. You sure you want to go back in there just now?" Pieter asked as he began to follow her.

"I'll be fine. And don't you come in, no matter what you hear."

"I think perhaps we should let him calm down first."

"No, he always says it's best to strike while the iron's hot."

"It's not the iron I'm worried about. It's the gardening shears."

"That was just a show for you. Sort of. Wait right here. I'll be back in two minutes."

"If you say so, I'll wait, but if you get in trouble, I'll be just outside."

"No. No matter what, don't you come in. For all his faults, he's still my father. I don't want to disrespect him any more than I did. Just wait. I'll be right back."

They finished their conversation at the base of the McCleash stoop. She ascended the stairs and went in the house while he waited, not so patiently, on the sidewalk.

Sean was not in the living room. "Father?" Monique called as she instinctively gave the pipe rack a once over. They were all accounted for so she went to the stairs and listened. Hearing nothing, she walked into the kitchen. "Father?" He was not there either, but the back door was open. As she walked to the screen door and peered outside she found her father on his knees at his flowerbed.

Monique hesitated on the safe side of the screen door and watched him working the ground around the bright colors. He was turning the soil with a hand spade, cultivating where it needed none, but working as briskly as if the long bed was overrun with weeds. She watched another minute, searching for courage and hiding the fear and inevitable pain that would come on the heels of the conversation she was about to launch. Courage was slow in coming, but pain stood at the ready. It would be easier to retrace her steps back through the house and join Pieter, but she knew an apology, even one refused, was warranted.

Meanwhile the major was pacing, drawing hard and long on a cigarette. Thankfully the misty rain had stopped falling on him, but he was still an easy target for the stares of neighbors and passersby. Even German soldiers who drove up the street stared, wondering on their faces what a major was doing warming the sidewalk as he was. He was growing more uncomfortable with each passing minute and found himself looking often at the door of the house. His presence was arousing suspicion, certainly from the locals, but also, quite possibly, from any passing German officer. If there was a trap to be set, a trap to be sprung, he would do it on his own terms. So Pieter walked on up the street away from the door through which this charming lady, new in his life, had passed, and also away from the problems his pacing might bring to the house of McCleash and perhaps, himself.

Sean paused ever so briefly when he heard the screen door open behind him. Rather than turn and let his eyes explain, he listened and heard slow, light footsteps followed by a familiar voice.

"Father?"

Sean would not answer. Not today. He resumed his burrowing with even greater enthusiasm.

"I wanted to apologize. I didn't invite him here."

The silent answer came back as before. Monique waited for an acknowledgement, a reply, any type of answer, even a tongue lashing, but nothing was forthcoming. She was discouraged, but had made the effort and righted her heart in doing so. There was little else to say or do.

"The flowers are beautiful," she offered as she turned to leave.

Sean never stopped his digging. "They're not fer the likes of you."

She felt the words run through her heart as surely as if they had been the spade in her father's hand. Ever so slowly, ever so painfully, Monique reached for the screen door latch. She opened the door and stepped back into the relative comfort of the house. The screen door closed behind her providing some security, and though the screen would have done little to prevent it, Monique did not look back into the yard.

For his part, Sean continued to stab the manicured ground around his flowers. He refused to look up, and his ears easily erased the finality of the closing screen door behind him.

When Monique came down her front steps, she discovered that Pieter was three houses up the street. When he saw her he came to meet her and she to him. She greeted him by taking his arm and the pair walked on, away from Monique's neighborhood and out from beneath disdainful eyes.

"I'm sorry about all that," she said without looking up from the sidewalk.

"No need. It's me who owes the apology. Next time I'll call first."

"That would be best."

The number of blocks between her and her house, and in another sense, her father, was growing. With the distance came a comfort and relaxation.

"Hey," she said abruptly. "What are you doing here? I thought you had to work?"

"I found someone to cover for me. I'm yours for the evening. That is...if you'll have me."

"I suppose that would depend on what you had in mind."

Pieter stopped and pointed down at her feet. "Are those dancing shoes?"

She answered by tightening her grip on his arm and cuddling close as they started up the street again. "Every pair I own is for dancing."

***

14

Across town at the safe house the fighters were lounging around, waiting for the go signal. Some were anxious, but others, more seasoned, appeared disinterested, though certainly they were not. They had seen much and learned much at such early ages that they now harnessed any anxiety and loosed it as anger when required. That anger, directed solely at the German occupiers, would erupt into wicked violence on demand. Those who had mastered this skill were readily visible among the others. Paul was at the pinnacle. He sat off to the side of the room, all but asleep, the excitement lost on him after countless raids and even more killings. Other less practiced guerillas paced or covertly checked their watches.

Michel lazily stirred a half-empty cup of cooling coffee. For her part, Claire sat dreamily watching Michel's cup, as if at any time it might do something other than hold the coffee. There was black boot polish streaked across her face. Few others wore it, at least not with the dramatic flair Claire gave it. Michel looked at it and smiled. Claire caught him staring.

"What's so funny?"

"Your boot polish. I'm trying to make out a design of something."

"You can stop looking. There isn't one."

"Most don't bother with it."

"I need it. The American Indians used to paint their faces before battles. Even the Scots over here. It's my war paint."

"I'd like to see you explain your 'war paint' to some patrol that stops you on your way back home."

"That's easy. I don't talk to patrols, I kill them."

"Why am I not surprised at that answer?"

The sounds of footfalls on the steps from the basement roused Claire away from the conversation. She looked up at the door just as it opened. Renault stepped out halfway and merely pointed to the street. All the anxious fighters moved at once. At least six piled up at the back door of the safe house.

Paul, not as asleep as he appeared, scolded them with his eyes apparently closed. "Hey! Ones and twos!"

The disjointed group stopped and collected itself. The briefest of organizational plans was struck which resulted in two members of the group passing out the back door. The others waited, still occasionally checking their watches, and drifted out in an unordered sequence one and two at a time over the next several minutes.

"Kids," Paul muttered before settling back in the chair and his uneasy rest. He would be the last to leave.

When the room was nearly empty Claire touched Michel's arm and stood up. She was well seasoned, but still felt an excitement rise up in her when the time to kill was drawing near. She did not envy Paul's coolness. She still relished the rush, the thrill of the hunt, and the mastery over her enemies when she killed them.

Michel was less passionate and more methodical. For him, he would have been happier with Renault, planning and staging. Going on the midnight raids was ever tempting fate. Bullets were made to kill, and the Germans had plenty. The Resistance had been doing well, especially this band, but German guns would be firing on the Clovington Turnpike tonight also. Sooner or later Lady Luck would turn her back on the young fighters and someone would not come home. Perhaps tonight.

Bullets and dying were worlds away from the conversation Monique and Pieter were sharing across a tiny table at the Café of Lights. Their conversations were forays into equal measures of distant fields of history and the future. They found common denominators between every word, each joined by a smile, a sigh, or an understanding look that quickly out distanced the time they had known one another. They laughed and flirted, danced and drank, bathed in the music and lights of the club's party atmosphere. Like new loves, they touched often, exploring boundaries yet unknown. With each slow dance they held each other closer, kissed each other deeper. Pieter would let his hands drop and run his fingers ever so gently over her hips. The crowd fell away with the touch and, to the couple, they were alone on the dance floor.

Monique caressed his face and neck then lightly skimmed his chest and tugged playfully at the waist of his pants. He held her tighter than before and pressed his hips into hers. She pressed forward as well, and the back of his hands skated up her waist and brushed briefly but purposefully against her breasts. It was time to leave.

When the song ended neither applauded. Instead she silently retrieved her purse from the table while Pieter tossed down a few German marks for the drinks and service. Then they picked up her coat and walked out of the club, more enthralled with each other, truer friends, more in love, than when they had entered just hours before. Though a real love was growing in their hearts, they both knew they were on the verge of frenzied passion, something so many others had gone in search of at the club that night.

The weather was damp. The day had not been long enough to take all the rain from the cloudy grey skies.

"I'm afraid I can't supply a moon for the walk home tonight," Pieter said as he searched the night sky.

Monique joined him in the search. "I guess we'll have to make do with the odd street lamp."

"They do give off a lovely glow."

"Lovely." She smiled at their comic attempt.

Pieter stopped and lifted her lips to his. "Yes. Lovely," he whispered, and they kissed in the misty rain.

The same rain was falling on the slopes above the Clovington Turnpike. It added to the disguise of the dark and shielded the creeping fighters.

"No moon," Claire whispered as she and Michel slipped down the bank.

"That's good and bad. Nice and dark, but we'll need flares to see down into the road when things get hot. Hopefully the first trucks will be burning. That'll help."

Michel took up a position about fifty yards above the road where several sturdy trees provided adequate cover.

"This is close enough, Claire."

"A few more yards," she said as she kept walking, a short machine gun in her hand with its sling dangling like the freed reins of a runaway horse and a rifle slung tightly over her back.

"No, you're getting too close. You want to be sitting on the driver's lap when those charges go up? You're apt to catch a piece of shrapnel."

"You're right," Claire said, disappointed, as she crept back up the hill to the trees near Michel.

They sat deathly quiet for a time, listening for the distant rumble of the German convoy. The Clovington Turnpike stayed quiet. There was nothing to do but check and recheck the weapons.

"Pretty quiet," Michel whispered.

"Sure is."

"I wonder if this is going to come off."

"Why would you wonder?"

"I have some doubts about the intelligence."

"Doubts? How so?"

"I can't really say. And don't repeat this to anyone, especially Renault, but it seemed to me he put an awful lot of credence in one tiny scrap of information."

"Oh, yeah?"

"We got into it last night."

"He knows his stuff pretty well, Michel. I don't think he'd send us out unless he was sure what was what."

"Could be, but this road is as still as a church."

Claire shouldered her rifle and looked over the sites onto the dark road below. "That it is, laddie," she said with a tickle of the Irish. "But the first German that comes within range is going to change all that. Guaranteed."

Back in the city, Monique accompanied Pieter to his suite. The choicest hotels in town had long since been commandeered by the German high command. The major's rooms had once been rented out by the day or the week for high prices, but now he would have them for as long as was necessary, as long as his army wished him to have it, and there would be no charge. His thoughts did not go to the wealthy hotel owners and the burden his presence and that of his comrades placed on them, but rather he considered those who once relied on his rooms for honest work and honest wages. He recognized that the women who now cleaned the rooms and did his laundry were doing so for pennies or less, and with that thought in mind he often left them tips for their labor. But even the money could not ensure good service or for that matter ease his conscience. The Nazis were largely despised, period, so often his attempts, though never refused, profited him nothing, neither service nor atonement, even if he pretended the latter was not his goal.

The daily presence of the hotel staff in Pieter's room was not readily apparent. Discarded shirts adorned the backs of chairs. Hastily removed ties, some still knotted, hung over the door handle to the bathroom and poked out from beneath rumpled shirts, having by necessity, beaten the shirts to the chairs. Near the bathroom door was a large cluttered desk, the top of which was rendered nearly invisible due to the volume of papers it held.

Desks such as this, having that disheveled appearance, would mislead many. Casual or occasional observers of Pieter's cluttered desktop had often shaken their heads at the untidiness of the owner, but had they asked for a particular item of the master of the desk they would have received it forthwith. The disjointed mess was orderly to the arranger.

The carpet in the room was thick and a little worn. In other years, in other circumstances, it would have been replaced. For now, until the Germans left or somehow reigned supreme, the carpet, like the heavy but faded drapes, would have to wait for brighter, fresher replacements. Most of the furnishings in the room followed suit. At one time each was state of the art, bright and new, in keeping with the aura of the fine hotel. The furniture, even the desk under the papers, had seen better days. The extreme was Pieter's makeshift bar — a converted dresser sporting water rings and moisture damage which had caused the corners of the wooden veneer top to curl. The lone exception to the shabby disarray was a tabletop radio on a nightstand across the room from the battered dresser. The radio was quite new and nearly impossible to come by given the present economic and political current.

Monique had been in this hotel before, but not this room, a fact that she was instantly grateful for. The times spent in this place and others like it in the arms of strange men was growing increasingly far away in her mind. There were moments when she forgot entirely what she did and what she had done for the Resistance and to herself. Though the present circumstance seemed the same - the uniform jacket Pieter had slipped off and tossed on the arm of a chair was the same grey color and had the same familiar collar ornaments as all the others — the air was different now. There was a twinkle in Monique's eye this time that meant more than simple triumph over a beguiled enemy.

After Pieter dropped his coat, he settled in at his makeshift bar, which had formed during his first days in the captured room. The mixing of drinks was followed by the click of the radio switch across the room as Monique played with it. The radio began to hum behind the yellow glow of its dial as it warmed up slowly.

Without saying a word Pieter carried the drinks across the room and slipped one into Monique's waiting hand. He held the glass for an instant as her hand caressed his.

"Thank you," she said.

"You're welcome. Sorry about the ice or, no ice." Pieter was relaxed and he smiled. "They tell me there's a war on."

"Oh, yes? I hadn't heard."

As they sipped the drinks their eyes looked out over the rims of the glasses like predatory big cats at water.

"Do you like it?" Pieter asked.

"It's not white wine."

"Do you object?"

"No. It's just stronger than what I usually drink. Makes me wonder what your intentions may be."

Pieter stepped ever closer and leaned to kiss her. The kiss was gentle, but his mouth engulfed hers. With his drink still in his hand, he circled her waist and eased her to him. He dragged the fingers of his free hand up her waist and ever so lightly began teasing her breast. Both hands fell away as the kiss ended. As a parting gesture, he very gently bit her lower lip.

"Perhaps," he said in a voice just over a whisper, "that clarifies my intentions."

"Very clear," Monique answered in a voice like flowing velvet as her hands, one still holding her drink, scaled his chest and rested on his shoulders.

The pair brought each other closer and kissed passionately. In mirrored movements, they moved their drinks away from the embrace and though fumbling blindly, managed to set the drinks on the table with the radio. As they did, the radio, as if cued, came to life from its warming, and the music of an easy waltz filled the room.

"Dance?" Pieter said between quickening breaths and rougher kisses.

"Not now," she breathed.

She brought up her silk-covered knee along the outside of Pieter's leg. He gripped her leg as the dress rode up her raised thigh. With one hand firmly around her waist and the other holding her thigh, Pieter effortlessly picked her up and carried her to his bed.

On the hillside overlooking the Clovington Turnpike things were heating up for Claire as well. The variation was the fuel. Up the valley road, Claire, Michel, and the others could see faraway flickering lights winking at them through the hills and the distant trees. Long before there was any sound from the convoy the trucks' headlights had given them away. A solitary pair would have raised little excitement, but a line of dim lights, lessened by shrouds that half-covered the headlights themselves, could only mean that Renault and the messenger had been right.

With the coming of the lights, Michel felt a peculiar sense of disappointment. A large part of him wanted to prove Renault wrong and thereby somehow take a step toward supplanting the old warrior. Michel's desire to take Renault's position was not born of jealousy in the conventional sense of wanting to garner power for himself. Rather, he had so tired of the raids that the insulation found in Renault's work appeared a very desirable alternative. These thoughts jumped about in his mind as the sounds of the approaching convoy began to filter into his ears. A rush of adrenaline shocked him as the trucks came closer and made him consider that another more compelling reason drove him to covet Renault's job in the Resistance — Michel was afraid.

As Michel struggled to focus on the approaching Germans, Claire fidgeted a few yards away. Her eyes were wide with excited passion. Her hands danced over the rifle in the miserable light and instinctively felt for extra clips of ammo strapped to the stock and jammed in her pockets. She tested and re-tested her footing, stomping the ground to secure her feet against the recoil she would soon feel. To Michel, Claire's actions brought to mind a bull pawing the ground, signaling its charge at the matador. The bull in the ring first charged out of anger, as they all had done. It was only later in the battle that the bull pursued the cape out of despair and perhaps fear. Then finally the battered animal succumbed to its inevitable death. Where along this orchestrated play was he? How near did he stand to the end of the taunting? And how long would it be before a matador's blade pierced his own heart? Claire's position in the battle ring was evident. There was still anger in her eyes, and even in the slightest of light Michel could see she was smiling, happy to charge the cape.

The roar of the trucks echoed between the hills making the approach louder, and to Michel, more intimidating. Claire, however, let the sound rush through her, the louder the better. It would only serve to drive her. They both gripped their weapons tightly and waited - one with dread hunched over his shoulders and the other with exuberance and passion rushing down her arms. They both knew explosions and gunfire would soon rock the valley, sending men by the hundreds, and themselves to and through both heaven and hell.

The headlights of the first trucks showed brightly now. In response, the guerrillas hoisted their weapons while Natei wiped his sweaty palms on his pants. Drier, but trembling slightly, Natei's hands clutched the detonators on the ground before him. Jon was nearby, his own hands prepared to set off the first blasts. He spoke to his brother in assuring tones as the trucks approached the kill zone. "Wait...Wait...Ready...Now!"

The explosions heaved the first trucks up off the road's back and left craters where they had been. A second round followed, leaving dead soldiers and those that longed for death trapped in burning, twisted metal hulks. Disabled and destroyed, the trucks had followed the Resistance fighters' plan and now successfully blocked the advance of the vehicles behind. The nearest trucks rammed the debris, unintentionally or in a vain attempt to escape, and succeeded only in blocking the turnpike more completely. As predicted, scores of German soldiers leaped from the trucks, some of which were burning, some wrecked, and others just forced to stop. Before the rocking of the first trucks had settled, fighters on the hillsides were peppering the cargo compartments of the trucks with small arms fire. As the German soldiers attempted to leave the conspicuous trucks behind and vanish into the perceived comfort and safe darkness of the hillside, Resistance flares filled the night sky.

Trapped like fish in a barrel, the Germans scattered, diving away from the trucks into the ditches that lined the road. Instead of safety, the soldiers found the trip wires. The exploding mines sent the soldiers, most now ripped apart, back into the road. Dismembered near-corpses, oozing blood and trailing their guts and limbs, rammed into soldiers still scampering in the road and knocked them off their feet. Some soldiers, thinking the flying torsos were attacking enemy, fired at them blindly, effectively killing the dead, the dying, and each other.

For the soldiers the road had become hell on earth. Exposed by the overhead flares, repelled by the mined ditches, and blinded to their attackers by the flames of their own trucks, they could muster little defense. They fired aimlessly all about themselves. It was the same over the length of the convoy.

The Germans' poor fight bolstered the bravado of the Resistance. Several fighters began to move from their guarded positions in the trees to spots where they could shoot unencumbered by cover into the German disarray. Claire jumped fearlessly into the open, firing constantly. Her lack of protection and the flash jumping from the muzzle of her gun, quickly gave away her position. Occasionally, clumps of dirt would jump nearby, the result of return fire. Claire either did not notice or cared less as she continued her assault.

When her machine pistol emptied, she let it fall to her side on its sling. She yanked the rifle from across her back to the front and to her shoulder in a blur. Beneath the sights of her carefully aimed gun, men continued dropping in and around the road. Within two minutes from the time the initial blasts went up, the screams from men hit and moans of the dying began to overcome the reports from weapons on both sides.

As the air settled around the fighters Michel let his weapon cool and breathed a sigh of relief. This battle was winding down. It had only taken minutes. The bull had cheated the matador one more time. To his left Claire was still firing, but to his right Michel heard the sound of a person running through the scrub brush of the hill and turned with his machine gun trained on the noise. Certain it was a misguided Nazi who had breached the mined ditch, Michel crouched beside his cover and prepared to dispatch him, but his heart was racing again. It beat against the walls of his chest and pushed up against his tightening throat. The matador's cape flashed in the brush, a man caught by the red glow of the flares above, and Michel's index finger began to squeeze the trigger.

Suddenly the figure fell forward, sprawling out of the brush yelling wildly, "Help me! I'm hit!" The voice belonged to Natei, and Michel turned away the business end of his gun, shaking.

Natei scrambled to his feet and ran past Michel on up the hill another twenty yards. He collapsed there, panting ferociously, writhing on the ground in the flickering light of the flares.

Michel left his position on the hillside and ran after him arriving along with a few others. As they began examining him, Claire kept up her firing far below. She did not notice two additional guerrillas emerge from Natei's brush. Nor did she see the body they were lugging as they passed behind her.

"Oh, Jesus!" Natei rambled. "I hit the charges right when Jon told me to! I swear I did! Then he stood up and started firing into the trucks. I was right beside him. Right beside him! I heard bullets whistle by my head. Then he got hit in the goddamn face! Jesus, he turned and looked right at me and half his face was hanging off! Oh, shit," Natei moaned. "I'm bleeding bad." He touched the blood trickling down his cheek and his head dropped back.

Michel shone his flashlight on Natei's face. Natei's eyes were white, rolled into his head. Blood was eking out of a ragged hole in his cheek. Michel wiped the blood away with his thumb, and fresh blood seeped out to take its place, but there were no other injuries he could find.

"Probably a fragment," Michel said as he wiped the blood away again. This time he pulled out a handkerchief and pushed it over the wound. Beneath the cloth he felt a sharp jab. Natei felt it too and immediately jolted into full consciousness.

"Goddamn it! You trying to kill me?"

Michel ignored him and reached beneath the white hanky quickly turning red. He felt around the laceration until he found the fragment.

"Christ!" Natei screamed and struggled against others who leaned in to hold him.

Michel produced the piece and held it under the flashlight. "Fragment," he said as he continued examining the half-inch long piece. "But it's not a bullet."

"Could be wood from the trees," a fighter said. "Hey, Natei, you got shot by a pine cone!"

The collected fighters began to laugh until the thud of a dropping body brought them from the joke.

"No," Michel said as he trained his light on the body. "It's not wood. It's bone."

"Christ, they broke my fucking jaw!"

"Shut your goddamn mouth, Natei!" Michel yelled. "If your face was broken you wouldn't be running your flapping jaws. That bone is from your brother."

The flashlight first found Jon's black pants and then moved up his body. The black sweater showed little evidence of blood though it was there, but when the light came upon his face, or what remained of it, there was a collective gasp.

The left side was intact, nearly normal as best they could see in the limited light, but the right side was a tangled mass of torn tissue, broken teeth, and splintered bone.

"Oh, my God."

"Pick him up," Michel directed. "Put him in one of the cars and take him to the spot, but don't dig yet. Renault will have to get the map."

It took several men to carry Jon with any semblance of dignity. As they struggled, Michel kicked Natei's feet. "Get up. GET UP! Help them!"

Natei got his feet beneath him and stood sheepishly. Only then did Michel let his sympathy show. "I'm sorry, Natei," Michel said as he put his arm on the young fighter's quaking shoulder. "Tend to your brother. But talk to Renault before you speak to anyone of this. Anyone. That includes your family."

Natei was wavering. "Jon's dead. My brother's dead, isn't he?" he asked as he began to wipe tears and blood off his face.

Michel grabbed him. "Hey. Hey! Listen to me! You have to be strong, Natei. Now more than ever! For your family and for Jon. You take this pain and carry it with you, never forget it." He pointed down the hill to the dying convoy. "Turn the pain on them, Natei." The young fighter was understanding and hardening with the passing seconds, but the tears were still flowing. "That's right," Michel said as he looked into the young man's face in a flare's light. "Go take care of Jon and then be ready to avenge his death. Always ready."

"I'll be alright."

"Yes," Michel said as he rubbed Natei's shoulder. "I know you will."

Natei jogged up the hill, wiping more blood and tears from his face as he disappeared into the trees behind his dead brother.

***

15

B ack in the major's bed, the lovers had breached the gates of heaven. Monique was still sitting astride Pieter, moving slowly, her eyes closed, smiling slightly between gentle bites on her own lip, her body bathed in sweat. As she leaned over him a bead of perspiration skated down her nose and dripped into Pieter's eye. He jumped slightly with the salty sting and turned his face away from any that might follow.

"Sorry," she whispered as she wiped another drop off the tip of her nose.

Pieter answered by dabbing at her face with the edge of the damp, twisted sheet. When he finished he limply dropped his arm and stared at his partner.

"Wow," was all he could muster.

Monique raised her eyebrows shyly. "Wow is good?"

"Wow is wonderful." He hesitated only long enough to take a deep breath and clear his head from the magic that had walked into his room on high heels. "Monique, that was absolutely-"

She stopped him with a finger on his lips. "Shhhh," she said as she lowered herself onto him and kissed away the compliment. The kiss was easy and was followed by her nestling her face against his chest. The couple rested silently, basking in the warm and comforting afterglow of the love they had made.

Meanwhile, Claire was ramming a fresh clip into her rifle. She racked the action and began firing, slower now, at glimpses of grey, each a man struggling to look invisible on and along the turnpike. New flares lit the sky, and she could see clearer the carnage she and her compatriots had wrought. The bodies of German soldiers were scattered everywhere. Remains of men draped out the doors of the trucks. Torn limbs littered the road, the result of contact with the mines. Many soldiers had tried to huddle beneath the vehicles and had died there. Others, repelled by the fire and smoke of the exploded trucks in the road and the mines to the sides, were shot as they ran about aimlessly.

Claire faintly heard an order being passed down the firing line to break for the barn, which meant to end the assault, vanish into the trees, and head for home. Now Claire lowered her gun, but not to cease her firing. Instead she looked down into the road, gathering a wider view than her gun sight allowed. She was scanning the road for movement.

"Let's go!" Michel said as he came up behind her, turning for the trees before his words even reached her. He was immediately stopped in his retreat by the cracking of Claire's gun. As he spun back to her, Michel saw Claire lower the gun slightly then snap it up again and squeeze off another round.

"Cla—" Michel began, before stopping himself, realizing that someone might hear the name. "Hey! Let's go!"

Claire did not hint at leaving, opting to continue her highly discriminate shooting. Michel hustled up to her as a German's bullet whistled by them in the darkness.

"C'mon!" Michel screamed at her as he grabbed her arm.

Claire roughly jerked away and sighted her gun again. "There's one moving behind that rear wheel...," she said slowly as she squeezed the trigger.

Michel jumped at the crack of the gun as though he hadn't heard a report in his life. His eyes followed the lay of the barrel and watched in a dying flare's light as a soldier rolled from beneath a truck. As he stared, Claire fired again, and the body twitched on the ground.

"Good shooting, huh?" Claire said coldly without looking up from the road.

Michel looked back at her. "That's enough! The others have already gone!"

"Let them go. There's a few left down there."

"You heard the order. Break for the barn!"

He grabbed her again and ripped Claire away from her killing. She balked, still looking down into the road, but reluctantly slung the rifle over her shoulder and gripped her machine gun. With her in tow, Michel ran up the hill into the trees. The hot barrel of Claire's rifle bounced across her back like a happy, playful child as she followed.

What few Germans remained along the convoy began firing blindly into the trees above the road, fully aware that the danger to them had passed. Though haphazard, their bullets occasionally came close, finding the trunks of trees along the Resistance fighters' escape route. Even as Michel and Claire made good their retreat, branches splintered beside them, impacted by German bullets. Michel ducked and cringed with each one. Claire laughed at him and the bullets as she ran on recklessly. In minutes the entire band had been absorbed by the countryside — these were their hills. One minute more and the entire contingency had disbanded. Even Claire and Michel split up, but not before Claire grabbed his neck and kissed him with a burning passion fanned by the gunfire still ringing in her ears.

Across the countryside passion had continued to subside in Pieter's bed. The couple had fallen into a peaceful coziness then drifted away into the arms of sleep. It was such as this, the sheets wrinkled and damp but worked from their tangles, the room so still save for rhythmic breathing over warm flesh, that the clock was permitted to click blissfully away unaware of the war in the world.

The clock had worked its way for a time before Monique began to stir. She rested for several moments, enjoying the scents of both Pieter, who breathed in slumber by her side, and the sex, which had been captured by the sheets. In time she slid without a sound from the bed, pulled one of Pieter's dress shirts from the back of a chair, and slipped it on. Its length discreetly covered her to her thighs, but it was the smell of his cologne that pleased her most. As she rolled up the sleeves to make them manageable she nuzzled the collar with her eyes closed and reflected back on the last few hours.

A loving glance back at Pieter, sleeping soundly while she gripped the collar of his shirt, and she made her way toward the bathroom. But when she passed his desk, a file resting on the top reached out to her. It was marked 'Confidential' in red. Outside the hotel room it was beginning to rain again.

Monique paused, halted in her steps by the red word that contrasted so brightly in the still burning romantic lights Pieter had lit. She read the brilliant letters then her eyes darted away as if she had done a bad thing or had seen something she was pretending not to have seen, as if looking away out of politeness from a friend's faux pas. But this constituted much more than a friend's mistake, and her eyes returned to the file.

There was a tug at her heart, and it came from the bed. Once again, Monique looked back at the sleeping Pieter. He did not move and continued his sleep, uninterrupted by the rushing battle Monique waged with herself. The cover of the file and the red word teased at her and enticed the French in her to push aside the bud of love that within the last several hours had begun to bloom in earnest.

Yet another quick check on Pieter, and Monique moved closer to the desk and the file. From as far away as her arm could reach, as if somehow it insulated her or concealed her intention, her soft hand flipped back the cover. Inside there was a short memorandum on top of several other papers. In the dim lights of the room she was unable to read the lead piece. Another look at Pieter and Monique moved in full force on the file, spurred on by French interest and commitment.

Even up close it was difficult to make out the words in the memo. She leafed through the remaining papers in the file and found them to be assorted lists of things, again things she could not make out in the poor light. Her frustration growing, she slipped the top memo from the folder and closed it, pressing it with her hand as if to be certain it remained that way. Then, clutching the memo and watching Pieter, she hustled silently into the bathroom.

Once inside she fumbled for the light switch. When she located it she touched its place with one hand, still holding the memo, and closed the door with the other. As it quietly eased shut Monique flicked on the light.

Monique translated the German easily, skimming hurriedly over the memo, her lips moving ever so slightly. Then in a whisper she repeated the highlights of the contents to herself.

"Armament shipment to Normandy via Castele Statine. Depart St. Laurens, 5 June – 2100 hours. Highest priority. Item listing and quantities enclosed."

She closed her eyes and recited quickly. "Armament shipment to Normandy via Castele Statine." Her voice instantly lost the words she had read. It was necessary to peek at the paper before she closed her eyes and continued. "St. Laurens. 5 June – 2100 hours. Armaments to Normandy. Castele Statine. St. Laurens. 5 June – 2100 hours." She cheated and looked again at the memo. "That's tomorrow."

With eyes wide open, Monique read again. Then she looked at the ceiling and repeated the cities and time in a whisper. "St. Laurens. Castele Statine. Normandy. 5 June. 2100 hours. Normandy. Tomorrow."

Content she had taught herself the intelligence in her hand, she turned off the light and quietly opened the bathroom door. As it swung away she looked in the direction of the bed. Pieter was sitting on its edge as though ready to stand, with only the sheet draped across his lap. Monique's hand, holding the memo, slid unnoticed behind her back in the darkness of the bathroom doorway.

"Hi," Pieter said softly.

There was little hesitation in Monique's voice. "Hi, yourself."

"What are you doing way over there?"

"Just powdering my nose. I didn't know you were up."

"I'm not," he said as he lifted the sheet off his lap and peered underneath. "But I suspect that may change at any moment."

"You're an awful man, Pieter Von Strausser," she said with a smile. "You should be ashamed of yourself."

"Oh, I am. I am."

"That doesn't appear the case."

"Appearances can be deceiving. Usually are."

Monique moved with an edge about her — instantly uncomfortable in the shadowed doorway. "Speaking of appearances I must look a fright."

"You look wonderful to me," Pieter said as he followed her shadowed legs with his eyes. "Come here."

"I bet you say that to all the girls."

"There are no other girls. Never will be either," he continued as he held out his hand to beckon her.

She let the words drift around in the romantic light as they were supposed to do then started her backward retreat into the bathroom. "Give me a second to get beautiful for you."

Monique began to slip back into the bathroom, but Pieter's words stopped her short. "Hold it!"

"What?" she answered, unable this time to hide the slightest of cracks in her voice.

The delay was much longer than Monique desired. She unconsciously shifted her weight. The tiny hairs on the back of her neck stood at attention and she felt a fresh chill race across her body. Pieter seemed to her to take a quick deep breath then just as suddenly, he relaxed on the bedside.

"Nice shirt," he said with a smile.

Monique hid her relief behind a relaxing smile and closed the bathroom door. No sooner had she done so then she turned and leaned heavily against it. There was a deep sigh, but it signaled only a temporary reprieve. The memo, the stolen memo, was still in her hand.

In a blur Monique threw on the light and jumped toward the vanity, shaking the paper slightly as if it were somehow stuck to her hand. She knelt down quickly and looked in beneath the sink. Finding nothing, she leaped up and opened the medicine cabinet, unsure in fact of what she was searching for apart from a deep hole in which to drop the memo. There being no gaping hole in the medicine cabinet, Monique spun away from it then around and around, still searching for a place to secrete the German intelligence. Mid-spin she saw the deep dark hole.

The toilet had been witness to her silent but frenzied attack on the bathroom. Now it would be her salvation. Without hesitating Monique dropped down beside it and began quietly tearing the memo into tiny pieces.

Pieter remained on the edge of the bed, the sheet still covering his lap. As he waited out his lover's return he listened for her steps. If there was anxiousness in his mind it was brought on by growing passion and nothing more. To him, in this state, the wait was too long and the bathroom too quiet. Letting the sheet fall away from him he stood and walked to the bathroom door, glowing with every intention of surprising his new love.

At the bathroom he stopped and turned an ear to the door. Though he listened intently, he could not make out a sound. The hard work of his ears took away from his eyes. They focused on nothing and drifted about in their sockets as though searching for a use. They soon found it on the desk. As Pieter continued to listen to nothing, his eyes brought his focus away from his ears and their failure at the bathroom door, to the desk and the ever so slightly disturbed 'Confidential' file.

The mischievous smile that had carried Pieter to the door faded. He moved to the desk and touched the red letters on the file like a medium reads the cards, as though the file itself would tell him how, and perhaps who, had disturbed it. When no message came to him he flipped the folder open and pulled away his hand.

Pieter recognized immediately that the covering memorandum was not in place. He bent over the desk now and leafed through the file. Not finding the errant memo he repeated the process, only slower. As the file did not cooperate he shoved it aside and began rummaging through the desk. The doors were all slid open and closed and the stacks of papers riffled. Only the sound of the toilet flushing caused him to stop his search. With the sound, he stared at the bathroom door and his thoughts locked on Monique just beyond.

The flushing noise abated. Pieter walked briskly across the room to Monique's clothes and purse. He searched them in seconds then returned to the edge of the bed and positioned the sheet as it had been just as the bathroom door opened in front of him.

"Miss me?" Monique said as she slipped seductively across the room and straddled Pieter's lap.

The answer came as Pieter's hands slid up her thighs and under his own shirt. "Definitely," he said as he became instantly aroused.

Her face was above his so he kissed her throat then fell to her breasts and began to caress them with his lips as his hands groped her bottom. One hand slipped around her waist and lifted her only enough to jerk the sheet off his lap. When he brought her back down to him he positioned her so that he effortlessly slid inside her. Monique arched her back and pushed up slightly with a faint moan then brought herself down full force onto him. She immediately began squeezing her legs together, lifting herself up and down very slowly.

The rhythmic caress of her hips was warm, but this would not be the time for gentle lovemaking. The passion was strong, as strong as when they had first entered the room, but this time Pieter felt a fierceness rise up alongside the passion, spurred on by betrayal. He tightened his grip around her waist, and in one movement lifted her and spun them both onto the bed. Pieter came down on her hard, driving himself into her with abandon. The thrusts that followed were near brutal as he drove deep inside her.

Monique felt the harshness in his hands and his hips, but gave back as good as she got for a time, sinking her nails into his back and biting his shoulder. But then the game did not seem a game, and she relaxed, content to have sex and not to make love as she had done so many times before. And yet, in this fury she still felt a veil of protection and, rather strangely, love.

Indeed, it was love alone that bridled Pieter. Without it, he would have been carried over into darkness. As it was, Pieter was finished. His muscles tightened and his deepest thrust remained until he had rid himself of lust and anger. As he relaxed he slipped off her and covered himself with the sheet, purged, but also awkwardly ashamed.

Monique was slightly dazed. The roughness did not frighten her, in it tremendous pleasures could be found, but now she hoped for reassuring comfort, a reminder that it had still been love though hidden in the disguise of sex. She did not suspect that she had been found out and believing such had actually brought about the change herself. So she lay quietly, listening as Pieter's breathing returned to normal. When it had, she felt his hand on her face gently brushing away her tangled hair. Her hand cupped his and she kissed it tenderly. Reassurance had come to both, but for Pieter it would have to do battle with his suspicions — and win — to remain.

He moved until he was lying alongside her, face to face. There were gentle kisses and comforting touches, but no words. After several minutes Monique braved the waters.

"Wow."

Pieter watched her another moment. "Wow is good?" he asked softly, mimicking her from a few hours before.

"Wow is different. Where did that come from?"

"Mad passion?"

"Mad certainly."

"No," he said apologetically. "Not mad. Just madly in love with you."

She bore deep into his eyes to see if the words were true. In his eyes she saw honesty, but she could not see the struggle to maintain it. Also in his eyes she saw her own reflection coming back at her, holding out the memo. Now it was she who felt ashamed. She kissed him in the hopes of brushing it away, but it was freshly born and strong. Behind her own eyes, deceit raged against new love. In her struggle she pulled herself closer to him and buried her face in his neck.

She felt tremendous uncertainty as to what she might say next. Could she really be on the verge of confessing and begging forgiveness in exchange for love? Words of repentance and love swelled up in her and were harshly forced down - back down her own throat like a bitter pill by the current Resistance and by conversations heard as she played beneath a kitchen table long ago.

"I have to go," she muttered hurriedly, afraid for herself and for love.

"Right now?" Pieter asked, not yet willing to have her leave, unsure if the damage he had caused had been successfully repaired and equally unsure if it should be.

"It's late," she said as she slipped out of his arms and off the bed. Before her hands left the sheet she continued. "But I could come back by tomorrow. If you'll have me."

Pieter propped himself up on an elbow and stared at her thoughtfully, not answering.

"What is it?" she asked.

Pieter rolled to his back and stared at the ceiling. "I was wondering if you're as French as your father is Irish."

"Why would you say that?"

He paused then answered as he dragged himself from the bed. "I don't know. I truly don't know."

Monique stood quietly and watched him as he slipped into his pants and began to pick up her clothes.

"How do you feel about the war?" he asked.

"I hate it. Nothing good can come of it," she said as she slipped off his shirt and traded it with Pieter for her dress.

"If it were not for the war, we'd have never met." Pieter held out her stockings and smiled genuinely.

She snatched the silk out of his hands playfully. "I'd rather you were a waiter or a garbage man."

"Is a German officer so bad?"

"My father thinks so," Monique said as she stepped into the dress and sat on the edge of the bed with her stockings.

"What does his daughter think?"

Rolling her stockings up her legs offered a moment to formulate the answer. Before it came, she put on her shoes and walked on high heels to Pieter's arms. "I used to agree, but now I'm not so certain."

"I see. So you've discovered that not all Germans are the monsters your Resistance propaganda would have you believe."

"Perhaps," she said as she kissed him.

Pieter dwelled with the kiss then took Monique's face in his hands. In his voice was resounding passion. "Oh, Monique. If you could see the Germany I know. It's a beautiful country, with beautiful people."

Monique left his hands holding nothing in mid-air as she turned out of his grasp and walked across the room. "France is beautiful, too. At least it was until it was overrun by grey."

The couple stood in silence, Pieter by the bed wearing only his pants, his hands slowly falling to his sides, and Monique ten feet away, though it could have been a thousand. They watched each other for a sign or for hope — and for love. They remained there for what seemed to both an eternity, looking at each other across the room and across the chasm of the war.

It was Pieter who first ventured out onto the thin ice. "We'll always come back to the war, won't we?"

"Perhaps not. Not if you could put aside that famous Von Strausser devotion to duty."

"And you? What would you put aside for us?"

Monique's answer was her silent stare. Pieter watched and waited. When the answer came as silence he held out his arms and she glided into them.

"It's not as easy as it sounds, is it?" Pieter said as he gently stroked her back and shoulders. "You do what you think is right and you do it for so long. Then one day it suddenly starts to look wrong, but it's become a part of you."

He moved her until he was holding her out in front of him. "Do you understand?" he asked in a voice that was growing in intensity.

"I do."

Pieter's grip tightened and he nearly shook her as if he were scolding a child. "Do you? Do you really understand what it is to believe in something, believe in it your whole life? Then one day, a word, or a person, or some goddamn thing happens and everything you've ever believed in, everything you ever thought was right, changes before your eyes?"

Monique grabbed him back. "I do understand!" She released him and clenched her fists as she spoke. "I do!" Then she quieted, opened her hands, and looked into her palms. "I do understand, Pieter. More than you can know."

Pieter snatched the open hands and pulled her into him. He held her tight and kissed her with abandon in the dim light as though they had just now entered the room. Rather than be consumed, however, a calm settled over them. The tension slipped out of the room, they relaxed completely, and lovingly stroked each other's arms.

"I really do have to go, Pieter. Will I see you tomorrow? Please say yes."

Pieter's answer was preceded by the softest of kisses. "I have a feeling tomorrow may be a difficult day, but I'll try. I'll try very hard." And he kissed her again. Then he smiled. "I'll definitely call first if I'm going to stop over!"

"Good!" And the couple shared an easy laugh.

Monique patted his chest and walked to her coat. As she picked it up, Pieter collected his shoes and began putting on his shirt. "Give me a minute and I'll walk you."

"Let's not go through that again. I'll be home before you get your shoes on."

Pieter stared at her, and his love was jostled by suspicion. Still, he dropped his socks on the floor. Without a word he walked to her and easily slipped the coat from her hands. As he helped her with it, love and suspicion continued to battle. When she had pulled the belt of the coat tight around her, and he had adjusted the collar, he escorted her to the door, opened it, and leaned against the frame. Monique took a half step out then turned back to him.

"Kiss me," she whispered. When the kiss broke Monique shuffled her feet slightly, contemplating her next words. "Pieter?"

"Yes?"

"Have you ever been in love?"

"Once."

Monique's chin dropped noticeable and she was a little girl. "Was she pretty?"

"Was?" he said as he stroked her hair and lifted her drooping chin. "Is. Yes, she is very pretty."

Monique's words could not stop themselves now. "You love me?"

"I think since that first night in the club. And you?"

"If I fall, will you catch me?"

Pieter's words did not trail so easily, but they somehow managed to come from his heart and mind, from love and duty, at one and the same time. "I don't know if I should catch you or not. Do you want to be caught?"

"I want to be with you."

"You love me?" he echoed.

"I do. Is there a way? Tell me there's a way," Monique said as she crushed herself to him.

"For us? For love? I hope so," he said as he stroked her hair. "I do sincerely hope so."

"So do I."

They stole one more kiss, turning the conversation.

"Call me then?" she asked as she primped his unbuttoned shirt.

"Tomorrow."

"Good night, Pieter."

"Good night, love."

A last kiss punctuated the day and the door slowly closed between them.

As Monique made her way out of the hotel, Pieter drifted around the room. He lit by the window and slightly pulled back the heavy drape. When he disturbed the curtain he could see the damage the sun had reeked over the years. The folds in Pieter's hand were deep blue, a very elegant color. The edges, exposed and unprotected, were baby blue, but also very pretty in their way. Independent from one another they were each wonderful, but side by side they did not match, did not work, were not compatible apart from each being blue. Exposure to the light had made such a profound change that the curtain was useless and the colors ugly. Pieter watched the heavy cloth as he let it slip from his hand. Unencumbered, unaffected by the change brought on by the touch of his hand, it fell back to its normal place and was somehow attractive again, made whole. He toyed with it for a moment and considered the power he had to move it from beauty to disgust with the brush of a hand. The two colors could not exist side by side. Only when left alone could the curtain continue with its intended purpose. If all brought together in the light, it would be torn down as ugly and destroyed in a day.

From behind the curtain's struggling colors, Pieter sneaked a look out into the street below. He watched patiently and was soon rewarded as Monique appeared and hustled across the empty road. When she disappeared around the corner Pieter let the drape fall back to its customary place and found himself staring at it again. Left alone, minus fluctuation in its idle routine, the curtain was fine. Change would lead to its destruction.

He turned and walked to his bed, picked up the edge of the twisted sheet, and bounced it in his hand as though testing its weight. Abruptly, he tossed it back on the bed and turned away.

Monique walked briskly up the street away from Pieter's hotel. Her hands were buried deep in her coat pockets, and her shoulders were hunched slightly against the dark and the damp night air. Above it all there was a glow to her face.

She replayed the events of the day and the night over and over, each frame snapping by with the click of a heel beneath her. Scattered between the laughter and the love scenes came flashes of the conflict they had muddled through and around. But as the sidewalk slipped by and home came closer than Pieter, the Resistance came closer as well, and love, like the concerns they shared when they were together, was held off to the side.

Out of worn habit, Monique looked over her shoulder. Seeing a clear street she slowed her steps and rummaged through her purse for a paper and a pen. She had done this so many times. She shook her head at the repetition of it all, but also at the fact that she was doing it at all after the wonderful day that was.

With her pen and ragged scrap of paper in hand, she stopped between shadows. She used her thigh and purse as a desk and wrote, reciting on paper the words she had memorized in the bathroom at the hotel. When she finished her hurried scribbling, she tilted the paper in the poor light and read to herself: "Armament shipment to Normandy. St Laurens through Castele Statine 5 June 2100 hrs."

"I can barely make it out myself," she said too loudly. There was a strange tone to her voice, almost disdain. She scampered up the street, stuffing the paper recklessly in her coat pocket as she did. But she had not ventured half a block when she pulled the note out and looked at it as she walked, accessing its legibility. "Good enough," she spat and rammed the paper back in the pocket.

In a few minutes Monique was nearing the street corner close to the safe house. As she approached she slowed her steps and listened intently. Again she glanced behind her and nearly stopped. Though there was no sound on the dark street she had grown more uncomfortable with each step. The events of the day had clouded her mind. She considered there was no point in tempting fate, and more importantly, no reason to ignore her sixth sense when it had served her so well in the past.

The corner of the safe house came and went and with it, the secret vent. She buried her hands in her pockets another time as the safe house drifted away behind her. In the pocket she felt the note. Frustration over it and all it meant was churning beneath the surface. Being unable to complete the drop only added to it. In a blurring whirl, Monique spun around and stomped off toward the safe house.

"Goddamn it!" she said aloud as her thoughts began a reckless tumble. "To hell with this waiting," she thought. "To hell with the Resistance, the war, the safe house, and that goddamn vent! This is the last time! The very last time!"

As suddenly as the silent conversion had begun it was over. Her steps dropped to a snail's pace. Then she stopped cold, well short of the safe house steps. Her head fell noticeably. In her pocket, the note caught the attention of her hand once more. "You're an idiot," her mind whispered to her. "Give it all up? Give all of them over? Surrender Claire? Because of Pieter?" Before the words had finished forming in her head, her feet had brought her around and she was once again headed home toward Rue Le Blanc.

***

16

At Monique's house, the McCleash patriarch stood a not too constant vigil for the return of his daughters. Both had been noticeably absent all afternoon and evening. Sean had begun to wait for them in the street early on, prepared to dress down at least one of them in front of the neighbors. Sean's plan was to demonstrate so profoundly that he would regain the face he had lost in the neighborhood because of Monique's practices. But night, gratefully for her, had intervened.

Several hours and numerous bowls of tobacco, each one enjoyed quietly in his chair as he skimmed a newspaper, had provided other thoughts which eventually relegated Monique's doings down the simple priority list in his mind. In fact, he was on the verge of dozing when Claire, in a wild rush, burst in the front door. This alone made him jump, but the sight of her, streaks of hastily removed black boot polish still on her cheeks and the smell of gunpowder reeking on her clothes, widened his eyes as she ran pell-mell across the room to him.

"Father! It was great! We hit them! We hit them hard!"

Estelle had been in the kitchen, but Claire's shouting brought her quickly to the living room, still drying her hands on a dish towel.

"Claire! Keep your voice down!"

Rather than offer any plea for forgiveness, Claire shot her mother a harsh look and returned to Sean with her tale.

"We were all set up, see. The road was mined like always. When those first trucks went up we turned loose on them with the small arms. They were jumping out of their trucks like rats out of a burning building!" she said with obvious glee. "And when they came out, we laid them down! Sent them all to hell!"

"Claire!" Estelle bristled. "That's enough!"

"Let her talk!" Sean yelled back. "Damn good news, I should think. Serves them jerries right. Ya done good, lass. Real good! I'm damn proud of ya! Now," he said as he leaned forward a bit in his chair and spoke over his pipe and paper. "Let's hear the rest."

"No! I'll not have it," Estelle stormed as she came further into the room.

"Damn it, woman! Let the girl speak!"

The rising voices had concealed Monique's entrance into the house. Unseen, but now heard, she yelled from the foyer. "What's all the shouting? You can hear the whole of you from the street."

The fracas enveloped her as soon as she stepped into the living room. Claire jumped away from her father and rushed up to her sister, so quickly that Monique leaned back.

"It was great, Monique! We hit a troop convoy tonight! Must have gotten two hundred soldiers! Maybe more!"

"That's two hundred less to worry about," Sean said proudly.

Monique's reaction was colder. Her forehead tightened over a biting grimace. "Oh, Claire, why must you do such things?"

The reaction was immediate. Claire bristled with defiance and literally straightened to attention. "Because I am a soldier!"

"No, Claire, no," Monique said softly as she touched the black boot polish remaining on her sister's dirty cheek. "And what's this black on your face?"

Claire recoiled from the touch of her sister's hand and leveled her own look of disgust at the remark. Before she could spit an answer, Sean chimed in.

"What would ya have her do? Be a common tramp? Like yourself?"

"Sean!" Estelle bellowed.

But he had already begun. "What would you call her? Her sister risks her life for France while she brings the swine pleasure!"

"Stop it!" Estelle yelled at her husband as she moved to Monique's side. With the move, Estelle supplanted Claire, all but pushing her aside. Claire felt the cold shame of her mother's back and with it her previous excitement faded beneath the black on her face.

"Our Monique is a fine girl," Claire heard her mother say in a soothing voice.

"A fine tramp is what she is!" Sean differed.

Estelle looked at him with the harshest eyes she had ever set on her husband. "I said, stop it!"

But Sean had been pushed enough and though never silent, he had had his fill of Germans and his wayward daughter, as well as his wife's protection of sin in his house. He crushed the paper in his hands and threw it as he leaped out of his chair. His face was crimson and the veins showed clearly in his neck.

"I will not stop! Goddamn it! My Claire here is a hero! And you!" he screamed at Monique, shaking his pipe at her so violently that the tobacco spilled out. "You are a whore to my enemies! you, are my enemy!"

The words settled around the family like an icy fog, but Estelle was as hot as her husband. She drove on Sean until there were only inches between their noses. Her own face was aflame and her fists were clenched. As she yelled, she motioned with disdain to Claire as though she were a stranger.

"And how many men did your hero murder tonight? How many died at your precious daughter's hand? This killer of yours?"

"This is war!" Sean echoed in anger.

"That's right, you damn fool! People die! Die like the Germans died tonight! And on some other night it will be her! Then what will you say about your fine hero? Our daughter will be butchered by Nazi guns. Then what? Will you tell me it's war? What will you tell me through your tears? That it's just war and people die in war?"

The cold element of truth behind his wife's words shook him. He sank backwards into his chair and held his pipe close to him. Estelle turned away and returned to hug Monique. Claire stood in the middle of the room, alone.

Minutes ago she had been in her glory. The excitement of the raid had carried her to her father in triumph. Now the moment, her moment, had been stolen by Monique and Estelle. She stared at her mother, consoling Monique, and began to shake her head no. Her eyes darted from person to person in the room, formulating a decision she would not back down from. Only minutes before, her eyes had been on fire with passion for what she had done. Now they burned with disappointment and anger. She settled on her sister and thoughts of Germans, nestled cozily between Monique's breasts, formed words in Claire's mouth.

Abruptly, Claire broke toward her father, still sitting, fondling his pipe reflectively. She rested her hands on his shoulders from behind his chair. Sean reached up, still clutching the pipe, and grasped her fingers.

"Father's right, Monique," Claire said with tremendous distance in her voice. "What you do is wrong. It's immoral."

Monique spoke for the first time in several minutes. Her words were slower than those of her military-minded sister and, though biting, still carried the relationship of family. "And you? Your bombing and killing is Christian?"

"It's a war, Monique. C'mon."

"Yes, it is a war. War for me, as well."

Sean released his hold on Claire's hand. His composure had returned. "Acts of war don't bring smiles to the enemy's faces or groans to their beds. Or babies to the bellies of stupid girls!"

It started again. Estelle spun from her daughter and leaned hard into her husband. "Damn you, Sean McCleash! Leave this child alone!"

"Child? She's no child! But that's what she'll leave us with... when she runs off to America to be a 'movie star,'" he said with cynicism as tart as venom. "True French, like my Claire, my soldier, kill Nazis! And that includes any bastards this whore of yours bears!"

Estelle moved at Sean with her fists, but her eldest daughter reached through collecting tears and caught her from behind.

"No, mother," Monique's voice cracked as the tears began to trickle out of her dark eyes. "It's alright."

Feeling the comfort of Claire's hands at his back, Sean could not be stopped. "See? See her tears? She knows she sins. She brings shame to our family and she knows it! Go on! Get out of my house, whore!"

The battle was over for Monique. She had resisted little. Under the barrage of insults from her father and the glare of her sister, Monique stepped away to the foyer and picked up her coat. Estelle was bewildered. She was torn between intense anger and concern for her daughter, indeed, for her entire family. Temporarily ignoring the anger, she followed Monique to the door. Tears began hinting in her own eyes as she caressed her daughter's shoulders. "Come back tomorrow," she whispered, her words holding all the love they could find. "It will be better tomorrow."

The bruised daughter smiled faintly through tears and kissed Estelle's cheek. "Thank you for trying, Mother. I'll be okay."

More words, as daggers, shot blindly into the foyer. "I said, go on, whore! Run to the beds of your Nazi lovers!"

Pain exploded from Estelle's eyes in tears. She hugged Monique tightly and turned the collar of her coat up against the insults and the drizzling rain that had begun to fall again. "Go now. Go."

Monique hurried out the door, down the steps, and up the street. She looked back briefly as she walked on and saw her mother, first fighting tears then wiping her face with damp hands as her oldest daughter ventured into the dark. Just as she vanished, shrouded by blackness, Monique stopped and turned. She raised a hand to wave, but somehow lost the strength. Her hand was suspended for a moment, as if giving a blessing. Estelle touched her lips to blow a kiss on a wave of her own, but it too was weak, drained by the words from McCleash to McCleash that had shattered her family.

Monique stepped backward into the darkness as Estelle watched. The matriarch gazed after her first born another moment then slammed the door and with the Furies behind her descended on the living room and the rest of her family.

Claire and her father remained as they were when they had banished Monique. Sean was sitting, though not too comfortably, in his chair. His soldier daughter stood ramrod straight behind him, her hands still resting on his shoulders. When Estelle marched into the room, Claire felt her father tighten beneath her hands. She gave a reassuring pat, but it did nothing to prepare the old man for what happened next.

Somewhere in the short steps from the foyer to Sean's chair, Estelle wound up and brought her hand down across his face in a blow that would have staggered him had he been standing. The slap stung his face and her hand and also both of their hearts, but the latter hurt would not surface for several more minutes.

"You son of a bitch, Sean McCleash! Don't you ever speak to her like that again! Ever!"

Sean's eyes were wide from the slap, but he believed what he felt and what he had said. On another day he would have fought to the death to defend Monique from a similar fate at the mouth of a stranger, but his was a familial right. Sean answered the slap and the threat with tremendous determination in his words as Claire stepped out from behind the chair.

"She is trash! She beds the Germans like a cheap prostitute! And a cheap prostitute is what she is!"

Before Sean had finished his defense, Estelle's hand was recoiling to strike again. But when it moved toward him, Claire reached up and grabbed her mother's wrist.

"That's enough, Mother," Claire said as she squeezed tightly.

Estelle turned into her daughter with her other hand raised, but Claire caught it as well. "I said, that's enough!"

The women and the family were locked in literal combat. Estelle and Claire's eyes were fused as tightly as their hands and wrists. There was anger in both. Estelle struggled in a quick jerk against Claire who held her mother in a vise-like clamp.

"Let go of me," Estelle threatened.

"No more, Mother. No. More."

Sean sat between the two. He saw the stalemate, and concern brought his hand up not to his wife but to Claire. He touched her hip and patted it softly as though trying to ease away her attention. When Claire broke her eyes from her mother, Sean shook his head no. Claire eased her grip.

Estelle ripped away her arms at the first hint of Claire's relaxing. She would not raise her hand again, but words were another matter.

"You," she said as she shook a finger at her youngest. "You think a gun makes you a soldier? Anyone can pull a trigger!"

"I fight to free France!"

"So does your sister!"

"I kill Germans! I don't sleep with them!"

Estelle hesitated a moment before launching her next words. "Where do you think the information comes from for your raids? Tell me that, Miss Hero Soldier? Where?"

Claire spun away from her mother when she found no suitable answer. "I don't know. None of us do. We just follow orders."

"From girls like Monique, that's who. You know it, and I know it."

"That's not so," Sean said. "Those girls are whores, given to foolishness and disguising it as work for the Resistance. They learn nothing except to be better whores. Nothing."

"It's play-acting, Mother. Monique and the others are afraid to fight, afraid they might get dirty or break a nail," Claire said facetiously as she looked at her own boot polish-stained fingers. "They'd rather dance with the Germans then fight them. They'd relish seeing all of us, all of France, screwing German officers."

Estelle pointed sharply at her daughter. "Mind your tongue."

"Or what?" Claire said as she came within easy reach. "You want to slap me, too? Will that make you feel better? Here," she continued as she snatched her mother's wrist and held it up by her own face. "Go ahead. Slap me and tell me I'm wrong for fighting for my country. Then slap me again and tell me Monique is right. Who are you trying to convince? Me or yourself? Monique does nothing but play games. She thinks she gathers intelligence. The Germans don't tell her anything! Do you think they're idiots? They impress her with lies. How does she know? And after they fill her full of lies, she lays down before them like a dog!"

"Stop it," Estelle said as she jerked away from Claire for the second time.

"It's true, Mother! Admit it!" Claire tormented. "She told me herself! She likes it, Mother! She'd do it without the war! She just likes to screw officers!"

"Stop it!" Estelle screamed and covered her ears.

Claire realized the first profane word uttered in the McCleash house had just come from her mouth. She blushed uncontrollably and retreated with her back to her mother. When she chanced a look at her father he slowly shook his head and a chastising finger at her.

"I'm sorry," Claire said sincerely before continuing on course. "I shouldn't use language like that. But she's wrong, Mother. She's wrong. And she's been wrong for so long, she thinks its right."

"That's true, Estelle," Sean echoed. "She's been plying herself for too many years. You know that much is true."

"I don't know any such thing."

"You do, Estelle, but you won't admit it."

"No! It's you that won't admit that what she does, that what she does for the Movement has merit."

"Love has blinded ya," Sean said as he adjusted himself in his chair.

"And hatred has blinded you. You can't even see your own daughter right before your eyes."

"Nonsense," Sean continued, with a quirky smile. "Me daughter is right here," he said as he stood and reached for Claire, touching her face. "She is here, proud, wearing the black badge of honor across her cheeks."

"You're a fool. Both of you are fools," Estelle said as she moved away from the pair. "Damn fools," she whispered before turning back toward the room. "How can you disown Monique for what she does, then praise the killing that comes from it?"

"She does nothing, Mother. And besides, killing is a part of war."

Desperation walked across Estelle's face as she tossed up her hands and marched around the room. "Why does everyone feel the need to remind me that war means killing and death? Am I that ignorant? I know what war is, and what it does, and what it means."

She moved toward the foyer, retracing Monique's steps from moments before. The attitude surrounding her became more subdued with each step. By the time she reached the foyer entrance she was speaking softly, almost reverently.

"When war came I thought I wouldn't be touched by it. With no sons to take from me, from my heart, I thought it would pass over this house - pass over it like the Angel of Death passed over the mantles washed with blood."

Estelle turned back to her family and stared at Claire as though confused, which she was. "Now I watch you paint your face black and disappear into the night. And I'm left alone with the thought that no one, regardless if there are sons, no one is spared when war enters in."

Estelle's voice picked up as she walked to her husband. "Sean, would you have her run guns, fight, kill, and die?"

"I won't get killed, Mother."

"Is that what you want, Sean McCleash? A martyr?"

No answer came to his lips, but one began to register on his face as Sean looked away from both his wife and the question.

"Not me," Estelle answered for him. "Not me. When this war is over, when the Germans leave us be, I want my daughters in this house. Both of my daughters. Both of OUR daughters. Not the memory of a dead hero."

Tears broke and trickled down Estelle's cheeks. "I want my girls in my arms, not the pity of neighbors as I carry flowers from your garden to a fresh grave."

None spoke. Estelle dropped heavily into a chair and began to cry in earnest. "Will you help me when the time comes, Sean?" she sobbed as crying overtook her. "Will you cut...will you cut your precious flowers to mark Claire's grave?"

Though she lurched in her chair, convulsed by the heartbreak she anticipated and the wedge in her family, neither Claire nor Sean moved to comfort her. The surface of Sean's cheek still stung with her slap, and Claire's sense of betrayal, deeper than her father's flesh, still burned. Captivated by their own pain, they ignored Estelle's.

Sean spoke over his wife's tears. The voice distracted Estelle and brought her slowly from the torment she was breeding. "Estelle, you speak of family. What of the pride of our family? What of our name? Monique brings disgrace to this house."

Totally exasperated, worn down by the fight, Estelle sagged under the weight and pleaded again. "She does what she can."

"She lays with men like a dime-a-dance girl."

Estelle's chin, still holding drops of tears, came up slowly as she squared off again with her husband. This time there was no anger, no violent urgency in her words. She spoke calmly and gently like one resigned.

"And what of it? Does it stay with her? Will a night out hang over her into eternity?"

"It may," Sean replied.

"And the killings carried out by your hero?" Estelle said as though Claire wasn't present. "What of them?"

While Estelle waited, Claire felt a strange chill. She looked at her father with hopeful eyes, trusting that he would have the answer that would exonerate her in Estelle's eyes and suddenly, God's. But she was left wanting. Sean stared at his wife, looking for time to think, looking for an answer. Estelle stopped him before he started.

"Tell me, Sean, which stays on your soul? Which stains the hands of our daughters more, the killing or the sex?"

The pause was as long as could be managed. Whoever spoke first would somehow lose. Finally, Sean just shook his head and retreated behind a familiar ally.

"War changes the rules of death," he mumbled.

"And other rules as well," Estelle shot back. Then, in a voice distracted, she continued. "But I guess I don't know anything anymore."

Claire stepped away from her father for the first time. The move was threatening to her mother and intended to be so. "Know this much, Mother. Without the Resistance — without our raids — this war is lost. There may be no France."

"I would have my family over all of it."

"Would you have your grandchildren speak German?"

"Claire, I hate the Nazis as you do, but there are nights when I'm afraid the war will leave me with no grandchildren of any language."

Sean spoke reverently, as though he had not heard anything his wife had said, "Without soldiers like Claire, France is dead."

"And our family, Sean? When death steals your hero and our family is less by one? Then what will you say of France and the Resistance? And what will you say of our family?"

"And when Monique leaves her filthy reputation and her German bastards at our door? What will you say?"

Estelle was worn. She rose wearily and trudged to the staircase, burdened by a broken heart. The walk was long and the staircase high. The steps were mountains to her feet, but she did not pause as she painfully answered, "I will say what any mother would say, 'This is my family.' I'm going to bed."

Father and daughter stayed on in silence in the living room until Estelle's shadow, real and imagined, faded completely. When it had, Claire pulled a chair up close to her father's and between furtive glances by both of them toward the upstairs of the house began again the story of the raid. This time, however, the volume if not the enthusiasm was greatly subdued. Sean soaked up each word. For her part, after the telling of but a few lines, Claire's vigor returned. She once again felt the glory. It was as if the row with

Monique and Estelle had never happened, but of course it had, and the ripples would echo through and around the McCleash family for a very, very long time.

Though Monique had been at the center of the storm, the total effect had not caught up to her as it had her mother. There had been other fights, other words, though perhaps not as strong. Now, as she jogged up the steps to the nunnery, she considered the heated discussion just another bout with her father. She had no way of knowing about the slap administered by Estelle and the biting words that followed from both sides. Nor could Monique sense how deeply rooted Claire's resentment had grown toward both her mother and sister. Lines had been drawn that hour in the living room, most of which could never be erased.

These things were suddenly distant from her mind as she was just looking for a place to sleep — a bed that would require no favor beforehand or duty after. In addition, there remained the hastily written note in her pocket. It demanded attention as well, if only enough to wad it up and drop it in the garbage. These were the things running through her mind as she rapped on the locked door of the nunnery.

When there was no answer from the dark building, she knocked again, a little louder, a little harder, and a little longer. With no answer forthcoming she knocked harder still, so much so that it hurt her knuckles. She resorted to a kind of desperate pounding with an open hand. No sooner had she begun this latest attack on the door then a dim light came on from somewhere deep within the old building. Monique stood quietly and was soon bathed in the outside light as it glowed to life above her head, revealing her to those who would unlock the door.

Unknown to Monique the light exposed her to someone else as well. A half a block away, cloaked by the darkness, Pieter stood watching. He had traced her steps home from his room, had even circumvented the safe house with her, and lingered long enough outside the house on Rue La Blanc to hear the loud voices. From there it was a short walk through the shadows to the nunnery. Here, he figured, is where she would spend what remained of the night.

If by chance she turned away, perhaps back to his hotel room, he would sprint ahead. As he watched his new lover patiently waiting beneath the light, Sister Arlene opened the door.

On seeing Monique the nun took her arm, hurried her inside, and closed the door. The sister's tone was harsher than intended. "Child, what in heaven's name!"

"I'm sorry to bother you, but I've had a bit of trouble at home."

"Why, the hour!"

"Yes, I know. I'm sorry to wake you."

Sister Arlene was fully awake now and was able to dampen her panic. She brushed at her faded bathrobe as if it were her pressed habit and calmly folded her hands in front of her.

"Yes, dear. I know you are. When folks come calling at this hour, it is generally bad news. We've had nothing else of late it would seem. You'll be needing your bed."

"Yes, please."

"Let's see if I've tucked any of my little rascals in it," she smiled.

As the nun turned away, Monique grabbed her arm. "Sister? There's another thing." Rather than say more, Monique held out the note from her pocket.

The nun didn't question it or look at it. "Of course," she said as she matter-of-factly took it from Monique's hand and slipped it into her bathrobe pocket. "That being the case," Sister Arlene continued. "You know the way. I've got the King's business to attend to."

Monique brought a hug up against the nun, but was playfully rebuked. "Go on now."

"Thank you, Sister. Thank you, again."

"I've done nothing. Now off to bed with you."

Monique did as directed and walked down the hall toward a familiar room. "Good night, Sis—" she began as she chanced a look back, but the nun had already vanished.

***

17

Fighters had collected to dig. In the dim light of a few hooded flashlights four men prepared for their work as unobtrusively as possible while Natei grieved. Michel pulled a dirty piece of paper from his pocket and unfolded it in the poor light. He turned it around and looked up at the trees in the woods then looked from the paper to the trees again and out toward the road over a hundred yards away.

"Let me see your shovel," he said in a whisper. A fighter become gravedigger offered up his leaning post and Michel took it and the paper and began moving systematically through the trees. He stopped now and then and pushed the point of the shovel into the ground. In places it bit the earth easily and deep. In others, the ground resisted. The waiting fighters paid him little attention and Natei saw nothing but the blood seeping through the white cloth that covered Jon's face. In a few minutes Michel returned to the diggers.

"Give me your back," he directed. A fighter pivoted, and Michel placed the paper on his compatriot's back. "Hold this," he ordered another and handed over his flashlight. Ahead of the order, the shovel's original owner took it back and resumed his leaning.

The light shown on the paper. It was a map of sorts. The main trees and landmarks were neatly laid out. Between them were numbers written in various handwritings. Illuminated by the light, Michel wrote, "27" in a spot held by his finger.

"Okay," he said as he folded the paper and tucked it in his hand. "Over here."

With that, the diggers followed him several yards deeper into the woods. Michel took the leaning post yet again and drove the spade into the hard ground. "Right here. But run in this direction," he motioned back and forth with the paper as a guide. "If you dig too far toward the road you may hit number six."

All eyes looked a few feet away from the shovel sticking in the ground to the spot nearer the road.

"Who's number six?" a whispered voice asked.

"I don't know," Michel answered the voice. "Renault keeps a list for after the war. He says they'll be moved to a hero's graveyard."

"I think they'll be forgotten," Natei said weakly. "We'll all be forgotten."

"That may be so," Michel said in the darkness. "I'm not going to lie, but our hope has to be otherwise."

Natei's words now spilled from a grown man and not the carefree boy who had gone to fight on the Clovington Turnpike with his brother. "They'll want to forget," he said in a stronger tone. "They'll forget because they'll have to. In order to move on. To rebuild France, as it was, or as a northern Germany. They'll have to forget and put all this behind them. Maybe someday someone will remember and build a little marker somewhere, but if they don't, we have to forgive them. Bad things are best forgotten, and this war is bad. We'll all be forgotten under the broad brush of the bad."

Michel put his hand on Natei's shoulder. "The Resistance, like your brother, is the goodness in all this evil."

"Maybe, but I think the numbers are too big." Natei motioned in the dark to the black form on the ground. "Jon is number twenty-seven of a hundred thousand. No one will remember. The tragedy of one death will be lost in the tally."

The group and the woods were as silent as Jon's body. Even Michel could not debate for he agreed. The men reverently mulled Natie's spoken thoughts, leaned on their shovels, and stood in a quiet tribute to number twenty-seven, number six not far away, and the others who lay in invisible graves all about them.

***

18

While Michel, Natei, and the others cared for the dead, Dr. Meceraux and Raquelle worked in the safe house basement to prevent more numbers being added to the graveyard map. Though the Clovington Turnpike raid had gone well, Jon had died in the effort and there had been other injuries. A few lucky fighters, lucky by inches, having caught a passing German bullet in the arm and not the chest, sat around the lower reaches of the house being administered to. One of these was Paul who waited his turn quietly, holding a white rag against his thick forearm. The wounds around the basement ranged from Paul's gunshot and other narrow misses to cuts from trees. Fortunately for the troupe none were deathly serious, and the doctor was making short work of what was required of him.

Upstairs, Sophie was returning early from a date cut short by the raid, her horny escort having been called away when the fighters attacked the column. When she learned of the wounded in the basement she went down to help as much as she could.

The room stayed quiet and busy as the fighters were patched up. One by one they slipped away toward their homes to recuperate. Sophie wandered among them talking softly, doling out praise and

reassurance for fast healing. Still dressed for her evening out, she
caught Dr. Meceraux's eye in short order as he examined Paul's arm,
which was being cleaned and held by Nurse Pravain.

David lowered his chin and looked out over his glasses at
Sophie. "Raquelle, who's that lady?"

The robust nurse looked quickly then returned her attention to
her work. "No idea."

Paul followed the doctor's eyes then locked on his face in
anticipation of the upcoming question. Raquelle's antiseptic burned
as she forced it into the bullet wound and Paul's arm instinctively
tightened.

"Hold still, you," Raquelle ordered.

Paul looked at the bloody hole through his arm and at the nurse.
She finished her work like she was massaging a piece of beef while
Dr. Meceraux prepared a suture. Only then did Raquelle look at
Paul's face. "I've put you back together a few times now, haven't I?"

"Yes, ma'am."

Then she softened and patted his leg. "You stop getting yourself
shot up. I'm getting tired of you."

"Yes, ma'am."

The doctor held the stitching needle over Paul's arm. "A bit of
Novocain, Raquelle."

"Save it for someone else, doc," Paul said.

"You sure?"

Paul looked at him silently.

"Alright," the doctor acknowledged. "Hold on."

The sharp needle, curved for the purpose, dove beneath Paul's
skin, across the hole left by the bullet, and back up the other side.
To the doctor's surprise, Paul did not flinch, did not move, did
not 'hold on.' To David's continued amazement, Paul watched
every turn of the needle through his arm. But while Paul saw the
thread begin to pull the injury closed, David saw a peculiar look
on his patient's face. What was registering was a look of apparent
disappointment.

The doctor was looping another stitch when he chanced a
question, an uncommon thing to do to known members of the

Resistance. "Do you happen to know who that woman in the dress is?"

Paul never looked up from the tightening thread. "No."

"She looks familiar," David said, but he could take it no further and though he suspected Paul had lied he felt the lie was justified and his asking of the question out of place.

Despite the lack of help from Raquelle and Paul, David continued to glance around the room to Sophie and was unnerved when she was not where he had last seen her. He finished with Paul just as Sophie came from behind and rested her hand on the fighter's shoulder.

"Hey. What are you doing here?" Sophie asked as she surveyed her friend's injury.

"Nothing," Paul answered as David's eyes bounced between the two.

"Anything serious, doctor?"

"Not too bad. He'll heal up nicely with a little rest." Assuming something other than what existed, David, envious of Paul, continued, "You may have to help him button his shirts for a while though."

"Hardly. He buttons his own or goes without." With that, Sophie pushed Paul's head away from her and walked on. The playful shove brought the faintest of smiles to Paul's sober face.

The degree of caring, sincere as it was, minus any displays of affection told the doctor that Sophie and Paul were not involved, and he was encouraged. He gave Paul's arm over to Raquelle and excused himself to supposedly tend to the next patient but instead maneuvered around the room to meet Sophie. The dress and her figure were alluring, sure enough, but there was also something in her face that whispered to him.

With nerves of the hopeful tingling through him, David smiled at Sophie, causing her to turn away from bolstering the courage of another fighter. "Your friend will be fine," David said. "He's a very tough man."

"Thank you for taking care of him," Sophie said before motioning all around the room. "And everyone else."

"We all do what we can, don't we?"

Her answer was a welcoming smile.

"David Meceraux. I don't believe we've met."

"Sophie," she said as they shook hands.

"I suppose I shouldn't use my last name. I guess I'm not well versed in the ways of the Movement."

Sophie smiled again as she chided him. "Nor should you use the word Movement for that matter."

"I am sorry! Perhaps I should keep still."

"No, just be careful. You're safe enough here."

"Thank you for overlooking my shortcomings."

There was a slight gap in the conversation, but Sophie's experience at making men feel at ease kicked in.

"I wonder how it is I haven't met you," she said. "I've heard quite a lot about your work for us, but I've never run across you. Not that I recall."

"Poor timing on my part apparently."

She smiled again. "Do you practice nearby?"

David looked around the room with an air of phony cautiousness. "Should I answer that, or is it a test?"

She laughed too loud, and the room looked in the couple's direction. Quieter now, she answered, "You can answer, but in a whisper."

David moved close to her, close enough to smell the perfume applied for a Nazi but now enticing him. "I'm at St. Louis Hospital."

"Very good. Now I will call the guards."

David was stunned for longer than he should have been. Sophie took his arm and leaned close herself. "Just kidding."

When she came close a recollection tried to gain a foothold in David's mind. He felt it there, as he had earlier, but it was greasy and slipped away from him, unfettered. But in its wake it left a long stare as David tried to find the source of the memory.

"Doctor?"

"Yes?"

"Is there something wrong? I apologize if I caused you concern. I only meant it as play."

"No. No. It's not that at all. You look familiar to me for some reason. Are you certain we've never met?"

"Very."

"As am I, and yet... I wonder if I've treated you or your family at the hospital."

"I've never even been to St. Louis."

"Your family perhaps? Your mother? A brother or sister?"

There were recollections of her own now and she was quiet.

"I'm sorry. I shouldn't ask about family."

"It's not that. My family is gone. That's all."

"I am sorry." This time it was he who reached out and held her arm. "I apologize for bringing it up." And a small smile from Sophie surfaced from the depths.

"Doctor," Raquelle interrupted, somewhat annoyed.

"Yes, Raquelle?"

"There are several more to see."

The nurse waited, ensuring David would follow. With the eavesdropper in place he was reluctant to ask for dinner. "Well, Sophie," he said as he extended his hand. "It's been a pleasure. Perhaps one day I will recall where we've met."

"Please let me know if and when you do."

David took that as an open invitation to call, which he would do just as soon as the war, the Nazis, the Resistance, and his patients allowed him. As he walked back across the room to his work shadowed by the diligent nurse, Sophie's dress and the disjointed memory of her face twirled away and up the stairs.

***

19

In the darkness outside St. Catherine's, Pieter continued to watch the door. He resigned himself to return to his room when Monique did not reappear. When the light above the door was turned off from within he concluded that the night had finally come to an end. No sooner had the decision been made then it reversed itself, as the sound of the door opening brought Pieter's attention back to the building.

The darkness that had raced in to shroud the steps when the light was extinguished prevented Pieter from seeing who had come out, but he heard the rhythmic click of a woman's shoes on the flagstone sidewalk. He strained his eyes and leaned hard against the corner of the concealing building in an attempt to see clearer, but he could not. As the figure descended the steps and moved up the street, Pieter looked around quickly for cover and began to again play the role of a tail.

Before several blocks had passed, it became clear to him that he was being led back to the safe house. He was so certain of it, and increasingly so angry, that he sprinted through the black night away from his target and on ahead. Two minutes later would find him positioned at the far end of the safe house street. Another minute passed alone before the object of the pursuit walked onto the block.

Pieter took several deliberate steps toward her, convinced that he would throw her masquerade to the ground in front of that damn house. And yet, his feet failed him. He brought himself up and huddled in the dark, watching. Given her stride and his distance, she would easily make the relative safety of the house before he could reach her. Perhaps it was just as well. Perhaps it was his plan in the first place. More likely the case, as he readily admitted to himself, he did not know what to do. To rush in on her would leave no doubts and no options. As he stood there in the dark and continued watching, she knocked and was immediately taken in.

"It is always best to have options," he mused. "Always options." But he understood that his were not options, his were choices that carried few opportunities for victory. When this thought settled in and grasped his mind, Pieter turned away from the safe house and walked to his room, his head down buried in thought.

By the time the streets gave way to his hotel Pieter had run a gauntlet of emotions foreign to him. He felt himself fluctuate between anger and hurt and bitterness and hatred and love so many times - literally a change with each step - that he was physically nauseous by the time he entered his room.

The door slammed behind him as Pieter ripped off his coat, wadded it in a ball, and threw it into a chair. He stomped to his desk and yanked open the center drawer. From it he tore his address book and leafed through until he found the number he was after. Then he took the book to the phone and snatched the handset from its cradle. He dialed forcibly with one hand while holding open the pages of the book. When the number began to ring, Pieter set the book aside and brought Monique's paper out of his pocket. On it were written her name and telephone number in her delicate handwriting and scribbled in his own, Monique's address as well as that of the safe house.

The phone continued to ring. "C'mon. C'mon. Answer the goddamn phone," Pieter said out loud. He looked at his watch. It was after 1:00 a.m., which immediately convinced him to hang up the phone without making a report, at least for now.

His eyes came away from his watch and onto Monique's note. Though he stared at it he did not read it. It was more that he was absorbing, again, all the things it held beyond the words themselves. The paper continued to hold him, but he walked slowly to his bed, kicking off his shoes as he drifted.

The twisted sheets, recent memories, greeted him as he lay down, still riveted on the note. As he followed the curved lines of Monique's writing his heart soared. Never had he been so captivated by a woman. She permeated him and he knew it. If it were only lust, only an infatuation, would he still warm at the thought of her? Recollections reminded him that he had fallen in lust before many times in many towns between here and home, but the feeling had lingered only until the sheets were wet and wrinkled. Likewise, an infatuation quickly cooled at the touch of a serious hand. At the thought, Pieter eyed his own handwriting at the top of the paper. This was a great deal more than merely serious.

At that precise moment Monique's perfume floated up from the note and caught him unaware. He brought the paper to his nose and deeply breathed in his new lover. Yes, this was serious, but it was also much more than infatuation. This was to be a sleepless night, eyes and mind held open by struggle.

Pieter adjusted the note, searching for the strongest scent. He found it and smiled behind the paper as his eyes fell to slits. He breathed it all in as if in the aroma there were answers. When his eyes opened he looked through his own cloudy haze for the stain of Monique's perfume. He touched it with his fingers, coaxing more from the fading fragrance. His eyes cleared slowly and beneath his fingers, shrouded by the stain, was the address of the safe house.

His throat tightened, as did his fingers. He slowly began to crush Monique's note. In a flurry he squashed it entirely and threw the crumpled torment across the room. Tonight, sleep may be slow in coming and restless, but in the morning he knew what he would do.

***

20

Early summer in France had always been a wakening call to artisans of various descriptions and varying degrees of talent. The spring rains lessened and allowed wares to be displayed with less regard for the elements. From the heart of Paris to wee villages, and the banks of the Rhine to the coastal roads, those with talent, and those in search of talent, or perhaps just a franc, sold their work or trinkets to any who would care to stop, look, or touch. A summer was acknowledged to be in full swing when the downtown squares across the country were lined, shoulder to shoulder in spots, with painters armed with watercolors running Notre Dame into the sky while textured oils waited to cure nearby.

Like so many pleasantries, a great number of the wayfaring artists had disappeared beneath the occupation. The younger men had been snatched up long ago by the military, many having already taken their talent to an early grave. Others had been driven into hiding, of person or talent or both, by an atmosphere vocally against expression. Still others had elected to withdraw from the streets because the people they had once courted had withdrawn as well. For those that remained, few in number, a new price of doing business was the cost of necessary permits imposed by the present conquerors. The money raised was destined for the war machine. For the artists it was as though they were buying the bullet that may one day kill them. For this, painters with licenses posted on their easels were not well regarded and their work was sold mostly to invaders, when it sold at all. More often the case, the art became the target of open theft because it had struck the fancy of an officer in black whose suggestion of "a donation to the Third Reich" was taken with a faint smile as opposed to dealing with the consequences.

Pieter found himself standing behind one such artist, an old man painting beneath a bleak sky and a tattered beret. They were near a street corner, and Pieter, clutching his briefcase handle tightly, was less admiring the work than waiting for traffic to part. The painter had positioned his easel to catch the best light possible from the fledgling summer day and was adding finishing touches to a simple street scene. It took a moment for the artist to notice Pieter absently looking over his shoulder.

"You like this, Major?"

To Pieter, he was looking at the painting for the first time while the artist took the glance as further scrutiny, a good sign of a potential sale.

"Special price for majors, sir."

Pieter smiled at the sales tactic. "Yes, I imagine so."

"Something else perhaps," the street vendor said quickly as he began retrieving other paintings from a satchel beneath the easel. He quickly and noisily replaced the street scene with a painting of flowers. Not finding the reaction he had hoped, he clapped another painting in front of the flowers — one of a woman with flowing dark hair. Pieter looked at it longingly, searching for a resemblance to Monique. They were plentiful.

Gauging promise, the painter pressed on. "Nice. Nice. Beautiful woman."

"Yes, she is."

"Perhaps your wife?"

Pieter smiled and shook his head no.

"A girlfriend then."

"Perhaps." Pieter's smile faded.

The vendor placed his hand in comfort on Pieter's arm. "No, not a lost love?"

Pieter looked down at the old man's hand resting on his uniform. Beneath each nail was a different color of the painter's rainbow. Pieter's sentiment was clear and the wrinkled hand withdrew.

"Sorry, sir. I believed I saw a sadness in your eye. Now I see I was mistaken."

Pieter shook himself from the painting and the touch of the old man. "You were," he said gruffly and he darted across the street, dodging traffic, his briefcase running beside him like an outrigger while the old painter simply stared.

Pieter reached the safety of the other side of the street and walked briskly down the sidewalk. Had he looked back he would have seen the ancient painter still looking after him. On the old face was a look of wonder and sadness. There was fleeting dismay over the loss of a sale, but it was outweighed by amazement at discovering that the men in uniform who surrounded him and sometimes stole from him were real; for he had not been wrong about the sadness in Pieter's eye and he knew it.

Up ahead of Pieter, a white stone building which had once housed city offices sent a wide staircase down to meet the sidewalk. Pieter approached the steps with as quick a stride as he could muster short of breaking into a literal run. The urgency around him was born out of the not distant knowledge that to hesitate would be akin to changing his mind. Duty and honor propelled him, and when he hit the steps he covered them two at a time.

When he broke through the heavy doors he stopped and looked back outside. His heart was pounding. It was as though he had raced into the safety of the building pursued all at once by things he did and did not know. Once inside, his mind made up and the course of action irreversible, his commitment was confirmed. Perhaps now he could relax and set about the business at hand, business which Monique through her own doing, he reasoned, had forced upon him.

The hallway was bustling though the day was still young. Low ranking soldiers — aides to officers, flew about the hall carrying brown leather satchels, manila files, and sealed letters tightly clutched in their hands. Women, employed French, moved in the hallways as well, but their steps were slower as they carried no dedication or devotion or need to impress to gain status or rank. They carried papers and files like the soldiers, but the heft was often more considerable and the delicacy of the documents far less so. The Reich would take few chances with important documents in the hands of the indigenous French, especially in this building, as Pieter was presently standing just inside the threshold of Gestapo Headquarters.

The hall was lined with offices. Doors opened and closed behind the fleeting soldiers and women with their bundles. Pieter had been in this building on a few occasions in the past but did not recollect business being this brisk. His concern and a hint of confusion were registering on his face as he read the hanging signs that stuck out above the numerous doors. He moved slowly, wondering to himself what had caused the upturn in activity. The concern kept thoughts of Monique's touch partially at bay.

Ahead in the hall he saw the sign he was searching for, Captain Rheinholt – Intelligence Div., the office of the phone number from his 1:00 a.m. call and a subsequent call at a more reasonable hour. Seeing the name brought him to shake free of his thoughts and march ahead with his sense of direction, literally and figuratively, restored.

Pieter did not knock at the door. He knew a secretary would be just inside. As predicted, a woman looked up from her desk as he entered, greeting him with a business-like, but pleasant enough smile. He recognized right away that she was German, no doubt brought to France to handle the clandestine work that crossed the captain's desk. The room itself was small and uncluttered, highly efficient, a sign as clear as any written that this office was focused, diligent, and dedicated to its task. The secretary's desk sat off center of a door behind it. By design one had to go through the woman and almost her desk itself to gain entrance to Captain Rheinholt's office beyond.

"Good morning, Major," the woman said politely.

"Yes, good morning. Would the Captain be in?"

"Yes he is. May I inform him who's inquiring?"

"Major Von Strausser. I phoned a short while ago."

"One moment, Major," she said as she picked up her phone and rang the inner office.

Pieter smiled a thank you and waited.

"Sir," the secretary said into the phone. "Major Von Strausser is here."

There was a slight pause and the secretary eyed the major as if comparing a physical description. "Yes, sir. Major Von Strausser... Very well, sir."

Before she hung up the phone she was already addressing Pieter. "The Captain will see you now, Major."

"Thank you."

The secretary moved from her desk and opened the door into the inner office. Pieter walked through, and she closed it silently behind him.

The mood of the much larger inner office was dark, brought on by rich, heavy paneling and thick crimson drapes pulled tight over the windows. The captain's desk sat well back in the room, forcing anyone who brought business to cross a wide expanse of open floor allowing Rheinholt time to size up or down an adversary. On the wall behind the desk was a lit picture of Hitler, graced on either side by twin red, black, and white Nazi banners that reached from the ceiling to the floor.

At the desk was Captain Rheinholt. He and Pieter were about the same age, though Rheinholt, with his crisp black hair and tight eyes, was considerably shorter. The desktop in front of the captain was extremely neat and instantly made Pieter think of the contrast with his own. A single pen and a blank pad of paper rested in the center. A few files were tightly arranged to the right, a shiny black phone to the left.

Each move the captain made was carefully calculated and readily offered that appearance. Few things were left to chance. His reputation as a cold yet efficient strong arm of the Nazi party was legendary. Though Pieter had never worked directly with him, he knew full well whom he was about to deal with. There would be no wasted minutes and few wasted words and certainly no games. Pieter's intentions wavered ever so slightly at the sight of the black uniform and the reputation it carried, but he forged ahead with the decision he'd made late last night.

Rheinholt stood as Pieter crossed the floor to his desk. Rather than salute, the captain extended his hand.

"Major Von Strausser. It's been a long time."

"Yes it has," Pieter said formally as they shook hands.

"Please. Sit," Rheinholt said as he motioned to an armless leather chair in front of his desk.

Pieter placed his briefcase alongside the chair and sat, adjusting himself more than once until he was as comfortable as possible in the chair designed to keep men tense. Rheinholt lowered himself slowly back into his own chair at the same time and did so without taking his eyes of his guest.

The captain spoke hesitantly, inquiring, as was his constant nature. "I must admit to having been somewhat surprised when my secretary said you had phoned and, in fact, were here. I was under the impression you had little use for the Gestapo. Perhaps I was misinformed."

Pieter smiled, a bit uneasily. "I'm sure the Gestapo has its purpose."

"Yes. Yes we do. Tell me, Major, what brings an administrative officer to Gestapo Headquarters first thing in the morning?"

Pieter eased back into his seat as though comfortable and confident, though he was neither, and as though his words had little meaning and less intention. "I'm interested in the Resistance movement here in the city."

"As am I."

"How active are they?"

"Oh, I don't know. Active enough, I'd say."

"Are they a threat to us?"

The captain paused for a noticeable moment then answered very deliberately. "No one is a threat to the Third Reich."

The reply was meant to be stern and it stymied Pieter. Graciously, the telephone rang and offered him a reprieve, time to prepare a suitable answer.

"Excuse me, Major," Rheinholt said as he reached for the handset.

Pieter did not reply as he gestured toward the telephone.

"What is it?" Rheinholt barked into the receiver. "Yes, yes. Patch him through. Rheinholt here... No, I'm out of patience." The captain's voice was rising. "Terminate them at once! At once, do you hear? Her first. And be certain he is made to watch... That does not concern me. I will leave that in your very capable hands." The captain laughed into the telephone having seemingly forgotten Pieter was even in the room. "Good. Advise me if the dog recants in any way... Fine."

Rheinholt hung up the phone, still incensed by the conversation and the ongoing events that caused it. "Damn these insolent French!" Rather suddenly, he took note of Pieter and began gauging the major's reaction as he searched for his own composure. Rheinholt tugged at his jacket, snapping it down sharp and neat. Then he picked up a pen and began twirling it in his fingers as he leaned back in his chair.

"That's two less members of the Resistance for either of us to worry about, eh, Major?"

"Perhaps, but it is also clear that they're something more than an inconvenience."

"Nonsense. Nonsense," the captain laughed as he moved his hands in the air as if to wave off the question and the Resistance with it. "A mere trifling. A nuisance. Nothing more. I assure you. That aside, what can I do for you?"

Pieter stood abruptly and picked up his briefcase. "It was nothing. I've taken up enough of your time."

"I'll be the judge of that," Rheinholt said coolly as he motioned for the major to sit.

Pieter did not move toward the door as he wished to, but there was defiance, and a measure of surprise, in his voice. "Am I to take it that you're ordering me to stay? You, a captain, ordering me, a major?"

"Not at all," Rheinholt said as disarmingly as possible. "Consider that this is merely the Reich asking for complete cooperation from one of the Fatherland's most dedicated officers and respected families."

Pieter was not impressed, but he understood the veiled threat behind the plea. Still, he moved neither toward the door or the chair and his hand fidgeted slightly on the handle of his briefcase.

"Please, Major. Sit down. Let's finish our discussion."

With hesitation enough to fully demonstrate his reluctance and also a dwindling attempt to regain the superiority his rank supposed, Pieter lowered himself with regal bearing back into the chair. Again, he placed his briefcase alongside. Then he waited, but Rheinholt was in no hurry.

"You wish to continue, Captain?" Pieter said deliberately.

"Certainly. Why the sudden interest in the Resistance?"

Pieter sat collecting an idea for a moment. He realized an answer, and not too ludicrous a one, was necessary. He began to dodge, something at which he was not well practiced at.

"I saw a woman the other day."

Rheinholt pulled the note pad closer and began to write. "Go on."

"It was the other day. She was...acting suspicious."

"In what manner?"

"Oh, I really can't say. She was lingering around a store downtown. It occurred to me that she might be making a delivery or picking something up, but in hindsight, she could have been stealing."

"The name of the store, please?" Rheinholt said as he continued to stare at his paper and scribble.

"The store...I believe it may have been a taxi stand."

"And the name of this taxi stand?"

"I can't recall. Don't think I ever really noticed."

"I see. And this woman. Do you know her?"

"No."

"Where she lives?"

"No."

Rheinholt snapped his pen down on the pad and continued the questions, not bothering to write answers he already knew. "Anything about her?"

"I'm sorry."

"Would you recognize her again if you saw her?"

"Unlikely. So many people in the city these days."

Rheinholt tore the top sheet from his notepad, crushed the dismal notes and threw them in the garbage can. "You don't have much information for someone so concerned, Major."

"I'm afraid this isn't my field of expertise."

"You've made that extraordinarily clear."

"Yes, well, now that I know what you require perhaps I can collect the proper information. Next time."

Pieter wanted to be finished. He wanted to walk outside and forget he had ever come. He also wanted Rheinholt to forget, but of course he would not. Pieter tried to relax in the armless chair, tried to show the confidence of his rank and breeding, but it was all too weak. The urge to rise was overwhelming. He knew he had placed himself under tight scrutiny from the last man in the war he wished to be watched by. So he sat, trading a long stare with a new adversary.

Rheinholt broke it, but with his voice as he did not look away. "Major. Tell me. Have you been to your office this morning?"

Pieter was grateful for a chance to speak. "No. I came directly from my hotel."

"With nothing I might add," Rheinholt snipped.

Pieter seized the opportunity to move and stood in a rush. He picked up his briefcase and headed toward the door, confident he could make good his escape.

"There is a tone in your voice I find most disturbing. This conversation is over." Pieter rushed the length of the room. "Good day, Captain."

Rheinholt shouted. "Did you know one of your troop convoys was destroyed last night?"

The volume did less to stop Pieter than the words. He froze with his hand on the doorknob. The blood drained from his face as he very slowly released the door and turned back to the captain. If this was a cruel hoax he might very well charge across the room. But pranks and jokes were unknown to men like Rheinholt. Pieter knew that what he had just heard was true.

"No. What happened?" His voice was already shaken and frail even absent the gruesome facts.

"Resistance fighters ambushed your troop transport on the Clovington Turnpike. The fatality rate was in excess of ninety percent. Of the few that survived, most were wounded."

As Rheinholt spoke, his words drew Pieter away from the door, across the room, and back to the desk.

"It seems this particular band of guerillas was very efficient," Rheinholt continued, "and very well informed."

Pieter's knees trembled under him. He tried to lower himself slowly into the chair, but his legs failed him and at the last second he slumped hard. His speech was almost slurred, his jaw slack, and his eyes glazed. "Ninety percent fatalities?" he echoed, more to himself than as a question.

"Ninety percent," Rheinholt repeated. "The attack was well planned and well executed. Obviously, as prepared as they were, we are forced into considering that they may have had prior knowledge." Rheinholt stopped himself and his voice became louder. "What am I saying? Of course they had prior knowledge. They knew everything! Everything! Which leaves one thing crystal clear — there is a mole somewhere on your staff. Perhaps in your own office."

"No," Pieter said hesitantly, still allowing the news to sink in. "I've handpicked every man."

"Yes, I'm sure you have. Regardless, I've already ordered an..., an 'investigation' shall we say, into the affairs of your department."

Pieter's head was clearing. "That won't be necessary."

"I'm afraid it is no longer your decision."

Rheinholt began scanning a file on his prim desk while Pieter looked across it, defenseless. As the captain read, he began addressing Pieter in a thick condescending voice. "I see you have orchestrated a substantial arms shipment for this evening."

"How did you know that?" Pieter said as his eyes jumped from Rheinholt to the file and back.

The captain leaned back in his chair and gloried in the major's surprise. He held his hands up and shrugged. "The arms of the Gestapo are very long, Major. Very long."

Initial distrust between the two men had given way to open dislike, which was racing ahead to something worse. There was little Pieter could do from his position in either the administration section or the armless chair. He would have to go along in whatever direction Rheinholt steered. Anything less would be hazardous to his career at the very least, his life at worst.

"And what of the shipment?" Pieter asked, suppressing his desire to quiz the captain further on how he learned of its existence.

Rheinholt leaned forward and leafed through the file. "It's too late to re-schedule or even re-route a shipment of this size. However, I have already taken the liberty of beefing up your security measures. Naturally, under the circumstances, I've used my own people."

"Have I been relinquished of command?"

The captain relished in letting the major wait for an answer. He rose from his desk slowly and turned away from it, stopping to adjust the picture of Hitler though it did not need it. As he passed one of the twin Nazi banners he pulled it from the wall and let it fall back into place. "On the contrary, Major Von Strausser. We'd like you to take an even more active role in the operation."

"How so?"

Rheinholt crossed the office and was near a side door. He was prepared to open it when he stopped to answer Pieter's question, as if it were an afterthought. "Why, you'll lead it, of course."

The captain left the office through the side door and closed it behind him leaving Pieter alone with his thoughts. The notion of leading the arms shipment was not unusual as he often did so. Pieter reasoned that there must be another foot yet to fall in this new stratagem and that, in all probability, Rheinholt was finalizing it at this very moment in the side room. He was right.

Next door, Rheinholt was addressing a lieutenant. "Major Von Strausser is in my office. Call him in here and go over the increases in security for tonight's armament shipment."

The captain walked to the primary door of the small office that led to the main hall. He opened it and called back to his junior officer. "Do you understand?"

The lieutenant looked at the common door between his office and Rheinholt's then to his captain. "Yes, sir."

No sooner had the lieutenant grasped the strategy then Rheinholt ducked out into the hallway. It was only a few strides to his own office door and when he stepped inside his secretary greeted him with a look of surprise. She couldn't resist a glance at the door that led to the captain's office. Just as she was about to inquire as to what had or was about to happen, Rheinholt held his finger to his lips.

The secretary understood that much at least. While she sat waiting, the captain crept across her office. He stopped at his own office door, pressed against it, and listened. From inside, he could hear the sound of the lieutenant opening the common side door.

As the lieutenant entered Rheinholt's office he snapped to attention and vigorously saluted the major. Pieter stood and returned the salute.

"Major Von Strausser? The captain would like you to review the security for tonight. I have the layout on my desk. Would you join me, sir?" As he finished, the lieutenant stepped slightly to the side of the door and waited for the senior officer.

"Yes, of course," Pieter said, grateful to the lieutenant for the opportunity to escape the confines of Rheinholt's office. He understood already that nothing he might say or do in the lieutenant's office would affect the modifications Rheinholt had enacted, but he was compelled to look. His years in the service of his beloved Germany had taught him a great many things, not the least of which was that the Gestapo did as it damn well pleased — blind to rank, name, or position — and no pedigree of service would protect him if he were found to be lacking.

Pieter stepped into the side office and was followed by the lieutenant who pulled the door closed behind them. As quickly as that door closed, Rheinholt slipped back into his own office via the main entrance. He hurried across the room, picked up Pieter's briefcase, and sat it quietly on his desk, watching the lieutenant's door as he did.

Rheinholt unbuckled the leather straps of the briefcase and began a systematic but hurried scrutiny of the papers inside. He looked briefly at each piece with an eye well trained in spotting what did and did not belong and what meant something to men like him that would have been lost on others. Nothing garnered more than a glance, even the "Classified File" of the night's shipment. Rheinholt was all but ready to close the briefcase when a scrap piece of paper caught his attention. He withdrew the wrinkled paper and unfolded it slowly. It was Monique's note.

Rheinholt read it in a flash. As he did, its perfume, so unintended for him, couldn't help but demand attention. The captain, as the major had many times before, brought the note up to his nose. However, as Rheinholt's nose inhaled the scent, his eyes locked on the lieutenant's door.

"We've increased the number of vehicles fore and aft of the actual transport, sir," the lieutenant said as he pointed out the route on a map laid out across his desk. "And we'll run empty lead trucks in case they're fired upon. In front of them will be the lead staff car and a special armored truck. From the aftermath of last night's raid we believe the mines are detonation type, not contact, so you'll be fine."

"Hmm," Pieter said, totally disinterested. His mind was wracked with thoughts of the disaster of the night before, the Gestapo investigation, and as always now, Monique. He knew what she was and even what she had done, through him, to him. As the lieutenant droned on, Pieter's thoughts replayed the incident in front of the safe house and Monique's betraying reflection.

"In the fifth, ninth, and fourteenth trucks we will have machine guns mounted for heavy return fire should it be required. We'll also have mounted lights to illuminate the hillsides and as many vehicles as possible will have side armor."

"Good." But the reflection played again. And then, through the back door of his mind, came Rheinholt's telephone conversation, "Terminate them at once!"

Pieter looked away from the maps and the babbling young officer. "Where's Captain Rheinholt?"

"He stepped out for a moment."

Pieter looked hard at the lieutenant then immediately spun toward the common door. "Your layout is sufficient, Lieutenant. Thank you."

"Excuse me, Major. You haven't seen the—" But the lieutenant's words were meeting nothing but Pieter's back as the major burst through the door into Rheinholt's office.

The captain was behind his desk, leaning back, very relaxed. The smug expression on his face was so pronounced, Pieter knew he had somehow been fleeced. His own face reflected as much, and Rheinholt drew a filthy grin across his mouth in response. Though he tried to resist, Pieter impulsively chanced an awkward glimpse at his briefcase. Behind him, the lieutenant entered, still stammering.

"Thank you, Lieutenant," Rheinholt said through his perverted smile as he dismissed the officer. "That will be all."

"Yes, sir." The lieutenant re-entered his office and closed the door leaving Pieter standing alone in the expanse of Rheinholt's office snare.

"I trust you find my modifications acceptable?"

Pieter walked casually toward the chair knowing he was not yet free to leave. "Overdone, but acceptable."

"I suspected as much," the captain added as he leaned backed even further in his chair. "And there is one additional change I neglected to mention."

"Which is?"

"I will be accompanying you. That is, if you do not object."

"Of course not. I have nothing to hide."

Rheinholt moved from behind his desk again and proceeded as before to the lieutenant's door. "If that is so," he said as he opened the door. "Lieutenant, if you would join us." The lieutenant immediately appeared in the doorway. "If that is so, Major, I'd appreciate it if you would permit the lieutenant to accompany you throughout the day. Perhaps assist you in any number of ways." Rheinholt slapped his hand on the young officer's shoulder. "The lieutenant is a very talented clerk. I'm certain he can be of service to your office."

"This is hardly warranted," Pieter said as he stood in objection.

"Again, Major Von Strausser, I'm afraid I'll have to be the one who judges what is and what is not warranted."

Rheinholt looked away from the disjointed major, who stood helplessly by, and gave his orders to the lieutenant. "Major Von Strausser is not to be out of your sight or hearing. Not for a single moment."

"That is not—" Pieter tried to interrupt, but the captain continued.

"Examine each and every dispatch that crosses his desk."

"Captain! I will not be subjected..."

"Major!" Rheinholt threatened. "You will do as you are told!"

"Who the hell do you think you are? I don't take orders from captains!"

"But you will take orders from the Gestapo! If you wish I can make a phone call and then you can receive these directives, and more, from a colonel, but I rather doubt that you would want the name Von Strausser being tossed about in Berlin."

Pieter stood as a stone. His teeth were grinding in response to the threat before him. Rheinholt stared back at him for a minute or more then abruptly broke for the telephone.

"Very well. Have it your way." Rheinholt picked up the phone and rang his secretary. "Get me Berlin." He waited and stared at his prey.

Pieter was still trapped in this office, still trapped by that black uniform. Rheinholt was right, of course. For now Pieter's problems were local. Perhaps with a successful shipment tonight the cloud over him would dissipate. If Berlin was informed, Pieter would likely be recalled from France. Then there would be little opportunity to clear himself. Also, Monique would be a thousand miles away.

"Wait."

Rheinholt held the receiver slightly away from his face. Pieter could faintly here a gruff voice answering Rheinholt's call. "Hello? Hello? Who is this?"

"There's no need to trouble Berlin," Pieter said softly.

The captain leisurely hung up the phone on the now irate voice. "A wise choice, Major. A wise choice. Lieutenant, do you understand your orders?"

The junior officer snapped to attention, his heels clicking beneath him. "Perfectly, Captain."

"Very good then. Gentlemen, have a fine day. I'll meet you in St. Laurens this evening to assist in the final preparations."

Captain Rheinholt immediately busied himself at his desk, shuffling his few papers and scanning files, ignoring the other officers. Pieter began to step toward the office door, with the lieutenant in tow, but stopped and turned back to Rheinholt's desk. "Captain, all this really isn't necess—"

"Good day, Major."

The captain did not look up from his desk. Pieter remained lost in the room. There was nothing more to be said. From the moment he'd arrived Pieter wanted to leave, but now standing before the exit, he balked, searching for another way out of the tangle he had immersed himself in.

"Captain…"

"Good day, Major."

With great reluctance, and the company of the lieutenant, Pieter walked out of the office. As the door eased shut Rheinholt snatched up his telephone and dialed. While he waited he produced a single page of notes from beneath his neat stack of memos. The notes were written in his hand and listed Monique's name, phone number, and address, as well as the address of the safe house.

"Captain Hemring, please. Walther? How are you?...Good. I believe I've located the mole in the admin section...Arrange for a tail to be placed on Major Von Strausser beginning tomorrow. And have someone sit on his apartment tonight. He'll be with me, I'd say until midnight...Yes. And I have a couple of addresses for you to, 'examine.'"

Rheinholt leaned back in his chair and laughed heartily. "That's just the answer I was looking for! And do it publicly. Make an example out of them, especially a woman. Her name is...How's that?"

Rheinholt hurriedly examined more paperwork on his desk, scrutinizing manpower lists. "No, Walther, I can't spare a single man. I've got every one tied up on this arms detail. It will have to wait until tomorrow then... No, I'll be accompanying the good major tonight. Just precautionary. I want to keep a very close eye on him... That's alright. I'll stop by your office late tonight, after we deliver the armaments to the coast. I'll have the names and addresses with me and give them to you then... No, tomorrow is soon enough. I'll see you tonight then. Fine. Good-bye."

The captain hung up the telephone and stared at Monique's name in his notes.

***

21

While her name was being read over and over, Monique sat at one of the child-sized tables in the day room of the nunnery. She, like Rheinholt, was reading, but hers was a storybook where the ending was well known and far less sinister. Essey sat alongside listening keenly to every word. Monique's knees were up high as she sat perched in the smallish chair, but she was more comfortable in that seat than in a padded booth in the finest restaurant in Paris. As she read and Essey listened, Sister Arlene approached their table.

"There's a telephone call for you, dear. A Lieutenant Mussel?"

Monique handed Essey the book. "Here. You keep going. I'll be right back."

"I can't read!"

"Yes you can, a little. Practice. Left to right. Left to right. Sound out what you can. I'll be back in a minute."

"Yes, ma'am."

When Monique moved away from the table Sister Arlene stepped up. Essey straightened considerably in her chair and diligently began running her finger left to right over words she did not know. The nun stood over her, hands clasped in front, and supervised.

The small office of the nuns was as simple and uncluttered as the rest of the nunnery. There was a battered wooden desk marked with nicks and chips and water spots. An old telephone and a lamp with a torn shade sat on top of it. The chair did not match the desk in any regard except its age and apparent misuse throughout its life.

The handset was on the desk when Monique walked in. She did not recognize the name or the voice, but pretended otherwise. "Of course. How are you?... Fine, just fine... Oh, I am sorry. That sounds like a wonderful time, but I've already made plans... No, I couldn't... Perhaps, but in truth, I may be moving to Paris soon... It is exciting, isn't it? Regrettably, I won't be around the club though... Well, thank you. That's very sweet. And thank you for calling...Bye."

She placed the receiver back onto its cradle and turned away from the desk. In the doorway, leaning against the frame, was Sister Arlene.

"Moving to Paris?"

Monique sighed heavily and sat on the desktop. "Hardly."

"Getting tired of it?"

"Very. And...I've met someone."

"Local boy?"

Monique dropped her head as she answered. "No."

"You've been through this before, remember? Don't you think you'd be better off to leave it alone?"

"I know."

"Nothing but troubles will follow. Your father, your work..."

"Yes, yes," Monique said somewhat irritated as she slid off the desk, folded her arms, and walked around the tight office. "I know you're right."

"But?"

"It feels so right. Even with all this around us."

"Feelings can be deceiving."

"That isn't much comfort."

"I'm sorry. Tell me, what is it that makes this one special?"

"I don't know."

"Well, that's a start. At least it's not just because he's handsome, or..."

"But he is handsome, Sister," Monique replied over a smile.

"I'm sure he is, but at least that is not the basis for these new feelings. Now, is there more?"

"Oh, I don't know. I don't know!" There was a growing frustration not so well hidden behind the fading smile. "You can't quantify a feeling, can you?"

"No, I suppose not, but you can examine your heart and look for signs that will tell you if it is love or infatuation."

Monique didn't answer this time. She drifted around the desk straightening the lamp and the phone, coiling its line.

The nun went to her and took her by the shoulders. "I am always here to listen, listen and offer what advice I can on the subject." She released one shoulder and tugged playfully at her habit. "Though I am scarcely an expert on affairs of the heart, I am an awfully good listener."

"I know. Thank you."

The sister patted Monique's shoulders and stepped away. "I'd better mind the children. Watch your step, dear. It is only temporary, the things you do. Don't reveal yourself too much to someone who will mean nothing with the change of the season. When we don't know why we feel like we do, we are the most vulnerable."

Sister Arlene was to the door before Monique held her up with her words. "He makes me have second thoughts."

"On what?"

"On what I do and...the Resistance."

The nun returned to her, wringing her hands. "Go on."

"I think I'd like to just go away with him. Be a wife, be a mother. Get away from this war, the Resistance, all of it."

"We all would like to get away from it, Monique, but we have responsibilities, to our people, our country...to ourselves."

"I'm just tired of it. Couldn't I just go away with him?"

"He's a soldier, an officer, am I right? He can never be far removed from war, this one or another, today, tomorrow, or in the years to come. So where does that put you if you are by his side?"

Monique could only nod her head yes.

"This is unlike you, dear. You've not had your head turned so easily."

"He's different."

"He's German. He is the enemy. Don't you forget that. If he knew your work, he'd pull the trigger himself. Believe me, he would."

"No, he wouldn't. He loves me. I see it in his eyes."

"Perhaps what you see is a reflection of yourself or perhaps only what you wish to see."

"Not this time."

The sister came to her and hugged her, rubbing her back generously. "Perhaps you should step away for a while. Take a vacation. Give yourself some time to see where God leads."

"There's a lot to do though."

"There is always a lot to do. If you choose to rejoin the fray it will be here for you. If not, well, if not, then no one can say you did not contribute more than your share already."

"That would certainly make my father happy."

"I believe it would."

"Until he meets Pieter again."

"Pieter, huh?"

Monique broke into another smile. "You'd really like him. He's very sweet."

"Yes, I imagine he is. I must get back to work. When you need to talk, I will need to listen."

"As always."

"As always," Sister Arlene echoed before continuing over the ringing of the phone. "But my sense is that you've already made up your mind."

"St. Catherine's," Monique said as she answered the phone. "This is she... No, I don't believe..."

Sister Arlene stepped once more toward the door, but Monique reached out and touched her arm, silently asking her to wait.

"Colonel Heinrich?" Monique shrugged her shoulders and looked puzzled at Sister Arlene, who responded by shaking her head yes and raising a level hand above her head.

"Yes, I know him," Monique continued. "Well, I don't know..." She cringed fiercely as she wrestled with the decision. "No, I... It's possible... How's that? At the club. Eight o'clock...Why the winery?...Okay. I'll try, but...Yes. I will. Thank you. Good-bye."

The handset dropped from her face slowly and she hung it up as though it pained her. Sister Arlene came up beside her and rested her hands on her shoulders yet again. Monique reached up with one hand and gripped the nun's fingers.

"What about Paris?" Sister Arlene asked gently.

"It's a colonel."

"You could have said no again. It would have been alright."

"I know, but a colonel..."

Across the city a German soldier sitting in a dimly lit office was hanging up a telephone. "How was that?"

"Perfect," answered his accomplice. "Perfect."

Monique was still trying to convince herself and Sister Arlene. "He said to bring a friend. That's a plus."

"Who'd you have in mind? Sophie?"

"None other," Monique said as she dialed the safe house.

"If you're not comfortable she'll get you out of it. She's a sharp one that Sophie."

"Hi," Monique said into the receiver. "Is Sophie there?...How long ago?... Hmmm...How about Claire?... Thank you."

Monique covered the mouthpiece and whispered to Sister Arlene. "Think she'll go?"

The nun raised her eyebrows and looked heavenward.

Over at the safe house Claire was picking the phone up from a counter. "Hello?"

"Claire? You busy?"

There was a noticeable hesitation in Claire's voice when she realized it was her sister. "Yes," she answered coldly.

"I only need a minute. I promise. Do you know a Colonel Heinrich?"

"I've heard of him."

"Well, I just hung up with his aide. I've got a meeting with the colonel tonight and he wants me to bring a friend. Want to be my friend?"

"No thanks," Claire answered quickly.

"He's going to send a car by the club to pick us up. He wants to meet at the old Juneau Winery. I guess he has a, you know, an 'office' or something out there. You know where it is?"

"On Plank Road."

"He's being pretty cautious. I suppose that's how he got to be a colonel, huh?"

"I said no, Monique."

"I really need a favor here. I'm not that comfortable with this anymore."

"Ask Sophie."

"She's out already."

"Too bad."

"But a colonel could be very valuable to us. I just don't want to go, not alone anyway."

"Forget it, Monique. My days of play acting a hooker for Nazis are over!"

"Can't you do this one little thing for me? It's the last time, I swear. Even I don't want to do it any longer."

"Yeah, sure. I believe that."

"Claire. I mean it. Go with me this one time and it's the last for either of us."

"You'll never stop. Father's exactly right. You do it because you like it."

"That's not true."

"Isn't it?"

"No."

There was an uncomfortable lull between them. In the vacuum Claire spoke of the thing nearest in her mind.

"Jon got killed last night."

"Oh, no."

"I can't believe it yet."

"How'd it happen?"

"Who knows. Just standing there like everybody else and got hit."

"How's Natei?"

"I don't know."

"That's so awful."

"Happens."

"Happens? How can you be so cold?"

"I didn't know him that well."

"Unbelievable."

The vacuum had been filled and pumped dry again.

"Claire, can you go tonight?"

"No. And neither should you."

"I have to."

"Bullshit. Tell the son of a bitch to go jerk off to a picture of Hitler."

"I know. I know. But a colonel, Claire. Think what we could learn."

"There's other ways."

"This works."

Claire hesitated. "Okay. Tell him you'll meet him."

"Thank you," Monique sighed.

"And me and Michel will be there waiting."

"Claire—"

"And we'll get him to tell us all we need to know. He'll be groaning, but not like he thought."

Monique ignored her. "Will you please go with me? Just to bait him? Then I'll turn him over to Sophie tomorrow."

"Christ, can't you hear? I said no! If I see your precious colonel, I'll kill him for you, but I won't FUCK HIM FOR YOU!"

Claire slammed the phone down and walked away.

Monique tried to cover the hurt. "That's okay. I'll see you later," she said to a dial tone as she hung the phone up slowly.

"No?" asked Sister Arlene, feigning ignorance of the answer she already knew.

"I guess she's already made other plans."

**

22

Dr. Meceraux was sitting at his desk examining the medical records and charts of some of the countless patients he ministered to. The wall behind him was lined with shelves of books, reference for his work. To one side sat a slightly smaller desk often used by Raquelle but at present piled high with bandages and medication. At the far end of this desk, against the wall, was a glass cabinet which would hold the medicines secure once they had been put away.

As the doctor swam through his paperwork Raquelle came in and seemed to David to emit a sort of rattle as she walked. The sound brought his gaze up from the papers before him and his eyes peered out over the ever present glasses on his nose.

"Raquelle? What's that noise?"

Relieved to finally be in the office, a tense look disappeared from the nurse's round face and was replaced with a wide mischievous smile. "We got so much!" she whispered loudly.

At that, Raquelle reached beneath her coat and produced a small amber glass medicine vial. "Morphine! And lots of it!"

David moved quickly from his desk, stuck his head out the door to look up and down the hallway, then retreated and closed the door behind him. Reasonably secure, he reached for Raquelle's bounty. He examined the first tiny glass bottle and discovered its label was written in German and boasted a small Swastika.

"Do I dare ask?"

"Found it in the street! Abandoned!"

"Did you?"

"I did."

David tapped the paper label. "These will have to vanish. If we're found with them, I doubt the Gestapo will believe you found them in the street."

The nurse turned to her desk and began unloading her treasure. "I'll make short work of it." As she continued to find bottles in her pockets, many of which were hidden inside her coat, she began to sing an unknown melody. David picked up two vials from the desk and watched in amazement as Raquelle's coat spilled bottle after bottle after bottle onto the desk.

"I can use these right away. My, Raquelle, someone was very foolish to leave so much medication in the street."

Raquelle smiled wider and sang a little louder as David stepped out of the office and began his rounds as he slipped the two bottles into his pocket.

The next hour would be full of hasty notes on changes in medications, what changes he could make, and changes in prognosis, most of which went from bad to worse. With the limits the war had brought, the doctor's skill was often hampered. It was only the secretive work of Raquelle and others like her, procuring supplies, that kept patients out of the gravedigger's hands. As the bottles of morphine clicked together in his pocket David smiled at the noise. At least for a few weeks he could drive pain away from the hospital door and deliver those who must die into the nether world without agony.

As David worked through a large ward attended by a few nurses, themselves bouncing between patients and juggling charts for the doctor, he heard a plaintive voice.

"Will it hurt?"

He began to follow the voice through the mumblings of those nearby. Slowly he came upon Val, nearly lost to him in the sea of afflicted.

"Rock me to sleep."

David was near her now and stared. Val was thinner than she had been when she was first discovered. Her hair had been crudely cut many times and what remained, barely enough to cover her ears, was ragged but clean. Her skin was pale and her muscles atrophied from lack of use, all of which caused the doctor to pause as he recollected this patient whose only illness, brain damage, negated him attending her very often over the years. With so many pressing cases, Val had merely existed side by side with them in the wards, shuffling from one bed to the next as space opened or was required. She had been fed and kept clean, but had lived in the cracks of the hospital, often unintentionally overlooked by those who sought to protect her as the burdens of the injured took precedence.

Valerie's eyes were as dead as they had been on that first day, but David saw in them the hints of an answer. The face, drawn down by her empty illness, still carried a resemblance he pondered yet again after all these years. The resemblance. He studied her with well practiced, objective eyes, moving closer as he did. Finally he was a few inches from her face. He could smell her breath, foul as it was, and see the smallest flinches of her eyes.

"Will it hurt?" Val asked him.

David ignored her and continued his examination. His proximity to Val brought stares from the nurses and other semi-well bodied patients who wondered what the doctor was looking for in this deranged woman without benefit of his instruments.

"Rock me to sleep."

He tugged gently at the grey bags under Valerie's eyes as he stared deep into her face. He stood abruptly then backed away. As if suddenly on a mission he walked across the room, but looked back several times at the woman who spoke only in two phrases. When he left the room Val said her good-bye.

"Will it hurt?"

Forty minutes later David was at the safe house. With the freedom his position allowed, he wandered the house asking after Sophie at every turn. Someone said she was out, and his heart sank. Others said she'd just returned, and it soared. At last he found her sitting with Renault at a table in the war room.

"Excuse me," he said quickly as he entered unannounced. Both Sophie and Renault were surprised to see him, but it was Renault who moved first as he stood with an anxious voice.

"Is there trouble?"

"No. No. There's no trouble. I'm sorry to break in like this, but I was hoping I might speak to Sophie a moment."

Renault shifted rapidly and, believing he was interfering with an affair of the heart, excused himself as he collected a few papers from the table. "We can finish this later."

"Thank you, Renault," Sophie and David said in unison, which brought smiles to all three faces.

As the door closed behind Renault, Sophie smiled in earnest. "What a wonderful surprise."

"I'm glad you feel that way and I hope you retain that sentiment."

"Why wouldn't I?"

David looked at her made up face and dress for the first time. "I apologize for keeping you from—"

"No. It's nothing. I've been stood up. It seems the entire German Army is busy with something tonight."

David grimaced slightly as he assumed Renault's chair. She leaned forward and touched his hand as it occurred to her that the reference to her work had offended him.

"What is it?"

He studied her face carefully with the eyes of a doctor, as he had Valerie's an hour before. His words were carefully chosen and well spaced. "Sophie. I understand that you don't know me well."

She relaxed, sensing that there was a proposal of sorts behind this pleasant man with the well-mannered awkwardness. "But I believe I'd like to."

"You would?"

"I would."

Temporarily distracted, David stammered his way back to the topic. "Yes. Thank you. I would, too. Would like to get to know you...better that is. In fact, I'd like to ask you about your family, if I may."

Sophie laughed. "That's the first time I was asked for a family history before going on a date!"

"I'm sorry. I didn't mean it that way. When we spoke before you mentioned that your family was gone. I took that to mean lost to the Germans. If you would indulge me, could I ask you how and perhaps when?"

Any smile, tenderness, or playful spirit disappeared from Sophie's manner. She was cold with the recollection of her sister and cool to David for the question, unsure as to what was behind it. He recognized the change immediately and tried to erase her new fear.

With abundant sincerity he reached across the table and took her hand. "Please, don't be afraid. And also, please don't be upset with me. I know we are not supposed to ask questions and those that do often have vile agendas, but I swear to you, from the very bottom of my heart, I would do nothing to harm you or anyone else. It is only that I-"

"I had a sister," Sophie said suddenly, assured by David's eyes and touch. "She was killed in a Gestapo raid."

"How long ago?"

"Four years or so."

"Do you know how she died?"

"She was strangled."

"And she looks a great deal like you?"

For the first time, Sophie hesitated and corrected David's apparent lapse in grammar. "She did, yes."

The pieces were coming together quickly. "Several fighters were killed that day, weren't they?" he asked with a tone that blatantly knew the answer.

"Yes, why?"

"I don't believe your sister was one of them."

***

23

The mood was grim in Pieter's office. News of the ambush the night before had spread like wildfire and generated havoc throughout the major's tightly run organization. The normally quiet and efficient machine Pieter had assembled had been turned upside down by the attack and the aftermath, which now included several black-clad soldiers meandering about the office suite. Pieter was surprised to find the Gestapo's presence so strong so soon. He secretly wished, for he dare not speak a word in the presence of his own shadow, that he had come to the office at first light as was normally his practice. But it was far too late for wishes.

The lieutenant hovered over Pieter's every move. Each dispatch that came and went, several on a normal day, innumerable on this day following the destruction of the troop convoy, was slowed and screened. Rather than fire off responses to inquiries and questions, Pieter was forced to stall as he sought an acknowledging nod from the junior officer in black.

His phone calls were first taken by the lieutenant. After the caller and intent had been documented, the call was handed over then listened to on an extension. As a result, Pieter could do nothing with the thoughts of Monique that scampered through his mind. When he gave himself pause over a coffee cup lunch, he wondered what he would do if he were able. Would he tell her he knew who she was, what she did, though in reality he had only pieces? Would he warn her that the Gestapo would be coming for her? Would he meet her somewhere and plan their escape? Or would he meet her to arrest her himself, possibly kill her? It all was gone for naught and he knew it.

With the Gestapo forewarned, Pieter could do nothing without risking arrest and execution himself. As more hot coffee seared his lips, he looked at the lieutenant and felt a sudden rush that was awkwardly grateful. The lieutenant's presence made any decision, right or wrong, good or bad, an impossibility. Pieter would try nothing, do nothing — nothing to either save her or stop her. He could blame it on the SS and the Gestapo. The coffee went down bitterly. For the first time in his career and in his life, Pieter felt like a coward.

The rest of the day passed as that. Pieter accomplished little. He occasionally entertained thoughts of grand elaborate schemes to warn Monique, but they vanished, run off by a devotion that outweighed love by duration if nothing more. When the office day drew to a close, Pieter straightened the few papers and files that remained on his desk. They were nothing more than minor issues, trivial matters, far from the work he would have normally dealt with following an attack. It had become clear to him hours before that anything of importance, anything of value, anything that had a true bearing on the affairs of the German military, were being diverted away from his hand and eyes.

The sentiment that he was untrustworthy weighed heavily on him. When he stood from his desk at the end of the day, and his shadow with him, it dawned on him that he might not be returning. The following days might find him on a train bound for Berlin and some nondescript secluded office, far from war, this or any other. Pieter looked back at his desk as he neared the door.

"Forget something, Major?" the lieutenant asked.

Pieter scarcely heard him as a coldness cascaded throughout his body. The cold did not pass quickly, like a shudder when an angel passes. Rather, it lingered and held him tight, uncomfortably so. The grip made him stop and look back as if he were reviewing a great many things the desk held for him. Should the night's events follow suit with what had happened recently, Pieter's career was all but over. He would not find the position that would enable him to show the rest of the world what he had tried to share with Monique. And the Von Strausser legacy, perpetuated by his grandfather whose apparition was now sitting in the desk chair with the ghost of Pieter's father alongside, would end with him. Not just end, as end all things do, but crash. The stigma would be more than a dark cloud over the surname Von Strausser. As a presumed traitor, Pieter would have damaged the Von Strausser family name to the point where it would have its literal throat cut and be allowed to bleed to death across all Germany.

A tear trickled down the face of the old specter in Pieter's chair. His father touched his own throat then nodded as his ghostly hand came away. Pieter recognized that whatever happened to him was of his own doing. He had hesitated for love and now he and his family must pay, like the soldiers along the Clovington Turnpike had paid even though the debt was not theirs.

The train for Berlin led to other places as well. Should he be required, he now understood that he must board without question. He owed that much dignity to the ghosts at his desk and those along the bloody turnpike. Life, as he had recently been reminded, held no certainties, "With this war around us…"

"Major Von Strausser? Are you alright, sir?"

Pieter shook his head and rubbed his eyes before looking at his desk again. It was as empty to him as it appeared to the bewildered lieutenant. Pieter resigned and took a deep breath. "I am now. I am now."

***

24

David and Sophie accomplished most of the trip back across the city in shocked silence. She was trying to absorb his story, and he was trying to bring her comfort as best he could. There was a possibility he was wrong. However, the more they talked, the more remote that possibility became. Sophie had cried at the safe house when David explained the woman's condition. She had resisted the notion that her sister was the near vegetable David spoke of. Valerie had been too young, too vibrant, too much alive to be the person he described.

Sitting in David's office at Nurse Pravain's desk, still crowded with bottles of morphine and bundles of gauze, Sophie waited for Raquelle to bring the girl from the ward. David waited with her and flipped up the edges of folders, not reading a word, wasting time and nervous energy. Sophie felt an admiration toward him for his careful compassion. Strangely however, she briefly contemplated that she did not know if she would love him or hate him if the news he'd brought her was true.

"Doctor?" Raquelle said from the doorway.

David motioned her inside. Raquelle stepped clear of the doorway and reached back to gently tug Valerie along. From inside the room Sophie saw a thin girl ease into the open door. First a hand, which could have been anyone's, then an arm, which belonged to every skinny girl in France. A shoulder and a leg, covered in a hospital gown. A profile of ragged dark hair and a neck as narrow as any she had seen. But then the woman turned and the face was her own.

Sophie stood up on legs that struggled to hold her. David hurriedly came from his desk and took her arm to steady her knowing instantly that he had been right. Tears broke from Sophie's eyes, and her hands covered her mouth and cheeks. As David held her she walked very deliberately to her lost sister.

Valerie did not move from the spot where Raquelle had let her go. Sophie reached for her with hands as tender as a mother's. "Val?"

There was no answer in the eyes that looked at Sophie as blankly as at any wall. Sophie took the frail hands in her own and spoke a little louder. "Valerie? It's Sophie."

"Will it hurt?"

Sophie took her sister by the arms and stood closer, spoke louder. "Val? Do you hear me?"

"Rock me to sleep."

"Val. Val. Do you remember me? It's Sophie."

"Rock me to sleep."

"Not now, Val. Listen close." Sophie slipped a finger into Valerie's palm, but Val's fingers didn't close on it. "Squeeze my finger if you understand me. I'm Sophie, your sister. Your name is Valerie. Remember?"

Val's fingers hung limp. Sophie snatched up the hand and squeezed Val's fingers around hers. "Like this, Val. Squeeze hard. Like this. Squeeze yes. Your name is Valerie. Mine is Sophie. We're sisters. You remember."

Sophie's eyes began to dart back and forth from Valerie's blank face to her hand, held in her own, looking, feeling for some signal of recognition. None came. Sweat broke through on Sophie's forehead, and her voice became frantic. "Val! Wake up!" And she shook her.

"Will it hurt?"

"Valerie! Stop it!"

"Rock me to sleep."

"STOP IT!"

"Rock me to sleep."

David stepped in with Raquelle. Each took a sister and pried them apart. Valerie stood as silently as before while Sophie turned and collapsed in David's arms.

The doctor motioned with his eyes for Raquelle to take Valerie back to the ward, but before she could be led away Sophie turned back to her.

"Wait! Wait! Valerie," she said with a forced calm as she again reached for her sister's hand. She stroked it compassionately and spoke slowly. "Do you remember Paul? Paul. Think about Paul."

Valerie was quiet, but there was no process taking place.

"Paul?" Sophie pleaded. "Who's Paul, Val?"

"Will it hurt?"

"No, it won't hurt. Just think about Paul. Remember him? He loves you. Paul loves you. Paul."

"Rock me to sleep."

Sophie slipped her arms around her sister and hugged her. "Oh, what did he do to you?"

David and Raquelle let her stay that way for some time, Sophie gently brushing Valerie's chopped hair with her fingers and examining her face for signs of life. Eventually Sophie stepped back and David held her up. Sophie touched his hand. "Thank you, David. I'm alright now."

"Let's sit down," David said as he walked Sophie to the nurse's desk. "Raquelle, please take Valerie back to her room."

"Okay, Valerie. Let's go back," Raquelle said as she took a skinny hand in hers as opposed to the arm hold she had used before.

"Good-bye, Val," Sophie called. "I'll see you again soon."

Raquelle escorted Val away, talking more gently than she ever had to a patient. "Valerie. What a pretty name that is, huh? I like it. Valerie. How about we walk around a little first, huh? What a pretty name."

In the office all was quiet as the voice and footsteps outside drifted away. Sophie sat hunched over the nurse's desk, absentmindedly playing with a bottle of morphine. She read the German label and bounced it in her hand. "I suppose you go through a lot of this stuff."

"Enough. There's a lot of pain here."

"There's a lot everywhere."

"Valerie's not in any pain. Physically she's sound, except for atrophy of her muscles."

"What is atrophy?"

"Weakness. Shrinkage from not exercising or being used. She has no concept of...of anything apparently. She doesn't know to walk unless you walk her. She doesn't seem to sense boredom. She'll sit, I believe for days, until someone moves her. She's not aggressive. She's not violent. She's not-"

"That's it right there – she's not."

"Yes."

"And she smells bad."

David knelt down beside Sophie's chair and took her hand. "I'm sorry. I'll have one of the nurses give her a bath."

"Why do you have to tell them that?" Sophie said angrily. "Shouldn't they do that on their own? Isn't that their job?"

"Yes, but it's very difficult. There are a great number of very needy patients here and a limited number of staff."

"Jesus, they ought to at least have her take a bath once a week."

"I'm sure they do, Sophie, but Valerie has to be fed. And...she doesn't use the bathroom."

"Oh, God."

"She's like a baby."

"Will she grow up? Like a baby does?"

"It's been four years."

"And nothing?"

"No change."

Quiet returned to the room as Sophie thought and David silently supported her.

"I'll take her home," Sophie eventually suggested. "Maybe when she sees her own things, it'll come back to her."

"It's going to be very difficult for you."

"What choice is there?"

"She can stay here."

"And get a bath maybe once a week?"

After several minutes, she looked hard at him. "How long will she live?"

The doctor came into his role and stood, stretching his cramped legs. "Who knows? She's as healthy as anyone, probably the healthiest person in the hospital – physically anyway. I don't see any reason why she wouldn't live out a normal life."

"Normal? That's not normal," Sophie said as she looked at the doorway.

"Age-wise, I mean. Valerie could easily outlive us both."

"Then who will take care of her?" Sophie said, not necessarily to David.

"The hospital. The staff. Same as now."

There was another pause as the thoughts of finding Valerie and finding responsibility raced through Sophie's head. "I need to talk to Paul," she said finally. "I don't know if he'll be in heaven or hell. I don't know where it's put me for that matter."

"You have your sister back. Take her home. Like you said, perhaps the familiar surroundings will spark something. And Paul, he and Valerie were close?"

"Very."

"That's the fella I stitched up the other day?"

Sophie nodded. "It'll kill him to see her this way."

"He'll be happy to find her alive."

"Not like this. Not knowing he did it."

"Did what?"

Sophie looked in David's eyes and waited, reading the trust and compassion she already knew was there. "Put her in here. He's the one who tried to kill her, to save her from the Gestapo. He was sure she was dead. Everyone was."

David was taken back. A moment and a deep breath aided his recovery. "It doesn't change anything. She's alive, and Paul will be there to help you."

Sophie reached for his hand and held it with both of hers. "David. As a doctor, wouldn't it be better if she didn't live, not like she is?"

"Better for whom?"

"For her. Better for her."

"She's not in any pain, Sophie."

"I understand that, but she's not alive either."

"Of course she is."

"Life isn't only breathing, David."

"In my profession, there is only life and death. I don't see grey areas."

"That's how you define life?" Sophie said as she pointed to where Valerie had stood. "I don't."

"What are you suggesting?"

"I don't like to see her that way."

"What about her? What do you think she would like? Life? Or death?"

"Let's ask her, shall we? David, she doesn't even know her own name."

"Not today. But perhaps eventually she'll come out of it."

"You don't believe that."

"Or some day there might be a new drug or treatment to help her. What about that?"

"Wishful thinking while she suffers."

"She's not suffering."

"She's not living either. That's what Paul will say."

David rested his hand on Sophie's shoulder. "I'm a physician. I took an oath to preserve life, not take it."

She snapped up from the desk and stomped into the heart of the room. "Haven't you ever had a patient who you truly believed would be better off dead?"

"As long as there's life then there's a chance."

"That is not life, David!" she uncharacteristically screamed as she pointed at the empty doorway where Valerie and Raquelle had walked away.

Sophie waited, but there would be no change in David's principle.

"No, Sophie. Go get Paul and bring him here. We'll talk."

David slipped up to her and put his arms around her shoulders. In the consoling hug, he spoke to her, "This has been quite a shock. Let it settle. We'll find Paul, and I'll help you talk to him."

She clasped his arm, leaned her head backward on his chest and whispered, "It'll kill him to find her like this."

***

25

The final leg of the German armaments' trip to the coast began in a monstrous converted manufacturing plant. The building, constructed on the huge scale as it was, proved an ideal jumping off point for the major's last convoy. Massive ten and twelve wheel trucks bounced into the open ended structure and left with springs taxed to the limit by the weight of weapons. Like ants, soldiers, stripped of anything soldier-like save discipline, formed human chains and passed box after box, crate after crate from nearby railroad cars and pallets up into the bellies of the waiting trucks. When the trucks had reached the limits of their own construction they pulled away slowly, engines and transmissions whining under the load. Others, rough-riding and empty, skated up to take their place and be burdened themselves.

Once loaded, the trucks, like the soldier ants, formed disciplined lines and waited to perform their part of the mission. The trucks, the weapons in them, and the men who loaded them, all discharged their duties with an eye toward a single goal: repelling the imminent Allied invasion of their newly acquired land.

Pieter's hands had been removed from the project along with his heart. His thoughts occasionally lingered over the fate of the transport, but his mind often raced ahead to the days that would follow. The concern was not for these nearby trains still coughing up their loads of bullets, but his train, the Berlin train, and its unfortunate destination.

The lieutenant was nearly as aloof from the scene as the major while the two stood near the main opening of the warehouse. The lieutenant watched the trucks, the railroad cars, and the soldiers scurrying with their loads with only a cursory interest. His attention rested on Pieter as his captain had directed, though the task proved increasingly boring as the major had been effectively neutered. Passing soldier ants coming within acceptable saluting distance still did so, oblivious to the major's new diminished role in the transport and possibly the German Army. Other soldiers, differentiated by their uniforms and demeanor, carrying sub-machine guns slung over their shoulders and cradled like loving children beneath their black arms, saluted as well, but addressed the lieutenant, one of their own, and not the man of rank in grey next to him.

From somewhere within the pack of weaving trucks a shiny black staff car suddenly materialized. It drove through the surrounding vehicles as though gifted with ambulance status. Weighted trucks locked up their brakes and skidded, shifting packed loads on their backs. The black car never took notice. Instead it blew an angry horn and sped away in the direction of the warehouse door.

The major and lieutenant spied the car and watched as it bore down on them. At a distance that had quickly become uncomfortable for the men, the car abruptly slowed, pulled to the side, and stopped sharply. As one, they recognized the driver to be Captain Rheinholt. When the captain stepped from the car, he was sneering.

"You needn't have been concerned, gentlemen. I knew exactly where you were."

The lieutenant laughed uneasily while Pieter stared again at the continued loading of the trucks.

"Are preparations in order?" the captain asked.

"You would know better than I," Pieter answered, still annoyed with the captain's attempt to rile him further.

"I suppose I would at that. Tell me, Lieutenant, how was your day?"

Pieter answered for him. "Uneventful and boring, I would imagine."

"True, Lieutenant?" Rheinholt inquired again.

"Yes, sir. Nothing to report."

"Oh, you mustn't put it that way. Major Von Strausser will misinterpret my having you accompany him. He will assume you were there to spy when in fact you were only along to help him recover from the trying ordeal of last night's butchered convoy. Let's hope tonight is far less disconcerting. Agreed, Major?"

"With you at the helm, Captain, I expect nothing less."

"I'm sure."

The conversation died a malingering death. Had the men been confined, words undoubtedly would have escalated to shouts and perhaps blows, but the scope of the transformed plant provided the option of stepping away, which the major did. With his hands clasped behind his back Pieter walked nearer the loading process. The lieutenant began to idly follow, but Rheinholt touched his arm and shook his head no.

"Forget it. He's finished. He just doesn't realize it. Tomorrow I'll file a report that will imprison him for a great many years. And that is if he is very, very fortunate."

The lieutenant did not respond. Instead he stood alongside the captain and mirrored his posture, following the beleaguered major now with only his eyes.

***

26

The safe house was lined with fighters. The go signal had been given and they had begun filing out in their customary fashion. Claire had several more minutes to wait and was still getting ready while Michel shadowed Renault. Paul was nowhere to be seen. Just as Sophie and David stepped in the back door, Renault and Michel emerged from the basement.

"Where's Paul?" Sophie asked excitedly as she almost ran into Renault.

"Out."

"Where?"

Renault looked at the doctor then back at Sophie. He was not worried about either, but practice formed the words in his mouth. "We're working tonight."

"Renault. Tell me where. I've got to talk to him right away."

"He's outside the city," he said as he glanced at his watch. "He's setting up for a hit. I imagine he's dug in on a hillside somewhere by now."

"Can you take us there?"

Michel jumped into the conversation. "Sophie, there's no way of knowing exactly where he'd be. He goes wherever he thinks he can do the best job. You know how he is."

"I do know how he is. That's why I have to find him."

Renault grabbed her arm and took her aside. Michel and David circled close behind. "What's going on?" Renault asked slowly.

"Valerie's alive."

The words took their time registering as Renault's hand fell away from Sophie's arm. "How?"

"She's in St. Louis Hospital. She's been there the whole time."

"Why weren't we told? Why didn't she let us know?"

"She couldn't. Let's go. I'll tell you on the way."

"We should wait until it's finished," Renault began to insist. "It isn't wise, for them or us, to be out on the roads nearby."

Now Sophie grabbed him and the tension in her jaw demonstrated her mood. "No. We have to tell him now, before the fight. One minute could be one minute too late with Paul. I know his mind."

"It won't be easy to find him. They'll be tucked in and scattered along the route."

"We have to try. Will you help?"

"Of course I will. But be mindful that an error now could jeopardize much more than a single person."

"I understand, but please let's hurry."

Renault turned over the mantle to Michel with no fanfare. "This part is yours tonight. See that everyone gets out of the barn on time. And back safe."

"I've got it."

"I know you do," Renault said as he shook Michel's hand. "Godspeed, son."

***

27

There was a small room at the nunnery that Monique had used on a great many occasions. In recent years it had become a haven of sorts when the temperature at her own home had driven her out as it had the night before. On other nights, when silk gifts were to be used against the unwitting giver, she had come to the room to prepare and then to recover. Tonight, Monique walked down the bare tiled hall and into the room with a cloak of sadness draped over her shoulders. Claire's rebuff was the fiercest yet, and the deteriorating relationship with her father was still ringing in her ears. It had survived in recent months on bare threads and scraps, but now it was as cold and ugly as dirty snow.

She walked into the simple room and sat on the tiny bed listening to her mind as it danced and fought with it all. Pushing to the front was Pieter. She was in love with him, knew it and felt it. The fall had been furious and she wanted it to continue. She wanted to sleep with him each night, wake with him each morning. Watch hand in hand as the days turned to months and years. While she felt these things in her heart of hearts she had still betrayed him, and it ate at her. How could she love him and use his love — his blind, trusting love for her — against him for the Resistance? She couldn't, and after tonight she wouldn't.

There was an understanding rising up in her that she could never bring back the Resistance fighters that tonight would set out against the Nazi column like wolves on the hunt. But there would be no more clandestine drops, no more notes on scraps of paper, no more stealing from untidy desks, and no more pillow talk on the affairs of the German military. Tonight she would go to the colonel as her parting gesture for the Movement. There would be no baiting for information. No plans for tomorrow night. And foremost, no sex. She would be company to a horny old man for a few hours, feign illness, and turn the colonel over to Sophie or someone else tomorrow. Tonight would be the end.

A smile broke across her face and her eyes came back to life, glistening and bright as the burdens slipped off her back. Behind the smile were the thoughts of how happy Claire would be, and her father, though he would require careful tending until he deemed fit to forgive her for past transgressions.

Pieter's handling would be even gentler. She could not confess the physical sins of the past or the choices she had made and seen executed at his expense. She would only love him day by day and year by year for the rest of her life. If it were in part a repayment for what she had done, so be it. Her past could never be erased with an apology and a tear. There would be no point in endangering through haphazard confession what they would make together out of the years to come. Though it occurred to her that these first days would be forever shrouded in lies, time would ease them she thought, as only time could. Perhaps one day when they woke to find themselves so firmly cemented together that the news from the past would settle around them like dust, only to be blown or brushed away, would she share with Pieter the events that transpired after they had per chance to meet. Or perhaps not even then.

The air surrounding her in the small room was clearer now, the dark clouds had been driven away by reason and decisions. There was renewed bounce in her movements as she slid across a small seat in front of the bureau dresser. As she rummaged through her makeup and began the careful application she winked at herself in the mirror. "You're retired, lady," she said with a smile. "It's over."

Like her sister, Claire was preparing for the events of the forthcoming night. But while Monique meticulously applied her makeup, all but humming to herself as she did, Claire was snapping the lid off a tin of boot polish with a large jagged knife. Monique eased rouge onto her high cheekbones while Claire coarsely streaked the boot polish across her face.

Claire was in the small bedroom at the safe house, getting dressed in the Resistance fighters' traditional black. The briefing had already been completed and through it Claire understood that tonight's raid was especially vital. If the information was accurate, and Renault had said it was, the Germans would be laying up enormous caches of weapons near the coast to repel an invasion from England. There was considerable uncertainty as to when the Allied Forces would attack, but little doubt as to the fact that they would. Where and how were also issues, but not to the Resistance. Claire and the others were only concerned with stopping German military might from reaching the shoreline. They realized that each bullet they could prevent from arriving at the coast was one less bullet an Allied soldier would have to stop with his blood.

Each sister continued getting dressed. Monique slipped into her silk stockings while Claire pulled on coarse black pants. The younger McCleash stomped her heels into her boots and laced them up tightly as her sister delicately eased into high-heeled shoes. Both sisters knelt by their respective beds and said a silent prayer for success and safety, then rose and crossed themselves.

As Claire stood from her brief communion with God, there was a slight knock at the door, and Michel stuck his head in.

"Hey, you decent?" he asked as he shielded his eyes and gazed at the floor.

"Nice of you to ask as you break in."

Michel dropped the chivalry charade with his hand visor. "Actually I was hoping you weren't."

"Oh, were you now?" Claire said with her much loved, but labored Irish accent. "Will you be knowing the traditional Celtic way of dealing with men who break into a defenseless lady's bedroom?" Claire raised an eyebrow as she picked up her knife and carefully ran her thumb the length of the blade.

"No I don't know it, but need I remind you that you're standing on French soil so your arcane laws mean nothing. Whereas I, being born and bred of France, feel obligated to educate you, a foreigner, to our traditions."

Claire waved the knife menacingly and forgot her accent. "I'm as French as you."

"When a man of high heritage enters a woman's bedroom," Michel said, ignoring Claire's words and her knife. "The lucky lady is presupposed to submit to his every pleasure."

"Is she now?" Claire said with a wicked smile as she put a foot on the bed and slid the knife into her boot.

"She is."

"And what would that pleasure be, your Grace?" she said as she dropped her foot to the floor and bowed low.

Before she could stand, Michel grabbed her and propelled them both onto the bed. They kissed recklessly, each running their hands through the other's hair and pushing their hips together in a grinding rhythm. When they paused for air, Claire laughed.

"What's so funny?"

"Look in the mirror," she directed.

Michel propped himself up far enough on the bed to see his reflection in the dresser mirror. His face was littered with black splotches of boot polish. She was watching beside him in the mirror until they both laughed and fell back on the bed.

"Let's go. It's almost time. I've pulled the job of hitting the charges," Michel said as he jumped off the bed. "Renault's not sure Natei is ready yet."

Now it was Claire's turn to prop herself up on an elbow. "That's the first time you ever got out of bed without taking off your pants."

"Disappointed?"

"Maybe."

Michel went back to the bed and knelt down alongside it so his face just cleared the mattress. For her part, Claire plopped back down on the pillow, her eyes even with Michel's.

"This is a real big one for us, Claire."

"I heard the same speech, remember?"

"Not that part. I mean for us. If this goes well I'm going to move into strategic work like Renault. He had to step out and left me to manage the house. When I move up for good, you're coming, too."

"Not me," Claire said as she sat up and slid off the bed. She went to the mirror and began reapplying the boot polish where it had been rubbed away.

"Don't be stupid. Look at what happened to Jon. He was an experienced fighter and now look at him. Dead. We'll still be doing our part, but we'll live to tell our children about it."

"We'd have to have sex in order to have children, and you just turned me down."

"Always have to say something smart, don't you?"

"Beats saying something dumb, like what you're saying right now."

"Claire, do you ever listen to General de Gaulle's speeches? He's asked us not to kill Germans," Michel said as he stood up.

"That was before."

"Do you know that the Nazis probably kill fifty Frenchmen for every Nazi officer we gun down?"

Claire turned away from the mirror. "You better catch up, Michel. That's old news. We backed off for a while, did what the General said, but the Germans don't kill prisoners any longer. They need men to work in Berlin and be their soldiers on the eastern front. De Gaulle knows that. We know that. And now you know it, too," she said condescendingly as she turned back to the mirror and ignored Michel's reflection behind her. "Unless you're trying to convince yourself otherwise for some reason."

"For possibly the first time, you are exactly right."

"About what?"

"I do have a reason for wanting out of the killing." Michel grabbed her and spun her around. "I want to live. And I want you to live. When this is over I want there to be an us. We can get married and have a family. Live normal."

"What's normal? All I can remember is Germans. Fighting them. Killing them. And I'd do it again. So don't preach at me, Michel. Right now is the time to kill as many Germans as we can."

He looked his young lover up and down. "What makes you think you're bulletproof?"

"What makes you think you're not?"

"Must you always play the smart-ass tough guy?"

Claire moved away from Michel to the door. "They haven't even mined the ore for the bullet that will get me. Okay?"

"No, Claire. It's not okay."

"We'll talk about it later, but I think we better find you another line of work."

"Claire—"

"Stop it! Will you just stop it?" She eased up at the door and managed to lower her voice as she turned back toward him. "If you want to be with me you better keep your gun because I plan on killing Germans for a long, long time. When everyone else is through with it, I'll still be hunting them down."

Michel shook his head. "Why, Claire? Because they're German?"

"Yes!" Claire said as though it pained her.

He didn't respond. He couldn't. Claire stared at him with eyes that seemed full of contempt. "You'd better be careful, Michel. If you think people like Renault don't get killed, you're wrong. The Nazis have taken as many Resistance fighters out of their nice warm beds as they've left bleeding from gunshots in the woods or alongside the road."

"That sounds strangely like a threat."

Claire's shoulders slumped hard. Her head fell backward, leaving her mouth hanging open. It was the look of a desperate lover. But she recovered, gave away her edge, and smiled as she approached the reluctant warrior.

"Goddamn it, Michel, you have become a pain in the ass!"

"Have I?"

"You have."

Her arms embraced him and rubbed his shoulders. "Now, listen to me. Everybody is a little tense over this one. You and I included. Let's get through tonight, then we'll talk. Alright? There isn't much more we can do anyway at this point. Am I right?"

"Naturally."

"Naturally. Is that anyway to talk to your future bride?"

He looked down at her, her eyes bright between the black polish. "Damn it, Claire, you're tough to figure out."

"Don't work at it so hard. Just enjoy me."

She kissed him delicately, and he flashed the slightest of smiles.

"Let's go," she reminded him excitedly as she reached for his hand and led him toward the door. "Are you with me?"

"Yes. But don't go getting us killed."

***

28

The Spartan nun's cubicle was left behind as Monique exited the nunnery and walked to the club. From a block away she saw an oversized grey staff car, presumably the colonel's, parked directly in front as promised. When she approached, a soldier got out from behind the wheel and jogged around to the curb and opened the rear door.

"Miss?"

"Thank you," Monique replied as she slid across the seat, knowing the soldier was discreetly admiring her silky legs as she pulled them into the car.

"My pleasure," he said as he closed the door then trotted around to the driver's side. "My pleasure."

The big car eased away from the curb and slithered along the city streets. Monique sat comfortably in the back looking out the windows, content that this would be the end of a difficult career. In the morning she would go to her major and piece together a shadowy life until the world's powers saw fit to leave them alone. The dream she harbored as she rode was encouraged by the twinkling lights of the fading city as they blinked good night to the car.

At the safe house, the guerilla fighters had nearly all gone. As Michel and Claire prepared to follow the exodus, Natei approached them. He was sweating and clutching a fistful of papers and a map Renault had given him.

"Are you ready?" he blurted.

The couple looked at each other with faces of disbelief. "Certainly," Michel answered for both, almost as a question. "We're the last out."

"Renault wanted me at the house to help him tonight, but then he disappeared. He wanted me to remind you of a couple of things," Natei said as he looked at the map in his quaking hands. "If the convoy is headed by a car or light truck, Renault said let it go. The heavy trucks will just ram through the wreckage. We'll never be able to stop them. We must wait. It's up to you, Michel, to detonate those charges at the proper time."

"Natei—"

"Otherwise Renault said we'll lose the whole damn thing!"

"Natei! We've got it."

"I know. I want to be certain, I mean, Renault wanted me to be certain, that's all. Remember, Claire, if there's a lead car, Michel will let it pass. Then you fill that son of a bitch full of lead. We'd love to get them all, but it's the armaments and trucks we're really after."

"Natei?" Claire asked with a marked gentleness that didn't match her black combat clothes.

"Yes?"

"We're ready. Trust us. We're ready."

As sudden as a thunderclap, Natei settled down. He looked at Claire and Michel through eyes that brimmed with tears. "I know. It's just...I don't think I can do this anymore. None of it. Not going out, not staying here."

Michel gripped his shoulder. "Relax, my friend. These have been difficult days, for you more than anyone. Give it some time."

"No. I've changed. I don't think any of this means anything anymore."

The words struck a harsh chord beneath Claire's painted face and as rapidly as the caring had come it vanished. "Hey, it means a lot!"

"Not to me. Not to Jon. No matter what we do tonight, tomorrow, he's still dead."

Michel stepped over Claire's gruff tone. "But we can save others."

"I don't care about others. Jon will always be dead."

Claire stepped away. "We've got to go. C'mon, Michel."

Natei looked up with surprise registering on his face.

Claire shot back to the look and her lover, "Hey, a minute ago you said we had to move!"

Michel tried to apply suave. "Natei, relax. We'll talk tomorrow. Let's all get through tonight first."

It was time to go. Michel took a step backward from Natei and judged the effect. Finding none, he turned and caught a glimpse of Claire's back as she slipped out the rear door of the safe house.

The lights of the city had disappeared from Monique's window. In their place was only the darkness of the French countryside. She had been picked up by underlings and driven to officers' hotels many times, but tonight the darkness seemed foreboding instead of cloaking her in its shadows of anonymity. Monique shook the feeling from her head, but it occurred to her that it was not just the dark, it was the quiet. Most drivers, either impressed or trying to impress, talked constantly. Many, no doubt under some guise of a friendly order from their masters, extolled the many attributes of their bosses, the men Monique was headed to see. Others, hoping against hope for a chance at her themselves, shared with her their many, generally fictitious, heroic exploits in the war. This driver, however, had yet to speak.

"You work for the colonel?" she asked, baiting the delinquent conversation.

"Sometimes."

"Where does he work anyway?"

"In the city, I guess."

"You don't know?"

"I'm not his regular driver."

"Where do you work then?"

"All over."

"How's that?"

"I'm a mechanic. I go where the work is."

"So, if we break down you can get us going, right?"

The driver didn't answer. Instead, they rolled along through the night in silence. That quiet was eventually interrupted by the rhythmic clicking of the turn signal as they approached Plank Road. The flasher lit up the front of the car in an eerie green light. Monique could see the driver's face bathed in the spooky glow. He seemed to be watching her as much as the road as the big car swung in a wide arc.

The colonel's car lumbered through the turn under the driver's hand and straightened out on the deserted road. From her place in the back seat, Monique strained to see into the dark ahead of the car's shaded headlights. In a few minutes she was rewarded when the outline of the Juneau Winery broke into view.

The driver reined in the car and turned again into the overgrown grass and dirt parking lot of the old factory. As it did, the car's lights shown on two widely spaced large German military trucks sitting in the lot. The trucks appeared only for an instant then vanished as the driver flicked off the headlights of the car. The engine was killed just as quickly as the car rocked to a stop.

The quiet driver immediately got out of the car and closed his door. Monique was temporarily blinded by the flash of the interior light as he did so. She could hear him walking around the car, but couldn't see a thing until the door opened next to her and the small overhead light glowed again. The silk of her legs preceded her across the seat, reversing her earlier motion. Predictably, the soldier's response was the same as before, but his leering was more blatant, protected as he was by the darkness.

When Monique stood up from the car she held onto the open door for a moment looking toward the winery. The rambling building was pitch black. She eased the door closed, but held it between where the interior light went out and the snap of the latch, with the thought that soon her eyes would adjust, but if they didn't like what they saw she could get back in the car.

"There are no lights on," she said inquisitively.

As an answer the driver pushed hard against the door, forcing it closed. The light went out. The soldier took her arm. "He's over here."

She took clumsy steps, hampered by the dark, her heels, and the pull of the soldier. After several yards the grip on her arm faded, and her eyes became more accustomed to the starlight. She could faintly see the driver walking on ahead of her. Anxious for the escort, such as it was, Monique tried to stop him with another lighthearted question.

"What's the colonel doing, hiding in the dark?"

As soon as the words hit the parking lot, so did the bright headlights of the trucks. Monique was standing dead in the middle of the lot, flooded from either side by the headlights. Instantly blinded, she shielded her eyes from the high beams of the trucks.

"Sorry, Frenchy," came a voice from beyond the lights. "No colonel here. Just us poor enlisted men."

As she looked into the glare, Sergeant Sneitz, Private Timic, and a corporal, stepped out into the lights to join her driver.

"Hi ya, Frenchy," Sneitz said as he flicked away a toothpick from his mouth. "Remember me?"

***

29

Not far away, Claire and Michel were in route to the raid site. As Michel drove along through the dark, Claire stared out the window as Monique had done over these same roads a few minutes before. Knowing the route like she did, and that Plank Road was not far ahead, brought to Claire's mind her sister. She attributed the thought to the proximity of the upcoming road, but as quickly gave it over to one of those not uncommon occurrences that happen between sisters when events push awareness to extraordinary heights. An unsettling feeling welled up further in her throat as each revolution of the wheels brought her closer to Plank Road. Finally, words burst from her so unplanned that they startled her as much as Michel.

"Swing down Plank Road."

"What?"

"Plank Road. It's coming up on the right. Pull down it. I want to check on something."

"There isn't time."

"It'll only take a second."

Michel's head flipped back and forth between the road ahead and his companion. "No, Claire. We don't have time. If we're not in position we'll lose the lead trucks."

Claire glanced at her watch and barely distinguished the time on its luminescent dial. "There's time. We'll make it. Please?"

Now Michel nearly ignored the road entirely as he looked at her with a stunned expression on his face. "What's wrong with you? Everything's planned down to the minute. Knock it off!"

When Michel raised his voice it fueled Claire's tendencies and excited her all the more. Plank Road was nearly on them as well. "Turn down the road, Michel!"

"Hell I will!"

The anxiousness in her throat jumped at Michel's strong voice. In a maneuver that seemed more instinctive than anything else, Claire ripped her 45 caliber automatic from her belt and jammed it at Michel's head.

"Hell you won't! Now, turn down the road!"

Michel's eyes lost their wandering nature and became glued on the road. When Plank Road came up, he did as Claire's pistol ordered. As the car straightened out he spoke softly, both hands on the wheel, eyes straight ahead.

"I never thought it'd be you. Not you, of all people."

"What are you talking about?"

"You. This. Isn't that a gun pointed at my head? I guess that's why you always acted like you were bulletproof. Did you have a signal or something so your Nazi friends wouldn't blow your head off?"

Claire eased the gun back into her lap. "Don't be stupid. Monique is down at the Juneau Winery. I want to make sure she's alright."

Michel chanced a look at Claire. "What?"

"Monique said she was going to meet some colonel at the winery. She asked me to go, but I said no. That ought to make you happy."

"Are you kidding? You stuff a gun in my ear so we can go watch your sister bang some kraut? And you call me stupid?"

"Don't say that," Claire said as she motioned ahead with her pistol. "There it is. Kill the lights and pull off."

"We're turning around right now."

"Michel. I'll run up quick. Make sure she's okay and we're gone. C'mon. We're already here."

Reluctantly, Michel turned off the lights and slowed the car to a crawl. "Damn it, Claire! We don't have time for this!"

"This is far enough. Stop the car."

***

30

"What is this?" Monique said with a hint of trembling in her voice for the answer was already clear. She held out for a reply in the pool of light while Sneitz and the other soldiers began to surround her. Each of the men flashed confident lurid smiles between themselves and through Monique as their eyes undressed her.

"We're gonna have us that little party we talked about. I had to leave the other night, kind of sudden like as I remember, but now it's just you...and me. No major. Oh, and a few of my closest friends."

"Take me back to the club this instant!"

Sneitz chuckled as he walked away from her toward the hood of one of the trucks. His shadow loomed out in gargantuan proportions across the parking lot as he stood in front of one of the headlights. The shadow jumped across Monique leaving only a black silhouette of the sergeant against the truck, but Monique could tell that the figure was taking off his gun belt. With a resounding thud and a metallic clang, Sneitz tossed his pistol belt on the hood of the truck and began descending on Monique with slow deliberate strides.

"Back to the club? I don't think so, Frenchy. We gotta have us some fun first. Right, boys?"

The men continued circling her like wolves. They were in no rush, and the circle did not tighten quickly. Instead, the men toyed and laughed, giddy over what was about to happen. They alternated going to the truck to undo their gun belts and soon all had been voluntarily deposed of their pistols.

"See, baby," the once timid driver said as he held out his empty hands. "No weapon." Then he grabbed his crotch. "But I still got a gun!"

The soldiers all laughed as the driver bounced up and down at Monique, fondling himself.

"Hey, Sarge," Timic laughed. "How'd that little poem go they taught us in rifle school?"

The sergeant cocked his finger like a pistol and held it in the air. "This is my weapon." Then he grabbed his crotch with his other hand. "And this is my gun. One is for shooting. And one is for fun!" The men all roared.

"Wanna see my gun, you fancy French bitch?" the corporal bellowed.

Monique kept moving in the now tightening circle. "Wait a minute. You don't want to do this."

"We don't?" the sergeant laughed as he slapped the shoulder of the driver. "Hey? Do you wanna do this?"

"You bet your ass I wanna do her. I mean do this. I meant, do this!"

Again the laughter soared, relieving whatever tension or anxiety remained within the pack.

"Listen to me a minute," Monique pleaded.

"No! I'm not listening to nothing! No more!" Sneitz screamed.

"Well," Monique continued anyway. "Maybe sometime we could—"

The sergeant stepped up and slapped her face. "We could what, bitch? Have us a dance?"

"Yeah, dance with her, Sarge."

Monique's attacker grabbed her neckline and with one sharp pull ripped the front of her dress down. The corporal grabbed her from behind around the waist and picked her up. When her feet came off the ground she kicked wildly at Sneitz, catching him twice but only with glancing blows. When the soldiers paused, laughing at Monique's flailing attempt at the sergeant, her manicured nails clawed the air behind, ripping into the face of the corporal holding her in the air.

Though her high-heeled shoes had essentially missed their mark, the fingernails found theirs and cut deep. The corporal, his face already trickling blood, tightened his grip on Monique, picked her up higher, and whipped her violently to the ground.

"You bitch!" he yelled as he dabbed at the blood collecting on his face.

The blood only served up more hysterical laughter from the other soldiers as they began tightening the circle around their victim.

***

31

Claire was silently creeping through the thin woods toward the winery. She stopped in the near black night and listened stubbornly to voices off in the distance. In her concentration she didn't notice that Michel had followed her, but a footfall behind her put her on full alert. With a move that would have been blurry in broad daylight, Claire spun and leveled her pistol at Michel's face.

"Goddamn it!" she screamed in a whisper. "Don't sneak up on me like that!"

Michel slowly pushed the gun out of his eyes. "Don't you ever get tired of putting that thing in my face?"

"Shhh! I hear voices, but I can't tell what's going on. We have to get closer to those lights over there."

Claire didn't wait for Michel to agree or not. She bolted off deeper into the trees and began to circle toward the parking lot. A reluctant Michel followed, but immediately fell behind when he tried to check his watch. Branches swept in on him as he looked down from the faint path Claire was blazing. He fought briefly with the tree limbs then broke clear and took off after Claire, frustration with the branches and his partner beginning to wear on him.

He caught up with her very near the edge of the parking lot, a hundred feet from the colonel's car. Claire was peering into the lot from behind a thin tree. She didn't look at Michel as he came up beside her this time, but craned her neck all the harder to see into the lot.

The pair could see the upper bodies of the four soldiers over the hood of the car. The men were shouting and shuffling their feet as they looked down at the ground.

"What the hell are they doing?" Claire whispered. "Where's Monique?"

"She's probably in the winery with the colonel."

Claire glanced in the direction of the building. "It's dark."

"So? Maybe they want privacy."

"Maybe."

"Could be she didn't even come. Though that seems unlikely. Maybe she couldn't find anyone to come with her and decided against it."

"I don't think she'd pass on a colonel."

"Forget it, Claire. We've got to go."

"Just a second."

Claire slipped quietly away from her tree just far enough to see the soldiers from head to toe. The sight of Monique on the ground shook her.

"Shit!"

Claire instantly tightened her grip on the pistol and took a rushed step toward her sister, but Michel lunged for her and pulled her back into the trees.

"No! We can't risk it!"

"That's my sister over there!"

"I see her. How do you know she's not there because she wants to be?"

"In the dirt? You asshole! Besides, those are enlisted men. Never!"

"We have to leave. Right now! They're not going to hurt her."

Monique threw a small stone from the ground and hit Sneitz in the face. He flinched sharply then retaliated by delivering a crushing kick to Monique's ribs. "Goddamn French whore!" he yelled as he undid his pants and dropped down on her.

"Like hell they're not!" Claire said as she again leaped toward the Germans.

Michel grabbed her gun hand and tackled her to the ground. She struggled against him silently, fighting her lover for her sister. Michel pinned her down easily and shook her.

"Claire! Claire! Think! If we're not at the rendezvous point to detonate those charges, the arms in those trucks will kill thousands of men in the invasion! Thousands, Claire!" Claire continued to fight beneath him as he continued the lecture. "We can't risk all those lives over this!"

"I'm going, Michel!"

"No!"

"They're raping her, you moron!"

"Listen to what you're saying! You're going to risk thousands against one! We don't know who's around here. They could alert the convoy. Goddamn it, Claire! They won't kill her! But Allied soldiers will die!"

Claire listened to none of it. She struggled more fiercely than before. Michel shook her violently, trying to get her to understand. "Claire, they're only going to take what she gives away every night anyway! Now let's go!"

Claire laid still for an instant and Michel relaxed his grip. As soon as he did, Claire broke free and rammed her pistol in his face for the third time that night.

"Say that about my sister again and I'll kill you right here!"

Michel was no longer impressed with her gunplay or intimidated by her temper. "Put that down. Let's get out of here!"

Claire realized she could not sway him. To accent a plea, she shook her gun at the Germans. "I'm not leaving her like that!"

"Why? Damn it, Claire! She was going to screw somebody! So it's a sergeant instead of an officer. Who knows how many soldiers are around here. One mistake and you could blow the raid. Hell, you could expose the whole Resistance!"

This time she did listen. The listening was slight, but there. She didn't listen while pasting together a reply, instead she heard each word and felt the bite as their teeth penetrated her skin and chipped her bones. Despite his poor timing there was truth in Michel's words that Claire could not deny. She looked hard back and forth from the messenger to Monique while the words and Michel waited.

"I've got to help her," she said.

Again, Claire didn't wait for an answer. She understood what it would be anyway. To wait any longer risked being tackled again, so as soon as she tendered her decision she jumped into the dark and sprinted away. Michel took a single step after her, of one prepared to stop, not help, then turned away. "Well you're going without me," he whispered into the dark.

Michel hadn't jogged twenty feet in the direction of his car before he heard Claire coming up behind him.

"Wait!" she said in the loudest voice she dared.

Michel stopped as a panting Claire broke in on him.

"Claire, that was the smartest decision—"

"Give me your pistol," she said as she held out her hand.

Without another word Michel pulled his 45 caliber automatic from his waist and shoved it into her hand. As soon as he did Claire ran off through the trees. He watched for a moment as Claire sprinted away toward the parking lot, a 45 in each hand. Michel ended his brief vigil and ran off toward the car, armed only with the feeling that he was doing the right thing, for the Resistance, himself, and the unknown Allied soldiers.

***

32

The German staff car and the soldiers flickered between the trees as Claire raced by through the trees. She circumvented the parking lot and came out of the woods and brush near the truck farthest from the men. The truck would be her cover as she fought it out with the Germans.

She crouched low and skimmed down the side of the truck until she was at the front fender near the headlamp. The bright light illuminated the parking lot and also shielded her from sight. She could have stood and not been seen as long as she stayed behind the light, though the men were so totally consumed with Monique that perhaps the bright light itself wasn't necessary.

Only when she was in position did Claire peek up over the fender at her sister. The scene unfolding in the parking lot staggered Claire so much that she felt a rush of dizziness come over her. Monique was splayed in the grass and dirt. Sneitz was on her, driving himself into her as he held her legs apart with his own. His hands held up her dress at her waist and his face was buried in her neck while his partners tore at her bra and groped her breasts and bottom between pinning her arms and legs to the ground. The soldiers' laughter mingled with Monique's stifled cries.

Claire teetered at the sight and sound and fell away from the fender. Her legs weakened beneath her as she spun on one heel and collapsed against the oversized tire of the truck. The back of her hands, each holding a pistol, came up to her face and rubbed at her eyes as though trying to wake from a horrific dream. When the sounds of the nightmare lingered, Claire, afraid of what she would see, once more peered cautiously over the fender. Only her eyes cleared the rounded metal, but that was enough.

Just as Claire caught sight of her sister, Monique managed to bite the sergeant's shoulder.

"You bitch!" Sneitz screamed as he reared up on her.

For her part, Monique spit in his face, but it only brought her more pain as the sergeant grabbed her by the throat with one hand and punched her like a hammer in the face. Monique went limp beneath him, unconscious.

The rest of the soldiers, on seeing her knocked out, released their vise-like grips on her arms and legs. Timic continued to fondle her while the others stood up from the dirt, dusted themselves off, and waited their turn, not so subtly rubbing the front of their pants.

Claire leveled both pistols across the fender of the truck. They too were shielded by the headlight. She understood that the flash of the weapons would immediately give her location away, but by then at least two of the unarmed soldiers would be dead.

"Like shooting fish in a barrel," Claire whispered to herself as she sighted in a pistol on Timic's back. But as she looked over the sights of the gun she also took in Monique, lying at Timic's feet. In spite of all the violence she was enduring, Monique was too near the line of fire to risk a shot and Claire suddenly knew it. A ricochet or fragment could easily kill her.

The impromptu training of the Resistance whispered in her ear. Claire needed a diversion, something to draw the men away from Monique so they could be dispatched to hell without risk to her sister. Whatever it was it had to come together quickly. Though Monique remained gratefully unconscious, the rape was continuing as brutally as before.

Claire dropped back down by the tire and inadvertently kicked an old wine bottle. Scattered around her on the ground were a few other discarded bottles, remnants from the active days of the winery. She jammed one of the 45's in her pants, snatched up a bottle, and crouching along the truck, hurriedly retraced her steps backward until she was hidden by the cab. Only then did she stand. Her hand gripped the old dark glass by its throat and tested its heft. She pulled her arm back preparing to heave the bottle across the lot, well away from her sister. When the soldiers moved to investigate she'd open fire.

Her arm was cocked, but once again Claire checked her actions. The bottle and her arm dropped to her side and Claire literally stomped her feet in frustration.

"Shit! Why not just tell them to go get their guns?"

Claire ventured yet another look at Monique's plight. The sergeant was rolling lazily on her, alternating his thrusts with seemingly gentle waves as he gasped for breath. His face was covered in sweat and dust, all turning to mud, as he rubbed against Monique's dirty cheeks and tongued her unresponsive mouth. Timic and the corporal began pushing each other and wrestling, almost playfully, as though warming up for their turn at the attack, or perhaps vying for status like animals in the wild — who would be next to mate after the alpha male sergeant.

The driver was standing quietly alongside Monique with his hand down the front of his unbuckled pants gently massaging his erection. He bent down to stroke Monique's naked thigh with his free hand, but Sneitz swung at his head. When the driver stood and stepped back, out of range of the swinging fist, Sneitz gripped the same naked flesh and possessively pulled it up closer to his own bare hip. The rush of the miniature conquest excited him and he began plunging harder into his victim. The sergeant drove Monique by quarter inches through the dirt and back to consciousness, her ragged hair bouncing over the torn dress and her exposed breasts with each thrust.

Monique's own flesh suddenly provided Claire with the makings of the ultimate diversion. Tears of frustration which had gathered in Claire's eyes were brushed away violently, along with the boot polish, onto the sleeve of her black sweater as the plan began to take shape.

The gun in her hand was the first to hit the ground, followed by the bottle and then Michel's gun from her waistband. Claire tore her sweater out of her pants and off over her head. She used the sweater like a towel to wipe the remaining tears, gathered sweat, and boot polish off her face. It was then haphazardly tossed aside as her hands ripped at her bra until it snapped free from her chest. She went to the ground with the bra tagging along looped over one hand. There she traded it for a pistol which she immediately stuck in her waistband at the small of her back. Her hands then sought out the second pistol and the old wine bottle.

Claire stood up and leaned back against the cab of the truck. The metal was cold on her bare skin and offered a moment's relief from the heat the events of the night had brought to her. Her leaning also pressed the pistol in the back of her pants deep into the small of her back, pinching her and reminding her it was ready. She took a deep breath and rolled her shoulders trying to relax. Her heart was pounding. She was sweating. For the last time she wiped at her eyes with the back of her very busy hands. The pistol she held smelled like burnt gunpowder. In her other hand, the bottle caught a shimmer of light as it passed across her face. It winked at her - the go signal. With one hand clenching a pistol behind her back, alongside the one in her waistband, and the other hand swinging the empty wine bottle, Claire stepped bare-breasted out into the lights of the trucks.

"Hey there. This a private party?" she slurred deliberately as she swung the empty bottle up to her lips. Claire wiped her mouth on her bare arm as the soldiers, each startled at first by another voice, quickly shifted gears at the sight of what had wandered in on them.

"Hell no. There's lotsa party for everybody," the driver said as he pulled his hand out of his pants. "Come on in."

Claire pointed with her bottle at the erection pushing against his pants. "You sure you got anything left? Looks to me like you was having your own personal little thing going on there. I wouldn't want to make your fist jealous."

The other soldiers cracked in laughter at Claire's joke and stepped further away from Monique who only now was beginning to stir. Even Sneitz had momentarily stopped grunting as he looked across the parking lot at the half-naked Claire.

"No, baby," the driver said smiling through his embarrassment. "I was just keeping it warm for you."

The driver walked toward Claire, but was stopped by the sergeant. "Where the hell did she come from?"

"Who cares?" the corporal muttered.

Claire picked it up regardless. "My friend said there was a party up here tonight."

"Yeah, Sarge. We told her to bring a friend."

"I got sidetracked with a couple of boys. They were cute, but just couldn't keep up I guess. They dropped me off up the road." Claire began to stagger a little and laugh. "I think I lost my sweater..."

The driver began unbuttoning his shirt, but in his aroused state found the buttons uncooperative. Instantly impatient and eager to push his bare chest against Claire's, he tore at his shirt, popping whatever remained of the buttons. As he took the shirt off he walked several yards away from Monique. One was now in position.

"Here, baby. You can slip into this if you're cold. Can't have you getting a chill, can we?"

Claire leaned demonstratively as though looking around the soldiers. "What's wrong with my friend? She drunk?"

"As hell," Timic said as the sergeant resumed his assault, having already forgotten about Claire.

"Looks like her dress got torn," Claire said as though puzzled.

"She wanted to play rough. Even bit the old Sarge there," Timic continued as he pointed and laughed.

Claire took another pretended drink from the wine bottle. "You guys like to play rough?"

The driver was getting closer, walking slow and dramatic. "Any way you want it, baby. Any way you want it."

The wine bottle became a pointer once more as Claire waved it at the lagging pair of soldiers. "How about your friends there? They waiting in line to get bit, or do they want something a little... friendlier?"

Claire tossed away the wine bottle to punctuate the sentence and undid the snap of her pants, leaving her thumb hanging provocatively in the zipper.

Timic and the corporal began walking through the lights, away from Monique and their guns. "This hellcat's all yours, Sarge," the corporal blurted out. "This other one's got her claws pulled back."

Two and three had almost fallen in line. Things were nearly right for the killing. Claire's grip on the pistol behind her back tightened and her finger slipped in over the trigger. She looked quickly at the pumping sergeant who was struggling again as Monique woke beneath him. With his pants around his ankles he was no immediate threat. He would be the last to die.

In order to clear her sister completely from the firing Claire stepped sideways in the parking lot, effectively aligning the three soldiers.

"Hey, baby? Where you going?" the driver sneered. "I've got something for you," he continued as he undid his pants.

"No," Claire said as her free hand slid nonchalantly from her zipper to her back and firmly gripped the second pistol. "I've got something for you!"

Both 45's snapped to the front like cobras striking. Claire was squeezing the triggers as they came around and the first bullets were on their way before the soldiers scarcely saw the guns. One round went through the driver's hand and deep into his groin. The first bullet from the other pistol hit him square in the chest. He and the others froze as more bullets exploded from Claire's pistols.

The driver pulled his hand away from his pants and looked with wonder and shock at his own blood. Before the pain could set in he fell over face down dead in the dirt.

The next rounds struck the corporal in the abdomen. As Claire continued to pull the trigger on her automatics the recoil raised the guns in her hands with each shot causing each succeeding bullet to hit slightly higher than the last. The pattern was obvious on the corporal's torso as bullets struck him in rapid succession from his belly to his throat. The impact of the 45's propelled the dying soldier backward through the air. He landed with lifeless eyes in a small cloud of dust a few feet from Monique's head.

Timic had turned away from the flames shooting from the pistols. He ran for the guns, but Claire's bullets out raced him. A trio slammed into his back. He arched in pain and dropped to his knees a few yards from the sergeant and Monique who had been brought to total consciousness by the reports of Claire's guns. Claire lowered one pistol and took careful aim at the soldier's back with the other. The report of the gun came, and Timic fell forward on his hands. He lifted his head, drooling blood, and stared through eyes filled with terror at Monique's face.

Claire lowered her pistol and walked deliberately through the acrid smoke of her guns toward the stubborn soldier. Timic labored back to his knees as she came up behind him. Claire stuck one pistol in the back of his head. The other she pointed at the sergeant and cocked her head to the side as he started to move.

"Uh unh," she said over the sights of the gun. The sergeant froze.

Claire never even looked at the bullet-ridden Timic, wobbling on his knees. Her eyes were locked on the sergeant. She scarcely saw her sister either or she may not have fired. But she did, without looking, point blank into Timic's head. Blood, brain, and bone splattered across Monique and the sergeant as the bullet detonated the soldier's head and face. His body slumped to the ground, and what remained of his brain oozed out and pushed away the grass and dirt before it.

The guns, dripping blood and surrounded by smoke, leveled on the sergeant. "Get off my sister," Claire said in a voice as cold as arctic ice.

Sneitz pushed himself up very gently off Monique, who scooted backwards on her heels and hands out from underneath him. As she did, her eyes were riveted on her tormenter, and she inadvertently stumbled against the corporal's body. She jumped, and the face that had been so beautiful contorted with insane fear.

"Monique," Claire said calmly. "Monique! Come over here behind me. And mister, you keep your ass on the ground."

The sergeant had pulled himself into sitting up. His hands were dusty, and his face was smudged with lipstick and dirt between droplets of splashed blood. He was struggling to get his pants up as he jabbered. "Ho...hold on a minute. She's not hurt. You can p-put them guns down."

Monique had made little attempt to move behind her sister. She was sitting in a stupor, surrounded by blood and dirt, trying to reassemble her torn dress over her bare shoulders.

"You okay?" Claire asked tenderly as she cast a fleeting glance at her sister while leaving the pistols trained on the trembling sergeant.

Without answering, Monique continued trying to slip her bruised arm through the tatters of the dress. She winced and moaned, but the pain brought her life. With great effort, like a newborn fawn, Monique clumsily got to her feet. She staggered away from Claire, the sergeant, and the bodies of the soldiers.

"Monique? Come back here, honey. Wait for me," Claire said as she took a step after her dazed sister.

"See?" Sneitz said rather gleefully. "She's alright. Probably just wants to get herself cleaned up." He suddenly reached into his pants, and Claire intuitively moved the guns forward. "Wait! It's just a wallet," he screamed. His head was down and he was holding the billfold up in a trembling hand for inspection. "It's just a wallet."

Not hearing a shot that would have meant his death, he fumbled through the wallet and retrieved all his money. His hands continued to shake as he held the cash out to Claire. "Here. It's f-for the dress. I...I got a little carried away, is all. Here, take it!" The money trickled out of his dirty hands onto the dust. "Take all of it," he mumbled as he dropped his head and began weeping like a child.

Monique had continued across the parking lot, erratically weaving through the headlights of the trucks. As Claire watched her, the sergeant was drawn by the silence and lifted his head. What he saw widened his reddening eyes. Monique was at the hood of the truck pulling his own pistol from his gun belt.

Sneitz brought his hands up instinctively as Monique turned the gun on him. "NO! Please!" he screamed as he jumped to his feet.

Claire fired as a reflex to the quick move. Her bullet blasted into the sergeant's hip and spun him around and back to the ground. As he writhed in pain Claire took a step toward him and brought both guns up to finish the job.

Sudden gunfire from the side caused her to jump away and drop to a knee, pistols at the ready, but it was Monique, blindly jerking the trigger on the sergeant's Luger P-08. Crying and covered with blood and dirt, Monique staggered at the sergeant, awkwardly pointing the semi-automatic pistol with both hands. The gun blindly jumped dramatically each time she fired, but as she came closer, her bullets began finding their mark.

The first rounds to connect struck the sergeant in the groin. He grabbed his crotch with both hands and lurched up from the dirt. As Claire looked on, Monique continued firing. Sneitz was getting hit in the arms and legs. Other bullets were narrow misses and sent puffs of dust up from the ground.

Monique's eyes were wide and wild as she staggered purposefully nearer the wounded man. She could barely see through her tears to shoot, but she pulled the trigger as fast as possible. Proximity proved her greatest ally. She was almost standing above the battered sergeant when the last of her bullets shattered the bones in his face and ended his torment.

The gun was empty, and the sergeant had ceased moving, but Monique kept tugging at the trigger and staring at her victim. Smoke from the gun circled her hands as the tears ran down her cheeks. They left clean streaks in the dust and mixed with blood until they fell as dirty pink water from her chin.

Claire eased one of her 45's into her waistband and stepped over cautiously to her sister. She reached up gently and pulled the smoking pistol from Monique's hands.

"It's okay, Mo. He's dead. He won't hurt you anymore."

Claire threw aside the empty German gun and slipped her arm around her sister. Monique began to cry uncontrollably, faltering as her arms collapsed to her sides. Claire held her and supported her to the ground until Monique sat in the dirt, crying on Claire's bare shoulder. With a hand still clenching her pistol, Claire tentatively patted her sister's back, trying to sooth away the hurt and stop the tears.

***

33

Other guns blazed in the French hills nearby. The raid that had been so precisely orchestrated ran head long into a German buzz saw. The convoy came along as designed, led by Pieter driving Rheinholt's car while the captain and the lieutenant rode along. The Nazi minesweeper was moving too fast to do much good, but the armored trucks that followed smothered the explosive charges Michel had detonated. His arrival nearly coincided with that of the convoy, and much to his surprise, he found Paul angrily manning the detonators. When Paul saw Michel scampering down the hill he abandoned the charges, picked up his machinegun, and bolted across the hill to a better assault position.

Michel called after him with all his might but was quickly drowned out by the advance of the German column and the explosions set off beneath his hands. Rather than block the road as had been done on previous raids, the explosions merely signaled the Nazis to attack. Tarps flew away from the backs of several trucks revealing lights and mounted machine guns. This time the soldiers stayed with their vehicles, utilizing them for cover and staying clear of the tripwires alongside the road.

The monstrous German lamps illuminated the hillsides and the startled guerilla fighters. The lights served to blind the guerillas and hold them as targets for the machine-gunners below. The fighters fired down into the road, but their muzzle flashes attracted more bullets than they sent. Like ducks in a row, the Resistance fighters began to fall under the heavy Nazi strafing. Paul, nearest the convoy, was one of the first to go down.

Michel was a hundred feet away flat on the ground. He had been down when he set off the charges and had stayed down when the Germans stepped out from behind their secret cloak. When Paul was knocked backward Michel began to crawl to him. Clumps of earth jumped between the men as the Germans poured it on. But other fighters, still standing, still firing, eventually drew the machine guns away. By the time Michel reached him, Paul was bleeding from several bullet wounds. The weary champion raised his head ever so slightly and touched the blood that oozed from his chest. He looked at the blood in the glare of the floodlights and, with a strange sense of pride and relief, showed it to Michel.

"Finally...," he smiled.

Michel could do nothing for him, and even if he could, he understood that Paul would not want it. Instead, he took the bloody hand and held it. Michel placed his other hand beneath Paul's head and cradled it while the firefight raged on around them.

"Hey, Michel...Look after Sophie and Claudine for me?"

"Sure, Paul."

"Tell them...I'm going to see Val...and I couldn't be happier..."

Paul's smile locked on his lips, but his eyes lost their focus as his body slipped beneath the scythe of Death.

"I'll tell them."

No sooner had Michel spoken then he heard Sophie's voice battling with the sounds of the fight, screaming for Paul through the trees.

***

34

C laire eventually looked over Monique's head around the parking lot now littered with bodies. "Monique. We can't stay here much longer."

Her sister continued to grapple with tears, but in time brought them under a modicum of control. Only then did she notice that Claire was topless.

"You're not wearing a blouse," Monique said with a tremor running through her voice.

"Yeah, you noticed that, too?" Claire smiled around the slightest of laughs. "It's over by that truck. Here," she said, pulling Monique to her feet. "Come help me find it."

After Claire had turned Monique away from the parking lot and the dead soldiers she brushed at her dress, knocking off as much dirt and grass as she could. She pulled the sleeve of Monique's dress together with the shoulder yolk and tied a tiny knot to hold it in place.

"There you are. Good as new," Claire said quickly, though she could see Monique's face was already swelling from the blows it had suffered. "Now that you're all covered up, let's see if we can find something for me."

Monique walked very slowly, supporting her ribs while Claire supported her. When they reached the truck, Monique sat on the running board while Claire felt around on the ground for her sweater. The bra turned up first, but she ignored it. When she located the sweater she pulled it on hurriedly and returned to the running board.

"There. That's better. Don't you think?"

Her sister didn't answer, she just leaned heavily against the truck door. Monique was weighted down by the injuries she had suffered, physical and mental, but also by the knowledge, only now striking her, that she had killed a man.

Monique looked up at her benefactor. "Claire. I shot that man."

Claire held up in her hurried attempt to leave, but said nothing.

"I killed a person," Monique whispered as she looked away into the darkness.

There was a moment's hesitation before Claire began to relieve her sister's burden. "No, you didn't. I killed him. You missed."

Monique looked up again, wanting to believe. "I missed?"

"You missed. Oh, you winged him a couple of times to teach him a lesson, but I think you only hit him in the foot. I was behind you emptying my clip into the son of a bitch. Didn't you hear my guns?"

"I don't know..."

Claire knelt down and took her sister's hands. "Look at these, all manicured and painted up. You couldn't hit the English Channel from the beach with these things."

"Is that true?" Monique asked slowly, still dazed.

"Sorry, Mo. You're no Resistance fighter yet. You have to kill a German first, and you're still batting zero. It's back to the Café of Lights for you."

Suddenly Monique got a wild look in her eye and almost lunged at her sister. "No!" she cried as her eyes sent new tears on their way. "I'm not going back there! I'm finished! I want to get married!"

Claire held her and stroked her hair. "I know, Mo. I was only teasing. You don't have to do that any longer. No more. No more."

Claire brought Monique back from her misery and eased her against the truck door. When Claire stood up she leaned over her sister into the truck and pushed every knob she could feel until the headlights went out. "There's bound to be patrols out after that armament shipment gets hit. It wouldn't do for them to find this mess. Are you ready to travel?"

The answer was Monique's feet steadying themselves beneath her. Only then did either sister realize that Monique's shoes were missing.

"My shoes are gone," Monique said like a little girl looking down at her feet.

"I'll find them."

"No!" Monique shuddered as she looked around at the long shadows of the parking lot. "Don't leave me!"

Claire took hold of her sister again, and they moved from the truck across the parking lot as though attached at the hip. Claire steered Monique toward the other truck and away from the bodies as best she could. When they reached it, Claire leaned her sibling against its fender.

"Rest here while I get your shoes," Claire said, but Monique snatched her arm. "It's okay," Claire comforted. "I see them. They're right over there. Here," she said as she slipped from Monique's grip. "You watch me."

Claire backed away from her sister into the lot. "See me? I'm right here. I won't go anywhere."

Claire glanced back and forth from Monique's frightened eyes to the ground. Her awkward steps caused her to stumble slightly against the body of the sergeant. "It's okay. Everything's fine. Here's they are. See?" she said as she knelt and groped with her hands as her eyes continued darting from her sister to the pumps in the dirt. "I've got them. Here you go," Claire said as she sprinted across the lot and began helping Monique with the once glamorous heels.

As Monique finished slipping on her shoes, Claire examined her pistols in one of the truck's lights. She released the clip on the first and estimated the remaining number of rounds from its side before thrusting the magazine back into the gun and the gun into her waistband. She repeated the same procedure on her second pistol.

Before she retrieved her sister, Claire snatched up two of the remaining German Lugers from the hood of the truck. She used the butt of one to smash out the headlight she had just used to check her ammunition. Then, with both of the slender pistols in one hand, she threw her other arm around Monique and helped her to her feet.

"Time to go," she said as she assisted Monique around the front of the truck. When they passed the other headlight, Claire stopped, sighted off the way to the colonel's car, then cracked the light with the Lugers. It burned out, giving up a slight puff of smoke in its dying orange glow as the parking lot and the bodies in it came under complete darkness.

As the pair limped across the lot in the dark, Claire thought of the raid for the first time since she had left Michel. Although her firefight had only lasted a few seconds she was reasonably certain the raid must have begun. She tried to look at her watch, but Monique's weight hampered her. Her mind argued with her that the convoy may have been late or the timing slightly off. Any number of things could have delayed it and left the door open for Claire to do the job she was supposed to do. But the weight of her sister, leaning on her for a change, whispered that even if the convoy drove to the coast unmolested because of her, she would do it all over again.

When they reached the car, Claire felt along its passenger side until she came to the front door handle. The interior light was blinding at first, as it had been to Monique what seemed like hours before, but it allowed Claire to gently set her sister on the seat before closing the door and racing around to the driver's side.

Once behind the wheel Claire tossed the pair of German pistols on the dash and fired the engine to life. "Here we go," she said as she flipped on the headlights and threw the car in reverse. The clutch popped, causing the car to leap backward where Claire's heavy foot on the brakes made the car skid onto Plank Road.

"Better hold on, Mo," Claire suggested as she ground the gears into first. The clutch popped again, sending a cloud of dirt and gravel flying from under the car's tires as Claire and Monique sped away toward the rendezvous point.

The car was soon careening down the country roads at breakneck speed. Several times it drifted onto the shoulders and fishtailed in the loose stones, but somehow Claire kept it going. With each bump in the road Monique clutched her side and grimaced in pain. Her sister caught it and grimaced along with her, but did not, could not, back off the accelerator. After several harrowing miles Claire noticed a fire burning on a far away hillside.

"We're too late," she said as she slowed the car. "They already hit it."

Claire was right, but even as she watched the fire, the fight was all but over. The Resistance had been battered from the opening bell and had fallen back rapidly. Renault had commanded everyone to head for the barn as soon as he arrived and witnessed the carnage his troops were enduring. The fighters retreated while Michel, Renault, and Sophie, all unable to grieve because of the intense gunfire laid down by the Nazis, dragged Paul's body into the hills. As the senior members and the wounded regrouped at the safe house, Renault tallied the cost. The toll was high.

Claire crawled to a stop at a crossroads and turned off the lights to better see the distant fire. Monique propped herself up in the seat and stared through the windshield with her sister.

"Damn it!" Claire sputtered. "Christ, am I in trouble!"

She turned off the car, and the pair sat in the quiet dark watching the fire in the distance. Claire rolled down her window and listened. Occasionally, faint gunfire could be heard from the hill. She had no idea the sounds were from German guns aimed at the backs of fleeing guerrillas as she drummed her knuckles on the car door and whispered. "Get them. Kill the bastards."

Monique had given in to the pain and was resting back on the seat. She did not see the headlights of a car approaching a few miles away coming down from the hill, but Claire did. Though her eyes followed the car lights as they flickered between far away trees, her immediate interest was on the raid as she continued whispering, "Kill them. Kill them." Her battle blood was beginning to boil.

"What now?" Monique asked.

"I don't know, but let's see who this is," Claire said, pointing to the advancing car.

Monique took little notice as Claire started the German sedan and backed out of the intersection. This time she left the car running. It was far enough back so as not to be readily visible by the oncoming car yet close enough to bathe it with her headlights when it passed. With the car in gear, her foot on the clutch, and her hand on the light switch, Claire waited.

The approaching headlights flickered and disappeared, masked by the trees and rolling hills. They reappeared, closer than before, only to blink out again. The wait gave Claire time to briefly access her sister.

"How you feeling?"

"Pretty bad. Hurts to even breathe."

"Probably got a cracked rib or two."

"That doesn't sound good."

"Not to worry. I've had a dozen of them. A little tape and some rest, and before you know it, you're good as new. Trust me on this one."

"If you say so."

"I do," Claire said as she looked back across the hill, looking for the headlights that had again temporarily disappeared.

"Maybe they went another way," Monique said weakly, hoping they had. She waited, as did Claire, for the lights to twinkle back to life, but they didn't. "Why don't we go home, Claire? I want to take a shower." She started to cry.

Claire looked at her sister, brushed the hair back from her eyes, and wiped tears off the dirty face. She couldn't refuse. "Okay, let's go home."

But as Claire reached for her own light switch, the once faraway headlights glowed to life a half a mile away. She didn't say a word. Her hand stayed perched on the switch. Monique heard the car approach and sat up straighter in the seat, instantly knowing the trip home, the shower, and the comfort and safety of her bed had been postponed.

As the car came nearer the women could see and hear that it was flying. Something had happened to make it run, most likely the attack on the German arms shipment. The thought stiffened Claire as though coiling to strike. The same thought weakened Monique.

In seconds the car shot into the intersection and Claire blasted it with her headlights. The passing car was illuminated for only a split second, but it was enough to expose the occupants. The driver was Pieter. Next to him rode Captain Rheinholt. In the back seat, holding on tight to the front, was the lieutenant. The black uniforms in the car signaled to Claire that there was a problem.

Monique literally gasped at the sight Pieter. She momentarily forgot her ribs and reached for Claire but was thrown back in the seat as her sister popped the clutch.

"Hold on!" Claire screamed as the car lurched out onto the road. It swerved dramatically as the tires spun, looking for traction, but Claire didn't ease up. "Goddamn it!" she shouted over the crying tires. "I'll bet that was my target!"

Monique braced herself in the car and looked out the windshield at the red taillights of Pieter's car. "Claire, wait!"

The plea went unheard as Claire's hearing had been rendered all but useless — all her energy was being diverted to sight and driving. Every bit of her focus was now channeled to the chase. As Claire continued to bare down on the major's car Monique anxiously looked back and forth from the red taillights to her sister.

"Claire, no! Let them go!"

"Are you nuts?"

"Please. Take me home. I hurt."

"I know, but I've got to try and stop that car! Did you see who was in there?"

"Yes."

"Gestapo! They wouldn't be along on an arms shipment unless something was up. They must have smelled something."

"I don't care about the Gestapo."

"I do! It was my job to take out—"

"The driver's not Gestapo!" Monique yelled over the sound of the racing engine.

"So what?" Claire yelled in return.

"I know him!" Monique screamed then bent over holding her side. "He's the one from the club that night you were with me."

Claire was watching the red lights get closer. "Yeah, well, he did a nice thing that night, but that's too goddamn bad. If he runs with Gestapo butchers, he's no good. He's no goddamn good, Monique. Understand?"

"No, Claire. He is good. He is good." Monique looked at her sister with eyes full of desperation.

"Jesus Christ, Monique. I can't believe you'd fall for a line of shit from a Nazi."

"Let him go, Claire."

Claire shot looks from her sister to the major's taillights and back again as she began to understand. In seconds, the curves in the road made her settle her concentration on maneuvering, but her mind was racing faster than the car she drove.

"Get us out of here, Major," Rheinholt said nervously as he looked past the lieutenant out the rear window into Claire's growing headlights.

"I'm trying," Pieter answered. Indeed he was, as the car raced pell-mell down the road, scarcely under control, but behind them Claire's knowledge of the country roads was beginning to pay off. The gap between the two cars was narrowing quickly.

"Monique, listen to me! Did you give us the information for this raid?"

Monique nodded. There was no more need for secrecy. "Yes."

"Did you get it from that major up there?"

"Yes."

"Okay, listen to me. Listen real good. The Gestapo must have known we were going to hit that convoy, or they wouldn't be around. And if they know, your major knows too. How long do you think it'll be before he figures out it was you, if he hasn't already? Then what do you think he'll do? He'll run right to the goddamn Gestapo with your name. Maybe he has already."

Monique could only sit and absorb Claire's version of the facts, filtering them through her love as best she could.

"He doesn't love you, Monique. He used you. Just like you used him. And as soon as those bastards in black figure out who used who more, they'll come after you! And when they get you, they'll get me. And then Michel, and Renault, probably even Charlemagne herself!"

"No, Claire. I've gotten information lots of times and nothing–"

"Did you ever fall in love before?"

Monique was quiet.

"My guess is a lot of information was passed...both ways," Claire continued though her eyes were locked on the road.

The words made Monique curl up on the seat. She sat shaking her head from side to side, crying, holding her side.

"Look, Monique. It's not your fault. It's nobody's fault."

"He's very special to me."

"Maybe, but he's only one person. If I let that car get away, a lot of people could hang. And you'd be the first." Claire floored the big German car. "And I'm not going to let them hang you."

"Pieter wouldn't do that."

"Don't be so sure. Once he gets out of bed he'll be thinking about his career, the 'Fatherland', and those black uniforms. Germans are Germans, through and through. You might be desperate in love right now, but soon enough the Nazi will come out of him. And he'll turn you over to save his own ass."

Monique didn't speak. She glanced out the window at the car they were rapidly closing in on as Claire's words flailed at her.

"Something is definitely wrong here or those sons of bitch-es wouldn't be in that car with your phony major friend. So he knows the gig is up. Did he call you today, warn you that he knew?" There was no response, apart from staring through the windshield.

"Of course he didn't. He's in league with those bastards, Monique. I'm certain of it." Claire let her words touch bottom before she continued. "He used you, honey. Just like those sorry assholes back there at the winery. But they'll never use anybody again, will they? And neither will these sons of bitches."

"No," Monique softly murmured.

Rheinholt turned and looked over the back seat as the major watched the headlights behind him bearing down in the rearview mirror.

"Can't you go any faster?" Rheinholt ordered.

Pieter flashed him a harsh look. "If you want to get a bullet in the head as you're lying in the wreckage against some tree, yes."

"Why do I think it could just as easily be you pulling the trigger, Major?"

"Think what you want," Pieter said as he fought the car through a sharp corner.

Rheinholt motioned to the lieutenant, and the underling immediately rolled down his driver's side window, flooding the car with the rush and noise of the night air. He thrust his pistol, too quickly, out the window and nearly lost it in the seventy-mile-an-hour wind. Lesson learned, the lieutenant leaned partially out the window, blocking a measure of the wind and allowing him to line up his sights. The Luger began spitting fire and lead at the pursuing car.

In one motion, Claire jerked the wheel violently to avoid the lieutenant's bullets and ripped one of the 45's from her waist. She thrust it out the window and, like the lieutenant, almost had it torn from her grip. To compensate, she held the barrel of the pistol against the windshield post. When she fired, the spent shell casings ejected into the compartment and bounced around, over, and off the sisters. Still bent on stopping the pursuit, Monique reached across the seat for her sister through the stream of hot shell casings. Once more, however, she was stopped by the pain in her side.

Suddenly the rear window of the major's car shattered under the assault from Claire's gun. All three officers ducked as the broken glass showered back on Claire's 45. Pieter swerved violently, but in exposing the driver's side of his car to Claire's bullets, watched as his window shattered beside his head.

Rheinholt was the first to recover. He pulled his pistol and began firing past the lieutenant through the now missing rear window. The lieutenant joined him, and the two men blasted away as Pieter drove on recklessly. He continued to weave erratically, in part to shake his pursuer's gunfire, but also in a failing attempt to keep his speeding car on the winding road. The speed and action hampered the shooters.

"Hold it steady, Majot!" Rheinholt screamed.

Claire's response to the heavy gunfire was to throttle into it. She crouched further against her door and yelled at Monique. "Take the wheel!"

Claire was partly out the window, pressing the accelerator with her toe and steering with one hand. "TAKE IT!" she screamed, but Monique stayed firmly rooted in her seat.

"Take the wheel, Monique! We stop them tonight or all hang tomorrow! Take the goddamn wheel!"

Reluctantly and painfully Monique slid across the seat to the steering wheel and wedged in beside her sister. As soon as she was near, Claire released the wheel, forcing Monique to grab on. Claire snatched the second 45 from her belt and leaned out the window as Monique's foot replaced her own on the throttle. Instantly, the car slowed.

"Hit it!"

"I can't!"

"Stay on the son of a bitch!" Claire screamed as she opened fire with both guns despite the fact that the car was rapidly dropping back.

"No, Claire! Don't!"

Despite falling away, Claire's accuracy was lethal. The lieutenant caught the first of her shots and collapsed across the back seat, dying as his pistol slipped from his hand to the floorboard. Rheinholt had ducked again, but when the lieutenant fell he leaned up and over the front seat and peppered Claire's windshield with bullets.

The response from the car was murderous. Claire, still leaning out the window, emptied both pistols in unison into the major's car. A round slammed into Rheinholt's right eye, drove through his brain, and took tissue and blood with it out the backside.

Pieter saw the blood splatter against the inside of his windshield just before the captain hurtled backward and fell to the floorboard without a voluntary movement or a whimper.

As the corpse looked on with its one remaining dead eye, Pieter crouched as low as possible in the seat and fumbled for his pistol. As he released the strap that held the seldom used gun in its holster, Pieter's body jerked forward three successive times. The steering wheel in his hands cracked, struck by at least one bullet that passed completely through his chest. He felt a numbing burn in his back and looked down to see a bloody stain already advancing across and down his white shirt.

When Claire's guns emptied and clicked harmlessly in her fists, she dropped back inside the still retreating car and shoved Monique to the passenger's side. Her foot drove down hard on the gas and she threw the empty 45's on the floor near Monique's feet. Her hands groped for the German Lugers bouncing along the dash as she attempted to see through the bullet-ridden windshield to the major's car.

She came up on it too quickly. It had slowed dramatically and was veering off the road as Claire roared near. She watched as the car continued down an embankment in front of her without the hint of a brake light.

"We got 'em!" she said through gritted teeth as her car rocketed by. She locked the brakes and slid sideways in the road, revved the engine, and spun out, returning to the spot where Pieter's car had veered off the road. Again Claire bound up the tires and skidded to a stop, leaving her headlights splashing across the pursued car that now sat quietly idling. She was out of her car before it stopped rocking, a Luger P-08 pistol in each hand.

The dead captain's car was lodged against a tree at the bottom of a gradual incline, a hundred feet from the road. The motor was humming slowly, not racing, and the headlights were on. Thick woods lay ahead of it and on the far driver's side.

Claire crept down the embankment in a low crouch, holding the Lugers out in front. She came up along the rear driver's side of the idling wreck. With the pistols acting in concert with her eyes, Claire peered in the broken back window. The lieutenant was lying on the floor of the back seat looking very comfortably dead.

Claire pulled back down alongside the car and crept further toward the front. At the driver's door she stood slightly and looked in the broken-out window. Rheinholt was jammed up under the dash. His head was fiercely perverted to the side, and blood was trickling from his ruptured eye.

"Looking for me?"

Pieter's voice froze Claire at the driver's door. She covertly adjusted the grip on her pistols, but hesitated, unsure where the major was and certain he would be utilizing cover. If she spun on him it would be suicidal.

She openly lowered one of the pistols to her side as she withdrew the other to her stomach, hoping the major wouldn't see the second Luger.

"Drop it!" Pieter ordered from the trees as he began stepping into the open.

Claire flagrantly tossed the hanging pistol to the side and began to turn toward the voice she was struggling to hone in on.

"And the other one, bitch!"

There was no other choice. Claire balked, but she knew she had been beaten. Her faced turned up to the night sky as she tossed the last pistol an arm's length from her feet. Assuming a position of surrender, Claire placed both hands, interlocking her fingers, on top of her head and slowly pivoted to face her enemy.

The Resistance fighter bore no resemblance to the dolled-up girl the major had met at the Café. Pieter didn't recognize her, but it mattered little as he had problems far more pressing. The bleeding had continued unabated, making it impossible to tell the color of his shirt save for the edges of the collar. The front of his pants were also soaked and so too the lapels of his open jacket. Pieter was faint and fading fast. He wobbled, his balance becoming impossible to hold as life very literally seeped out his chest.

When Claire turned and saw his condition she relaxed. There was comfort in knowing that she could count another dead German in her tally regardless of what might happen to her now.

"You're a dead man, Major," she smiled. "You won't last three minutes."

Pieter straightened his arm and pointed his pistol at Claire's head. "Neither will you..."

"NOT SO FAST, MAJOR!" Monique screamed from the top of the embankment. The punctuation was the click of the hammer of Claire's empty 45 caliber pistol as she held it in both hands. She stood on the side of the road in the fringes of the glaring headlights.

Pieter knew from the delivery and the click of the hammer that there were teeth behind the order. Though terribly out of context, he also thought he recognized the frenzied voice. When it came to him again, he knew it.

"Put the gun down, Pieter."

Pieter kept his pistol aimed at Claire but turned toward the voice. When his eyes confirmed what his ears had told him, his gun dropped slightly.

"Monique," he whispered, the words and breath coming as much through his chest as out his mouth.

With his attention completely diverted, Pieter became an easy target for Claire. She dove for the pistol near her feet, rolled through the grass and came up firing. The major squeezed off several rounds in the sudden exchange, but he was too weak and too overcome with the sight of his lover to prove much of a threat to the quick moving fighter whose aim would cheat him out of his last few minutes.

Claire continued to jerk the trigger on the Luger until it was empty. She watched across her sights as the impact of the bullets drove the major off his feet and he fell backward onto the slope. Suddenly, behind him, up the bank, Monique's hands dropped. As Claire peered up from the grass, the empty pistol slipped from

Monique's hand. The sisters looked at each other in the twilight from the cars' headlights across the bloody body of Pieter. Then Monique collapsed to her knees.

"MO!" Claire screamed as she scrambled up the embankment on her hands, one still clutching the empty German pistol. The sight that waited for her at the top made her tremble in fear for the first time in her life.

The look on Monique's face that met her sister was of silent shock. She was pale and sweating, dabs of her own blood graced her chin and cheeks, transferred there by hands that were covered. For now, those hands had slipped from her chest and were resting in her lap as she sat on the ground. Above her hands, much like Pieter's shirt, her dress was soaked in blood.

Her breathing became difficult, and her eyes blinked back tears whose headwaters were pain.

As Claire kneeled over her sister, shock settled over her as well. Monique had been shot, that was clear enough, and shot badly. Blood oozed from the bullet wounds in her chest, but Claire didn't see it. Her eyes refused to tell her that her sister was dying right in front of her. Instead, Claire noticed the rips in Monique's hosiery caused when she dropped to her knees on the gravel roadside. She set the Luger down alongside Monique's leg and began flicking away the tiny stones caught in the torn silk.

"You ruined your hose."

Monique looked at the ragged stockings and began tugging weakly at the silk with her blood-covered hands, but the pain suddenly overtook her body. Her hand ignored the torn stockings and gripped to grip Claire's fingers, coating them with warm sticky blood.

Claire quivered, but the shaking served to bring her back. She looked wide-eyed at Monique who raised her face and whispered, "Help me."

"Oh, Christ! I shot you!"

Now Claire's hands were all over her sister, touching the bloody dress and her bare arms, accessing the damage as her own tears rushed into her eyes.

"No," Monique whispered as she labored to shake her head. "In the car," she said as she feebly pointed at the windshield behind her. In it, Claire saw three well-placed bullet holes, directly on the driver.

"Let's get you to a doctor. You'll be alright. I think they just nicked you."

Behind Claire, down the bank, Pieter stirred slightly. Claire was lost in her sister and Monique in her pain until she saw Pieter, lying in the short grass, begin to raise his pistol and take aim at Claire's back. Monique's face gave away what she saw without saying a word. Claire instinctively turned and glanced down the path of her sister's frightened eyes and into the rising barrel of the major's gun. In a blur she reached for the Luger at her sister's knee, aimed, and pulled the trigger. Click. She cocked the upright receiver of the gun and pulled the trigger again. Nothing happened apart from the sound of another empty click.

As Pieter struggled against death to steady his pistol, Claire snatched up the empty 45 Monique had dropped, pointed it at his head, and pulled the trigger. Nothing happened. She quickly racked the action of her gun and tried again, but the pistol clicked harmlessly.

By now, Pieter had lined up his sights.

Claire lowered her gun and began to slide gracefully in front of Monique to shield her, but she was halted by her sister's bloody hand.

Monique's eyes sought out Pieter's. His own remained trained on his target, the Resistance fighter who would claim his death.

"Pieter," Monique said to him, from a chest damaged nearly as bad as his own. "Pieter."

His eyes jumped from one sister to the other and back again until they finally came to an uneasy rest on the woman he loved. There in the gravel and grass, illuminated only by the night sky, a clouded moon, and the headlights of the cars, the couple looked at one another, separated by both Claire and the pistol.

"No, Pieter. No," Monique pleaded faintly as she reached down the bank. Her hand stretched out to him and the pistol. All her meager energy permitted her to do now was sadly shake her head no and mouth the word as her hand tried to reach with bloody fingers down the bank to her lover.

Eternity passed within each of the three as they reclined alongside the desolate road. Years as a sister gave way to the wants of a lover only to return to ties of blood.

Pieter's time spent in dedicated and honorable service became only a memory.

For Claire, the fear of facing death at the business end of a gun, so long poked and teased and laughed at openly, gripped her throat, only to be overcome in front of her without a battle or another shot fired.

Love had moved Monique to protect her sister, ignoring the specter of death herself, though it already stood steadfast at her right hand. True as life and love was the move of her hand and the thoughts behind it. The hand had remained graceful in its filth and now strained to pull to her shattered breast, the love of the man her dreams had settled around.

For Pieter as well. The dreams brought on by the woman with the trembling, pale, and dirty outstretched hand had warmed him and changed him. In the brevity of days, a passionate kiss and the touch of that now bloody hand had waved over him like a magician's wand and evoked a newness that ran the breadth of his being. But tonight, on the cooling grass of the slope, the warmth was seeping out of him, pumped away by his own heart. And while the standard contents of the heart continued to drain, it became full again to bursting as Pieter looked in Monique's watery eyes. There was enough there, he realized. More than enough. The life would have been glorious beyond this ravaged land. For what would have been, would certainly have been, Pieter lowered the gun.

"I didn't...I wouldn't...have told...," he cried softly.

Monique swelled up in pride and to muster an answer for her beloved. "I know. I know."

The breath in Pieter's chest was nearly gone. The gun slipped from his hand, and he raised a timid finger toward his lover's feet.

"Are they...dancing shoes?" He smiled as the tears plummeted down his cheeks and into the corners of his blood-filled mouth.

A weary smile broke across her face. "For you."

Pieter nodded with tremendous effort, ever so slightly, then lowered his head to his arm with no fanfare and stared upon his lover's face until she was just a hazy picture surrounded by black. Then the eyes could no longer hold her image. The picture faded further, his chest relaxed, the confused heart ceased to beat, and Pieter died.

Sobbing overtook Monique, and she surrendered to Claire's strong shoulder. The lurching of her crying brought great pain, and it became impossible for Claire to distinguish the cause of the greatest suffering, not that its source mattered. As she held her inconsolable sister, Claire looked down the hill at Pieter's body. She still did not understand completely, but the sight of the grey uniform did not bring with it much of a desire to comprehend further. Of course she had killed the major, but only to protect Monique from him and the Gestapo. Even if it was as he had said, she still felt little remorse. Her sister had apparently loved this man and he her, but he had been a Nazi and would have turned on her one day like a dog that bites its caregiver. Monique would grieve but recover and be the better for it. The major was now as Nazis should be, turning cold as the stench of death enveloped him.

"C'mon, Mo. Let's get to the car."

Monique was weakened by the loss of both blood and love. She had little strength to stand and even less desire to do so. There was a commitment in her to remain on the embankment and die alongside Pieter.

"I'm too tired."

"No you're not. Up you go," Claire said forcibly as she strained to lift the bulk of her sister. Monique pushed her feet out and stood stiffly, her legs untested like a new foal's. She was miserably faint, but still caught sight of Pieter's body in the grass.

"I don't want to leave him."

Claire looked quickly down the bank at the dead. "I'll come back for him."

"No you won't, Claire. Don't lie."

"If you want me to, I will."

"I do."

"I swear. Right now, let's get you to the doctor."

The pair stumbled around the car to the passenger door. Claire held her sister with one arm, braced by the roof of the car, as she fought with the door. When she flung it open she hurriedly but as gently as possible dumped Monique inside, slammed the door, and ran around to the driver's side. As she did she noticed again the bullet holes in the windshield. Their placement couldn't have been much better. Two must have passed through the center of the steering wheel, as though it had been a bull's eye target.

When Claire hit the front seat, the slight shifting of the car brought Monique slumping over toward her. "None of that," Claire said compassionately as she straightened Monique in the seat. But when she took away her hands they were bloody. She stared, slipping back into shock herself. Her hands turned over in front of her as Monique swooned across the seat. Claire sat motionless, her hands suddenly ice cold. She shivered though the warm night air didn't warrant it.

"Stop it!" she yelled at herself and pounded the wheel. Her bloody hand slapped her own face, to be sure she was cognizant — to bring herself back to this bitter reality.

Monique's blood was still coming. Claire pulled the knife from her boot and slashed at the seat, ripping open a wide gash. Her sticky hands tore at the cushion until she had pulled out a huge handful of padding. She dropped the knife and plunged the stuffing as a makeshift bandage down the front of Monique's soaked dress. Then she took her sister's hands and pressed them gently against the bunch.

"Here, Mo. Try to hold this on."

"Okay," Monique answered.

With her reckless first aid complete Claire threw the car onto the road and sped away from the major and the black car, now pressed into service as an impromptu Nazi coffin.

The car flew with more abandon than when it had hunted the fleeing Germans. The immediacy was more severe, and it was not lost on Claire that the thing she had tried to avoid by the killings now brought her to risk her own life and what remained of Monique's in her mad dash down the twisting country road. The driving was hampered by the bullet holes in the glass in front of her. Claire ducked to see around the fractures as best she could, but they radiated in all directions, reminding her of how bad Monique was likely hit.

While the road continued to disappear beneath the spinning wheels, Monique came in and out of consciousness. Her disjointed moans were like music to Claire's ears compared to the silence that cradled them on either side. When the road and the silence remained too long Claire nudged her sister and tried to rouse her.

"Hey! Almost there," she lied. "Stay with me, okay?"

There was no response.

"Monique? Monique! Wake up!"

"Are we home?"

"Almost. Hold my hand. Can you squeeze my fingers?"

Monique fumbled slowly and blindly in her lap for her sister's finger and gripped it as faintly as one would caress fine crystal. Claire felt the slight touch and also the damp blood, but it was the cold of her sister's hand that shocked her into pulling away. Her mind raced in a whisper that said it was the curve of the road that caused her to jerk away, but Monique hadn't noticed, whatever the reason.

Claire spoke to ease the tension from her mind. "We're going to the safe house. There are people there with more experience patching up nicks and cuts than all the doctors in France. Know what I mean?"

When Monique did not answer, Claire reached over and pushed the hair off her sister's face. She saw Monique move.

"Hey? You know what I mean?"

"Yes."

"Good. Good. Stay awake, okay? I think that would be good. Just stay awake. That's your job. I'll drive, you stay awake."

As before, Monique said nothing, but Claire heard her breathing, wheezing, and for now that was enough.

***

35

The room was absolutely still. Occasionally an unconscious sniffle would erupt and seem like an explosion of sound. Renault was sitting in a worn, overstuffed, red leather armchair. His legs were crossed at the knees, still muddy and damp. He sat back deep in the chair's comfort but found none. One arm rested limp across his lap while the elbow of the other pressed into the chair's arm, holding his hand up to his face. A single finger pressed against his lips, and the thumb gracefully held the old man's chin. His eyes were cast down and saw nothing in the room and everything beyond. Memories flashed. Most were good, others less so, but each was as vibrant as if it were happening again right now, right in front of those distant eyes.

Sophie was curled up on a small bed a few feet away. Her knees were pulled up to her stomach, and both hands clutched a dainty handkerchief with a frilly lace border to her mouth. Her once exquisite makeup was all over her face, and her eyes were red and swollen. The fingers fidgeted with the handkerchief as if feeling their way for something.

Renault had been to the woods already. He had knelt beside Paul's torn body and wept as his hands clutched the bloody black sweater of the young man he had at first mentored then come to love as a son. He was unable to provide the normal direction to the grave diggers. It didn't seem to matter any longer.

"Renault?" Sophie called from the bed for the second time.

"Yes, dear? I'm sorry. What did you say?"

"Did he suffer?"

"No. Not for moment."

"That's good," she commented slowly as though trying to find solace in the cold facts. "He suffered enough."

Renault barely nodded.

Several more moments passed in silence before a hesitant knock came at the door. Before either could answer, it opened slightly, and Claudine stuck her head in. Her hands gripped the edge of the door tightly as if she could buttress the wood and shield herself from what waited on the other side. She wanted to ask if what she'd heard was true, but one look at the tear stains on Sophie's face and the question was no longer necessary. Without a word she burst in and fell across the bed into Sophie's arms. They didn't speak, but held each other as both began crying for the other's loss.

Renault stood and walked by. As he did, Claudine reached for him and gripped his arm. Neither spoke. Renault only nodded again, patted her hand, and slipped away deeper into his grief as he closed the door and wandered around the room.

"How? Why?" Claudine questioned from behind a veil of trembling tears.

"I don't know, honey. I don't know," Sophie answered as she hugged the girl now left fatherless for a second time.

Minutes melted into the better part of an hour before Sophie sat up on the edge of the bed and brushed the hair from Claudine's face.

"What about Valerie?" Sophie asked Renault.

"Valerie?" Claudine asked, torn from her grief by the name she had long lingered over. There was a question in her voice that suggested the mention of the name at such a moment as this was tantamount to sin.

"She's alive," Sophie said to her as if it were an afterthought before returning her attention to Renault. "What do we do now?"

Renault waved his hand in front of him, as if in search for words, but none came. His throat was tight and bone dry.

Sophie saw his struggle and released him from the constraint to answer. "Maybe tomorrow, or the next day."

He shook his head yes and sighed. Renault spoke in a raspy tired voice. "Dr. Meceraux is downstairs. Terrible. It's full of wounded. I'll speak to him about her. Like you say, tomorrow or the next day we'll go to St. Louis and bring her home. After this mess settles." He walked to the door as though his joints hurt and indeed they did. "I should go to the war room. Charlemagne will need me."

"And I should be helping David," Sophie said as she too struggled to move. "You rest a little while," she said to Claudine. "Why don't you try to take a nap? I'll come back up and check on you later."

"No, I can help," she said, showing sudden resolve. "I think I'd rather be doing something."

Sophie held her arm down. "It can be pretty ugly sometimes."

"I'll find you something up here," Renault offered, but not strongly.

"I'm ready," Claudine said stoically.

Sophie looked to Renault for the final word. "If she gets tired, bring her back up," he said diplomatically before slipping out of the room. The women painfully followed him with their arms around each other, wiping the drying itching tears off their cheeks.

***

36

The lights of the city began to tease Claire on from a distance. Her speed was such that before the lights could continue their game for long she overtook them. Now she was forced by confining streets to be more moderate with the accelerator, but only slightly. What few cars she encountered suffered at her passing. Though it occurred to her that the manner in which she drove and the car itself — a colonel's staff car with a bullet-ridden windshield — would draw the attention of any patrols, she could not bring herself to waste anymore time. Worse than the attraction of the car and her driving, Claire intended to wheel right up to the safe house, effectively leading any pursuers right to the heart of the Resistance. However, the needs of the Movement were very distant at the moment, driven there by Claire's love for her sister who was collapsed across the seat.

As Claire rounded the last corner onto the street of the safe house the tires squealed like playing children, and the rubber left a smell that drifted over the sidewalk. The tires sounded like a siren to all who could hear that trouble had come to the street. They signaled again as Claire bounced over the curb onto the sidewalk, nearly hitting the safe house stoop as she screeched to a stop.

A number of fighters were milling around inside. Some, fresh from the basement, wore bandages while others, led by Michel, were pushing discussions into arguments over the losses they had suffered in the ambush and the obvious readiness of the German command. Tension was high. No one knew the extent of the German intelligence information or if the Resistance might soon be on the defensive. Claire's grey car and the ruckus she was causing out front brought several fighters to the windows and seemed to provide the answer.

"Germans!" Natei barked out on seeing the grey car that still bounced on the sidewalk.

Men and women scattered in all directions. Some grabbed maps from the center table and ran down the stairs to the war room shouting the alarm the entire way. As quickly as they descended to the war room others were running up, automatic weapons jostling in their hands.

Renault was one of the first to emerge from the basement. He raced to the windows armed with a short shotgun just in time to see Claire leap from the car. Other fighters were descending on the windows and door with weapons as well, ready to open fire on the encroaching enemy.

"Stop! Stop!" Renault ordered. "It's Claire!"

Claire ejected herself from the car before it stopped rocking. She scurried around to the passenger door and flung it open and immediately began tugging Monique from the front seat.

Renault dropped his shotgun on a chair and pushed hurriedly through the confused fighters to the door. "What in the hell?" he muttered to no one.

Claire was still struggling with Monique's limp body as Renault jumped down the steps to the car. Fighters, watching from the doorway, looked nervously up and down the street, then hurriedly followed to the car. Renault hesitated only a second when he saw that Monique's dress, torn and tied at the shoulder, was covered from neckline to hem with blood. "Jesus Christ," he said as he gently took Monique's shoulders from a weary Claire. "Get her inside. Quickly, quickly!"

Claire gave up her role as litter-bearer and followed the strong arms that now whisked her sister over the secret vent, up the steps, and into the safe house.

Renault snapped at Michel who was holding the door for those carrying Monique. "Get rid of that goddamn car!"

Claire swept by Michel after Monique and the mob that carried her. Though he stared at the bloody dress and after at Claire, she never glanced in his direction. Instead, she was taken in by the house while he went down the steps two at a time and jumped in the still running grey car.

As Michel powered the car off the sidewalk and raced up the street, quickly putting as much distance as possible between the safe house and the commotion, he looked through the bullet holes in the windshield. Like Claire had moments before, he ducked and shifted with the road to see around the radiating fractures in the glass. Alongside him, the dark stain of Monique's blood covered the front seat. On the floorboard were his and Claire's 45 automatic pistols.

As soon as the car escaped the street, the air of the sidewalk cleared of the smell of rubber and grew still. The safe house slid back into the anonymous row of nondescript homes, and the street breathed a quiet sigh of relief. For the moment there would be no firefight on this quiet avenue. Inside the safe house, the story was much different.

Whatever remained on the wide table in the main room was knocked to the floor and replaced by Monique's blood-soaked and limp body.

"Get the doctor up here!" Renault demanded.

Claudine was standing at the top of the stairs. "He's just finishing putting stitches—"

"Tell him now!" Renault screamed, knocking the young girl back down the stairs in a rush. "Aand get Charlemagne!"

"You'd better get a priest, too," someone whispered.

Capable hands began cutting away Monique's dress and picking off Claire's makeshift bandage. Someone eased her head up and slipped a pillow beneath it. Others brought blankets and tucked them under, around, and over Monique.

"Get some more dressing!" Renault shouted his directions as his hands moved quickly. "God, this girl's a mess."

Claire was lost in the buzzing crowd around her sister. She slipped away from the table as David, already bloodied, shot into the room from the basement followed closely by Sophie and Claudine. Raquelle was behind them with a tray of medical tools — some of which, like the doctor's hands, showed the signs of having already been used.

David went to work in a practiced frenzy. While Monique was haphazardly rinsed by Raquelle in order to locate the entry wounds in the gore that had been her upper chest, David administered a massive shot of morphine. The warm water from Raquelle's washing momentarily settled in several small holes in Monique's flesh until it was flushed out by a weakening pulse. The laboring physician began to probe the bullet wounds while Sophie, already crying new tears for yet another love, dabbed Monique's face clean.

So many people gathered and worked on and around Monique that Claire lost sight of her sister. No one noticed her sink back and slump into a soft couch well beyond the table at Monique's feet. And no one noticed either her reaction when the esteemed Charlemagne came up the stairs from the war room surrounded by a small entourage. Claire could not see her at first, but could hear her being addressed in the dizzying quiet.

"Her name's Monique, Charlemagne. She's an intelligence officer. We haven't been able to ascertain what happened to her, but she's very bad off."

Claire stood to see for the first time the woman she had long admired from afar. The beehive of activity over the table and the crush of Charlemagne and her aide-de-camps created a maze of bodies in front of her. As Claire moved back and forth, permitting her eyes to weave their way through the crowd, she heard a familiar voice make an elaborate request with a single word.

"Doctor?"

Above the anxious faces, Claire caught the sweaty and furrowed brow of Dr. Meceraux move from side to side. "I can't tell yet, Char. I just can't tell."

Claire moved more than her eyes now. She stepped into the throng around her sister and worked the maze until she found the source of the familiar voice — and an even more familiar face. Standing at the right hand of the doctor was Claire's mother. Estelle was Charlemagne.

Estelle wiped at Monique's pale face with a shaky hand, her own face already ashen. She whispered to no one special, "Help her."

David's tired hands, unaware of what drove the special request, stopped for a second. "Char, please. I'm doing everything I know."

The head of the Resistance snapped back to her position and touched the doctor's arm reassuringly. "I'm sorry. Thank you," she said firmly as an aide pointed to Claire who continued to approach, though in shock nearly as much as her mother and sister.

"This girl brought her in. She's one of our finest fighters. Her name is—"

"I know who she is," Charlemagne said decisively as she moved down the table away from one daughter and toward another.

Claire reached for her mother to hug her, but Charlemagne caught her arms, turned her gently and guided her back to the couch. She eased Claire down and sat beside her while her aides settled in nearby.

"What happened, Claire?"

"You. You're—" Claire murmured in wide-eyed disbelief.

"Never mind that now. What happened?"

Claire shook her head and let her eyes drop away from her mother to the floor. This night had been too much. Her mind was fragmenting. It took Claire several moments of heavy concentration to push aside the overwhelming dark tunnel of confusion within her mind and recall the events that already seemed ages ago.

"Monique was supposed to meet some colonel at the old Juneau Winery. She asked me to go." Her face came up and she locked eyes with her mother. "But I told her no. I wouldn't go, Mother. I wouldn't go."

The nearest aides exchanged perplexed looks when Claire called Charlemagne, 'Mother'. Even more so when their leader replied without a comment.

"You had a job to do. How did she get hurt?"

As before, Claire sought the support of concentration offered by the floor before she could muster an answer. "She went to the winery. There were soldiers waiting for her. I made Michel drive me there so I could check on her. And the men...they were kicking her. And—" Claire's eyes reached out to her mother yet again and begged her not to have to say it.

"I understand," Charlemagne said softly as she patted her daughter's knee. "Go on."

"So I killed them. And Monique killed...No, I did it. I did it. They're all dead."

Claire's face dropped, as though ashamed of what she had done. The shame was honest, but was rooted further back than the execution of Monique's attackers.

Charlemagne motioned for Renault. He rushed up to her side while the aides closed tighter around her to listen. Claire listened, too, in wonder as her mother doled out orders as fluidly as she made her tiny finger cakes.

"Send a contingency out to the old Juneau Winery. On Plank Road. Correct, Claire?"

"Yes."

"There are bodies out there to be disposed of. Vehicles and weapons, too, I imagine. Take the vehicles to the warehouse. Have one of the girls wash the uniforms and deliver them to my house. I'll throw a quick stitch or two in the bullet holes. We may have need of them very soon."

Claire's jaw fell slack and her shame deepened along with her amazement.

"Renault," Charlemagne continued. "The Germans will be swarming like bees whose nest has been poked with a stick after what we did tonight. Send good men to the winery and tell them I want them to be shadows. And if you would, please go to my house and tell Sean what's happened. Would you wait there with him? I'll have someone call with an update."

"My honor," the old fighter answered.

"Thank you."

Renault began to step away when Claire blurted out more details of the night. "Mother, there's another car just outside of town along the way to Plank Road, down an embankment. There's a couple of dead soldiers in it. They're the ones who shot Monique."

"Fine," Charlemagne said as she prepared to address Renault and her staff.

"And there's a major on the slope next to it," Claire interrupted. "He and Monique were friends. More than friends. I guess they were really in love, but I shot...I don't know. He said he didn't tell..."

"See to it, Renault."

"It's done," Renault answered. He motioned to Natei as he turned to go, but stopped, stepped back, and patted Claire's knee. There were no words fitting in his mouth or mind. He could only touch his young friend and nod his head. Claire understood and clutched his hand for a moment. She looked at the wrinkled fingers caressing her own then noticed the dried blood that still covered her hands. Renault saw her eyes fixated on the blood and vigorously rubbed her hands, as if warming them, effectively brushing away the majority of the red flakes.

"You stay strong, Claire. We'll need you." Then he looked over his shoulder at the table and the crowd of people still working feverishly over Monique. "She'll need you."

Then he took Claire's hand and placed it on Charlemagne's. The women gripped each other's fingers and Renault stepped away, followed by a quartet of senior aides. He talked quietly to them as well as Natei, then slipped out of the house like a puff of smoke.

When Renault and the others had left them, Claire and her mother turned their attention back to the table. They each said quiet and hopeful prayers. Claire even quoted a part of one in the old Irish that she remembered her father saying years ago when the invasion first began.

"More morphine," David ordered impatiently.

Raquelle did as directed and pulled the drug into the syringe from one of the bottles she had gotten the day before. She stopped at two cc's and looked at David.

"More," he said emphatically.

"She's already had four."

"Make it four again."

Raquelle balked.

"Four, please, Raquelle," he said softly. "I want her without pain."

Sophie, standing with her arms around Claudine at the bloody table, understood the meaning behind David's words. She squeezed the young girl tightly as Claudine looked from the needle in Raquelle's hand to Sophie's tears. When the needle disappeared into Monique's skin Claudine looked away.

The youngest McCleash wiped tears off her cheeks as she looked at the people gathered around the table. Sophie was standing at the far side on the fringe, tears raining down her face, but being very still. Claudine was in front of her, closer to the table with a look of confusion and fear on her face rather than tears. When someone inadvertently bumped her she jumped and then disappeared from the room into the basement.

A few battered fighters remained there, waiting for the doctor to return. Claudine walked briskly through them all but unnoticed. She stopped when the room ended and found herself at the last table where David had been in attendance. Blood-soaked gauze littered the makeshift examining stand and captured her eyes. Paul was dead. Monique was near the same black door. And then there was the shocking reappearance of the pretty ghost from her past. While her eyes continued to look on, Claudine's hand stole onto the table and picked up a used syringe and full vial of Raquelle's pirated morphine. She slipped them in her pocket then looked at her fingers and saw the blood transferred there from the syringe.

In the room upstairs, the driest eyes beneath the wettest brows belonged to Dr. Meceraux and Raquelle. They were too intent on the task to fret at the moment but knew from experience that the time for tears may come to them later. The elbows of the pair flashed through the group from time to time, and occasionally Claire would hear metal instruments hit against each other as David directed the procedures he attempted.

"Will she be alright?" Claire beseeched her mother.

All Estelle could do was nod toward the doctor. "He is the best France has. His talent is his gift to the Resistance. Like so many others, he does what he can."

While the pair of shaken women watched from the couch, David's hands began to slow. It wasn't so much the change in pace that frightened Claire, but the crying that now began at the very edges of the table. In another moment, those that had tried so hard began to slip away from the table, and David hesitantly came to Charlemagne.

"I'm sorry," he said softly as he wiped blood from his hands on a towel already damp with red. "She's got two bullets deep in her chest. Plus a half dozen fragments of lead and an equal number of glass shards. She's lost so much blood. I don't know how she's held on this long. I'm sorry."

As Claire and her mother listened in disbelief, Sophie, fighting the urge to wail uncontrollably, came up behind David and spoke softly but clearly to Charlemagne. "She's asking for Estelle."

Charlemagne slapped her hands on her knees and stood abruptly. "That'd be me," she said as she moved straight to the head of the table. Claire trailed behind her mother while Sophie walked around the table until she was at Monique's head opposite Claire. David followed Sophie and reached to comfort her, but stopped and looked at his hands covered with drying blood. He chanced a touch and said he was sorry with his eyes. Sophie leaned her head against his face for a moment then held his arm until he stepped away and returned to the basement and the other waiting wounded. When he moved, Raquelle followed down the stairs carrying a pan of bloodied instruments and filthy gauze.

At the table, Estelle gently eased Monique's wet hair back from her forehead. She felt the coolness of her daughter's skin as she did and bit her lip to stifle the fear. "I'm here, Monique. I'm here."

Monique's face was alabaster save for her lips which were ice-cold blue. Her chest was a patchwork of bandages and tape and heaved sparingly against its restraints. The heretofore highlighted and meticulous eyes that had so often mesmerized many an unwary man were closed but opened to slits at the sound of the voice.

"Mother?"

Estelle took her daughter's hand and held it between both of hers as she leaned low on the table.

"Yes, dear. I'm here."

"Where's Claire?"

"I'm here, Mo," Claire said as though speaking to the deaf. She huddled close to her sister, reached across the treated chest, and held Monique's other hand.

"Where's Estelle?" Monique asked as she feebly tossed her head from side to side as though looking around the faces at the table as the women surrounding her exchanged troubled glances.

"Mother's right here, honey," Estelle said louder.

Monique pulled her hand from her mother in slow motion. She held it off the table parallel to the floor in the measure of a small child. "Essey," she whispered.

Claire caught up her sister's hand and brought it back to the table then whispered, "She means some kid at the nunnery."

Monique visibly relaxed, shook her head, and smiled slightly. But the smile lasted only long enough to make it. Only minutes remained and she sensed it. She labored to lift her hand from the table's edge and pointed to her sister.

"Look after her for me, Claire."

Tears were erupting from Claire's face, but there was an untimely harshness in her voice.

"No, I can't—"

Monique grimaced hard against the pain coming from her body and her sister. "Yes you can," she sobbed.

Estelle gripped Claire's arm and squeezed it tight, bringing Claire's attention to her. A mother's stern look corrected the tone in her youngest daughter's voice as well as the answer itself.

"Okay. I'll look out for her," Claire said with more than some hesitation, staring at her mother as she answered. "But you'll be back there real soon."

The attention of those that remained around the table left Claire and returned to Monique. Blood was escaping the bandages on her chest. Her breath was growing increasingly shallow and worked around a reoccurring cough that brought pink foam to the corners of her mouth. The skin of her face blanched as even the blue of her lips became more pale. She opened her eyes fully, but it was apparent she could not see. The eyes blinked hard but had lost their purpose and could only squeeze more water out the sides.

"I just wanted to dance," Monique said with a sudden burst of strength.

"You will, Mo!" Claire shouted as she leaned over the table and grabbed Monique's bloody shoulders. "Soon the Americans will come! Then you and me will go off to your Hollywood! Just you and me!"

Monique's eyes glazed over as she looked through Claire and whispered. "Hollywood..."

An odd gurgling noise rose up from Monique's throat. Those in the room who had witnessed death steal a compatriot on other sad days recognized the death rattle for what it was. They — and Estelle was counted among them — knew Monique was gone. Even the shallow breath stopped as death's pallor slipped over the pretty face.

"Mo? Mo! Din't leave me!" Claire screamed, shaking on her own as she shook her sister. The excited fighter roughly grappled with her sister's body, trying to rouse her, but Monique's quiet form was limp beneath her.

"Mo!" she shouted louder as the shaking tossed Monique's hair over her face, closing her off from the world.

From behind Claire, Estelle slowly but forcibly took a hold of her arms. "Claire," she said, trying to muster some reassurance for her remaining daughter. But the fighter was ready for none of it.

"No!" Claire screamed again. She tore herself free from her mother and began to climb onto the table with her sister. Sophie came around the table and with Estelle's help grabbed Claire from behind and tried to bring her off the table.

"It's okay," Sophie said as she extended the obligatory comfort.

When Claire's feet hit the floor, she spun on those around her, flailing her elbows to free herself and instantly exploded at Sophie.

"It's not okay! And it won't be okay until I kill every German I can find!"

Her face was red beneath the boot polish, dirt, and blood of her sister. She was nearly growling as she breathed through clenched teeth. Then she turned away from Sophie and her mother, leaned close to Monique's ashen face, brushed the damp hair back, and whispered to her. "For you. I'll kill them all for you."

As the words settled in ears that could no longer hear, Claire gently kissed her dead sister. The cold skin held Claire's kiss and cooled her lips as well as the anger behind them.

Refreshed by a renewed determination, but still skating near shock, Claire averted her face from Monique. Once again her mother cradled her, yet this time she met no resistance. The subdued Claire stood stoically for nearly a minute then rapidly collapsed into a pile of tears on her mother's chest.

Estelle had been crying herself, but bucked up for the needs of her remaining child. Sophie, herself an emotional disaster, put her arms around both grieving women and gently guided them away from the table. Charlemagne's aides followed, holding and comforting, while still sharing looks of astonishment at the relationships they had learned of only tonight. Not one of the caregivers looked back, nor did Claire or her mother. If they had they would have seen a dark blanket traverse the length of Monique's torn body and settle over the perfect face with the ghost-white skin.

The lamenting women were taken into one of the house's small bedrooms down the hall from the main room and the death table. Their escorts immediately left them except for Sophie who remained for several minutes, alternating from giving comfort to receiving it.

"I'm going to miss her so much," Sophie cried.

Estelle found a smile for her and rubbed Sophie's shoulders. "You've always been a wonderful friend to her."

"What a beautiful person she was. Inside and out."

"That she was."

Claire moved away from the polite talk and sat on the bed. Sophie felt the slightest shift of change and realized it was time for family to be with family. She hugged Estelle and slipped toward the door. "I'll see to her," she said purposefully.

"Thank you," Estelle breathed as Claire, slipping into a foggy haze, continued to sit quietly.

The door closed silently and left the McCleash women alone with their grief. Tears had run their course and had deposited their stains under red eyes. Now there was only energy for soft introspection and stroking the warm flame of memories. It was a time when words meant nothing and were habitually not heard if offered. When the touch of a hand or a kiss on the forehead relayed thoughts and sentiments far more efficiently. Words were difficult to form and equally difficult to comprehend. Hence, the pair of sorrow-filled women sat quietly, touching gently, moving little, and speaking not at all.

Minutes passed into twenty and on into forty until more than an hour had vanished. The dried tracks of tears on Claire's face itched and reminded her she was still alive, still human. She brushed them away and took a deep breath.

"How long?" Claire asked. "How long have you been, you know, Charlemagne?"

Estelle answered by blowing her nose. "From the beginning," she said between wiping away the overflow of tears.

"Why didn't you tell us?"

"Wasn't safe. Still isn't. Those of us who fight to free France lead shadowed lives right now. Someday, soon perhaps, that will change. But for now we must stay low and do what we can."

The words rekindled a memory and forced Claire's chin to her chest. The words fell from her mouth directly to the floor. "Like Monique."

Estelle's eyes settled on the floor as well. "Like Monique."

The moment passed, grief resumed control for a time, then was again pushed aside. Without a warning to her mother, Claire's head popped up and she was instantly excited.

"We'll give her a huge funeral!" she smiled. "Lots of flowers. And music. And dancing! She would like that. Lots of dancing."

Estelle waited a moment to let the rush pass her by. "We can't, Claire."

"Why not?"

"There won't be any funeral. They draw too much attention. The Germans would know she was a part of the Resistance. And through her, you. And then me. And the others."

"But Mother—"

"No, honey. That's how it's done. We have the place in the country. The men will take her there tonight. Then it falls to us to explain her disappearance. We usually say the girls ran off with a soldier."

"Oh, no."

"I'm sorry, dear. There's no other way. There's no other place that's safe. For her or us."

The words dove into Claire's mind and rested there. The night had already given up lessons on a great many things, some accepted, some rejected. One lesson well learned, was the special nexus of blood and the rarity, even with it, of the care Monique had demonstrated toward her little sister. In the classroom that had begun under the kitchen table all those years ago, Claire had watched, listened, and learned. She had railed against her teacher's hand many times, but never more so than in these last few days. And now the commencement had taken place on an earthen embankment near Plank Road, and with the moving of the tassel Claire knew she could not abandon her sister as readily as had been suggested.

"Father's flower bed," Claire said clearly, looking steadfast at her mother. "Monique could be there. Be with us."

"Oh, I don't think—"

"Yes, Mother! Please? Then I can look after her."

"But, dear..."

Claire jumped to her feet and marched to the center of the small room, the Resistance fighter still very intact in her black clothes and steel manners. "I can't leave her alone in some goddamn deserted woods in the middle of nowhere!" Then the march became a walk, and the voice lost its thorny tone. "She saved my life, when I tried to save hers. Please, Mother?"

Estelle was lost in thought and looking away from the request. "It's against every doctrine of the Movement."

"They'd do it if Charlemagne said so. I know they would."

As though on cue, there was a subtle knock at the door. It granted Estelle time to formulate an answer, which was again delayed as the door opened slightly and Sophie stepped partially inside.

"Charlemagne? Monique is ready."

Estelle rose and walked to the door, running her hand down the length of her daughter's arm as she passed.

"Mother? Can you-"

"Wait here, Claire," Estelle said authoritatively. "I must speak to your father."

"Renault is still with him," Sophie said as the two women stepped out of the room and left Claire alone. In the hall they passed a hurried Michel who was searching for Claire. He was muddy over the length of him, but the women paid him no mind as they passed. Michel, however, stopped at the sight of Estelle in the safe house.

"I have something I'd like you to attend to," Charlemagne said to Sophie as they walked by. "And I need to call Sean. I want him to hear it from me."

Michel recovered and interrupted the conversation as he reached back and touched Estelle's arm.

"Mrs. McCleash? I'm very sorry."

"Thank you, Michel."

"She was a very special person."

Estelle nodded, patted his arm, and pointed down the hall. "Yes she was. Claire's in there. Perhaps you could sit with her for a few minutes until I return."

He didn't answer but stepped away, anxious to be with his lover.

The door was still open as Estelle had meant it to be. Michel walked in and found Claire leaning forward, her elbows on her knees. Movement brought her eyes up, but the sight of Michel turned them down again. He closed the door behind him, and the young couple was alone as they had been in the car and in the woods alongside the Juneau Winery's parking lot. The anxiousness Michel carried into the room did not leave readily. He buried his hands deep in his pockets and stayed some distance from his lover.

"Claire?" he began slowly.

"Don't say a word. Not a word."

He waited but was compelled to finish. "I'm so sorry."

"Just shut up. You think I've forgotten the things you said about her? You didn't like her and that's that. Don't insult her or me by pretending you give a shit."

"That's not fair."

"Fair? What the hell do you know about fair? My sister's in there on a table, dead, because you wouldn't help me save her. Fair. Son of a bitch. Get out of my sight."

Michel retreated to the door then stopped and wheeled around. "Don't try to put this on me. I did exactly what I had to do, exactly what I was supposed to do."

"Are you deaf? I said don't talk to me! What you were supposed to do! My sister's dead!"

"I know that! But there's nothing I can do for her, is there? It's you I'm concerned about."

"Bullshit. If you were so concerned you would have stayed and helped me."

"Why? Why, goddamn it? So a thousand men could get killed?"

"No! So my sister could live!"

There was a minute that Claire relished, confident she had done and said the right things that would forever put Michel in his place and shoulder him with the burden that lay so heavy on her heart. Michel allowed the minute to hang, almost prepared to allow Claire to have her triumph, but he wanted her back and understood that there was a journey, a painful one, to undertake first.

The first steps of the trip were slow but gathered speed quickly and in another moment were at full throttle. "Natei was at that embankment getting that car. I talked to him. And I stopped at your house and talked to Renault on my way back from the winery. Monique didn't get killed by those soldiers in the parking lot."

"I know that. Leave me alone."

"What happened in that car, Claire?"

"You go to hell."

"I'll tell you what happened. You forget, Claire, I know you. You saw that car and knew it was your target. You screwed up, Claire, then tried to make it right, so don't put it on me."

"Shut up, Michel."

"No, Claire. You tried to get that car, and Monique was just along for the ride."

"Shut up!"

"She didn't have a gun. Didn't know shit about fighting. And you drove her right up on three armed men!"

Claire leaped across the room leading with her fists and began punching him.

"Trained soldiers!" he tormented.

"I'll kill you!"

Michel grabbed her and spun her around. He held her tightly, pinning her arms across her chest in a coarse hug. "No, you won't kill me," he whispered in her ear.

"Let me go!"

"You won't kill me. And you didn't kill your sister," he stabbed as Claire continued to struggle. "You didn't kill her!"

The struggling eased slightly, but Michel held on tight, recalling her feigning attempts earlier in the woods. "You didn't kill her."

The thrashing stopped. Claire now held the arm that held her. "Yes, I did," she began to cry. "I killed her."

"No, Claire. Don't even think like that. It was all a horrible accident."

"No, I might as well have shot her myself."

Michel loosened his bear hug and turned Claire into him. He now hugged her as tight as he had restrained her. "No, you didn't. No, you didn't," he consoled as he stroked her hair.

But Claire pushed him away slightly and stared through his eyes. "I did. I chased that car when I could have let it go. I...I thought that maybe they would come after her so I was trying to save..." Any words that remained were lost in the choking back of tears.

"Yes, you were."

"But I ended up killing her instead."

"No, Claire. You're wrong. The Nazis killed her, not you."

"But if I'd let them go-"

"They might have killed her tomorrow, and a lot of others."

"No. He said he didn't tell."

"Who didn't tell?"

"Doesn't matter," Claire said faintly as she stepped out of his embrace and turned back to the room.

Michel walked with her, tenderly eased her down on the edge of the bed, and then sat beside her. "You didn't do it, Claire."

All she could manage was a shrug of her shoulders.

"You were supposed to stop that car, and you did."

"Look at the price."

"A terrible price, but one we're all prepared to pay. We know it every time we go out."

"She didn't know that. She wasn't like us."

"I think she was more like us than you know."

In the quiet that filtered back into the room, Claire continued to search herself for answers amid all the questions. In an action repeated so many times that night, she roughly wiped tears off her streaked face.

"I'm going to make them pay," she said in a low voice.

"I know. And I'll be your sword-bearer if you'll let me."

Claire leaned into him, and he slipped his arm around her shoulders, holding her in the quiet room. From the comfort of his chest and protected by his arm, Claire spoke to him in a voice that yielded all her thoughts and feelings.

"I can't be mad at you."

"Let's not-"

"Just listen, please. I did the same thing I tried to blame you for. When you left me in the woods you did the right thing, but so did I. And when I went after that car I did the right thing, too. I had no idea he really loved her. If I'd known I would have let them go, would have let him protect her. He would have done a better job." And the tears began anew.

Most of the one-sided conversation was lost on him, but Michel performed the best task a friend could do and listened with a mind concerned only with listening and not working up answers. When her voice trailed off against his chest, he kept still save for a gentle tightening around her shoulders which signaled that he understood, which he didn't, and that all would be well, though that too remained in doubt as sirens wailed across the city.

***

37

stelle and Sophie did not knock before they re-entered the room. Mrs. McCleash's sudden appearance caused Michel's arm to begin a hasty and involuntary retreat from Claire's shoulder as any young man might be prone to do when the mother of the object of his affection chanced to come upon them. The arm and the caress were of no concern to Estelle, whose hand remained on the doorknob, but she did motion for Michel as Claire continued to rest against him. With tremendous care, he stood and brushed Claire's hair away from her face.

"I'll be by tomorrow," he said with a soft smile. "We'll start right away."

"Thank you," Claire answered as her hand touched his in a lover's good-bye.

The door was held open for him, but Estelle took hold of his arm as he passed and held him up. She spoke to him in a hushed voice as Sophie listened in. He took his orders in silence though his face questioned, then stepped further into the doorway as Charlemagne issued a last-minute instruction.

"Renault is still at the house with Sean. He'll wait for you."

"Yes, ma'am."

Sophie's hand replaced Estelle's. "Come with me," she said to Michel. "I'll explain."

The door began to close behind him, but Michel stopped unexpectedly, pulled up his black sweater, and retrieved Claire's 45 automatic from his waistband.

"This was in the car," he said across the room to his battle companion as he slid the pistol onto a battered nightstand by the door. Claire nodded then let her eyes drift away from the gun and all it reminded her of.

"Good night, Claire. Mrs. McCleash."

"Good night, Michel, and thank you," Estelle said as she closed the door.

The two women were alone again, surrounded immediately by the void Monique's absence had already created in their lives. Estelle's steps into the room were light as feathers and just as quiet. She walked toward her daughter but then diverted to a far corner where she stood absently adjusting an old lace cover on the arm of a tired chair.

"Monique will be going to our house," she said as her eyes and fingers examined the lacey spread.

Her daughter nodded but answered with a question. "How's Father?"

Estelle breathed deeply and shook her head. "Broken."

"We should go home, Mother," Claire said as she stood up from the bed, rubbing her arms as though to warm them. But rather than join her, Estelle simply turned toward her daughter, tears streaming down her face.

"I'm so sorry, Claire," Estelle let out as her arms dropped limply to her sides. "I'm so sorry."

As daughter moved to comfort mother, Estelle turned away. "It's not your fault, Mother. It's no one's fault except the Germans. They're to blame for all of it. Every goddamn bit."

"No. Not everything. It's me," Estelle sobbed as Claire held her from behind. "When you girls were little, Monique was always in such control of herself. But you, you were so wild and reckless. God, I loved you both so much. So much."

Nearly breathless from her weeping, Estelle was forced to stop and regain her air. Like Claire, she wiped at her face again and again before she continued. "When the Germans came, I knew you'd pick up a gun. I was so afraid for you. You and your recklessness would kill you. I was certain of it. I tried to keep you from it. Tried to get Monique to make you change your mind, but you wouldn't listen. There was no stopping you."

Estelle rotated in a small circle until she faced her daughter. Then she deeply breathed the breath of one about to confess a grave sin.

"Claire, I purposely pushed you away from me to keep me from being hurt so badly when the news would come that you'd been killed. I didn't want to know what you did. I didn't want to know you, for my selfishness. And all the time I moved further and further away from you, waiting for the news." Estelle sank heavily into the chair, falling away from her daughter. "I always thought it'd be you."

Claire's arms circled her mother and caught her tears as the woman lamented for forgiveness. It came on Mercury's wings as Claire dropped down in front of her mother and pressed their tears together. "It's alright. It's going to be okay."

"I love you so much, honey. I always have."

"I know you do, Mother. I love you, too."

They settled in on the chair and the nearby floor. Tears had run dry in both mother and daughter. Forbidden by nature to cry any longer, they stayed that way - Estelle on the edge of the old chair and Claire curled up at her knee, until time once again rescued the drifting souls.

Estelle stood first then helped her remaining child to her feet. There they held one another's faces and brushed away the stains.

"Let's go home," Estelle whispered.

"Yes," came Claire's echo. "Let's go home."

With their arms around each other's waists, the pair strolled toward the door. There, the 45-caliber pistol looked up at them from the table. Claire hesitated, unsure of her mother's position after the long night.

"Go ahead," Estelle said with some resignation. "I know tonight has only fanned the flames for you."

The fighter picked up the heavy gun and tucked it beneath her sweater. "Just for protection," she said as she went out the door ahead of her mother.

Estelle swatted her playfully on the bottom. "Don't lie."

Claire waited for her mother and they held each other again, smiling at their little joke, but the smiles instantly faded when the wide table of the main room came into view. It was empty now, void of everything that came before or after the McCleash sisters rolled that German car onto the sidewalk out front. There were no used coffee cups, no maps, no ammunition clips, no bandages, and no blood. The table was cleaner than it had ever been. Certainly for now, it was far too clean. Had it held its standard fare it would not have appeared so stark. In their concern to rid it of the reminders of death, Sophie and the other well-meaning fighters had stripped it bare, which left it holding nothing but the memory of Monique and the last minutes Claire and Estelle had spent crowded around her.

The Resistance fighters themselves had long since disbanded, instructed by Renault to vacate the safe house for fear of reprisals by the Nazis. Should they come it would be better for the Movement to lose individuals rather than clusters. So the house was empty except for the ghostly memory hovering over the table.

To ward off not the apparition, but the pain that came with it, the women clung to each other tightly and escorted one another rapidly to the back door. Only when it closed behind them and they were swallowed by the darkness in the alley did either woman begin to breathe again. That breathing and their steps were the only sounds until the front door of the McCleash house creaked open under Estelle's sturdy hand.

A soft light was filtering down from upstairs, warming the otherwise dark room. Estelle habitually flicked a switch in the foyer sending bright light out into the living room, over the chair and the man crying in it. The women could not see Sean, but they did hear his shattered voice.

"Turn it off, please."

The light was extinguished without question. Claire and her mother took its place. Even in the shadowy glow from upstairs they could see Sean sitting stoically in his chair, his hands resting on his lap, palms up, submissive. Had the dim light been stronger they would also have seen the streaks on his face and his drained eyes.

Fittingly, his wife approached him first. She leaned over and hugged him. By doing so she felt the dampness on the front of his shirt, the resting place of tears. All that moved on the old man was his arm that came up slowly and stroked the encircling embrace of his wife.

"How's my Seany boy?"

The answer was slow in coming, and when it did it rode on a voice wracked by pain. "They took me girl, didn't they?"

"Yes they did."

Sean's hand came back to his lap to rest. "They robbed me of me chance, Estelle."

A tender hand stroked the hair from his forehead and replaced it with a kiss. "I know."

"I wasted all this time being against the thing I hate instead of being for the thing I loved."

Estelle supported her husband's confession with more soft kisses.

"And now the chance to make it right's been stole from me very heart."

"She knew the truth, Sean."

"Did she now? Small wonder, when all she got from me was guff."

"Father?" Claire said in her softest voice as she inched toward him. "She did know. We talked about it."

"What did she know?"

"That you loved her."

"Then she was wrong."

His words struck the women like a cold north wind.

"Don't the lot of ya see nothing a'tall? That's the rub of the whole goddamn mess. I hated what she did so much, I hated her."

"No you didn't, Sean."

"I did! Damn right and I did! Now I've got to bear the burden of it. And don't be trying to lighten the load with your sugar talk of what she did or did not know."

"Sean, you loved Monique as much as I did, maybe more, and you know it's the God's honest truth."

"Did I?"

"You did."

"Then guess what? Doesn't amount to a tinker's damn now, does it? If ya love someone ya show it. And if ya don't, that shows, too. Woe to those who love and hide it or let trifles crowd up in their gullet so far the love gets choked right out of them. No, goddamn it, she knew." Sean pointed a bony finger into the air in front of him. "She knew goddamn well. She was too smart for your words, that Monique."

"She told me she loved you," Claire chirped.

"What?"

"She said she loved you, despite..."

"Despite what?"

"You know, that you were mad at her a lot."

"Is that true, girl?"

"Yes."

"Don't be mollycoddling an old man."

"I'm not! She told me her own self, as I'm standing here."

Newborn tears formed in Sean's beleaguered eyes. "All the worse shame for it then," he said as his lips trembled. "She loved the hand that laid her to waste."

There was no consoling Sean in his grief. Estelle was worn down by her own suffering and couldn't bear Sean's any further tonight. "God forgives," she said with resignation as she patted his thin shoulder.

"He shouldn't. I hope He doesn't. That's me prayer. That He doesn't forgive me. I have no warrant to deserve it. And I will not ask. How can I ask me heavenly Father for forgiveness, when here in this world, a daughter looks for forgiveness from her father and

I turned me head? May God turn His face from me as well and punish me."

Estelle's hand reached for his, gripped it tightly for a moment, then fell off. "The punishment has already come," she said. "But in God's punishment there's always a promise. Who can know what it is?"

Sean didn't move, but had heard. "Tonight," he said with a voice grown hoarse by crying, "and for years to come, I will only feel the lash."

Weighted down by the tragic events of the night, Estelle trudged heavily toward the stairs. She stopped only briefly to hug Claire and kiss her goodnight for the first time in several years. "You won't go out again tonight, will you?" she asked of her daughter.

"No, Mother, not tonight. I promise."

"I think I'll try to sleep. Sean, are you coming?"

"I'll be along."

"Claire?"

"I'll sit with Father a minute."

"Goodnight all," Estelle said wearily, and she slowly disappeared up the stairs, taking each step in pain.

Claire was still standing in the center of the room in the spot where she had attacked Monique a day before. Sean was in his chair, also as before. Estelle had gone to bed, surrendering as she had on the night Monique had been run out of the house. It was not simply a mood difference on this night, however. If it had been only that it would have been sobering and ended. This was a vacuum. Claire would never fill it — this was something different she realized already, so there would be no attempt to try. The family would ride a crest of anguish over the loss, perhaps forever, but the old man would suffer most. The mother had been unerringly supportive, the sister a combative friend until the final days, but the father? He had said it himself: "I wasted all this time being against the thing I hate instead of being for the thing I love." His actions had become a specter that would haunt him to the culmination of God's punishment.

Sean looked over at his surviving daughter and raised his arms. She flew to them, and the two found consolation from their sins in shared failings. In the middle of the embrace Sean felt Claire's pistol beneath her sweater. The old hand moved as lightning and tore it from her waist. Claire clutched it with both hands, eyes wide in fresh fear, thinking her father would attempt to shortchange God on the pain. But the wiry hands were strong and ripped the pistol away only to slam it down on his table. The nearby pipes rattled in their starting gate, trembling in the presence of the gun.

The hand that smacked the weapon down trembled as well, but calmed as Claire touched it. "It's a necessary evil, Father."

"Is it?"

Claire didn't answer directly. Rather, she stood up straight and eased her father to his feet. "Enough for tonight. Time for bed," she said as a mother.

Sean shook his head in agreement, and they walked away from their blue steel guardian. When they reached the base of the stairs, Claire hesitated. "You go on up, Father. I'll be right along."

"What is it, child?"

"I'm going to get a drink, is all. Go ahead. I'll be up in a minute. Goodnight," she said as she kissed his furrowed brow.

"Goodnight, sweetie pie. Daddy loves ya so."

Her acknowledgment came as a second kiss and a warm embrace that drove enough of the chill out of Sean's bones that he would be allowed to sleep.

For her part, Claire was not yet ready to permit slumber to end the day. She looked after her father's steps then moved backward into the living room and turned toward the kitchen. But the promised comfort of her father's chair called to her. She ignored the kitchen and the drink and walked across the quiet room. The instant she lowered herself into the worn soft leather she felt the heat left by her father. It felt good, as though a strong comforting arm had encircled her.

She sat that way for several minutes, thinking everything and nothing. The events of the preceding hours played like a dream, a nightmare, before her. It began with a rejected phone call and ended with a plea for life. In between, there was Michel and the winery, the soldiers and the killing. The chasing of that car and more killing. The major on the slope and his dying declaration that meant love to Monique then and to Claire now. The flight to the safe house and that goddamn table.

Somewhere during the night Charlemagne had stepped into the dream and promoted her mother from seamstress to general. Michel had stepped in and out, only to be allowed back in again. And then there was Sean. Pain oozed from him like wax from the top of a candle, forged in a searing flame. Even as she sat in his chair Claire understood that her father would never be the same, even near it, and she wondered too if she would be.

When she woke from the tragic daydream her hands were cradling the white clay pipe. Monique had done the same a short time ago when she had reminisced of other days. Perhaps it was genetic that a McCleash be brought to this thing as a talisman, a comforter, a portal to dreaming, and she suddenly wondered what her father thought of when he held it.

In time she slipped the special pipe carefully back into its distinguished place at the end of the rack, just beyond the reach of the resting gun. With her hands free once more, along with her mind, Claire rubbed her palms on her thighs as to warm them. She stood stiffly and walked through the plain archway into the kitchen and clicked the light switch. The light seemed especially bright.

She went to the sink and watched as the water took the remaining dirt and blood from her hands. The faucet also refreshed her face and took away the last of the boot polish, previously washed with tears. With her hands clean, Claire cupped the water and drank as the water continued to run. She used a nearby dishtowel to wipe her hands and the counter near the sink, but let the water drip from her chin, perhaps to disguise any tears that might come on the way to bed.

Claire opened the icebox but only stared at its contents. She closed it without getting anything and turned away, content now to go to bed.

When she reached for the light switch the floor beneath the table caught her eye and imagination. Time spent in play with Monique flooded in. Remembrances of her sister under the table, running from room to room, chasing up and down the stairs, and dancing in the backyard flickered by her mind's eye like pictures in a cinemascope. Then the machine stuck on the dancing, and the backyard, and her father's flower bed.

Drawn to the back door by a strange combination of curiosity and reverence, Claire opened the solid door and then pushed the screen door to the side. She stood there, still in the kitchen, staring down the small steps across the tight lawn to the large flower bed, her father's pride and joy, which now was slightly raised.

The kitchen light did its best to reach across the dark yard. Claire used it to see the freshly turned soil all around the bed that had once been only for flowers. The entire arrangement seemed to be nearly a foot higher than it had been. The strange notion came over Claire that it shouldn't be that high as Monique was such a small girl. But she let the thought pass away from her and stepped cautiously as though testing ice down the stairs into the yard.

As Claire got closer she saw too that the flowers, yesterday so neat and upright, were disjointed and bent, the after-effects of being so rudely uprooted. Claire knew how they felt. Her hand dipped to the flowers and ran through them gently as she walked the length of her sister's grave. At the end of the bed she paused and let another odd notion borne from being wrung out physically and emotionally creep into her clouded mind. Where were Monique's feet? At which end was her head? After she made a mental note to ask Michel, the thought slipped out one of the many cracks in her mind.

Settled, but still unsure, Claire knelt in the lawn at the middle of the flower bed. Fresh dirt, spilled onto the grass during the burial, quickly added to the collection of blood and debris her pants had captured throughout the rough night. The position was one for prayer, but Claire had no words for God, no desire to ask for a blessing, and no energy to ask why. The only words that came were for Monique, and even they cracked painfully as they escaped Claire's lips.

"I'll make it right. Tomorrow I'll start. And I will never stop."

She touched the upturned dirt with a tender hand, brushing it smooth and patting it down. This would become a familiar spot, she reasoned. The plan grew in her that each night she would come here and recount the day's events — in essence, provide the body count to Monique. Armed with this deadly strategy Claire crossed herself, granting the plan a blessing herself as though God might bestow it.

She stood slowly, aching all over from the trials of the night and the increasing damp cold. The weather was fitting as she stepped away from the grave and up the few steps into the house. The screen door closed behind her, and she turned for a last look through the mesh while closing the main door. Her hand stopped, however, and she pushed the solid door open again, as though Monique would follow later or so as to not close her out of the house entirely.

"See you tomorrow, Mo," she whispered into the backyard. Then, carrying the fresh promise with her, she turned out the light and went upstairs.

She passed by her own room and went further down the hallway to her parents', but was met with their closed door. She pressed her ear against the old wood to eavesdrop long enough to hear soft voices of comfort. Rather than interrupt, Claire turned away, but in doing so found herself face to face with Monique's bedroom door.

The knob turned easily in one hand while the other pressed lightly against the door itself. When the latch gave way Claire restrained the door from opening as though she was sneaking in the room, trying not to wake her sleeping sister. The door creaked out a warning, however. When she was able, Claire slipped inside the door and closed it behind her. She stood in the room in the dark, her hand fumbling for the light. When she located the switch she held it, finding comfort in the security of knowing that she could flood the room with saving light should the need arise.

In the shadows and dark forms Claire could make out all the things of the room. Even in the dark Claire knew the color of each thing as well as its texture and scent. This room was as comfortable to her as her own, perhaps more so, as it was here under the wing of her older sibling that she had learned so many of the things necessary to be a young woman. Here is where she came to ask simple questions. Here is where she sought the answers to harder questions others would not, could not answer.

Laughter had somehow found a way to echo between these plain walls on nearly every occasion, including that terrible night when Claire's body first told her that she was now a woman. How Monique had laughed at Claire's notion of being near death. Most every trouble could be solved in hours-long conversations stretched out across Monique's bed. Claire absolutely knew that days would soon come when she'd have need of this bed and the wisdom that always accompanied it, but she knew just as truly that those days were gone, robbed from her by Nazi guns.

As she surveyed the room a minor fear of the dark clung to her but was overcome by the memories. There was also an odd trepidation of the dead, even though she had loved her and was loved in return. Still, death carried that damn scythe and draped itself in a cloak of black, demanding respect if not fear. But the room brought her such comfort that Claire's hand left the light switch unused, and she went to the bed enveloped by the darkness.

She sat on the edge and ran her hands out on the bedspread in all directions. Perhaps it was the proximity of the bed, but Claire was suddenly exhausted. Very deliberately she bent over and groped at her bootlaces until they cooperated. She worked her feet out of the black boots, and they fell to the floor in successive clunks. Then she eased herself up fully on the bed and lay down on her side, curling up in her black and dirty clothes like a little child. Her hands circled one of Monique's pillows and pulled it up tightly under her face. The scent of her sister's perfume immediately filled her head and drove out the last tears of the day. However, in a few minutes Claire's breathing grew deeper, the tears subsided, and she slipped off to a fitful sleep.

***

38

Darkness had long come to the wards of St. Louis Hospital. Outside its cloistered halls, sirens continued to wail against the night as the Germans, fresh from their victory on a deserted road, pursued the Resistance through an imposed civilian curfew. The population was behind locked doors, tucked in their beds, though many were not asleep as the alarms reminded them that control of France rested with the Nazis. The sirens also signaled that there would be payment due for the alleged transgressions of a few.

A sole figure defied the curfew and now walked as quietly as possible in echoing halls. The click of her shoes careened between the walls, announcing her steps to anyone who would have listened, but there were few ears to hear and none who cared. Single lights burned dimly at each bend in a corridor. So faint was the light that it gave up halfway down the long halls only to be taken up again by light stretching hard from the opposite end. She stopped at a double swinging door that advertised that the woman's hospital ward lay just beyond.

Once inside she listened to the sounds of coughing, snoring, and soft moans surrounded by the antagonistic scents of urine and antiseptic. The large room was crowded with over a hundred patients, some sleeping and others longing for it. Medication had brought dreams to most, but some, held awake by pain of mind or body, looked at the young woman with curious eyes as she wandered between the beds. She walked close to each and stared at their faces, lingering over many, cocking her head from side to side, studying the features before her. Those whose faces were partially covered had their blankets carefully pulled back to allow her inspection. With each bed, with each face, the examination came and went, then she moved on.

At the foot of the beds hung charts with the occupant's name in bold letters across the top. Her eyes scanned these as well, but she concentrated on faces as she looked for a reminder of a horrific afternoon years earlier. Three beds ahead she thought she found it.

Valerie was lying in her narrow bed with the pillow wadded behind her neck, propping her head up in an awkward position. Her empty eyes were open, and she seemed to half follow the person who was working toward her. There was no hint of recognition on her face. The years that had passed since last these two saw one another and the fleeting nature of that run by Valerie and Paul through Claudine's living room would have erased the faces from even a well mind. Valerie looked out blankly from her bed. Claudine's pulse, however, quickened at the sight of the woman who, in her mind, had brought death to her mother and brother.

The name on the chart at the foot of the bed read "Valerie" in bright black letters. Beneath it, old and faded, was the name "Jane Doe." Claudine ran her fingers and her eyes over the name before she looked up again at the vacant face.

"Do you know who I am?" she asked. "I know who you are."

Valerie blinked away the answer.

"You used to be pretty. That's what I remember most. And that's why the Nazis were chasing you. They wanted you, not Paul. They always want the pretty ones. If you hadn't been pretty, they wouldn't have come. And wouldn't have done what they did."

Claudine walked closer to the bed as she continued. "Do you even know what happened? I wonder if you remember? Or if you even care. Did you care, at all, even then?"

The silent answers came as before.

"I know where you were hiding. I heard later. You must have heard the shots. I still hear them. They wake me up at night, and I can't sleep anymore."

Valerie stared, remembering nothing, understanding nothing.

"I always wondered if you were watching the street when they shot my mother. I was. I saw it all. And when they shot my brother? I saw that, too. He was only eight."

Valerie blinked, but she continued watching the girl who now eased down onto the bed beside her. Claudine smiled, almost laughed. "I can't believe you're alive! All this time everybody thought you were dead. Paul thinks you're dead. But he doesn't go out with anybody. He doesn't like pretty girls, same as me. They cause trouble. Like you did."

Claudine reached into her pocket and pulled out the morphine bottle and the syringe. "But you're not going to cause any more trouble, are you?" As she talked, Claudine poked the needle into the bottle and steadily withdrew the plunger. "You can't just show up and take him back. He doesn't need you. The Movement needs him. And I need him. Not you. He wouldn't love you anymore anyway," Claudine said, the words becoming her own lost denial.

She stopped pulling on the syringe when it was completely full. "You're skinny and ugly now. And stupid. You can't talk, can you? You couldn't say, 'I love you, Paul.'"

"I love you, Paul," Valerie blurted out.

The surprise shook Claudine and the bottle in her hand. It fell to the floor and shattered as she jumped away from the bed still clutching the syringe in a trembling hand.

"Jesus, you can talk! Do you understand me? Do you know who I am? Do you remember what happened?"

"Rock me to sleep."

"What?"

"Rock me to sleep."

"Sleep?" Claudine said as she noticed again the loaded syringe in her hand. "Do you want this? Do you want to die?"

"Will it hurt?"

"I don't know! You didn't care if it hurt my brother and my mother! Why should I care about you?"

Valerie was as expressionless as ever, but Claudine had been placed on guard.

"I thought you'd be asleep or goofy medicated or something. Or just out of your head. I suppose this won't work like I planned now. If you fight me, I'll hurt you. I know how. Paul taught me."

"Rock me to sleep."

"Jesus, you do want me to kill you, don't you?" Claudine stepped backward, frightened by the perceived conviction she read on Valerie's face.

The length of the bed separated the women as they looked at each other through eyes that were miles from understanding. Across the chasm Claudine realized that other eyes were watching them as well. She turned slightly and found several pairs of eyes belonging to Valerie's neighbors watching the play unfold in the ward.

"She's crazy," Claudine said to no particular face as she motioned to Valerie.

"We're all crazy," a pair answered. "But if you try to take her, and she doesn't want to go we'll kill you."

Claudine moved the syringe out in front of her and held the point toward the voice.

"You're wrong, young lady," another voice said calmly. "She's not crazy. She's hurt. We are all hurt. Like you. The war has hurt us all. But my friend is right about one thing. If you try to hurt Jane, we'll kill you. So maybe you should put the needle down and go away."

Claudine looked into the dark room and saw at least a dozen bodies propped up on elbows in narrow beds and nearly as many sitting up on the sides.

"She killed my brother and mother!"

"Like that? She doesn't even know her name."

"Before! She ran through my house and brought the Nazis with her! They killed my family trying to find her and her lover!"

The voices whispered mingled condolences. "I'm sorry. I'm so sorry for your loss. I lost a brother, too."

"We thought she was dead all these years."

"She has been dead. Look at her."

"Not like my mother."

"No, not like your mother, but perhaps worse."

Claudine looked down at the syringe and slowly lowered her hand. "Maybe so, huh?"

A quiet minute passed as the shapeless faces looked out for one of their own. Finally, another voice rose up.

"What of her lover? Have you killed him, too?"

"No."

"Will you?"

"No."

"Why not?"

"It wasn't his fault. They were after her. They always want the pretty ones."

"And it's you that loves him now."

"Yes. He has always helped me. He's like my father."

"What does he say of Jane?"

"He doesn't care about her anymore."

Claudine nearly fell in the hole created by the lie until a voice threw her a line.

"He doesn't know, does he?"

"I think he does. Now..."

"You think?"

"They say he died tonight, but I don't believe it. He's the best. He always comes back. Always."

"We heard the sirens. He didn't come back tonight, did he?"

"No."

"Your friend is dead."

Claudine didn't speak to the voices any longer. She went back to the bed and sat next to Valerie, fidgeting with the syringe in her hand. Intent changed in her heart as she touched the needle point.

Tears begin to slip from her eyes. Valerie watched her movements with no regard while the voices silently listened. Several minutes passed as that before Claudine's voice, true and tender, struck a new chord and disarmed all the faces around her.

"I'm sorry, Valerie, but I've come to tell you that your Paul is dead. He died a hero tonight, fighting for us and this country of ours. He'll be waiting for you, if you want to go to him."

Claudine looked into the voices and heard nothing. She lifted the syringe and watched, but there was no movement in the shadows.

"Paul is waiting, Valerie. What do you say?"

"Rock me to sleep."

"Okay." Again Claudine gauged the reaction of the shadows before she moved the needle close to Valerie's arm. The voices were as still as before and all had eased back in and down to their beds. The needle pressed lightly against Valerie's pale skin and brought her eyes down to it.

"Will it hurt?"

"Just a tiny bit. But then you will go to sleep. And when you wake up, you'll be with Paul. Won't that be nice?"

"Rock me to sleep."

"I will."

Claudine pressed the needle into Valerie's arm then eased the plunger down, and the mammoth dose of morphine slipped away and began its work.

Emptied, the needle emerged. Claudine cupped Valerie's face with both hands, the syringe pressed lightly against the dying woman's cheek. Claudine leaned close and kissed Valerie's lips with great tenderness.

"I forgive you. I want you to take that with you. I forgive you. And when you see Paul, tell him I love him. Goodnight, Valerie."

***

39

The morning's dawn was hampered by an overcast and threatening sky. Its grey light found Claire asleep on Monique's bed, still dressed, but covered with a blanket supplied by loving hands during the night. Next to her lay her mother, also asleep, also still in her clothes from the day before. Both women had come to the room seeking comfort and to hold onto a special someone for one more night.

While they slept the early morning hours away, thunder rumbled across their city and their house and into the room. When the noise came again it nudged Claire from her restless sleep. She woke with great effort and stretched on the bed. For an instant, she was confused as to where she was, then came the why, then came the realization and the remembering.

Before the pain could fully clench its fist around her heart the rumbling broke again, driving the last vestiges of sleep from her eyes. Yet another distant thunderclap and she sat up in bed, tilted her head to the side, and concentrated on the sound. A slow powerful rumble came again in seconds, far too quick for thunder. Her senses had been so keyed on the strange noise that only now did she notice her mother still sleeping beside her. Claire's gentle smile and soft pat on her mother's shoulder was interrupted by the sound again echoing over the hills outside.

She tossed the blanket aside and gently slipped from the bed so as not to disturb her mother. One sock had nearly worked its way free from her foot so she tugged at it, coaxing it back on while she walked and hopped to the window. With the sock again in place Claire pulled aside the heavy drape, Monique's buffer against the sun when a late night begged for a few more hours of sleep.

The scene outside was nearly as confusing as the rumbling, which had continued unabated throughout Claire's move to the window. The street below was chaotic. Grey cars and trucks were dashing up and down, jockeying for position in the road which was quickly becoming lined with the beleaguered citizens of France.

Claire opened the window and stuck out her head, still a little foggy from the sleep and the lingering effects of a night that would forever haunt her. Not all but many of the vehicles she saw were streaming to the north and to the west. The thunderclaps waited there for them, at the coast.

Suddenly it dawned on her. This was not a storm of rain and lightning at all. The noise was the shelling of the beaches by Allied warships in the English Channel. The Americans had come!

Claire jumped away from the window and clamored to the bed, nearly pouncing on Estelle. "Mother! Mother! Wake up! The Americans are here!"

The rumbling sounds of the invasion filled the room like music as Claire dropped to the floor and hurriedly pulled on her black boots.

"Do you hear it?" she said excitedly from the floor to a drowsy Estelle who could barely focus on either sight or sound. "Those are battleships shelling the coast! Knocking the hell out of them by the sounds of it!"

Claire leaped to her feet and stomped her way into the boots as she went back to the window. She alternately put each foot on the sill and wrapped the long black laces around her ankles and quickly tied them off. As the final loop of the last lace was being pulled between her fingers, the frantic pace suddenly slowed. She pulled the lace tight as a look of enormously deep thought fell over her face. Her eyes were as vacant as an empty shell casing and temporarily as useless. Behind the eyes her brain raced ahead of the sounds of battle and settled on what it meant. With the coming of the Allies the Germans would leave. There would be battles, ruthless bloody battles, but the Americans would prevail. Claire knew it. And soon the Germans would be gone.

She leaned far out the window and took in the raucous parade and the sounds of ships' cannons as if to confirm it all again. "No," she said to herself softly. "Not today. Not now." But her words did nothing to impact the cars or halt the Allied landing craft that even now were hitting the beaches only a few miles away.

As Estelle stood up from the bed, her daughter rushed by in a blur and raced down the stairs, screaming the entire way. "No! Not today! Not today!"

"Claire? What's wrong?" Estelle shouted after her as she gave chase.

But Claire didn't stop to answer. She hit the living room on a dead run and launched herself on through to the kitchen. The back door was still open from the night before, but the screen door was closed. Claire drove into it so hard its hinges tore loose from the frame and the door spiraled out into the lawn with Claire scrambling over top of it. When she cleared the broken door she threw herself down on the flower bed. Her fists began to pound the fresh dirt as tears of frustration splattered on the flowers.

"No! Goddamn it! Just one more day! One more day!"

Estelle appeared in the doorway hot on the heels of her youngest. Before her lay the broken door and beyond her broken daughter, flailing at the flowers, throwing fistfuls of dirt. She ran to her tormented child and tried in vain to pin the wild girl's arms down.

"Claire. Claire! It's over. The war's over. There's nothing you can do for her now."

The lost girl settled for a moment and looked at her mother with tears streaking the dirt on her face. "If she'd have lived one more day, just one more day. She'd be here. It'd be over."

"I know, dear. I know. Please," Estelle said as she looked around the yard while the sound of the invasion played on. "Please come back in the house. It isn't safe yet."

In a savage burst of energy Claire pushed her mother away and leaped to her feet above the flowers. "NO! They can't run from me! I'll hunt them down like dogs!" Before Estelle could recover, Claire sprinted across the yard and the broken door and flew into the house.

The racing fighter rocketed past the chrome-legged table into the living room and fairly dove for her pistol that was lying on her father's end table. In her careless fury Claire's hand forced the gun hard into the pipe rack, sending the delicate and carefully aligned pipes scattering into the air and across the room.

Sean's everyday pipe bounced along the floor like a skipping stone and settled against the far wall, none the worse for wear. The walking pipe was spared entirely as it was accompanying its master on his morning constitutional. The Sunday pipe was cushioned by the rack, whose brittle wood cracked apart when it struck the bare floor. Other pipes skated off in assorted directions, some wounded, others unscathed, much like soldiers who endured the same fire fight, never understanding why or how one survived over another.

The white clay pipe from Ireland, so revered and protected, suffered most. Predisposed to dream-making, its physical makeup would never withstand a blow. Hard, brittle, and beautiful, the clay would fail the first test of strength. When the rack was sent piling across the hardwood, the special pipe was launched from its throne at the end of the holder as if it had been in a catapult. It gained a remarkable height for the blow and crashed to the floor long after the other of its number had come to rest. Tiny shards of clay splintered from the bowl as it absorbed the collision with the floor the best it could. A stiff bounce flipped the pipe on end and snapped the mouthpiece off as neat as a pin. Only after it was reduced to two pieces and a few scattered splinters did the pipe stop its convulsive dance.

Claire never saw the rack hit the floor nor did she see the damage she had caused. Her pistol was leading her into the foyer while the white clay pipe, though airborne, was still whole. The sound of it dying was masked by the tearing open of the front door as Claire and her pistol exploded into the street.

The avenue that greeted her was awash in grey cars and trucks. Though hardly a main thoroughfare, Claire's street was heavy with traffic. Some drivers were struggling to bring reinforcements and supplies to the coast, while others were looking for a shortcut out of the congested city and away from the advancing horde of Allied soldiers. While the cars raced by, collecting citizens began showering them with garbage. Gunshots being traded between the sides rang out sporadically across the congested streets as well.

Claire, her 45 in hand, jumped to the sidewalk from the top of the steps. The landing was harsh, and Claire went to her knees, but she scrambled to her feet with the pistol still leading the way. The sights dropped down on the passenger compartment of the nearest passing grey car. The wide-eyed driver ducked onto the lap of the soldier riding alongside him who was suddenly face to face with Claire's automatic. The shocked German had no time to react.

Claire's aim was lethal, and at the close range of the street, the German was a dead man, but when Claire's finger tightened on the trigger the pistol clicked harmlessly. The soldier was so close he heard the snap of the hammer fall on the empty chamber before speeding on. He would undoubtedly forever tell the story of how he was spared on this last day of German supremacy in France, and perhaps even savor the rest of his life as a gift from God, as indeed it was.

Claire instinctively racked the action on the pistol and fired again as the car ran up the street. As before, nothing happened. The fighter was forced to withdraw slightly as she ripped the clip from the weapon. She stared at it in disbelief — it was still empty from the night before.

In total disgust, Claire threw the clip at a passing car as she screamed, "GET BACK HERE AND FIGHT, YOU SON OF A BITCH!"

She jammed the worthless handgun into her waistband as Claire looked to improvise a new weapon. As she scoured the street,

Estelle stepped from the foyer. The women met as Claire converged on a hapless garbage can sitting comfortably alongside the house. Claire snatched it up despite Estelle's attempt to stop her.

"Come back and fight, you cowards!" Claire bellowed as she hoisted the garbage can and ran toward the street. Estelle was just behind her daughter as Claire heaved the can into the side of yet another grey car. The can left a mark but bounced back onto the sidewalk nearly knocking Claire off her feet. Undaunted, Claire stepped into the street and pulled her pistol on the harried Germans.

"I'll kill every one of you Nazi bastards!"

Estelle lunged for her daughter and jerked her onto the sidewalk as a truck screamed by, missing the out-of-control girl by inches. But the narrow escape did nothing to squelch her threats. As had happened so many times already that morning, Claire broke away from her desperate mother, and sprinted up the street brandishing her toothless 45.

People were running and shouting everywhere in the city, showering the parade of grey vehicles with a barrage of bottles and trash. Claire joined in the running, but while others were celebrating she was in torment.

"Fight me!" she yelled as she spun around on the sidewalk, running in every direction and none at the same time. The spinning and anger combined to make her delirious and disoriented. The traffic and crowds only added to her madness. She grabbed her hair with both hands, one still clutching the empty pistol, and screeched like a crazy woman: "Come back and fight me!"

Lost in her insanity, Claire stood still on the crowded sidewalk and began aiming the gun at every German uniform she saw. Some soldiers who were close enough ducked while others returned real fire to Claire's imaginary bullets. But like the speeding truck moments before, Claire took no notice of the bullets whistling by her head. Instead she took careful aim and squeezed the trigger on the empty pistol time and time again. With each pull of the trigger, the gun jumped in her hand simulating the recoil of the powerful handgun.

The fire that Claire was drawing from passing Germans sent anyone near her scurrying for cover. Nazi bullets screamed by and sent puffs of stone and dust up from the sidewalk near her feet, but she stood fast and dropped the impotent hammer over and over, sending German soldiers to hell in her mind with every shot. Over the sights of her gun Claire saw heads explode as her rounds slammed into the faces of the enemy. Soldiers were falling dead all around her, instantly oozing huge pools of bright red blood beneath the dull grey of their bodies. Soon the street and sidewalks of the city were littered with grey and red soldier corpses.

Captured by the tricks of her dementia, Claire began running again, chasing down the fleeing Third Reich. Her black boots splashed through puddles of crimson German blood while in reality her own countrymen were jumping out of the path of this lunatic girl in black sprinting with the big gun.

A single soldier, mirroring her in SS black, peeked at Claire from around a corner of a building somewhere in her mind. Claire set a blistering pace up the street after him, still shooting countless Germans with the pistol she would never have to reload. When she rounded the corner in pursuit of the nonexistent soldier he was already at the end of the block, leering and laughing. Claire dropped her head and raced the wind to catch and kill the symbol of occupation that was still torturing her.

As before, the soldier vanished when Claire came on him. The mind of the fighter was reeling, on the verge of irrevocable collapse when it was casually spared by her physical failure. Like a racehorse that had given its all to nose the wire, Claire's body was ready to give out. The endless running, the twisting, and the brutal effects of the game her mind had played, served to sap her of the energy necessary to even stand.

Claire staggered near the street, teetering from side to side as though drunk. She arched backward and looked up at the grey morning sky. Her hands were stretched out in true crucifixion style, one still loosely holding the gun as she screamed at the clouds, "Fight me!" But the body and voice were weakening rapidly. "Fight me. Fight...me..."

When the clouds did not answer, Claire's arms collapsed to her sides, and her head fell to her chest. In the subtle fall, her mind slipped gently back into place and the gun hung limply at her side, scarcely able to cling to her hand. Torn down, Claire slipped the gun under her sweater, stood silently with eyes closed, and breathed deeply. As the turmoil continued around her, Claire fought for her breath and then began meandering away deeper into the city.

The rushing Germans were no longer interested in the stumbling girl in black. Without her weapon showing, she was just another one of a thousand civilians craning their necks to witness the last stand of the foreign military. On any previous day, her clothes and dirty face would have been a signal to the German military, and she most assuredly would have been questioned.

People around her were also less cognizant, many simply convinced the girl with the stutter in her walk was drunk from reveling in the Allied invasion. When Claire drifted to the wall of a stone building and sank to the sidewalk next to a row of garbage cans, no one, French or German, took notice. And when she curled up like a baby against the building, shaded from easy sight by the garbage cans, the assembly continued to wheel and walk by, oblivious to the girl on the sidewalk, the hurt in her heart, or the tears in her eyes.

Claire stayed that way for almost an hour as all around her, Nazis fought for their lives while the French felt the first stirrings of theirs return. In time, the stone sidewalk reminded her that she was flesh and bone, and she was forced to move. She pushed herself up from the ground and sat leaning against the wall, letting the blood pump back into parts of her left cold and stiff by the stone. From her lowly vantage point she watched the parade.

Several soldiers, rushing up the street on foot, stopped at the corner and spoke hurriedly with a German captain who had pulled his car up next to the curb. Claire heard them talking about regrouping to the east beyond her coastal city. She thought for the briefest of seconds that there may still be fight in these bastards, but the look on the soldiers' faces told her that the fighting with the Allies would move inland quickly. Perhaps she could pick a fight here and there in their withdrawal and kill when she could. And there was her vow to Monique. She had promised to make them pay. No matter how far they ran, how deep the retreat, Claire would never stop carrying her hatred of the Germans with her. But for all the hatred, she understood that at least for the moment she too must regroup.

With one hand on the building to support the attempt, Claire began to rise. The wall steadied her for a short while before she stepped away and looked around, trying to regain her bearings. Only then did she notice the lightest grey of a shadow, a pinnacle shape, thrown by the overcast sky, stretching out in front of her across the sidewalk and into the street. With her head and mind cleared as much as they had been on this short day, Claire turned and looked up at the building. The shadow belonged to the towering spire of St. Catherine's Cathedral.

It wasn't a true conviction that held her fixated by the tower and the church that lifted it to heaven. She felt no spiritual connection or drive to make her do what she did. But in that deep part of her where a soul might survive, there was another promise, much resented even at its making. So, moved by that damn compelling promise and a spark of curiosity, as if drawn to the face of horror, Claire slowly paced off the length of the cathedral and began walking up the stairs to the nunnery.

Her quaking hand touched the latch as if it might be hot. When she tested it there was a secret hope that the door would be locked, but it welcomed her without a grievance. As her steps brought her inside the door, she felt removed from herself, wondering and confused still as to what had brought her here.

The world of the nunnery was much different from the only other time she had been here just days before. Today the wide room was loud and boisterous, the excitement of the Allied landing having filtered down to the wee ones. Children were running everywhere, all being tailed by scurrying nuns who alternated between trying to corral the youngsters and squealing with delight themselves at the liberating invasion.

Claire scanned the big room somewhat uncertain of what she was looking for and totally uncertain of why. Repulsed by the blonde-haired bouncing children, Claire took a step back from the room. The dirty black clothes made her stand out, as Monique's dresses had often done, but Claire's untucked sweater dangling off her, hiding that big gun, and her disheveled hair around that blank face, brought every eye to her. Sister Arlene had spotted her the moment she walked in. Essey, standing close to the senior nun, saw her as well.

The little girl took off for Claire, who was still watching the room through hollow eyes. Essey ran the first several steps but slowed to a walk as she came closer to the woman who had rejected her just days before. By the time she crossed the busy room Sister Arlene had caught up. The approach of the pair brought Claire's attention to the little girl who looked up at her with red and swollen eyes tucked in a tear-stained face.

"My mother," Essey said softly, then slapped a tiny hand over her mouth and looked at the nun with wide fearful eyes. "I mean, Monique," Essey continued as she turned her face into the nun's habit.

Sister Arlene placed her hands lovingly on the little one's shoulders and slowly turned her around to face Claire. "That's alright," the nun said firmly. "Claire knows about the secret."

Essey looked up again at Claire who was locked in a daze. "My mother went to heaven last night," Essey said in a voice of unique understanding only a child brought up as she could muster.

The stupor that surrounded Claire jumped through a hoop of disbelief as she looked from Essey to the nun. There were a hundred questions painted on Claire's face, but the answers were not readily forthcoming. In fact, Sister Arlene only smiled.

"You and Monique were not the only type of sisters in the Resistance, Claire."

That alone would take several minutes to fully register, but the nun gave her another dose. "And not all fighters carry guns."

Essey was listening, not comprehending at all, but Claire understood perfectly. "Yes," she said in a whisper as her eyes moved back to the little girl. "I know that now."

While Claire began scrutinizing the child, examining the tiny face for traces of a McCleash, Sister Arlene touched Essey's shoulder again and gave her a gentle command.

"Go fetch your things, child."

Essey immediately did as directed and scampered away across the floor and disappeared through the archway. Each of her steps were carefully monitored by Claire. Long after the arch had swallowed the girl, Claire continued to stare at it. While her eyes were captured by the archway, her voice sought out the nun for more answers.

"Is she really Monique's daughter?"

"Yes she is," Sister Arlene said proudly as she too joined in the watching of the archway.

"How?" Claire asked as she shook her head no in ongoing confusion.

"Oh, the usual way." The nun smiled, but understood that more answers must follow Claire or she would never believe, and if she did not believe, she would not take charge. "Several years ago your sister came to me, still a child herself, and told me of her trouble. She came here to stay with us for a time."

Claire's brow turned into a wrinkled field as she thought back into her sister's past. "She went to Paris. To school for a while."

The nun shook her head no. "She was here with me."

Claire joined her in shaking her head, more in disbelief this time than in disagreement.

"I'm certain your mother knew," Sister Arlene continued. "I believe your father as well, but it pained them deeply. Especially your father. When the baby came it was a very difficult delivery. We almost lost your sister more than once. When it was all over we had little Estelle there, but Monique was left barren. I think that is why she...why she did the kind of work she did for the Resistance. She knew she would never be able to have another baby. Essey would be her first and last child."

There was a tremendous malingering in Claire's words. "But I can't..."

"Oh, yes you can," the nun pronounced strongly. "You can and you must. You need her now as much as she needs you."

"Well, what am I supposed to do with her? Come here and read her stupid stories?" Claire laughed cruelly.

"No, you're to take her home. She's your family."

"She's not my family. She's German."

"She's your blood."

"She's a Nazi bastard."

"She's Monique legacy to this world. And she entrusted her to you."

In the heat of the growing debate, Essey came running across the floor. A small knapsack was slung over her frail shoulder and bounced along with her blonde hair. Her face still carried the tracks of sorrow, but there was a slight smile of excitement on her lips as she approached the two combating women.

"I'm ready, Aunt Claire."

"Don't you call me that!"

"Claire! She's just a child!"

"You little Nazi ba—"

"Claire! You're in the House of God!"

The Resistance fighter was seething behind clenched teeth. Her eyes were fierce as she stared at the nun while Essey adjusted her knapsack uncomfortably. But Sister Arlene stood ramrod straight and bore holes into Claire's cold eyes. The women were locked together, neither one about to break off and lose the battle they felt placed on earth to win. It was Essey who ended the silent battle by tugging at the nun's long habit. Pulled out of the fight by a tiny hand when a tank could not have done the same, Sister Arlene was compelled to look down.

"It's okay," Essey began softly, but unintentionally loud enough for Claire to hear. "Mother told me that Claire wouldn't like me much at first, but after a while she would. Mother told me that."

Sister Arlene knelt beside the little girl and aligned the knapsack. "Who told you that?" she asked tenderly. The question was for Essey, but the answer was clearly meant for Claire.

"My mother. You know, Monique."

As before, the entire notion incised Claire's temperament, but the thought of it forced a distraction that temporarily stymied her anger. In the gap, the nun primped the collar of Essey's dress and brushed the front flat.

"Estelle," she said sternly. "You behave yourself. And be sure to come back and visit me."

"Oh, I will!"

"Promise?"

"Promise promise!"

"Good," the sister said with a broad smile, which hid more than a slight concern. She hugged her tiny charge and felt the skinny arms embrace her then stood up over tired knees. To bestow a blessing and leave the door open should it be necessary, the nun hugged Claire as well, but the Nazi-killer's arms just hung at her sides. Sister Arlene held her for a long uncomfortable moment, felt the pistol in Claire's waistband, then slowly released her after realizing what she had long known, that the embrace would not be returned. Again, Essey would be the one to coat the sting. She tugged the nun's habit a second time and shielded her mouth from Claire as she spoke in a hushed voice.

"She's not much of a hugger."

The Sister smiled and put her arms around the little girl for the last time. "I'm going to miss that charming wit of yours, young lady!"

"I'm going to miss you, too, but mostlies I'm going to miss my mother."

Claire spun on her heel at the remark and marched toward the door. Sister Arlene grabbed Essey and quickly pushed her off behind Claire though the fighter was already clearing the nunnery.

"Hurry along, child! And stay close to Claire! She'll help you! I hope."

As the words echoed around the room Essey struggled with the heavy door. Then in a flash she disappeared on the other side. Sister Arlene made the Sign of the Cross toward the door and the child on the far side now out from beneath her protection. Then she bit her lower lip and wondered if she had done the right thing.

The sounds of the invasion greeted Essey outside the nunnery, but they didn't concern her. She discovered that Claire was already on the sidewalk moving swiftly up the street, and she knew she'd be hard pressed to catch her. Gravity helped her down the stone steps to the sidewalk but then worked against her as she grappled with the unruly knapsack on her shoulder. In a dead run Essey eventually caught the long striding woman in black, but in less than half a city block she was tiring and began to lag badly.

Claire stopped and spun on the girl who was some thirty feet behind. "Go back to the nuns!"

As Claire scowled with her fists thrust out by her hips, Essey ran up alongside panting like a puppy. A timid smile from the little girl was like a starting gun to Claire. She wheeled away from her ward and jetted up the street faster than before but was forced to hold up at the end of the block before crossing the street.

Traffic, both foot and vehicular, was heavy. In the wait for the street to clear Essey caught up again. She stood next to her unwilling protector and lowered her bag to the sidewalk to rest. Claire looked down disgustedly.

"I suppose you think I should take your stupid hand and help you across the street."

"If you want to."

Claire looked straight ahead. "I don't."

Without waiting any longer for the traffic to lighten Claire jumped into the street, intent on dodging her way across and perhaps losing Essey for good in the bargain. But when she moved, Essey caught the hem of her sweater and trailed along behind like the tail of a kite.

Though Claire could have easily slipped out of Essey's grasp, she did not. Instead she felt the tug at her sweater come up into her shoulders and tickle a frozen heart.

The feeling of being wanted and needed ran with the tug. It was not a feeling Claire was ready or prepared to embrace. Her heart was too full of rancor, revenge, and sadness to accept anything more. When they reached the safety of the other side of the street, Essey let go and pranced up alongside her troubled and reluctant aunt.

As the unlikely duo — the little girl in the flouncing dress and the dirty soldier in black — marched toward home, Claire was wrestling with crushing feelings of hurt and loss, both well seasoned with hatred. The fighter's eyes began darting back and forth between the Germans in the street and the child who continued to struggle to keep up, jogging at her side. Claire's eyes began to fill with tears, forced out by the overwhelming despair of the last twenty-four hours and an anger that had festered for years.

Merely by her presence, her unwitting heritage, and being a living reminder of Claire's own fallacies, Essey became the flashpoint for that anger. In a blurring rush that frightened them both, Claire dropped down and grabbed Essey by the arms.

"Listen to me! I don't like you! I never will like you! I hate Germans!" Claire shook her as the anger poured out over the hapless child. "I've killed hundreds of Germans, and I'm not finished yet! Do you hear me?"

"Please don't kill me!" Essey screamed with quaking lips.

Such was her rage that Claire growled like an animal. She could see the fear in the girl's eyes. She turned her back on the petrified girl. Her fists were clenched so tightly they convulsed in front of her as she yelled at heaven through gritted teeth.

"Goddamn it! How could you do this to me?"

The little girl stayed very still, frozen by fear, but uncertain she would run even if she could convince her feet to do so. Claire did not move either, save her chest, which heaved as she inhaled deep breaths of frustration. Essey watched the black sweater across Claire's back expand with each breath and wondered in her innocence when the next tirade would drop on her. She thought about the safety of the nunnery and looked over her shoulder. The nunnery was out of sight, but in her mind she caught a glimpse of it and remembered a lesson her mother had taught her there.

To Essey the storm appeared to have settled as Claire had not yelled at her in almost a minute. She knew a screaming bout or worse might not be far away, but she risked a chance at re-igniting it. "I'm only a little bit German."

The gentle words caught Claire unaware. A reflex made her look over her shoulder down at Essey, trembling on the sidewalk.

When they locked eyes Essey was at first more frightened than ever, but she soon saw in Claire's eyes the birthing of new tears. She relaxed ever so slightly and pointed a tiny finger at her heart as her face pleaded with the fighter towering above her.

"Mother said that in here I'm French and it's what's in here that really matters."

Claire swallowed hard and years of anger went down her throat.

"Is that true, Claire?"

Claire looked away from the child and up at the sky. The tears flowed to the corners of her eyes and trickled down the sides of her head until they lost themselves in her auburn hair already darkened by sweat. Her heart relaxed, and the tension slipped off her shoulders. Now it was Claire's lip that began to quiver.

Essey watched again as the black sweater expanded in the deepest sigh yet. Perhaps even quicker than before, Claire spun and dropped down in front of the little girl and threw her arms around her.

"Don't hurt me!" Essey screamed.

Though she was shaking herself, Essey soon felt the strong shudders of Claire's crying and, though confused, relaxed to just this side of fear for the first time in several minutes. She loosened her grip on fear entirely when Claire spoke to her between sobs.

"I won't hurt you. I won't ever hurt you. No one will ever hurt you as long as I'm around. Promise promise." In the tight embrace, Claire whispered, "I've got you, Mo. I've got you."

In the heat of the press, Essey felt the same intense love that had surrounded her when her mother held her. She knew instantly that the harsh time Monique had spoken of was already passed. She squeezed her new protector as tight as she could until Claire eased her grip and held Essey out at arm's length.

"Essey, what I said before, about not liking you. I didn't mean it like that. I'm sorry."

"I know you didn't mean it. It sounded like you mean-did it, but I know you didn't. You just don't like Germans. My mother told me so. I'm sorry I'm a little bit German."

"No, you don't have to be sorry for anything. You are who you are. You're my sister's little girl."

Claire stumbled over her words as fresh tears fell from a new place in her heart. "You are...my family and...and I love you."

"I love you too, Aunt Claire. Oops! Is that okay? Can I call you that sometimes?"

"To tell the truth it makes me feel kind of old. How about just Claire?"

"Okay. I like that."

Claire hugged the little girl again and felt the warmness she'd been missing.

"Goshes, Claire! For someone who doesn't like hugs, you are really good at 'em!"

Suddenly Essey's feet left the ground as Claire hoisted her effortlessly up into her arms. The little girl buried her tiny face in Claire's long unruly hair, closed her eyes, and enjoyed the ride as they stepped away down the street.

"Let's go home," Claire said. Then she took a deep breath with her steps and wondered if she could keep her promise and protect Essey from her own father.

***

40

The only sounds in the McCleash home were the rumblings of the distant landing and an occasional clink of dishes as Estelle painfully rinsed two teacups and two spoons in the kitchen sink. The cups could have waited — could have sat on the chrome-legged table or next to Sean's chair until a helpful neighbor dropping off a pie or a casserole tended to them. But for Estelle the distraction was sorely wanted, and as she finished, she wished the piled up dishes of a Christmas dinner waited for her idle hands. Slowly, as though trying to help time do what it does best, she dried the delicate cups and put them away.

Estelle hung one of the cups on its thin hook inside the door of her neat cupboard. The cups, in proper pairs, were two deep. Most things in the McCleash kitchen were this way, except the finer china reserved for those holiday dinners when friends and extended family packed the house. But when strictly purchasing for her brood, the years had given themselves to collecting items by fours — four daily plates, four sets of everyday silverware, four plain glasses, and the four teacups.

Estelle dried the last cup and began examining it thoughtfully. Was this Monique's cup? There were no names, of course, and everything in the family kitchen was interchangeable, but the thought of Monique's hand on the cup collapsed the woman who had aged immeasurably since the night before. Her fingers ran over the rim and caressed the handle. She gently brought the cup up to her face and closed her eyes as her cheek nuzzled tenderly against the side. Her mind whispered the painful thought that she no longer would have the need for four.

Sean had finished his tea long ago. His morning constitutional had taken him far afield well before the tea in the darkness of pre-dawn. He was absorbed by the countryside and his mourning when the first sounds of the Allied warships reached his ears. The distraction, like Estelle and her dishes, was short-lived but accompanied him most of the way home. When he arrived, his tea was waiting by the chair, but Claire had already gone, deep into her rampage.

The morning tea with his wife passed in complete silence. Like the night before, Estelle was too battered to support the demise of her husband's tortured soul. Had she spoken to him she would have discovered that he had few words for her to bear. The long night had driven the thoughts into his heart so deeply that they would not easily spill out on his cheeks or on those nearest him ever again. He understood God's punishment and had set his feet against it. His heart had steeled and he would accept the burden of having failed his daughter. The punishment would begin and end inside him. No one else need be chastised for his shortcomings as a father.

When the teacups were empty Sean sank deeper in his chair. Practiced habit brought out his sitting pipe, and he tried to clean it in preparation of the traditional after-tea smoke. However, his hands were not in it. The easy cleaning, as the pipes were all spotless, seemed a chore, and the pipe weighed ten pounds in his tired arms. Sean slipped the pipe back in its place and rested his hands on his lap, but his eyes stayed on the rack a few minutes longer.

There was a harsh nick in the rack itself where the supports had splintered off the base when Claire's morning attack had begun on the Germans. The casual pipes again held their places and showed no signs of their adventure to the floor. The same could not be said of the white clay. Back in its spot at the end of the repaired rack, the special pipe clearly showed the effects of Claire's miscue with her pistol.

Estelle had glued the stem back on the bowl as carefully as she could. The fit was accurate, but the repair would always remain a repair. The thin shards of clay chipped from the bowl were forever gone. And though it might have looked quite good to one who did not know the pipe before its death, it was much different, much worse, to those who had known the delicate instrument in its prime.

The old man lingered over the clay pipe for a long time before he carefully removed it from its place and maneuvered it through his bony fingers. He held it to his nose and was repulsed by the smell of the glue which had vastly overtaken the rich scent of special occasion tobacco. The piece was still glorious though and now would require even greater care if Sean should ever hope to used it again. He touched the break like a soldier touches an old scar, but his thoughts were not of the damage done to the pipe. No, he was aflame with the thoughts of German grey and what the Nazis had taken from him. Deeper still, almost beyond the killing of his beloved daughter, was again the fact that they had stolen away his opportunity to ever set things right. Monique's death was a crime. Sean's treatment of her was sin. The old man would forgive neither.

The quiet of the house was interrupted by the sound of the front door. Sean didn't stir from his chair but slipped the pipe which had provoked so many thoughts in his family, many of which he knew nothing about, gently back into its place.

Estelle however, called from the kitchen then followed her own voice into the living room. "Claire? Honey, is that you? We've been—"

The voice lost itself near Estelle's mouth and was replaced by her hand as Claire and Essey entered the heart of the house from the foyer. Sean was drawn away from his private loathing of both the Germans and himself by the silence and looked across the room. Claire was standing behind the child, holding Essey by both shoulders to steady herself more than the girl.

"Mother. Father," Claire began slowly. "This is little Estelle. She's come to live with us."

Claire held the girl a moment longer as she tried to gauge her parents' reactions. Her mother could scarcely breathe — Claire could see as much from across the room. Estelle's hand remained at her mouth as though trying to prevent her from speaking and saying words that might be right to some ears and wrong to others. More important to Claire was her father. He sat as a stone except for his face which reddened slightly around a tightening jaw as it turned away from everyone.

Completely unsure and unprepared as to how to proceed, Claire knelt beside the little girl and pointed to her mother. "Essey, this is-"

But before Claire could finish, Essey dropped her satchel and bounced across the floor to her grandmother. "I know who this is," she blurted out as she stopped in front of Estelle to curtsey, a bit off balance. "You are Gran'ma'ma!"

Essey held up her index fingers pushed together with her tiny thumbs in the shape of a little box. She worked hard to close one eye then looked closely through the finger box up at Estelle. "You make wee tiny cakes! My mother said..."

As in the nunnery, Essey slapped her hand over her mouth. She ran back to the safety of Claire's side and buried her face in her guardian's neck.

"It's okay. It's okay," Claire comforted while Essey resisted being turned back to Estelle and Sean. "They know the secret."

Essey peeked out from Claire's neck at Estelle. "It's alright, Gran'ma'ma?" she asked tentatively.

Estelle swallowed very hard and began a fight against tears. She felt she could not speak but quickly nodded her head yes.

Still anxious, Essey asked again, "No more secrets?"

This time Estelle cleared the lump from her throat and answered in a choked whisper, "No more secrets."

The words, and the growing but cautious smile behind them, brought Essey away from her fear. She smiled brightly and threw her arms around Claire's neck. "Then this is my Aunt Claire!" she said as she gritted her teeth to squeeze all the harder. Claire smiled, as did Estelle, and the little girl released her brand new aunt from the embrace. "But I just call her Claire 'cause she's not that old yet."

Essey then took up a position next to Claire and placed a skinny arm over her aunt's shoulder while proclaiming to the world, "She is a great soldier! My mother told me so."

Estelle smiled at the decree and answered as proudly, "Yes she is."

But Sean had not moved. His daughter looked at him closely and, though speaking to Essey, was watching him as she continued the declarations of pride. "And your mother was an even greater soldier."

The exuberant child followed Claire's eyes and went without hesitation to Sean's chair. Claire rose quickly and took a step forward, ready to snatch her away if need be. Estelle took two steps toward her husband to be in position as well.

"And you are Papa," Essey quipped. "Know how I know?"

She didn't wait for an answer, though one was far from coming. Instead she ran back to her pack and rummaged around inside until she produced a small photo album. She ran with the book back to Sean and thrust it onto his lap. His hands were in the way, and he made no attempt to move or accommodate the album. Essey didn't notice the disregard for her and her book and immediately began flipping through the pages. When she realized the pictures were upside down to Sean she picked the book up quickly and spun it around, dropping it again on his hands. As Essey started pointing at pictures Sean sat numb, as rigid as a stone.

"See!" she exclaimed. "There you are! That's how I know you!" Her little hands flipped the pages hurriedly. "And there! And there, and there. Look! There's you with my mother when she was little like me. See, Papa?"

Sean allowed his eyes to fall to the pages. When they did, the ice around the embattled heart began to melt, and the water ran from his eyes. Essey saw the tears and stopped turning the pages. "You're sad about my mother. Don't cry, Papa. Sister Arlene says she's in heaven teaching angels how to dance."

Almost unknowingly, Sean shook his head yes. For her part, Essey returned with the attention of a child to the photos.

"See this one, Papa? Mother's hair was light like mine when she was little. She said mine will get darker when I get big."

The old eyes began to move from the photos in his lap to the little girl at his knee. A tired hand crept out from beneath the book and moved languidly up and touched Essey's blonde hair.

"Do you like my hair, Papa?"

Sean swallowed hard and cleared his throat of excess tears. "Yes," he said in the faintest of whispers.

Essey responded with much flamboyance, fluffing her hair and shaking her nose in the air. "Thank you so very much! You need nice hair to be a movie star. That's what I'm going to be, Papa. I'm going to Hollywood, America, and be a star!"

The women hid their faces slightly to hide the anguished memories that were slipping down their cheeks, but Sean remained still, mesmerized by the little girl.

Without warning Essey pointed excitedly to the pipe rack on Sean's table. "And there's your pipes! I know every one!"

As Essey moved around her grandfather's knees to the pipe rack, the little photo album began to slide from Sean's lap. He caught it and held it dearly while Essey pointed to each pipe.

"That one's your everyday pipe. And that's your walking pipe. The next one is for Sunday," she said matter-of-factly. "And that last one there? That white one? That's your special special pipe. It's from someplace far, far away. Mother said I must never touch it. Never never! No no!"

Sean answered in a new grandfather's voice, very soft, a little anxious, but tender, "Maybe, if you're very careful, you could hold it sometime."

Claire and her mother exchanged looks of wonder and shock then watched as Essey turned away from Sean and sprinted across the room to the stairs. She leaned heavily on the first steps and peered up and around the landing as though looking down a well.

"Right up there? That first room? That's Claire's."

As soon as the words were said Essey jumped away from the steps and ran behind Estelle into the kitchen. The rest of the family heard her shoes tapping across the tile floor. "And here's the kitchen. And out there's our very own yard! And Papa's flowers!"

The tapping returned, louder and faster than ever as Essey raced back into the living room and over to Sean. She grabbed his hand with both of hers, oblivious to what the old man's thoughts had been, and tugged until he got up from the chair.

"Papa! Come see the flowers! They're just like Mother said they would be!"

With a tiny hand wrapped around one of his old fingers, Sean obeyed, set the photo album carefully in his chair, and was summarily led out of the living room and through the kitchen. He did not look at Claire or his wife as he passed, but kept his eyes fixed on Essey as though he was unprepared just yet to let the world see the change. Though they were ignored by both the youngest and most senior McCleash, Claire and her mother fell in behind the parade.

The broken screen door was leaning precariously against the door frame as Essey and her grandfather walked by it down the short steps into the yard. Essey ran straight to the raised flowerbed and began waving her hands through the colorful bouquet as Sean followed. The women paused in the doorway and watched the unlikely scenario unfolding before them.

"Aren't they pretty, Papa?" Essey said playfully as she continued to move up and down alongside the fresh dirt.

"Yes, they are," Sean answered slowly as he knelt beside the bed and began tidying the disjointed blossoms.

"May I pick one?"

Claire grimaced and gripped her mother's arm in the doorway, but Estelle patted away the concern and motioned to Sean who was already clipping the biggest and brightest flower. He handed it carefully to his granddaughter as Claire shook her head and smiled.

Essey would never repair the break in the old man's heart entirely. Like the clay pipe — once broken, though repaired with as loving and tender a hand as God had ever made — the signs of damage would remain and some function would forever be lost. But unlike the pipe, hearts heal, and with this fresh chance at redemption, God and Sean McCleash came to terms.

In the far-off distance, the monstrous Allied guns banged out an irregular beat. Essey slipped the flower between her teeth, tossed her head back, and spun around in an off balanced, exaggerated fandango whirl. Claire and Estelle cradled each other in the doorway while Sean, tentatively at first, began to softly clap his hands once again for his tiny dancer.

THE END